PROJECT FIVE FIFTEEN

first light

By Samantha Summers

Project Five Fifteen - First Light
Copyright © 2012 by Samantha Summers
www.projectfivefifteen.com

Published May 2012

ISBN 978-0-9873288-0-9

For My Nan
Valerie Elizabeth Bristow.
Miss You

CONTENTS

PART I

PROLOGUE

JESSE KNEW HE WOULDN'T BE ABLE TO HOLD OUT
MUCH LONGER. He'd been running for so long his
muscles were finally threatening to give way. A fence
three times his height loomed ahead. It didn't faze him. Fluidly
he leapt up, scaled the wire mesh and somersaulted to the other
side, springing straight back into a run. But every movement
was laboured now, everything slowing down. If his pursu-
ers had been civilians, or even the police, he would have had
nothing to fear. But they weren't. They were just like him, only
better. Running now merely delayed the inevitable.

Still he pushed on, forcing his body over holes, branches
and debris on the forest floor. When he least expected it, on the
jump across a small stream blocking his path, his limbs finally
buckled. His usual speed and graceful precision failed him and
he toppled into a clumsy fall. It cost him only seconds, but he
knew it would also cost him his life.

He steadied himself on the bank where he'd landed and
closed his eyes in resignation. After running for two hours

through the wilderness he allowed himself to stop and enjoy the cool air on his face, the rhythmic sound of his blood pumping in his ears. For what he knew would be the last time, he let himself smile.

He could hear them clearly now; they were very close. So, with some regret for a life he would never know, he turned to face his murderers as they came at him brandishing their nine-millimeter weapons. *Okay,* he told himself, *you tried your best.* He always had. Even in the darkest moments of his short life, Jesse had done what he could to be number one and today would not take that away from him. He would die with as much pride as he had lived.

They slowed as they closed in on him.

He placed his hands behind his head. 'Took you long enough, boys,' he nodded to those he knew. Some had trained him; some had taken care of him when he was a child. Tomorrow, he would have turned sixteen.

'Well, you gave us a good run, J. Not that we expected any less.' The one who led them broke away from the unit and inched forward.

'You know me, boss, I don't do things by halves.'

His tormentor smiled. 'How true. No hard feelings, lad. You know you can't go free. You're a danger to the world – a liability.'

Jesse forced a tight laugh. 'It's funny how you can smile as you say that, Barker – you made me what I am. So perhaps you should be standing here instead of me?'

'Perhaps,' the man shrugged and lifted his gun, Levelling it at Jesse's forehead.

It took all his remaining strength but Jesse stood as tall as he could and held his head high so that it pressed against the steel barrel.

'Barker,' he spoke loudly so all could hear, 'cowards always manage to weasel out of what's coming to them, but I promise you, your time will come. K is going to mess you up.'

His words clung to the air around them.

'Until then,' the man said… and pulled the trigger.

1 — FUNERAL

I WANTED TO BE SOMEWHERE ELSE. ANYWHERE ELSE. Blocking out unpleasant experiences usually came easily to me. I'd simply picture my hero – my knight in shining armour – and have him rescue me. Dreaming was my forte. Usually. For the past three years it had got me through the dullest of school days and the hardest times of my father's illness. But today was different. Today, try as I might (and oh boy I was trying), I couldn't disappear inside my head. I was forced to watch helplessly as my father's body was laid to rest.

I swayed. A tidal wave of grief crashed over me. The rain was pouring relentlessly, rattling against the plastic of my umbrella, the dark grey sky mirroring my mood. The priest was saying whatever priests say at funerals. It must have been particularly moving because all around me people wiped their eyes and sniffed into hankies. Funny, because not one of them came to visit us during the months Dad lay dying.

I shut my eyes. In spite of being outside, I felt suffocated. I took a deep breath, but it wasn't enough — no matter how hard I tried, I couldn't get enough air. I began to panic, but as my eyes flashed open, something caught my attention:

Underneath a tree on the opposite side of the cemetery stood a boy dressed in black. It wouldn't have been too distracting, except that he was, without a doubt, the last person I expected to see at Dad's funeral. I didn't know his name, but I knew of him – he and four other boys had moved to Clanots Ocean a few months back and rumours had been rife ever since. No one knew if they went to school, or who their parents were, but the consensus was that they were bad news.

The boy had no umbrella and, despite the downpour, made no move for shelter. His dark hooded jumper and converse trainers were completely soaked yet he barely moved; he simply stared, in what looked like my direction. I tried to come up with a good reason for him being there. Perhaps he was passing by and had some morose fascination with death, or maybe he was lost. But something about the way he was staring told me otherwise. He looked affected, as if he were really grieving. *He had to have known Dad,* I thought.

The distraction helped me through the rest of the service. The priest carried on talking, but I found myself glancing up from behind my dark sunglasses to check if the boy was still there.

Everyone began to disperse and people wanting to offer their sympathies flocked around me. When the crowd ebbed away, I looked back over in the direction of the boy, but he'd gone - the landscape, empty and grey once more, showed no trace of him.

As people began to make their way back to our house, our neighbour, Maureen Carpenter, took my left hand in hers and squeezed it, breaking me out of my trance. I had to concentrate to take in what she said.

'... Going to be okay, Ronnie, love?'

I hadn't seen Maureen for over a month. Usually, she was the type of neighbour you couldn't get rid of. The stereotype, peep-out-of-the-curtains-and-run-round-for-a-cup-of-tea-to-gossip, nosey neighbour, but since Dad had fallen ill I hadn't seen her at all.

'Thanks, Mrs Carpenter, I'll be fine. Rachel and I have each other for support.'

'Oh,' she stammered, 'it, it's just – I saw Rachel leave five minutes ago with her lovely boyfriend. She seemed so upset, poor dear, she obviously couldn't bear it any longer.'

Ah. It wouldn't be too surprising to learn my sister had left without waiting for me – at twenty-six, despite being nine years older than me and having a child of her own, she'd never been the typical adult, but leaving without me today would be a bit much, even for her. I peered over towards the exit. Rachel's blonde hair stood out within a crowd of people by one of the cars. I let out a small sigh of relief, but I didn't want to push my luck and linger too long.

'He's a lovely lad. So handsome,' Nosey continued. 'I know you're only young, Ronnie, but you should try to be like your sister now. Get a nice man who can take care of you.'

I dipped my head in agreement, pondering just how screwed up our tiny family would be if I did, in fact, decide to be more like Rachel. At the same time, I saw my best friend making her way towards me. I made my excuses to Maureen and let myself enjoy a warm hug from Mae.

Then, with a deep breath I braced myself for the evening to come.

2 — WHITE KNIGHT

'**W**HAT ARE YOU DOING STILL IN BED?**'** My sister's voice was shrill. I'd been awake for hours, but couldn't find a reason to get up. I moved the pillow from my face and squinted at her.

'It's only ten.'

'You can't let this get you down, Ronnie. We need to be strong and carry on. It's what Dad would have wanted.'

'I'll get up soon.'

'Well, the house is a mess after the party.'

'The wake.'

'What?'

'The wake, Rachel, it wasn't a party.'

Rachel rolled her eyes. 'Yes, Ronnie, that's what I meant, don't be melodramatic, please. It needs to be cleared up anyhow.'

I sighed, trying not to let her get to me, this was standard Rachel. Dad always said she was more like our mother in both looks and personality: beautiful, passionate… volatile. I don't remember my mother, but Rachel does. She'd stuck around until I was three, when one day she packed her things and left, never contacting any of us again.

'I'll clear up soon. It wouldn't hurt you to help out a bit.'

'Yeah, I need to sleep though. I've only just got in. Yesterday was so awful it took a lot out of me. I'll have a thirty-minute power nap then I'll help.' With that, she flounced out of the room, her champagne blonde hair bouncing as she went. I listened to her brushing her teeth before going to her old room, closing the door and turning her music up so loud I couldn't make out what she was doing.

I covered my face with the pillow again, trying to block out the brightness around me. I used to love my lemon-coloured walls and sheer white cotton curtains. My room in our old farmhouse was always bathed in the first rays of morning sunlight. Dad called it the Happy Room. Today, however, the sunshine was in sharp contrast to how I felt. I threw back the covers and forced myself out of bed, heading downstairs. The floor was cold under my feet. I'd have to remember to put the heating on timer from now on.

Glancing around at the plates and glasses strewn about, I sighed. Taking a dustbin bag from the kitchen, I began swiping up left over food littering the living room, cleared a broken glass and set about getting a red wine stain out of the cream rug. As I cleaned, my spirits began to lift. I thought: *if I can just keep busy, I might be okay.* Keeping my mind occupied had always helped me avoid things that upset me. That's where my hero fantasies had come from. That's what the trauma counsellor told my father, anyway. I saw her a few times after I was attacked on the beach three years ago, taking a detour home from Mae's late one night. In hindsight, walking along the beachfront after midnight seems like a stupid thing to do. But, hey, I was fourteen.

The rain had begun as a light drizzle and, as I walked, the sky thundered around me. I was wearing my cherry-red plastic raincoat, a present from my dad, who had no taste in clothing but a strong sense of practicality. *'That big hood will keep you from getting wet. And it's a nice bright colour so drivers can see you if you're out at night, Ronnie.'*

I pulled it tightly around me, tugging the hood down to cover my face. But the rain was so severe I was getting soaked anyway, tipping my head down just to keep water out of my eyes.

I hadn't expected anyone to be out walking, so when someone barged into me I almost apologised. But I received another blow – only this time far more powerful – to the side of my face. I fell, landing on the low wall that stopped the sea coming in too far at high tide. My back cracked against the stone. I cried out, but a gloved hand shoved across my mouth muffled the sound.

I thrashed out against the huge figure holding me, but I couldn't break free. His hand blocked my nose and mouth so I couldn't breathe. My hands scratched at his, my feet slipped against the wet ground. We both fell over the sea wall onto the beach below. He pinned me to the damp sand and ripped at my wet clothes.

The police said my attacker had raped and murdered four teenage girls from neighbouring counties. That night, however, I was lucky – luckier than the girls before me, anyhow. I told the counsellor and my father that my daydreams weren't my way of coping with depression or trauma. I was never depressed! I was just incredibly frustrated, because on that night someone saved my life and, to this day, I don't know who it was.

The police issued a statement to the press saying my attacker had drowned, having fallen from the pier when he was disturbed by a passer-by. But I'd told them until I was blue in the face that someone had not just *passed* by. He'd intervened.

I was filled with fear at the time, but I know what I saw: someone hauled my attacker off me, someone moving quickly in the shadows. I scrambled to my feet, peering through the torrential rain, to see the monster and the stranger fighting. The tussle didn't last long and I'll never forget the image of my attacker's huge body dropping lifelessly into the ocean and how, shrouded in darkness, my saviour looked back briefly in my direction before sprinting off into the night.

He was the reason I was still alive. But no one believed my story, because according to the police there was no evidence to support my statement. Apparently trauma does that – makes you a liar. Or, according to my counselor: *"Alters your perception of reality."*

I didn't see her for long. Dad insisted at first, but I hated every minute of it. So I kept myself more alert while I was around him, dreaming only when I was alone and never talking about the phantom hero. After a while – abracadabra – I was cured. Ever since that night, however, I've secretly prayed that one day I'd meet the one who saved me, that my knight in shining armour might come to my rescue again.

Gazing out of our living room window, holding a plate of leftover sausage rolls covered in congealed tomato sauce, I felt that now was as good a time as any.

3 — STRANGER

I PACED THE KITCHEN. Dad's hand-carved wooden furniture, the pile of his dirty clothes I'd yet to wash and the coffee in the kitchen that only he drank. All of it was too painful to look at. I needed to get out.

I took the quickest shower in history and pulled on my usual jeans and long-sleeved top. My sister still hadn't emerged from her room so I grabbed my hat, scarf and jacket and almost hurled myself out of the house and went into town.

Clanots Ocean High Street is basically a string of dated amusement arcades and a small circuit of shops touched white by the salt from the sea. I headed for Tom's Diner, which is actually more of a coffee shop than a diner, but has an open fire and an awesome view of the ocean. It's a good place to kill time. Ordering a slice of homemade cherry pie and a hot chocolate, I found myself a vacant seat by the window. I managed to while away what I hoped was at least an hour before my cup was empty, lingering over the milky foam dissolving. Christmas shoppers filled the streets. Colourful shopping bags and smiling faces held my interest for a while, but I knew I couldn't avoid home for ever and there was a queue of people lined up outside waiting for a table. Reluctantly, I took the bill that had been left on the table and dug into my bag for my purse.

To my horror, it wasn't there.

11

I continued to search, but I knew I wouldn't find it - I could picture it sitting on the kitchen counter at home. Mortified, I rose from my seat and tried to quietly explain my situation to the waitress.

'What do you mean?' she asked with a high-pitched nasal sigh. 'You can't pay?'

My cheeks filled with blood as the eyes of every customer flicked in my direction. Curling into myself, I replied as quietly as possible. 'I come here all the time. I've left my wallet at home, but I'll go there now and get it.'

Her face scrunched up and she popped her gum as she mulled over my words. 'I don't think I can do that. You say you come here all the time? I've never seen ya.'

Though I kept to myself, I found it hard to believe someone wouldn't know who I was – who anyone was for that matter – if they lived in our tiny town. I knew her; she'd been two years above me in school! I glanced around the café and, to make matters worse, the boy from the funeral sat in the far corner, looking over at us intently from beneath a pair of dark eyebrows. My whole body grew hot as my humiliation intensified. I didn't think it could get any more embarrassing, but then someone yelled over:

'Hey Lynn, lay off of her, her dad just died.'

I couldn't take any more. Positive I was about to cry, I turned to run from the café, but at the same time as I spun away from Lynn, she was grabbing my arm to stop me.

Just when I thought I would fall in a heap on the ground and let myself rot there, a hand appeared from behind me, handing a twenty-pound note to the waitress.

'Keep the change,' said a low, smooth voice, 'and buy yourself some tact while you're at it.'

I had just enough time to see Lynn Horton's face twist in shock before I looked over my shoulder to see who'd helped me. The boy from the funeral stood looking down at me. His dark eyes locked onto mine for a fraction of a second, but he looked almost as embarrassed as I felt, and glanced away quickly. I tried to thank him, but before I could form the words he'd already turned to leave, the line of customers parting as he walked past them.

All around me, people sat in shocked silence. I should have felt humiliated, but I noticed everybody's interest had shifted from my having no way of paying, to the stranger who'd helped me.

I fought back a smile and, with what I hoped was my most disapproving look, I said, 'I'll let Gail know what a big help you were today, Lynn.'

Holding my head high, I marched out. The owner, Gail, had known my dad well. If she'd been working the new waitress wouldn't have got off so lightly. I walked out feeling shame-faced, but the lump in my throat had dissolved. It could have been a lot worse.

I wandered aimlessly through town after that, thinking about what had happened. I'd only seen the mysterious group of boys a couple of times in the three months they'd been in Clanots. The first time, they were running along the beach early one morning. There was nothing remarkable about that – a lot of people ran in the mornings – though I did notice they appeared to be quite regimented; how I imagined army cadets might be. The second time I'd been taking a detour along a back street behind the old abandoned supermarket in town when, as if out of the sky, a boy dropped down in front of me. I leaped backwards. Oranges scattered as my shopping bags fell from my grasp, and a boy around my age rose from the crouch position he'd landed in and stared straight at me. He was athletic, with a cap turned backwards, covering most of his shoulder-length blonde hair. He didn't smile, but he didn't look threatening either, so I let my gaze shift from his blank face to see where he came from. There on the roof above, another boy stood looking down at us. Before I could wonder what he was doing, he

13

descended as if walking off the edge of a cliff. I flinched again, amazed as he caught the guttering on his way down to steady his fall, dropping the rest of the way and landing as gracefully as a cat. The one I had now seen twice in two days stood up straight and looked at me, his dark eyes animated, as if he were hiding a smile.

After picking up and handing me some of my fallen fruit, the pair had turned and darted along the alleyway towards the street ahead, one of them somersaulting over a dustbin in his way. I'd collected the rest of my things and continued home and that had been that. I never bumped into any of them again, so seeing one of them at the funeral, as if paying his respects had really got me curious. I decided to look for him and give him back the money. That would give me a chance to find out if and how he knew my dad.

Inside my duffel coat, my phone vibrated. I fished it out of the silk-lined pocket.

'Hello?'

'Ron, it's me.'

'Hey, Rach, what's up?'

I heard her tut on the other end of the line. 'Where are you? I go to sleep for thirty minutes and you've run off. I need you to babysit, you know I have Yoga on Saturdays.'

'I didn't think you'd go to yoga this week, after everything that's happened—'

'Don't try to make this all about you, Ronnie,' she snapped. 'I'm just as upset as you are, but we have to try to get on as normal. For my daughter's sake more than anything. She was looking forward to seeing her aunt and you've let her down.'

I muttered an apology. I really couldn't be bothered arguing. 'I've just left town, can you pick me up? I'll have her for the whole afternoon.'

Rachel hung up with a grunt, but I knew that was a yes and I only had to walk about half a mile before her silver BMW shot

14

round the corner.

'Really, Ronnie, because of you Jared's late for an important meeting,' she complained, as soon as I slid into the car. Rachel had the heat on full, so I began shedding my layers of clothing, as I considered what office supply manager would have a meeting on a Saturday afternoon. As always, I kept my thoughts to myself.

'Hey, do you remember Lynn Horton?'

Rachel's glossy pink lips pulled to one side, the way they always did when she was thinking. My sister and I could not look more different. Rachel was the sort of girl who turned heads wherever she went. With alabaster skin, pale blonde hair and crystal blue eyes, she looked just like our mother. My own dark brown eyes and auburn hair that I inherited from our dad were dull in comparison. The only thing we had in common were those lips she was chewing, yet somehow, what looked sultry and sensual on Rachel Rose still managed to look nothing more than clumsy on me.

'Yeah, I remember. Cat Horton's little sister,' she said eventually. 'I went to school with Cat. She was a moron. What about her?'

I lifted my shoulders and stared straight ahead. 'Lynn works at Tom's now. I forgot my wallet today and she made a big scene about it.'

Rachel looked at me then, her mouth dropping open. One thing Rachel could be counted upon was to be angry if someone she didn't like had something to say to one of her family. She was loyal that way, like a terrier.

'Oh, did she now? Both sisters will no doubt be waitressing all their lives. Useless witches! Next time I see her I'll give her a piece of my mind.'

'No, don't,' I insisted, but only half-heartedly. I'd never really have told Gail what happened, but I didn't think it would hurt Lynn to get a mouthful from Rachel.

15

'What about those boys who arrived here a few months ago?' I was going for casual, but Rachel wasn't buying it. Her eyebrows lifted as she cut me a sideways glance.

'Why? They don't work there too, do they?'

'No,' I said, ignoring her sarcasm, 'it's just, one of them kind of helped me out. He paid.' I was beginning to wish I hadn't said anything. Her pretty features fell in a mix of disgust and alarm.

'Ronnie, stay away from them, I've heard terrible things. Oh and now you owe one of them money! Is this what it's going to be like now? You attracting trouble wherever we go?'

I let my head fall back against the seat, wondering what trouble I had attracted – ever. I decided not to mention I'd seen him at Dad's funeral.

'Don't worry, I'll give him the money back tomorrow,' I said.

'Well, make sure you do. And don't talk to him. I mean it, Ronnie, just give whichever one it was the money and leave well alone. Yes?'

I stared out the window without answering, but I could feel her glaring at me. Eventually I nodded my head to show I agreed. For the moment anyway.

4 — WHO ARE YOU?

MONDAY MORNING, the weather had returned to its standard December grey and the wind was blowing up a gale. I dug out my wool-lined boots from the back of my cupboard before I left the house and jogged the five-minutes to the bus stop to help me keep warm.

I'd been putting off going back to school for weeks. They'd given me a pass because of Dad, letting me complete most of my assignments from home, but there were only so many re-sits I could do before they were going to force me to repeat the year. I wasn't sure I could handle that. Everyone would be going to uni and I would be left behind. The thought made me slightly queasy.

As soon as I walked through the gates, the curious stares and whispers began. Expressions filled with pity from literally every person I passed – including the faculty – were enough to make me cringe.

'Oh my goodness. Ron? What are you doing here?' Mae's brown eyes widened as I walked into class. I managed a small smile, though I didn't feel it. Especially when I glanced around to see the seating had changed while I'd been away. Mae now sat with Cheryl Matthews and Toni Gillings, two of the most popular girls in school. I hadn't expected that. They had barely said two words to Mae or myself in the six years we'd been at

Clanots County High. But for the moment, Mae's new friends were the least of my concerns. From the looks of it the seating hadn't just changed, I now had no seat at all.

'Here,' Greg said breathlessly as if he'd been caught sleeping on the job. 'Sit here.' He pulled up his own chair and shoved it on the end of Mae's desk. Greg was our form tutor. Up until a year ago we had called him Mr Northmoore, but apparently when you enrolled for A-Levels you were at school through choice, so you had the privilege of using the teacher's first name. I still hadn't got used to it.

Not wanting to attract any more attention, I plonked myself down, letting my rucksack fall to the floor. Greg hesitantly began taking the register from his standing position back at his desk and eventually the other kids' focus fell away from me. I knew most of them meant well; they couldn't understand why I was back so soon after Dad's funeral. I wanted to announce that it was so I could try to get back to normality and their staring at me like I was an alien with two heads wasn't helping the cause. Instead, I focused on my timetable and pretended I couldn't sense their curious glances. Mae squeezed my leg under the table. The touch of her hand made me relax some. Things would get back to normal soon, I told myself.

The day passed much the same way and by the end of my classes, people's interest in me had waned a little. I figured they were waiting for some sort of mental breakdown. I must have been a disappointment.

I found Mae in the common room before I left. She was with Cheryl.

'...Christmas break is in like, a week. She should have just waited. Come back in the New Year...' Cheryl trailed off as I approached. Her high cheekbones flushed pink but she wasn't one to dwell too much on awkward moments. She looked at me fleetingly before planting a kiss on Mae's cheek and leaving the room. I stared after her. Petite and pretty with a tiny nose that turned up slightly at the end, she was captain of the girls' netball team and co-founder of the first-ever cheerleading squad at Clanots County High. Mae hated sports and cheerleading wasn't something I had her pegged for either. Cheryl was possibly the last person I expected her to have taken up with. Mae had lots of friends, usually the studious book types – types like me, but I hadn't seen Mae talk to any of our usual social group all day.

'Something I said?' I asked.

'Sorry about that, Ron, she's just worried about you.'

'Yeah, I bet.'

'I'm worried about you. She's right, you didn't need to do this.'

I sighed and lifted my shoulders. 'What else was I gonna do?'

'You wanna come over tonight?' she offered, looping her arm through mine as we headed out of the building into the cold winter air.

'Thanks, but I have homework.'

Mae didn't respond, but I could tell she was a little relieved. It wasn't that I wanted to be alone, I just hadn't figured out how to be around people yet. And no matter how much they tried to pretend otherwise, I could see in everyone's eyes they didn't know how to be around me either. I just hoped time would fix the rift in my life and I wouldn't be forced into being a complete social recluse for ever.

The following morning I had two free periods, so I headed back to Tom's Diner before class. Not wanting the wallet incident to have a negative impact on one of the very few places in Clanots I liked, I pushed aside any humiliation I felt and strode in. To my surprise Lynn was especially nice to me. As soon as I ordered she almost fell over herself to apologise.

'Ronnie, I'm sorry I didn't recognise you. Even so, I shouldn't have said anything out of turn after you were honest enough to come over.'

19

I couldn't work out what had prompted her change of heart, there was no way Rachel would have said something and not come home to gloat about it, but as the thought crossed my mind, Gail walked past and shot Lynn a disapproving look. It seemed I didn't have to tell on her after all; word really did travel fast in small towns. I paid up front and went to my usual table in the window experiencing a glimmer of satisfaction that made me feel guilty just as quickly.

I stared through the window and picked halfheartedly at my cherry pie. In the end, I was just playing with my food, pushing pieces of pastry around the plate. I was getting up to head over to school, when two figures dressed in dark clothing emerged from a side street across the road.

My stomach flipped. I leaned forward so my nose was almost pressing against the window and watched the pair pass the shop, turning down onto the high street.

'Gorgeous, aren't they?' came a voice from behind me.

I jumped, turning to see Gail wiping the table next to mine, her curly black hair falling in her face. Her voice was deep and gravelly, as if she had a permanent sore throat. 'I find it so bizarre how they never talk to anyone, though. You know, I heard they don't have any parents–' Her face fell and her eyes grew wide. 'Oh, Ronnie, I'm so sorry, I didn't mean anything by that.'

'That's okay, Gail,' I said hurriedly before she could explain further. 'I understand what you mean.' I wasn't sure where my sudden surge of confidence came from, but I wanted to get outside before they disappeared from sight, so with a quick goodbye I swiped up my coat and rushed out. I had to skip my steps to catch up without running, but after a small desperate scuttle I managed to overtake them and turned to face the one I'd been looking for.

He was at least six-foot, so I had to look up and the moment our eyes met, my mind began to cloud. He wore a sweater that clung to him like a second skin and my eyes were drawn to his lean frame; strong without being bulky. His friend, similar in build, but with longer hair pulled back into a ponytail, stared vacantly at the ground, tucking a strand of his sandy-coloured hair behind one ear.

I reminded myself to breathe as the boy looked at me blankly, pretending not to know me.

'Can I help you?' he asked, with a smooth impassive voice.

'Yes,' I answered, much less calmly, 'I saw you at my dad's funeral.'

For a moment he just stared. I wondered if maybe he hadn't heard me, but then he turned to the longhaired boy and with a curt nod, told him to leave. His friend walked away without question or even a glance in my direction. Before I could consider that for too long he looked at me and frowned.

'Okay,' he said, taking my hand and walking purposefully in the direction of the seafront, 'let's talk by the sea. You can yell at me then without prying eyes. Or ears.'

I was shocked at the contact, but I found myself trotting after him anyway. 'Why would I want to yell at you?' I demanded.

'You tell me, Red. I have radar for irate women. I can see you're irate.'

'Don't call me Red,' I said self-consciously. I wasn't a massive fan of my red hair and I definitely didn't want to be referred to by it. A slow smirk formed on his face and I snatched my hand away.

When we reached the beach – which was cold, empty and grayer than usual – I took some initiative and stopped, sitting myself on the lowest point of the sea wall. He stopped too, looking around us both as if to check for onlookers. Satisfied, he perched next to me and stared out at the sea.

I studied him. I couldn't tell his hair colour because a black woolen hat covered it, but he had an intense frown, made more prominent by dark eyebrows and I couldn't help noticing a pale scar below his right eye. It held my attention, but didn't detract from his looks. Irritatingly, I had to admit Gail was right: he was totally gorgeous.

'I saw you at my father's funeral,' I said eventually.

'Did you?'

'Yes, you saw me too, you were staring at me.'

'Oh.'

'What do you mean, oh?'

He didn't respond. I fiddled nervously with the top button of my coat as the silence lingered. 'What's your name?' I asked when I couldn't take it any longer.

'Kalen.'

Kalen. I repeated the name in my head. 'Do you have a last name?'

'Smith.'

'I'm Veronica. Ronnie actually... Ronnie Rose.'

'How old are you?' he asked as if I hadn't spoken.

'How old are *you?*' I retorted.

He resumed his silence. His indifference was irritating – I wanted to shove him off the wall.

'Seventeen,' I grumbled. 'I'll be eighteen in February.'

'You live alone?'

'No,' I said, a little too quickly. 'My older sister lives with me and her boyfriend's there quite a bit too.' The lie rolled off my tongue. Something about him screamed danger, I wasn't sure I should trust him.

He nodded. 'Does she take care of you, then?'

'Ha! Hardly. She has a little girl, she barely takes care of her.'

'Who does?'

'Who takes care of her daughter?'

'No, who takes care of you?'

I was about to tell him I could look after myself, since that's what I'd done for as long as I could remember, but I stopped short, realising he had so easily led me into such a personal confession. Instead, I left the conversation with a shrug.

'You've avoided my question.'

'Yeah, I guess I have.'

'But you did know my dad?'

Another extended silence passed. I dug into my pocket for the twenty pounds I owed him, when he looked over his shoulder expectantly towards the road behind us.

'I have to go,' he said, as though he'd heard something I hadn't. His eyes met mine for the first time and I was instantly taken aback. They were the most intense dark blue, like the ocean at night, and while they showed no particular emotion, something in his stare caused a stir in the pit of my stomach.

'Thanks for what you did the other day!' I blurted. Aware I was gawking like an idiot. 'Here's the money I owe you.' I shoved the note towards him.

'I don't want your money, Red. Keep it.' With a wink, he leaped over the wall, turning back to me and arching one eyebrow suggestively. 'Tomorrow morning?'

'O-Okay.' I answered hesitantly.

He jogged down the bank towards the road and I was left wondering what had gotten in to me. He hadn't told me a thing, yet I'd agreed to meet him again, no questions asked. I was considering running after him to tell him I'd changed my mind, when a huge black motorcycle roared by. It slowed as it passed him. Fluidly, he swung onto the back and it tore off into the distance.

I stared after the bike, trying to figure out what had just happened. All the while, ignoring the voice in the back of my head, screaming at me to stay away from him.

5 — DESCENT

DESPITE HAVING LAID AWAKE MOST OF THE NIGHT TRYING TO TALK MYSELF OUT OF IT, I was taking time over my hair and applying my sister's mascara and blush ready to go and meet Kalen. It was more effort than I'd made, ever, and I had no idea why I was even going. Not only that, but I was missing a class to do it. Third day back. Nice one. I waved away the negative thought; considering every teacher practically fell off their chair when I walked in the room anyway, I didn't think my absence would be a big deal.

I didn't have much to go on, so I went back to the beach where we'd sat yesterday at the exact same time.

He didn't show.

I perched on the seawall with my legs dangling onto the damp sand for almost an hour, feeling so foolish that warm tears stung my eyes. Furiously, I squeezed them back and walked the two miles to school instead of getting the bus.

I didn't see Mae for the rest of the morning. She was missing in French, which was the one class we had together. I eventually found her in the cafeteria sitting with Cheryl and Toni. I weighed up my options: I could go find some of the girls Mae and I used to hang out with, or I could stop being a baby and sit with my best mate. I took a breath and headed over.

Toni was flicking through a hair magazine looking for a new style.

'That wouldn't suit you,' Cheryl was saying.

'It's the same as yours,' said Toni with a pout.

'Well, you're not me are you? Your face is too long anyway, go for something shorter.'

Mae nodded along in agreement and I wondered at them all. Six months ago, Mae and I would have been testing out our French skills or deciding on which countries we were going to travel to in our gap year before university... or some days, having our own private jokes about girls just like the ones she was BFF with now. I considered telling Mae about Kalen, but scrapped the idea almost immediately. They would have questions about my dad I couldn't answer. Plus I'd have to tell them he'd stood me up. Somehow, that wasn't something I wanted to share in front of Cheryl Matthews, who had probably never been stood up in her life.

The rest of the week passed slowly. The days I could handle; even hanging out with Cheryl and Toni was a breeze compared to the nights on my own. If it were possible, the house felt more silent with each night that went by. Rachel had moved into her boyfriend's apartment months ago, before Dad had become ill, but from time to time she still came home and stayed in her old room. Lately though, her visits were becoming more infrequent.

I was trying not to let it get to me, but ever since our solicitor had told me that Dad's secret gambling problem meant the inheritance Rachel and I assumed we had coming was gone, I felt a weight had fallen on me. To top it off, in typical Rachel style, she hadn't made it to the solicitor's meeting, so it was up to me to tell her we were going to have to sell the house. I wasn't looking forward to it. I wanted to crawl under my bed and never come out.

On Friday night, the perpetual ache in my chest made it impossible to sleep. Hours ticked by so slowly that eventually

I was counting each minute. My radio alarm clock taunted me from my bedside table.

Tick-tick-tick.

I tried thinking of Kalen. Replaying in my mind the moment he'd given the waitress the money, to when he winked at me and said he didn't want it back. But it would always bring me back to the fact that he had dealings with my dad and I didn't know what they were. Considering Dad had ended up with so many debt problems, which were now my problems, I couldn't help but wonder if the two were related. The ache grew.

Tick-tick-tick.

Tossing the covers aside, I went to my window and stared out. A thick layer of clouds covered the night sky, making it darker than usual. But as my eyes adjusted I could make out the rolling fields behind our back garden and the forest that had haunted my dreams as a child. I still felt like a child, but what good would it do me now? Now I had to be an adult, whether I liked it or not.

Tick-tick-tick.

Back on my bed I watched back-to-back sitcom re-runs until finally, dawn shimmered into my room. I hadn't slept at all.

Tick-tick-tick-tick-tick-tick – BOOM.

I found myself walking through the dense undergrowth of the forest that sat beyond the edge of our land before I was fully aware of my decision to leave the house. My clock radio lay shattered in pieces on my bedroom floor. I managed to find what I was after without much trouble. The small cabin my father had built was not far into the canopy of trees, nestled on the edge of a clearing.

The hut felt colder inside than out, so I was thankful for the portable gas heater Dad had left in the corner of the room. That and a foldout bed was everything inside. A plastic window looked out onto a frost-covered spider's web. I wiped it with the cuff of my jumper to let in some more light, then I pushed the ignition on the heater until a small orange-blue flame replaced the clicking noise. Glancing around, I perched on the icy bed, pulling my knees up to my chest and waiting for the air to warm.

When my toes no longer felt numb, I emptied my small bag on the bed. Three books, a packet of biscuits and a bottle of water fell out. I lay back and began reading, becoming distracted by a large house spider in the room with me. It made its way from the floor to the ceiling and positioned itself in a ray of early morning sunlight. I wondered if my dad had looked at the same spider. The pain in my chest returned.

Walking around outside, the fresh air helped a little. Eventually though, the cold forced me back inside and in front of the heater. My stomach growled in appreciation as I crunched down on the first of what was to be many Jammy Dodgers. Midday came and went. I stacked my books, un-stacked them and read each back cover at least five times before arranging them on a cardboard box, using two small rocks to hold them in place.

As I finished my last biscuit, I wondered if anyone had noticed my absence at home. The thought got me through a few more minutes and finally I curled into a tight ball and managed to fall asleep.

When I woke it was getting late. Soon, the whole cabin would be plunged into darkness. I cursed my stupidity and looked under the bed. *Surely Dad had a way to light the place in here somewhere?* Pushed up against the far wall was a small box of candles. Rummaging through it for one suitable, the sound of footsteps approaching outside catapulted me upright. I held my breath, trying to hear over the pounding in my chest. Maybe Rachel had sent Jared to look for me.

The door creaked open and I bit back a gasp. I hadn't expected Kalen.

He scowled at me from the doorway. 'You've had people worried.'

'Oh, it's you. What do you want?' I said, feigning disinterest and tossing the box of candles back on the floor.

He walked in, closing the makeshift door behind him as much as the out-of-place hinges would allow. Because the room was so small he could either sit on the bed with me or stand by the window about three feet away. He chose the window. Trailing one finger across my improvised bookshelf. I didn't repeat my question, though he made no move to answer it either.

'Kalen?' I said. Enjoying saying his name a little too much. 'You stood me up the other day.'

'I tried not to,' he replied.

It sounded like an honest answer, but I wondered what he meant. As far as I was concerned if you didn't want to stand someone up, you didn't. 'Why are you here?' I asked with exasperation.

He shrugged.

'You don't speak much, do you?'

'Sometimes.'

Sometimes what? 'How did you find me?'

'I'm good at finding people.'

'Okay then, *why* did you find me?'

'Why here?' he asked suddenly.

I followed his gaze out of the small window.

'My dad used to come here,' I said before I could think. I clutched my stomach as a sharp pain rushed through me at the memory. 'He thought we didn't know, but sometimes late at night he would sneak out of the house, not coming back until dawn. I followed him once. I don't know why he liked it here, but I suppose it just gave him some time away from us. I didn't consider it much, but it must have been hard having to bring up two girls by himself,' I reflected sadly, 'Rachel doesn't know, please don't tell her.'

'I don't know your sister.'

I couldn't see his face, but I thought his voice sounded kinder somehow. I stared at him while his back was turned. Without his hat, I could see his hair was dark blond, cut short with no particular style. He was dressed entirely in black, like before. Timeless clothes. He didn't dress like anyone our age – or anyone older for that matter. He definitely had his own style. I tried to put my finger on it. Practical? Still, the fitted sweater clung closely to muscles hiding beneath; I doubted there was much he wouldn't look good in.

He turned around and I averted my eyes.

'You need to get home,' he said. 'Being alone in the woods is no place for a young girl. You of all people should know that.'

'Why me of all people? And who are you anyway? You haven't told me anything I want to know, but you expect me to leave here with you. Are you mental?' I was serious about the last part: he definitely had me questioning his sanity.

His face broke into a wide grin. I hadn't seen him smile and the transformation was startling. He had without a doubt, the best smile I'd ever seen. Bright and disarming with deep-set dimples piercing each cheek, it lit up his face and I was forced to look away to catch my breath.

'I do expect you to leave here with me. I'll make you if I have to.' His smile continued with an arrogance I wanted to hate, yet found myself blushing at.

'Tell me how you knew my dad,' I insisted.

He seemed to think it over and then with a measured tone said, 'You told me you have responsibilities at home – your sister, your niece? I don't think you'll stay here long, Red. If you insist, I'll stay with you, to make sure you're safe.'

I pulled my hair back from my face and let out a lungful of air. But I knew I was no longer mad. I actually wanted to go home. I wasn't even sure why I'd left in the first place and I definitely didn't want to stay alone in the woods after dark. I refused, however, to have some smart-aleck stranger tell me what to do.

'Stay, see if I care,' I retorted.

He hesitated, then shrugged and kicked off his shoes. 'Awesome, I was looking for a way to kill some time anyway.'

Sitting on the rickety bed, he bounced lightly on the springs and arched his eyebrows. 'This is going to be tough to sleep on with two of us,' he noted. Lying back, he closed his eyes. His long legs hung to the floor.

While I knew he wasn't really sleeping, I was a little lost for words at his calling my bluff. 'You can't sleep on the bed with me.'

He opened one eye and looked straight at me. 'Where should I sleep, the floor?'

'I don't want you to stay here.'

'I don't want *you* to stay here.'

'Get out,' I huffed.

But he'd closed his eyes again, stifling a smile.

I changed tact. 'Kalen, why are you here? Why do you care what happens to me if I stay by myself in the woods all night? Stop evading my questions and I'll let you take me home.'

He kept his eyes closed for a while longer and silence lingered in the room, broken only by birds outside and the wind picking up through the old oaks.

'I stopped by your house,' he said finally, sitting up straight. 'I overheard your sister talking on the phone. She was... worried. I wondered if you were okay, so I came to check.'

With a gulp, I asked the question that was on the tip of my tongue, 'Why?'

'Young girl, father just died. I had nothing better to do anyway.'

I pressed my lips together – I would never get a straight

30

answer out of him. 'Hey, hang on. You were at my house? How do you know where I live?'

'No, my turn to ask a question.'

I folded my arms across my chest, trying my best to look cross.

'What is the point of this?'

'Of what?'

'Of, this…' he waved one large hand towards the room around us. 'Being here, not telling anyone. What is it you want to gain?' He gazed at me with genuine interest as he waited for my answer. I thought it over and suddenly felt very ashamed of myself. I had no idea what I wanted.

'You know you overheard my sister?' I began, trying my best to explain. 'You said she was worried…'

He sat up straighter, shifting in his seat.

'She wasn't worried at all, was she.' It wasn't really a question, because I knew the answer.

He chewed his lip and I could see he was selecting his words. 'You told me your sister doesn't take care of you anyway,' he answered carefully.

'So, she was mad right? Moaning that I'd gone off somewhere and she wanted someone to take care of my niece.'

He studied me for a moment, a question in his eyes that went unasked. 'It's dark,' he said, without taking his eyes from mine. 'Will you let me take you home?'

I nodded, because it was all I could do. My eyes were heavy and my heart the same.

'You know,' he said, pulling one hand down his face as if trying to decide whether to continue. 'I'm an orphan too. I know how it feels to be lonely.'

I sat very still for a moment in case he continued, but after a minute or so of silence he stood up. I pushed my arms through the sleeves of my coat while Kalen swiped up each of my books, helping me put them in my rucksack. Then he led us out into the darkness.

As I stumbled around I couldn't help but laugh out loud, picturing myself alone in the cabin at night with nothing except the spider and the ever-increasing sounds of the forest. I thought I saw Kalen look back as he wove down towards the gap in the trees, but he didn't ask what I was laughing at. Nothing seemed to move him emotionally. He came across cold and detached for the most part, but still, none of that frosty exterior could take away from the fact that he had come to take me home. It was a pleasant notion that nestled warmly between many painful ones.

When we arrived at my back porch he told me to sleep well and turned to leave.

'Hey,' I called before he disappeared into the darkness.

He turned and looked at me.

'Um... so, how do I contact you?' The thought of him disappearing from my life had me strangely desperate.

'I don't have a phone,' he said, apologetically. But I guessed it was a lie – who didn't own a mobile phone?

'I'll see you soon though,' he added. Then, with an impressive leap over my side fence, he was gone.

I lingered for a while in the chilly night air, contemplating Kalen Smith: who he was, where he came from and what he wanted from me. Finally, my stomach got the better of me and I went inside, the prospect of food, a bath and bed suddenly infinitely more appealing than they'd been for a long while.

6 — SEARCH

HAVING SLEPT THROUGH AN ENTIRE NIGHT FOR THE FIRST TIME SINCE THE FUNERAL, I felt positive about the day ahead. I'd prepared pancakes for breakfast and was just sitting down when Rachel burst in through the back door.

I got up to grab some more eggs from the fridge.

'None for me, Ron, I can't stay long.'

'Hi, Rachel,' I responded quietly.

'Morning Aunty Wonnie.'

That was Cloud, Rachel's three-year-old. I have no words for how I feel about the name, but her father's surname is Johnson, so I'd taken to calling her CJ.

'CJ, aren't you looking lovely today!'

Cloud held her tiny fingers up to her wispy blonde hair. She was like a mini version of my big sister, all blonde hair and big blue eyes – heartbreakingly beautiful.

'Would you like some breakfast with me?'

My little niece nodded.

'I assume that's why you're here with her then?' I directed at Rachel, who was rearranging her own silky hair in the mirror.

'Yeah, look, I have to shop and you know I hate to do that

33

with her. I'll only be an hour, I couldn't get a sitter at such short notice.'

'Did you try?'

'Ha. Ronnie you're so funny, but really, after not being here yesterday, you shouldn't be difficult right now.'

With that, she air kissed my cheek and her daughter's and rushed back out the way she'd come. CJ sat down at the kitchen table and smiled up at me. She was shamelessly cute and really, I couldn't resist her. My only hesitation was that I'd wanted to go into town and look for Kalen. I needed to be strong and find out what my dad was involved in. I quietly prayed it was nothing that would mar my opinion of him.

I handed Cloud a plastic spoon and the pancakes I'd cut into small squares, with a side of defrosted raspberries, before sitting down in front of her with my own.

She mumbled a thank you.

'You're welcome. What do you want to do today?'

'Beesh?'

'No sweetheart, the weather is no good for the beach, how about we do some painting inside where it's warm?' Cloud whooped with joy over the new idea and squishing raspberries into her mouth she flashed me a big red smile. Kalen can wait, I thought adamantly. An afternoon of riddles and answer swerving was not a priority over my family.

Cloud and I spent the morning with our fingers in an array of paints I had laid out on our huge kitchen table. Once we had drawn several paintings of Mummy, Daddy and Scat the cat – who was the cat Cloud wanted, not one she owned; Rachel would rather die than have pet hair anywhere near her – it was already midday. I began clearing away the brushes and splattered newspaper until at last only our paintings and one brush clutched in her small hand were left.

'Come on now, why don't we watch a movie?'

She shook her head repeatedly.

I laughed. 'Really?' I feigned disbelief. 'You don't want to watch Toy Story?' It was sure to work, it was her favourite film.

Her interest in paint faded and the brush fell to the floor as she ran to me with outstretched arms. I scooped her up and, after washing her hands I found the DVD and sat back with her on the couch to watch it.

Just as it was ending, my iPhone buzzed loudly at my side. It was Mae.

'How are you, hon?'

'Not bad,' I told her.

'What you doing today? Mum and I are going shopping.' I heard her mother, yelling for me to go with them. I felt myself smile at the sound of Mrs. Jensen.

'Rain check? I'm babysitting.'

'Really? When will Rach be back?'

'Ha, your guess is as good as mine.'

'Okay, well, if you need to get out, just call me, okay?'

'Thanks.' I was about to hang up when a thought occurred to me. 'Mae–'

'Mum, I said wait!' she yelled at the other end of the line. 'Sorry Mum is rushing me, what's up?'

'You know those guys, the older boys we sometimes see in town.'

'Yeah, Chel doesn't stop talking about them lately. To be honest they give me the creeps – I don't care how hot they are. Some of the boys reckon they're dealing.'

'Drugs?' I blurted.

'No Ron, candy floss.' I could almost hear her rolling her eyes.

'Right.'

'What about them, anyway?'

'Oh, nothing,' I bit my lip.

'Nothing, equals something.'

I cringed. 'Well, I met one of them the other day. His name's Kalen.'

'Ommigod!' she exclaimed. 'How? When? I want details!'

'It's no big deal, but–' I heard Mae's mother calling her again on the other end of the line.

Mae sighed. 'I have to go Ron, but this isn't over. You got his last name?'

'Yeah.'

'Perfect, look him up on Facebook. Buzz me later okay?'

'K, bye.'

We hung up at the same time as I heard a car coming up the driveway. My mind was reeling as I peered outside. Rachel was back. The whole drug concept would have to wait – I guessed now was as good a time as any to tell her about the house, but she burst into the living room with a stormy expression that gave me second thoughts.

'I've had the worst day!'

'Wow, for a minute there, Rach, I thought you might take up all of mine.'

'Don't start with me, Ron, I am not in the mood. Look at my hair. The stylist completely used the wrong colour on my highlights.'

Cloud ran to her mother and held her hands out. Rachel swiped her up and started cooing at her.

'I think your hair looks nice,' I said. It didn't look any different to me.

'Oh, what would you know, you've never even dyed your hair.'

I took a deep breath so I wouldn't say anything I'd regret. My sister was a brat, but arguing with her never got me anywhere. Rachel had been most affected by our mother leaving

36

because she'd been a teenager at the time and was old enough to feel immense rejection and abandonment from it. I knew that's why Dad had always let her run wild, while I had to behave myself and take care of the home. I expected it was also why, to this day, I still felt protective of her – she'd had it rougher than I did. The news that our inheritance was gone was not going to be welcome. It could wait until after Christmas at least.

'By the way, did you give that boy back the money you owed him?'

The question caught me by surprise. 'Um, yeah, sort of.'

'Sort of?' she snapped, lifting her perfectly plucked eyebrows.

'He wouldn't take it.'

'What does he want then?'

'Nothing,' I shrugged and sat back. 'You staying here tonight?'

'No, I'll be at the flat, don't change the subject either. He obviously wants something?'

'What, because he bought me a hot chocolate? It wasn't a marriage proposal, Rach.'

She flashed me a sarcastic smile. 'I don't want you getting led astray, especially now I'm not here that much.'

'You could always come round more often,' I pointed out.

'Oh don't be selfish, Ronnie, I have a family to think about. Dad wouldn't approve of you hanging out with them you know.'

Hot anger boiled inside me at the mention of my father. I resisted the urge to tell her that she had no idea what Dad would approve of. Instead I said something I knew would get rid of her.

'Speaking of Dad, can you help me get the Christmas decorations down from the loft?'

Her eyes widened as she considered helping me do something that could get her dirty or potentially break a sweat. I smiled.

'I would, but I have to go. Christmas is in a week. You'll cook right? Just let me know what I need to bring.' She hurried out.

When she was gone I pulled out my laptop and waited for it to spring to life. I wasn't as up-to-date as I should have been with Facebook. Dad had a strict rule of only one hour Internet per night, which for me was usually taken up with assignment research, but even I had my own page. I logged in and typed in Kalen's name. The search came up blank. I checked Google for any sign of him. Nothing. Not even a My Space.

I was oddly frustrated. Had he lied about his name? I snapped the computer shut. Who didn't have a phone or any social network? Something about him was off, but more annoying was how badly I wanted to know what it was. I needed a distraction. I took out a pad of paper and started to brainstorm what to do about the house. In the middle of the page I drew a circle and wrote Ronnie in the centre. The first thing I scribbled down without even thinking was, JOB. That was it – I had to get a job! The idea was appealing and the more I thought about it, the more perfect it seemed. Perhaps if I could contribute, Rachel and Jared wouldn't mind getting a mortgage in their name and we wouldn't lose the house. The possibility of losing the house I'd grown up in, so soon after losing my dad, was scrambling my brain. It wouldn't compute. If I could work weekends and during the holidays maybe I could save it. It might mean giving up on uni, but I wasn't sure there was another way.

Not letting my mind dwell on the depressing side of things, I focused on the good. One step at a time: a part-time job for now and I would try and work everything out between now and university enrollment. I'd already been tentatively accepted into my first choice and I knew the offer would be there as long as I didn't flunk out on all my exams.

I began to wonder what sort of job I could get. I'd always wanted to travel, but it didn't seem as important to me as keeping something William Rose had worked all his life for. Maybe if I worked in the travel industry I could go to college part time and study tourism. That would help me see some of the world while still keeping our home.

The thought lingered. It was a long shot, but it was better than no shot at all. As I stared at the wooden table Dad built with his own hands, I knew I had to try.

I showered and washed my hair, dressing in the only shift dress I owned and teaming it with a pair of Rachel's heels. Feeling marginally more confident with my new appearance, I left the house. The weather was cold and dismal, as usual, but the rain had subsided. A good sign, I told myself.

I was boarding the bus, when a text beeped through on my phone from Mae.

Christmas Kick Off. White Lies 2mrw nite! xx

The Christmas holidays had begun, so everyone our age would be out celebrating a Sunday night with no school the next day. It was a long-running tradition in Clanots, but one I'd never been part of. Mainly because we'd never been old enough, but White Lies was the only club in town where they rarely asked for ID so I knew that wouldn't be a problem. Though I didn't feel it was really my scene, I wasn't in a position to be picky. I texted back that I'd see her at nine.

I spent the afternoon picking up application forms for retail work, plucking up the courage before I left to go to the only travel agent in the town centre. There was no sign of the boy I quietly had my eye out for, even after repeated trips to the seafront, but the Travel Shop owner seemed interested in seeing me again. The old Greek owner said I reminded him of his daughter and to pop back after Christmas for a formal interview. With my much-needed good news, I was more excited about my evening out with Mae.

7 — DROWNING

I WAS GETTING READY FOR THE CLUB WHEN I HEARD A CAR PULL UP OUTSIDE. I peered out the window on the landing. Rachel's BMW gleamed from the driveway.

'Hey, Rach,' I chimed from the top of the stairs as she walked in.

She sprinted up to me. Her long hair was piled on top of her head and she wore a light grey tracksuit with charcoal-grey UGG boots. She looked like she'd just stepped out of a winter catalogue and I couldn't help but feel slightly envious at her effortless glamour.

'How are you?' she asked.

'Pretty good,' I said. 'Not that it isn't good to see you, but why are you here?'

'It's my house too Ron, I don't need an invite to come over.'

I resisted a roll of my eyes and went back to my room, running mascara over my lashes.

'I need a favour,' she added, following me in.

'I can't tonight Rach, I'm going out.'

'Ronnie, I'm desperate. Just for a few hours.'

'I can't. I haven't been out of this house since... well, for a long time and tonight, for once, I have plans.'

Her eyes narrowed as she stared at me. 'Plans with who?'

'I'm not dignifying that with an answer.'

'Veronica, I'm in charge now that Daddy's gone.'

'I'm going out with Mae, okay? With Mae!'

She eyed me skeptically, looking for a lie. Finally, with a huff, she gave up trying to wear me down, muttering to herself as she claimed a hair dryer and brush from the bathroom.

'I just can't rely on anyone! My stupid babysitter had an argument with her boyfriend and is refusing to come out of her room. I've been left completely in the lurch. That's what I get for trusting a school kid.'

Rachel stood at the door waiting for me to change my mind like I usually did. I refused to give in. I had to start taking control of my life and that meant getting one. Mae and I needed a night out and even if technically I was breaking the law by a few months, I was going.

Eventually, Rachel left, slamming the door behind her, but not without telling me how I was ruining her evening. I wanted to point out that perhaps if she hired a more mature babysitter in the first place I wouldn't be held accountable for night ruining, but I didn't bother. I had enough bad news to share with my sister without arguing over trivial things. I could handle a Rachel tantrum. I booked a cab and continued getting dressed.

***

In White Lies, Mae was sitting beside me looking at me like I was mentally challenged. She drummed her long fingernails on bar in front of us.

'Ron? You're not listening, are you?'

I'd managed to lose myself in one of my fantasies while she was talking to me. Quickly, I tried to recall what she'd been saying. I had nothing.

'Um, sorry, I guess I was just thinking about Dad,' I ventured.

'No, Ronnie, you don't think about what's actually going on. You never do. I know what you were thinking about, it's the same as always. I'm trying to help you have some fun and you're dreaming of a guy that doesn't exist.'

'He does exist!' I gave myself away of course, but it was annoying that my own best friend didn't believe my version of events as to how I was saved four years ago. It was bad enough that everyone else thought I was crazy, without her believing it too. I focused on her face, trying to be more attentive, but her eyes had glazed over.

'I wasn't thinking about him anyway,' I insisted. 'I was just in my own world. Sorry.'

'Fine, I'm sorry too,' she said with a pursed smile. Pulling her thick shiny curtain of black hair over one shoulder, she continued with a softer tone. 'I was saying that my mum said you're welcome to stay with us for a while if you want. Save you being in the house on your own, so soon after, well, you know – so soon.'

I could tell she was struggling; she had really liked my dad. Mae had known him for as long as we'd been friends and was practically family.

'Charlotte's living at university now so you could have her room.'

'Thanks, but I have to stay and take care of the house. Lord knows Rachel won't.'

'Ron, the house doesn't need taking care of, you do. For once, why don't you let someone help you?' She took my hand and squeezed it. Then her face brightened. She stood up, waving frantically towards the door. I swiveled on the bar stool to see Cheryl and Toni wave back from the entrance. Cheryl was laughing with a door attendant while Toni made her way towards us. Toni had gone for a dramatic hair change. Her normally mousy brown colour was now a bright yellow-blonde, straightened in a perfect middle parting so looked like it was cemented to each side of her face.

She ignored me as she sat down, talking directly to Mae as if I weren't there. I plucked up the courage to say hi and she just sort of, *sniffed* in my direction.

I felt invisible. I had on a pair of tight jeans and my favourite green top that complimented my colouring – the dressiest items I owned. I'd even kept on Rachel's heels. I thought I looked okay, but the mass of shimmering glitter and microdresses around me made me acutely aware of why I wasn't part of the in-crowd. I half smiled at Mae across the table. She looked back at me apologetically after Toni's rebuff.

Cheryl joined us shortly afterwards and I got a marginal acknowledgement from her, though it felt more of an appraisal. Her eyes lingered on me a moment longer than necessary and her glance swept me from top to bottom. I heard my father's voice in my head saying if someone wasn't polite to you, you could sure as hell guarantee they were just jealous. It was a sweet thought, but I was certain Dad hadn't a clue about the psyche of teenage girls. I bit my lip again, this time to cause a pain other than the one in my heart at the thought of him.

I ordered a round of drinks, hoping it might break the ice. Turned out I was right. As the drinks flowed they actually began to include me in their conversations. And the drinks really did flow.

Growing up, I'd been allowed the odd glass of champagne on special occasions, and there had been times when Mae and I had sneaked red wine from Rachel's room. Back-to-back schnapps shots, however, had not figured in my childhood. So, while the girls appeared to be seasoned veterans, I felt myself quickly and drastically losing control.

The club filled up with people; a smoke machine created a permanent fog all around us, while the heat from all the bodies crammed into a confined space enveloped us like a cocoon. Somewhere in the middle, I was dancing like crazy and didn't want to stop. I took the drinks handed to me and let the liquid burn the back of my throat. With each one the pain in my chest grew easier. I continued to twirl and shake my hips. Mae looked at me in concern, but Cheryl and Toni offered me what I needed: shallow, temporary comradeship that allowed me to drown my sorrows.

Then, out of nowhere, a white tablet was handed to me. I stopped dancing. The floor kept moving around me as if I was at sea. Despite the haze of too much alcohol, I knew what I was doing wasn't me and that my father would have been devastated. I rocked back and forth in my stupor. A man I didn't know had his hand on my waist, yelling something in my ear about how much fun I was. I smiled, trying to focus on his face, which was no more than a watery blur.

Looking at the pill in my hand, it suddenly occurred to me that I wanted my father to be mad at me. I wanted him to come yell at me, ground me and force me to leave the club. But he wasn't coming. He was never coming.

With that thought, I lifted the drug to my mouth.

8 — WATCHMAN

THE MOMENT THE SMALL TABLET TOUCHED MY TONGUE A LOT OF THINGS HAPPENED ALL AT ONCE. An arm wrapped around me, lifting me high off the floor, the man with his hand on my waist cried out in pain and a glass shattered on the table beside me. Then, I was floating across the dance-floor towards the toilets.

Once inside a cubicle, I blinked against the stark white light and two fingers were shoved down my throat. I squirmed frantically, gagging against the obstruction in my mouth, but it wouldn't budge and I was held tightly in place until after a few more moments of pointless thrashing, I vomited into the bowl.

It didn't take long for me to dry retch. I hadn't eaten all day. But once the alcohol, drug and all other contents of my stomach had emptied, I was released. I fell back against the cool tiled floor, dizzy. As the fog began to clear I could make out the person standing above me. I expected Mae, but should have known she wouldn't have had the strength to hold me. I squinted up at Kalen's face. He was talking to someone outside the door.

Mae was shouting to be let in and threatening to call the police, while he was telling her to calm down.

He helped me stand and with a grunt of disgust, said, 'I'm

getting you out of here.'

I thought about telling him where to go, but something stopped me. Instead, I leaned against him and let him help me out. I stared sheepishly at Mae and the crowd of whispering girls around her.

'You her friend?' Kalen asked Mae abruptly.

'Yes. Who the hell are you?'

'I'm taking her home – you too, come on.'

'No, let go of her!' Mae shouted. I was about to tell her I was okay when two bouncers appeared in the doorway.

'What's going on in here?' the smaller and stouter of the two asked, directing his question at the only thing holding me upright.

'This is my girlfriend,' Kalen answered casually, without pause. I saw Mae open her mouth to speak and I widened my eyes at her desperately. With a dark stare she quieted.

'You ain't allowed in the ladies' toilet, mate. I suggest you get your drunken bird outside before we throw you both out.'

I felt Kalen tense beside me, but he politely agreed and said all he wanted to do was get me outside. Before I could say, *'What the hell's going on,'* we were walking out of the front doors into the icy night air.

He led me to a nearby bench and told me to sit as he went to the McDonald's on the opposite side of the road. He returned with a bottle of water.

'Drink this,' he said coldly.

I took it from his hand, half temped to throw it back at him. But I unscrewed the lid and gulped it back. When the bottle was practically drained I turned to face him. As usual, he was dressed in dark clothing, with a round-necked sweater that seemed to cling tightly to the muscles beneath. I swallowed the last of the water and tried to focus on what he'd just done, instead of how good he looked.

Mae's ringtone broke the silence. Flushing, I located my phone in my purse and held it to my ear.

'Er, what the hell?' Mae yelled over the music inside.

I cringed. 'I'll explain later, okay?'

'Are you okay? I can get the bouncers–'

'No! I'm fine, honestly.' I looked at Kalen, who was leaning his elbows on his knees and staring at the ground.

'I'll call you later, okay?'

'Do not go home with that guy, Ronnie, are you crazy?'

'I won't. Speak later.' I ended the call and stared at Kalen. 'Why did you do that? Why are you here?'

'I could ask you the same questions. I won't be around every time you wallow in self-pity, you know.' He leaned back on the bench and stared straight ahead. Some people tumbled out of the club and their laughter carried over to us.

'I mean, why are you following me around?'

His eyes narrowed. 'Don't flatter yourself. This dive is the only place to go in this ridiculous town, right? It's not that big a coincidence.'

'So what, you were just out?'

'Something like that,' he said acidly.

'Maybe you're my guardian angel.' I ventured.

'Guardian angel?' he snorted. 'And she asks me if I'm mental! No, you couldn't be more wrong. I am most definitely not your guardian angel.'

'But maybe you are and you don't even realise it.'

He looked indifferent once more. Just when I thought the conversation had ended, the way they often seemed to do with him, he sighed and spoke again. 'I saw you dancing and people crowding around you. I left you to it at first, but then I saw what you were about to do. Kind of irresponsible, don't you think?'

It was my turn to scowl. 'I'm allowed to be irresponsible.

47

I'm tired of being dull and responsible all the time. Anyway, everyone else does it!'

'Everyone else,' he said with disdain, 'are sheep.'

'You're not a people person are you?'

'Depends on the people.'

'Well, you don't know me and I can do whatever the hell I like now–'

'Now that your father's dead?'

The bluntness of his response was brutal, but I'm certain he wanted to shock me. I sucked in a breath, a painful lump in my throat. I wasn't sure how to respond.

He said more gently, 'I'll drive you home.'

'I can't get in a car with you, you've been drinking,' I muttered.

'I don't drink.'

'You don't drink? I don't know anyone who doesn't drink.'

'You do now.'

9 — ADMITTING DEFEAT

I WAS SHOCKED WHEN HE OPENED THE DOOR TO A BLACK AUDI. It didn't seem like a car for anyone our age, but really, I didn't even know how old he was. It all seemed rather insignificant anyway, when he pulled away from the kerb.

To say he drove fast didn't do the word justice. I found myself clutching the door as if it might give me some protection if we veered off the road. I wanted to tell him to slow down, but instead I bit my lip and stared out the window at the dark landscape flying past us at what felt like light-speed.

When we arrived in front of my house, I let out a breath I hadn't realised I'd been holding. He came around to my side of the car and helped me out.

'How are you feeling now?' he asked me when we were at the porch.

'Fine.' I wobbled.

'You don't seem fine,' he spoke from behind me as I unlocked the front door. He was so close his breath on the back of my neck sent shivers down my spine.

'I guess I'd be better if I wasn't standing in front of you with vomit in my hair,' I mumbled.

'I hardly notice,' he said lightly, but I could hear a smile in

49

his voice. 'Sleep well, Red, I'll come check on you tomorrow.'

'Aren't you going to come in?' I blurted, spinning to face him before I could stop myself.

He hesitated and looked back at me over his shoulder. 'I'm not sure that's a good idea.'

I shrugged, but my disappointment must have been obvious, because a slow smile spread across his face. The effect of it had not diminished; I was momentarily overwhelmed.

'Come to think of it,' he added, with a voice like liquid gold, 'I should probably check everything's okay in your house before I leave.'

He leaned against the doorframe and ushered me in ahead of him, his grin never leaving his face. My stomach fluttered.

'Are you hungry?' he asked, following me inside.

'It's after midnight.'

'That wasn't my question.'

Hearing his confusion, I laughed. I was hungry and I guess the time made no difference. I turned and stared at him for longer than was appropriate. With such a large frame and a sharp jaw line, his whole being screamed, man – yet when he smiled, a boy shone through.

'I'll make something to eat after I've showered. I'm not sure my hands should be touching food after hugging a toilet bowl.' I fled upstairs, desperate to look in a mirror. The sight was worse than I imagined: my hair was a matted bird's nest and my mascara had smudged under my eyes. Cursing, I jumped under the stream of prickling hot water until my skin felt numb.

When I was done, I rubbed scented moisturiser all over me and rough-dried my hair, pulling out the knots with my fingers until it ran smooth.

As I pulled on a pair of boyfriend jeans and the only fitted sweater I owned, my phone beeped. It was a message from Mae.

WTF?!! Are you home or what?

Tempting as it was not to respond, the last thing I wanted was for her to think something bad had happened and call the police.

Yes, all gd. Will explain 2mw x

I threw my phone on the bed and headed downstairs. He was in the kitchen when I got there, leaning lazily against the counter, his blue eyes taking me in. I quickly glanced away, heading to the fridge as a distraction and hoping there would be something in there to eat. I scanned the expected emptiness and when I looked up he was next to me, surveying the contents as well. Our faces were so close they almost touched. If I lent in just an inch, I could've kissed him.

'Minimalist?' his smooth voice sliced through the tension in the air between us.

'Yeah, sorry. I can make you a cheese sandwich if you like?' I flushed and stood up straight, unsure what was happening between us. Every nerve in my body seemed electrified when he was around.

'Sounds great,' he said gently.

I took out the butter and cheese, grabbed a loaf and a kitchen knife and set to work. I was acutely aware of his eyes on me. Sweat trickled down my back, my palms too and as I cut the cheese, the knife slipped clumsily from my grasp. It clattered on the worktop then tumbled towards the floor and in the split second it took to fall, I stared at my bare toes, my brain accepting I might lose a few. But the pain never connected. Kalen was placing the knife on the counter and moving away before I even had a chance to yell.

I laughed nervously. 'Quick reflexes.'

'Perhaps I should make the sandwich?' He asked with a half smile.

'I can do it, thanks. It's you, making me nervous. Quit staring at me!'

'I make you nervous?' he asked, taking a step closer.

'I wish you wouldn't sound so pleased about it.'

'Fine,' he chuckled, 'I'll wait in the living room, but seriously, go for a smaller knife.'

I turned back to my half-made sandwich, unable to contain my smile, when I felt his hands encircle my waist. I jumped, sucking in a breath. My heart rate accelerated as I wondered what to do next.

Slowly, he turned me to face him, looking at me in so intensely that I trembled. His dark eyes held mine as he slipped his hands under the hem of my jumper, resting his thumbs on the waistband of my jeans. A flourish of goose bumps ignited on my skin. I closed my eyes in an attempt to calm my racing heart.

'Better,' he whispered, his lips hovering next to my ear.

'What's better?' I asked, my voice breathier than I'd wanted.

'You, without make up, just how you are right now.' His lips grazed my cheek and found my lips. An intense rush flooded through me, so I had to concentrate not to lose my footing. This wasn't right: I barely knew him and he was in my house... in the middle of the night. A clamp of fear tightened around my stomach, but I relished the sensation – any feeling other than the numbness I'd been living with over the past few months. Instantly, I pushed my body against his. In turn he maneuvered me back against the kitchen cabinet, taking my waist in his large hands and lifting me so I was sitting on the worktop.

I reached my arms around his neck as his mouth pressed fiercely onto mine. My lips tingled in response. It was rough... intense. It was everything I needed right then and there. As if a light switch had been flipped off, however, Kalen turned to stone in my arms. After a moment's pause, he stepped away and I found myself asking him timidly if he was okay. At least I must have done, because he answered the question I thought was in my head.

'Sorry,' he breathed, looking disappointed with himself in some way. 'I shouldn't have done that.'

I hopped off the counter and turned from him, taking up the knife and slicing furiously through the cheese. I didn't know if I was angry or embarrassed. Did he like me or was this all a game? Too many questions on the tip of my tongue, all serving to hurt the pride I hadn't been aware I had.

'Ronnie?' his voice was tepid behind me.

'Yep?'

'Are you okay?'

'I'm fine.'

'Look at me, please.'

'No.'

Oh my god, no – tears! I looked up towards the ceiling and blinked to fight them back. There was no way I wanted to cry in front of this boy, but one lone tear escaped and trickled its way down my cheek, falling onto the bread I had haphazardly sliced. As I watched it fall – almost in slow motion – I knew immediately that one tear was one too many. More followed, faster than I could wipe them away.

He spun me to face him and touched one of my wet cheeks with his thumb. He closed his eyes, his mouth pressing into a tight line of frustration.

Looking at me once more, he took my arms in his hands. 'Ronnie. I don't want to hurt you.'

'Then let go of me.'

His hands fell to his sides and he stepped back. 'I didn't mean like that. Sorry.'

I let myself slide down the cabinet until I was sitting on the floor with my knees up to my chest. I dropped my head in my hands.

'You miss your father,' he stated from above me. 'It was terrible timing of me,' he struggled. 'I don't know why I even

53

care, but I would be taking advantage and I don't want to do that with you. That's all I meant. Of course I would love to... I think you understand this better than you make out.'

I stared at the black hole I'd created under my canopy of hair and realised just how right he was – about one thing at least: I missed my father so much. I'd been trying to live with distractions for the past two weeks, not allowing myself to pause, but in reality, I missed him so much, no amount of pretending was going to make the hurt go away. A pain swelled like a fist inside my chest at the realisation and came out in a single pitiful sob.

I felt Kalen sit down beside me. His fingers intertwined with mine. More tears overflowed from my eyes and dropped on his hand. I stared at them without blinking.

'It's okay, Red,' he whispered into my hair as he pulled me closer to him. 'Everything's going to be okay.'

The small act of kindness was too much for me and I could no longer fight it. I let him pull me into his embrace and let out what I had pent up for the last five and a half months. Tears flooded, thick and fast, my breathing escaping in uncontrolled sobs.

I wasn't sure how long we sat that way, but he held me tightly as what felt like an ocean flowed out of me. At some point, though I don't remember the exact moment, I fell asleep.

France – May 2003

He spent his thirteenth birthday at an airport in Paris, accompanied by two thirty-something adults whom he'd never met.

'Mom, can I carry my own bag?'

'Of course, dear, be careful you don't lose it okay?'

'Thanks, Mom.'

The immaculately dressed blonde woman smiled widely, showing a set of perfect veneers as she passed K his rucksack.

'Give the man your passport, son,' said the tall dark-haired man as he nodded politely at the French border security. They passed through the gates with no problems and the man hailed a taxi to take them to their hotel. They rode the taxi in silence, apart from K asking if he could see the Eiffel Tower, to which the driver smiled and nodded enthusiastically. 'It's a beautiful structure. The tourists, they love to see it!'

'Yes, this is our son's first time. He's always wanted to see Paris,' the pretty lady gushed. Patting her fake son's knee.

'You are American, yes?'

'Yes, that's right, from Baltimore,' she replied with an overtly sweet smile. K stared out of the window. He'd done his bit; the phony conversation for the sake of the taxi driver could be limited now, all he wanted to do was get to the hotel and out of the company of the two actors, whom he found revolting.

The hotel was beautiful, of course. It was his first trip abroad so if he'd been a normal boy it would have been an exciting moment. He had, however, already memorised the layout of the hotel and a map of the city. He knew every street and side street as well as the hot spots for police activity. He wasn't interested in croissants and coffee, all he cared about was the man staying in a room directly three floors above who would be checking-in to the hotel in less than thirty minutes. One thing at a time, every step accounted for – enjoyment was not part of the plan.

K stepped out onto the small ornate balcony and looked over it. As far as cities went, Paris was vastly different to any in America and almost sparked a glimmer of interest inside him. It evaporated quickly when someone spoke from inside the room.

'We'll escort you to the airport tomorrow at the agreed time.'

They didn't wait for any acknowledgement or goodbye, but then, K didn't offer any. He didn't need to be told. He stared blankly as they left, closing the door behind them. When he was alone he unloaded his bag onto the bed: pants, vests, sneakers, a tennis ball and a Nintendo Gameboy – none of which belonged to him. Inside the casing of the console lay a small syringe. He pried the outer shell apart and took out the needle, placing it carefully on the bedside table before going to wash up.

When he returned to the grand room he sat on the edge of the bed and switched on the television. It was his first time and he could not deny he was nervous. He wouldn't admit that to anyone, of course, but he made a conscious effort to keep his hands from trembling. After a few minutes of meditation, they became deathly still. He exhaled. Trying to focus on something else to pass the time, he looked at the picture in his passport and the name next to it: **Kalen Smith**

It was the first time he'd seen a name next to his picture. He took a moment to consider how it made him feel. He wasn't sure. Nerves were getting tiresome, but K knew if he couldn't pull this off he would be no use to the unit. If he was no use to the unit, he was nothing – there was nothing else except the unit.

Thirty minutes passed; it was time. K took the syringe in his hand and slid it into the front pocket of his black sweater. Silently, he left the room.

He avoided the few cameras in the hotel without much trouble, gliding to the stairwell and up to the floor he wanted and moving swiftly along the typically French Damask corridor until he reached the room.

He entered using the key he had been given before he left the US and crept into the room. He could hear the shower. Perfect timing. He slipped into the bathroom, following the sound of running water.

Mistakes are to be learned from. If the result of that mistake is not death, then the lesson can be a useful tool for survival. The shower was empty. He hadn't expected that. Of course, he shouldn't have expected anything and he knew it. Could it be the brightest student in the whole team, the head of the class, the strongest, smartest and most able of all of them had forgotten the first rule of assassination on his first day on the job? Assumption was the mother of all...

He had something on his side though. Had he been an adult caught snooping in the apartment of such an important person, the man holding the gun to his head would have fired it without thinking twice. K would have been dead before he had a chance to turn and face his killer. His childlike frame, however, had prevented such a reaction.

K turned and let his eyes grow wide with faux fear.

'What the hell are you doing in my room, kid?' the American man bellowed, removing the safety on his Glock 23.

'S-sorry, sir,' Kalen stuttered, pushing a strand of his chin-length hair behind one ear, as he felt for the item stowed within his pocket. 'I-I must have the wrong room. Sorry to have disturbed you, if you don't mind, could you help me find my parents?'

The target lowered his weapon. It was the last thing he would ever do.

10 — FOUR MORE

MY HEAD FELT AS THOUGH IT WAS CEMENTED TO MY PILLOW, held down with lead weights - and an avil. At first I wondered what was happening. Was I ill? Had I hurt myself? Then the evening's events dripped slowly back into my mind and the reason for my pain became clear. I had a hangover.

Ergh!

For all the times I'd heard Rachel complain and thought she was overreacting, I said a silent apology.

I was closing my eyes again, when something stirred in my en-suite. At the exact same moment a disturbing thought crossed my mind: *I don't remember getting to bed.* I shot upright, ignored my throbbing skull and yanking the quilt around me. Kalen walked casually out of the bathroom wearing nothing but his jeans.

'Good morning,' he said, sitting on the edge of the bed and flashing me a bright smile.

'I'm half naked,' I exclaimed dumbly, aware that all I had on was my underwear.

'I undressed you.'

Desperately, my mind searched for a memory of what had happened, but everything was hazy. 'That's so rude! How dare you?'

'It was necessary,' he answered, as if my question was ridiculous. 'You fell asleep, so I put you to bed. I promise, I hardly looked, and I slept on the floor.'

'Oh my goodness!' I wailed.

'It's okay, I've slept on worse.'

'Kalen, that's not what I meant.'

'Call me Kal.'

That threw me. 'Really? Do your friends call you that?'

'No.'

'Oh, well why –' I closed my eyes, my fists clutching the duvet. 'Kalen, Kal, whatever, don't try to confuse me. You can't be here. You can't stay over at a girl's house or undress her without her permission!'

'I'd better go then.'

'Yes, you better had.'

He grinned widely and left the room. I listened to his footsteps as he went down the stairs and the slam of the front door. Finally sure he was gone, I leaped out of bed and looked in the mirror. Surprisingly, I didn't look too bad for an evening of crying. I felt both relieved and ridiculous. I should have been mad, but somehow I couldn't stop thinking about his firm and sculpted torso – tanned, strong and vastly more appealing than any of the boys at school. Mostly, I was picturing the large milky scar that ran from the base of his neck to the middle of his chest, almost like a continuation of the small one on his face. As I wondered what could have happened to him, my anger melted away.

The house phone rang, startling me out of my reverie. I answered it carefully; my whole body felt fragile. On the other end of the line, Mae sounded furious, hurling questions I didn't want to answer. To buy some time, I invited her over. I used the minutes to take some painkillers and pull on some clothes. In my favourite tracksuit, I curled up on the sofa and waited.

When she arrived she stared at me with her arms folded. 'So, are you gonna fill me in on the guy from the club last night? Was that Caleb?'

'Kalen.'

My stomach churned and I didn't know if it was from the mere mention of his name or an aftereffect of my alcohol-fueled night. 'I told you the other day that I met him.'

'Met him where?'

'He was at Dad's funeral.'

Her eyes grew wide, her mouth forming a little O. 'That's weird.' She sat down. 'Where was he? Did he know your dad?'

'He was standing over by the lake. He stood watching for ages. And, I don't know if he knew Dad. I think so.'

'Um, hello? Have you asked him?'

'Yes,' I frowned. 'But it's complicated. Anyway, now I guess, we hang out sometimes.' I shrugged, trying to make light of it.

'What do you mean you *hang out*?' she asked with exasperation. 'Don't you tell me anything any more? I can't believe you're falling for the whole bad-boy thing. How tacky.'

I sighed. 'Have you ever had a problem with any of them?'

'Well, no. But I've heard–'

'Yeah, but have you ever noticed it's always a friend, or a friend of a friend, who knows something about them? No one's ever had a run in with the boys personally – it's always someone they know. I dunno, I suppose I'd like to keep an open mind.'

'Did he tell you what he does for a living?'

She had me there.

'Exactly,' she said, when I didn't answer. 'You're only defending him because you think your dad knew him and you don't want to believe your dad would have been mixed up in anything bad. But think about it, what do they do all day? Why don't they work or go to school? Who are their parents?'

'Look, I don't know what he does, but I know it's nothing to do with drugs after his reaction last night. Plus, he doesn't even drink! And we don't all have parents, do we?' I retorted.

A blanket of awkward silence nestled itself between us. I could think of nothing else to say.

'Fine,' Mae continued eventually with a flick of her hand, 'tell me about him then. What have you two been doing? What's he like?'

I smiled, feeling my tension dissolve while I considered her words. I couldn't describe what he was like, because I had no idea where to begin with anything deeper than aesthetic details. I told her he hadn't told me much yet, but I was working up to finding out, which was mainly the truth.

She eyed my curiously before shaking her head and changing the subject. I wanted to be honest with her, though until I knew more about him myself I wasn't sure how to do that.

***

When Mae left I decided to spend the evening cleaning. It would help keep my mind off of a certain hot, but potentially dangerous, boy whom I knew nothing about. Were Mae and Rachel right? Was he bad news? So far he'd been around when I needed him most, I couldn't see what was so bad about that.

I brushed the thought away and spread some toast with a thick layer of Marmite. Not much of a dinner, but I didn't see the point in cooking just for me. Once I'd swallowed it down I began to feel marginally better. I got some rubber gloves and cleaning spray from under the sink and took myself upstairs to the en-suite.

I made it all the way to my bathroom before my mind caught up with what I had glimpsed at my bedroom window. I whirled around.

Kalen.

'What are you doing here?' I wanted to sound angry, but it would have been a lie.

'You seemed annoyed with me earlier, I wanted to apologise.'

'Why are you at my window instead of the front door?'

'I thought it would be romantic.' The sarcasm in his voice made it obvious he was poking fun at me. That was fine, I could hold my own.

'Romanic or class-five stalker behaviour?' I countered.

He chuckled silently, but I noticed he didn't deny it.

'Nice gloves by the way.'

I tugged them off and threw them on the bed.

'Can I come in?' he asked.

'I don't think that's a good idea.'

'Okay.' He shrugged, though I could see he was a little taken back. 'Wanna get out instead?'

'And go where?'

'Wherever you want.'

Despite my best efforts, I couldn't stay mad at him. My mood was lifting already, but I did need to know more about who I was hanging out with. 'Fine, I know what I want to do.'

He lifted one dark eyebrow, waiting.

'Where do you live?'

'Ah.'

I glared at him. Eventually, he sighed, leaning back against the window frame. 'Right now, I live on the other side of town.'

'Who with?'

'Some friends.'

'*Some* friends... plural?'

His perpetual frown knitted together even tighter than usual. 'Yes, as in, there are four of them, plus myself.'

I knew he was cross, but he'd said I could do whatever I wanted, so I chose to ignore his change in mood. 'Are they all our age?'

'You don't know how old I am.'

'You can't be much older than me,' I said smugly.

'I'm two years older than you.'

'Oh!' My spirits lifted at the snippet of information. 'Well, I'm eighteen in February so that's only a year.'

'I am twenty in May, but years don't often mean much.'

'Are you saying I'm immature?'

He smirked. He might not have said it, but he definitely meant it. I folded my arms. I knew he was trying to throw me off by making me angry.

'So,' I said breezily, 'are the others all nineteen too?'

'Thereabouts. Except Ace, he's only fifteen and Nash is nearing twenty-one.'

'Well, you don't sound happy about your friends, don't you like them or something?'

'Or something.'

Okay, now I was getting irritated. 'I'd like to meet your friends.'

'I don't think so.'

'Why not?'

'My friends are a bit... complicated.'

'Fine, I have things to do, so if you don't mind. Are you able to see yourself out?'

It worked. He seemed to contemplate for a few moments and then he shook his head with a silent laugh. 'You win, Miss Rose.'

'We can go?'

'Yes, but don't hold it against me when you're bored – you chose this.'

Based on my life of late, it was impossible I'd be bored. 'Give me five minutes, I'll meet you downstairs!'

With a one-fingered salute he turned and left back down the roof. I gasped and ran to the window, but he'd already disappeared. Shaking away the image of him leaping from the top of my house, I swiped some dark blue jeans and a cream woollen jumper from my cupboard and brushed out my hair. It fell in long waves past my shoulders, a bit flat, but it would have to do. I pinched my cheeks to bring some colour into my face then grabbing my purse, I dashed downstairs.

Outside, he was leaning against a small sky-blue car; a rusty three-door Fiesta that looked as if it might turn to dust at any moment. He held the passenger door open for me and soon we were driving into town. It was the first time I was doing something I wanted to do, instead of what was expected of me. I felt a bolt of excitement.

We turned off the main road and drove up a long winding gravel driveway that left me lost for words. I forced my gaping mouth shut. I'd assumed they'd live in a caravan, or a small bungalow sleeping two to a room, but I knew this house – everyone did. It sat on the highest point of town, on the cliff-edge overlooking the ocean. Far apart from all other houses, the old Taylor mansion was surrounded by high fences that prevented anyone seeing what went on inside. We never saw the infamous Mr Taylor who owned it. Rumour had it he was an international millionaire who was never in town.

'We rent it from him,' Kal answered hesitantly when I voiced my surprise.

'How? Do any of you work?'

'Sort of,' he said, cocking his head to one side as if he found something amusing.

'Is it expensive?'

'Here we are.' He pushed at the front door without answering my question, letting it swing open. 'You ready for this?'

I smiled. It took every ounce of composure I had not to skip on the spot.

Inside, the house was as enormous as it looked on the outside, but eerily empty. In each room we passed, white sheets were draped over furniture and clumps of dust gathered in the corners of the floorboards. It was as if no one had been there for years. Then we reached the kitchen, the only room in the house that was warmly lit and reminiscent of how a home should feel. The smell of pizza wafted from the oven.

The room was remarkably tidy, given that five boys lived there alone. Of that fact there was no traditional sign, bar all five of them being there.

On stools by a marble worktop sat three of the four friends Kal had mentioned, and on a beanbag in the corner of the room what looked like a male model was stretched out with a book. He was the first one to look up and his smile was immediate and telling, forcing me to wonder if perhaps there had been bets on my coming to visit.

'At long last!' his deep voice boomed with an American accent I hadn't been expecting. That's when all remaining heads turned to face me.

One belonged to a boy who was definitely younger than the others, with a mop of black hair against dark skin and even darker eyes. The second face I recognised from when I'd first met Kalen. He was fair, with long hair that he wore back in a ponytail and he was wearing a sports cap turned backwards. The last boy held my attention, his blond hair almost white and his eyes a cold frosty blue. Though he was lean like the others, his body looked tense – the muscles in his arms, veiny and hard. He glared at me. The hairs on the back of my neck prickled and I quickly let my gaze fall back to the other boys. They were all so different, yet the same; something about them was so similar but whatever it was, I couldn't put my finger on it.

'Boys,' Kalen stepped in front of me, 'this is Ronnie Rose.'

'Awesome, Ronnie!' the little one declared, standing and

bounding over with a bright smile. 'So cool to meet you.'

The second American, I noted with interest as he shook my hand and pulled me in for a hug. I liked him instantly.

'Ronnie, this is Ace Jones.' Kalen held the young boy back with an outstretched arm and Ace backed off.

'That's Nash Philips,' he said, pointing to the one with the ponytail, who half got up from his stool and with a silent nod hello, reached a hand out for me to shake.

'And this is Laith Williams.'

Ah, the scary one. Laith looked at me when his name was mentioned, though he didn't get up from his seat, and when he spoke his voice was thin and razor-sharp.

'Ronnie?' he announced with a degree of disgust. 'That, is a boy's name.' His accent was British – completely normal for where we lived, though maybe a little more well-spoken than I was. He sounded just like Kal.

'It's short for Veronica,' I defended meekly.

'Dude?' Kal shook his head at his friend and looked at me apologetically. I smiled at them all nervously in return, but the tension was quickly diffused when the big one got up from his low seat and bowled over. He was at least six-four and had the sort of chiseled features you only saw on a movie star. Brushing his brown hair out of his eyes, which were the brightest of blues, he took my hand and kissed it, with a sideways grin towards Kalen.

'Good to finally have you hanging with us, gorgeous – I'm Denver. Ignore Laith. We all do.'

Laith eyed Denver briefly before turning away and continuing to watch a television show they were all engrossed in. Four lionesses were mauling a dead Zebra carcass.

'Let's go to my room,' Kal said into my hair.

Kalen's bedroom was similar to the rest of the house, only he'd removed the dust cover from his bed and replaced it with a small brown blanket. The rest of the room was sparsely furnished with a reading lamp and a small pile of books. I walked towards them, aiming for the only thing I could use as a talking point.

He was leaning casually against the wall, with one foot over the other, his dark eyes fixed on me. My pulse picked up speed. Being so close to him again, and in his bedroom, I was caught in a strange limbo between excitement and confusion.

'Do you like these books especially?' I asked, hoping to keep my cool. Unfortunately the pitch of my voice let me down. I coughed to clear my throat.

He shrugged. 'Why do you ask?'

'Conversation. I was just wondering why these books are on your shelf out of the thousands of books there are in the world. Lord knows, something is lucky to get a place in your room by the looks of it!'

He smiled the sort of smile that normally turns into a laugh, but he kept that part back. 'You're in my room, you must be pretty lucky.'

I rolled my eyes.

'Sorry. Okay, well the first book: *The Count of Monte Cristo*. I like that one a lot. It's about a man who's sent to prison for a crime he didn't commit, only to escape and take vengeance on all of those who put him there.'

'Wow, that's the first time you've said you like something.' Picking up the source of his enthusiasm, I scanned the pages. 'It's in French!'

All trace of amusement left his eyes. 'It's by a French writer,' he stated flatly.

'You can read French?'

'Um, yeah. Want to go eat?'

'No, thanks, where did you learn?'

'At school like everyone else.'

I put it back on the pile. When I straightened, he was next to me.

'The second book: *Veronika Decide Morrer,* I like the Author. He has an interesting way of looking at the world.'

'What's *Veronika Decide Morrer?*' I tried to pronounce the words in the same way he did.

'Veronika decides to die.'

I swallowed. 'That's my name.'

'Yes, I'd noticed that actually.'

I couldn't think of an appropriate response so I mumbled that I thought it sounded morbid and walked to the window. 'And what language is that one? And the others?' I asked, doing my utmost to seem blasé, though I was slightly uneasy at the coincidence.

'It's Portuguese. The others you won't have heard of or be interested in.'

I stared at him, wondering at the boy who could obviously speak at least three languages.

'You're really smart,' I said, stating what was becoming blatantly obvious. 'Where did you go to school?'

His eyes flashed towards the door. 'Ace, what's up?'

The youngest of his friends peered in and looked at Kal before entering.

'Hey!' I smiled

Ace straddled a chair he'd brought in with him, so his arms were rested on the back. 'So Ronnie, do you live near here?'

'Yeah not far, a bit further out from town. What about you, where are you from?'

'I grew up in New York, I've lived in a few different places since then,' he said.

'So how do you guys know each other?'

'K's like a big brother to me.'

'Oh? How did you meet?'

'Ace,' Kalen interrupted before Ace could respond, 'I think you should leave us alone now *Little Brother.*'

'Laith's being a jerk, I'd like to stay here with you guys.'

An awkward silence followed. Kal didn't look at either of us, but his stance was clear, even to me.

'Fine, see you later, Ronnie, it was good to meet you.' With that, the youngest boy got up and slouched out.

'That wasn't very nice,' I said when the door had closed.

'He needs to toughen up.' Kal bit his lip as he looked at me, as if thinking something over. 'How're things at home?'

'Okay.' I lifted my shoulders, but a weight seemed to bear on them at the thought. 'It's Christmas next week, it'll be hard for my sister and Cloud.'

'What about for you?'

I hesitated. What did it matter how hard it was for me? 'I want to keep things as normal as possible. I haven't decorated yet. Dad used to do that.'

'Will your sister will help you?'

'Rachel doesn't do house stuff, she's not good with manual.'

'She's older than you,' he said, as though it were the answer to everything.

'Yeah, but she had a hard time when we were kids.'

'How so?'

I perched on the edge of his single bed. 'Well, our mum ran out on us all when I was young. Rach was a teenager, but I was only three so I don't remember her really. Rachel took it badly and Dad never knew how to make it better for her.'

'He was a good father,' he said thoughtfully.

For what felt like the hundredth time, I realised that I still didn't know how he knew my dad. My father was a good one, but he'd kept a lot from us in the end. Could Kalen have been one of his secrets?

He took a step towards me. I instinctively stood up. It halted

69

him.

'I just–' I hesitated, 'we can't let this, whatever this is between us, keep happening.'

'Like what?' His eyes narrowed. 'Me, holding your hand? Being there for you while you cry?'

'No, yes – any of those things – all of it. You undressing me for a start! I don't even know you.'

'You know me better than anyone else does.'

'That's not saying much,' I scoffed. 'Why can't you tell me anything about who you are? Is it bad? There's a lot of talk going around about you guys.'

He let out a dark laugh. 'And what do the people of Clanots Ocean have to say?'

I shrugged. 'I don't listen to rumours.'

'Maybe you should.'

For a moment I thought he looked incredibly sad, but just as quickly his eyes turned to stone.

'Why are you being like this? I'm just trying to be your friend,' I said quietly.

'Well, I'm not your friend.'

I flinched. Refusing to let myself cry, I snatched up my bag and headed for the door. 'If you're not my friend then why is it every time I turn around, you're there?'

He laughed then, a sharp dark sound that made me recoil. 'I've been asking myself that very question.'

Stung, my brain fought with my heart as to what to do. My head won. 'I'm so out of here.'

I hurried down the stairs and through the front door so I didn't have to pass his friends. Outside, I broke into a run and only when I was far from the wrought iron gates of the mansion did I let my legs slow down. I kicked a small stone, watching it rattle along the pavement. Instantly I tried to conjure my hero, imagining him slipping his hand into mine. He was tall and strong, everything about him wonderful and good... but something didn't feel right. The daydream didn't calm me as it usually did. In fact, it had no effect at all. I shook the image away, the sound of someone calling my name catching my attention. A group of boys from school were standing at the bus stop by a small row of shops. The smell of fish and chips filled the air from the take away opposite. My stomach growled.

'Hey, Joel.' I was a little miffed; Joel Turner had barely said two words to me in the six years we had gone to Clanots County High together, now he was smiling widely, like we were best mates.

'How've you been? I was sorry to hear about your dad,' he continued as I stopped beside them.

I glanced at his friends. They seemed to be hanging on every word.

'Thanks, I haven't been too bad.'

'Good,' he said, nodding as if there was more he wanted to say. Then one of his boys with him – who I didn't recognise – shoved Joel from behind, forcing him to continue.

'So,' he grinned, 'that guy who dragged you out of White Lies on the weekend. He hangs with those other lads, right? The ones from the Taylor mansion?'

I resisted the urge to roll my eyes. 'Yeah he does,' I replied, checking my watch. Ten minutes until the bus rescued me.

'What's their deal? How do you know him?'

'I don't – I mean, not really.'

One by one, their interest waned. 'See,' said one, 'she doesn't know them. I told you guys you were full of it.'

'But he did carry you out of the club though, right?' Joel persisted, his tone suddenly unfriendly. 'My sister saw you.'

I thought about how to answer. They obviously thought I wasn't cool enough to know one of the infamous boys and, to my own annoyance, it hurt to know people thought I was such a loser. The sound of a car approaching at speed behind us saved me from the conversation. The passenger door to the black Audi swung open as it pulled to a stop beside me. With a quick look back at Joel and his friends, I leaned down to look inside.

'I'll take you home,' Kal said, his eyes narrowing in on the boys, who were all craning to get a better look at him.

Thinking better of my inclination to tell him to get stuffed, I climbed in, giving the group a small wave as we sped away. The tyres screeching was an added bonus, one I enjoyed almost as much as watching their gaping expressions in the side mirror.

I didn't mention the exchange to Kalen and by the time we neared my house it no longer seemed important. He turned off the engine and stared at the wheel. I didn't move. I felt compelled to say something, to try to make things better, but I was still too angry. Eventually after a prolonged silence that neither of us appeared able to fill, I opened my door to get out.

His hand reached out and rested on my arm as I swung my legs out. A jolt of electricity passed through me.

'Please don't walk out on me into the night like that. It's not safe.'

'You we're being an idiot.'

'So you endanger yourself?'

'I just walked to the bus stop, Kal, and it's only nine.'

He was silent again. He chewed his lip and stared out the window before speaking in a voice that was barely more than a whisper. 'I shouldn't have let you go... I'm not used to explaining myself, especially my emotions. It's new to me,' he struggled. 'I want to spend time with you but, it's so complicated. I'm not a good person to know, Ronnie.'

'Do you mean you're dangerous?' I asked, my own voice tight.

'I would never hurt you,' he looked at me, his eyes serious. 'But I'm not good for you.' He emphasised each word, sending a shiver through to my core. I felt a strange surge of disappointment, but something about him seemed in so much pain that instead of worrying about the danger he was talking about, I felt sorry for him.

'You should get inside,' he said finally, letting his hand fall from my arm as the first drops of rain began to fall.

My heart ached more than ever, but I forced my legs to work and stepped out into the damp air.

'Ronnie–' his voice sounded from behind me.

I looked back. He was out of the car, leaning against the doorframe, a level of misery in his eyes that I couldn't understand. 'Friends then?'

I smiled. 'You tell me.'

He smiled in return, his lips pressed together. I turned to go inside, at the same time as the clouds opened above us.

Closing the front door I blocked out the outside world and listened to his car speeding away. Soon, all I could hear was the rain beating on the deck. No one was home. It was the first time I was actually relieved to be alone.

Lisbon – September 2006

Four of them were enjoying an afternoon of sunshine outside the small town centre when Ace arrived, letting his moped fall to the floor as he ran up to them.

'They're here,' he said grimly.

They'd escaped from America almost a year before and had had no problems until now, so they all knew they must have let their guard down: going round in a group of five more often than they should; staying in one place for more than a few weeks. It had been good in Portugal. Life had felt okay for once.

They all rose from their seats on the pavement, Nash moving swiftly to Ace's side as he checked him for injuries.

'I'm fine,' the twelve-year-old said. 'I was playing back-gammon with the old guy from the market. I saw a car pull up outside our apartment. They cased it for a while. I managed to slip down a back street. I don't think they saw me, but I can't be sure.'

'Damn,' said Kalen. Although he'd known all along this day would come, he'd wanted his freedom to last a bit longer. He was fond of the little one especially; Ace didn't deserve to go down for things he hadn't even done.

'Okay, we knew it was just a matter of time,' he continued.

Laith cursed their former bosses under his breath and Kal silenced him with a look.

'I know how you feel, but that won't help us now. We all know the drill. Ace, you're with Nash. The rest of us will split up. Stick to the plan, we'll try to meet in Morocco in two weeks – take care,' he added as an afterthought.

Each boy nodded, struggling to express his fear. No words were spoken, but as the sun set over the horizon, igniting a blood-red sky, they parted at the street corner knowing they may never see each other again.

11 — SURPRISE VISIT

THE MORNING WAS CLOUDY, still heavy with the rain that had been falling all night. I took a quick shower, pulled on a tracksuit and caught the bus to the gym. All the while I tried, unsuccessfully, to think of something other than Kalen. I knew he was telling the truth when he said he was dangerous, it wasn't an act, I was sure of that. But I didn't think it was drugs, or anything else the people of Clanots Ocean had come up with. Whatever the truth revealed, I wasn't sure I could ignore him now even if I wanted to.

I dialed Mae as I walked. 'Kickboxing?' I asked.

'Um, can't today, Ron I have plans with – Mum.' She sounded awkward. I was sure she was lying, but I let it go. "See you soon, then," I said and hung up.

Kickboxing class was therapeutic. I enjoyed smacking the pads and practising my roundhouse kicks, but the trainer, Taz, was especially attentive today. Constantly fussing and asking if I was okay. I found it curious. I guessed he'd heard about my father – like everyone else in town – and wasn't sure how to treat me.

The temperature had dropped by the time I stepped outside, so I pulled my scarf out of my gym bag and looped it around my neck. As I headed from the bus along the long winding road that led to my house, I stopped. Ahead, a dark car was driving towards me. It's blacked out windows sent my pulse into a panic. I'm not sure why I did it, but I scooted to the side of the road and ducked down beside a thorny bush. I felt dumb, but I waited until the car had passed before coming out of my hiding place. I spent the rest of my walk hoping it wasn't a debt collector, or anyone from the bank. I had been putting off the inevitable, desperate to wait until after Christmas to tell Rachel about the house. I figured I could hide until then.

On my porch steps, a boy sat leaning up against the front door with his eyes closed. I felt my face pull into a wide smile. 'Ace! What you doing here?'

The youngest of Kalen's friends sat up straight and smiled shyly. 'Hey, Ronnie. I was just hanging around, thought I'd stop by and say hi.'

'Great, come on in.' I unlocked the front door and led us through to the kitchen.

Tucking his dark hair behind his ears, Ace glanced around, his eyes searching, taking everything in.

'Want some tea?' I threw my coat and scarf on the back of a chair and took some mugs from the cupboard. He nodded. His eyes had yet to meet mine.

The kettle whirred to life.

'So,' he said, peering round into the living room. 'I was thinking I could put up your Christmas tree, or if you don't have one, I can go get one?'

'Ah,' I let out a short laugh. 'Kal sent you didn't he?' After Kalen's incessant questions regarding my sister helping me decorate for Christmas, I should have guessed something like this might happen.

'No, I wanted to come.'

I sighed. 'Well, I'm not sure, Ace. I'm not really feeling up to it this year.'

His face paled, a look of distress flickered across his features. He was concerned, I supposed, about not doing something that had been asked of him. Did Kalen really have so much power over his friends?

'But, I'm sure my niece Cloud would love it,' I amended quickly. 'I do have one. It's fake but really nice. So if you wouldn't mind getting it down from the loft?'

He was up the ladder before I could blink.

'You know,' he mumbled from the hole in the ceiling, 'Cloud is a strange name.'

'Ha! You can talk, *Ace!*'

'Yeah, I guess so.'

He grinned as he jumped down and placed our box of tree decorations on the floor.

'You guys are quite athletic,' I noted.

'Yeah, I um, train a lot with the boys.'

'Train for what? I take kickboxing classes.'

'Do you?' His mouth pressed together. Though he still wasn't looking at me, I could see he was trying not to laugh.

I frowned. 'Why's that funny?'

'I just can't imagine you fighting, that's all,' his grin widened. 'But it's good to be able to defend yourself,' he added.

'Well, you shouldn't judge a book by its cover, Ace. Maybe I'm kick-ass!'

He laughed out loud, before scooting back up the ladders.

'Do I really look that feeble?' I yelled upwards.

'No comment,' came a call down.

A minute later, he landed back on the floor with the tree over one shoulder. 'I could teach you some self-defence, if you want. Probably more than whatever you're learning at a gym.'

'Really? Like what?'

'Actually,' he backtracked quickly, as if he wished he hadn't mentioned it, 'K, would be a better teacher.'

Leaving the kitchen before I could question why he'd changed his mind, he positioned the tree in the corner of our living room and began decorating it with white lights, baubles and tinsel. I left him to it, cleaning the kitchen while he worked. By the time he'd finished the living room looked like a grotto. My hand flew to my mouth. Ace looked pleased with himself, glancing at me for approval and meeting my eyes for the first time.

I nodded. 'Best tree ever.'

With a grin, he flopped down on the cream leather couch and flicked through channels on the television.

Not wanting my company to leave just yet, I said, 'I'm making chicken casserole for dinner. Want some?'

He leaned forward in the chair. 'Oh wow, are you sure?'

'Of course.'

'Okay – thanks.' He seemed hesitant, but after a few moments he threw his feet on the coffee table, his eyes fixed on the television once more.

Gathering up some ingredients from the pantry, I set to work. For the first time in what felt like forever, my kitchen was alive with the sounds of boiling, chopping and blending.

We sat watching Christmas movies for the rest of the evening. Not much conversation passed between us, but I assumed that was just how they all were.

***

Ace had left late and when I woke up I was on the sofa with a blanket covering me. The tree lights winked and glistened from the corner of the room. I smiled. Cooking for Ace had cheered me up. I had even almost forgotten about the strange car coming from my house. Before I knew it, I was heading out to do the Christmas shopping I'd been putting off. The temperature outside had dropped to sub-stupid and I passed my father's car, experiencing a pang of disappointment that I still hadn't taken my driving test. The bus it would have to be.

In town, I pushed a trolley around Tesco, tossing in food as I went. A small turkey, potatoes, parsnips and some sprouts. I took a tin of Quality Street chocolates, putting it back when I saw the price and I was toying with the idea of making my own cookies, when out of nowhere a strange feeling crept over me. Tiny prickles fluttered against the back of my neck, it felt like someone was watching me. I spun around. I was the only person in the isle, but a shiver ran up my spine all the same. Shoving the cookie mix back on the shelf, I hurried to the checkout.

The beep of the cash register was familiar and soothing, but the creepy feeling refused to leave me. I stared at the notes as I handed them over, thinking: the sooner I get a job the better. Taking the carrier bags full of shopping, I was glad to get out of the store. Especially when I stepped into the car park to see Kal's black Audi parked with the engine running. A warm feeling replaced all others but, as I approached, I noticed he wasn't in the car. It was Ace, Denver and Laith. Ace opened the door and bounded over to me like a happy Labrador.

'We saw you walk in,' he said brightly. 'Thought we'd help you with your groceries.' He took the shopping bags from me.

'Thanks.' I didn't know what to make of it, but I climbed in the back of the car with him. As the door closed I wondered at what I was doing. *It wasn't like I knew the boys particularly well, yet I was getting into a car with them.*

'Hey, Ronnie,' Denver greeted me from the driver's seat as we pulled away. 'Ace was kinda going on about you when he got in last night, and the awesome dinner you made him,'

My cheeks flushed. 'Um, I'm not a great cook, but you guys are welcome to stay for dinner if you want?'

He flashed me a smile in the rear view mirror. 'By all accounts, you're great.'

'They wanted to come, Ron,' said Ace, almost apologetically, 'we don't ever get nice food cooked for us. They were jealous.'

'I wasn't,' said Laith.

'Why are you here then, L?' Ace cut back. Laith didn't reply and I fidgeted in my seat to hide my embarrassment.

Denver's driving was not fast like Kal's, yet undeniably he handled the car well – another thing I could see they all had in common.

'Were you guys in the supermarket just now?' I asked, remembering the eerie feeling I'd had.

'No, just outside, waiting for you,' said Denver with a frown.

'Oh, it's so weird it felt like someone was watching me. I must have imagined it.'

I caught a look Denver flashed at Laith in the front seat: the corners of his mouth pulled downward. Laith shrugged.

We arrived back at my house and I led them through the back porch into the kitchen.

'Denver, where's Kal?'

'He has some things to take care of out of town with Nash. He'll be back soon.' He rummaged through the fridge, taking out a tub of coleslaw. 'Can I eat this?'

'Yeah, sure. It's Christmas the day after tomorrow, do you think he'll be here then?'

He shrugged and my mood plummeted. Laith laughed darkly from the doorway.

'Veronica, you really think highly of K, don't you? You're not the only girl who does.'

As casually as I could manage, I leaned on the counter to steady myself.

'Maybe when he returns, you should ask him what he's been doing the last couple of days.'

'Laith, shut up,' Denver snapped.

I was too unsettled to reply anyway. I gathered up some food while around me the boys found things in the house they could fix. They changed light bulbs, took the rubbish out and made a start sweeping leaves in the garden.

Just as I was dishing up lasagna for dinner, Rachel arrived with Jared and Cloud. At first I hadn't noticed, but then I heard the commotion outside. My sister's high-pitched, irrational voice, I could happily ignore, but what followed sent me racing from the kitchen. Jared was yelling.

12 — BODYGUARD

I THREW OPEN THE DOOR IN TIME TO SEE DENVER AND LAITH WRESTLING ON THE LAWN and Jared about ten feet away picking himself up from the grass. My eyes flicked across the scene: Jared limping in pain, Rachel helping him, uncharacteristically silent, and Denver whispering something into Laith's ear while he pinned him to the floor.

'What the hell's going on?' I looked at Denver. Ace appeared behind me and I felt him slump.

'Ronnie, I apologise for Laith.' said Denver, all six-foot-four of him struggling to hold onto his smaller friend. 'We'd better be going. Ace, let's go.'

'Yeah, that's right, run away before I call the police and have you thrown out,' Rachel said.

'Rachel!' I yelled. As usual, she wasn't helping the situation.

She glared at me. 'Veronica, you've really lowered yourself lately. I have no idea who you are any more, but today you've overstepped the mark.'

As my sister and I glared at each other, I wondered how she could judge me so harshly. Cloud was weeping, so I picked her up. She flung her arms around me, burrowing her face into my neck, but Rachel snatched her away.

'Ace, none of you have to go,' I said as he walked past me. 'Rachel, let's all go inside and talk about this.'

Laith stormed out the front gate without looking back and Denver stared at Ace until he followed suit.

'Sorry, Ronnie,' Ace mumbled before jogging off down the front steps after his friends.

'Ronnie, thanks for cooking us dinner,' Denver said. 'I'm sorry we couldn't enjoy it. Good to meet you Ms Rose.' He flashed Rachel his hundred-watt smile and I could see she was momentarily caught off guard. It shut her up for all of five seconds, then Jared opened his mouth.

'You lot aren't welcome in this house, do you hear me? Next time I'll call the police.'

'I'm sorry you feel that way,' Denver responded with a politeness that would have made the Queen proud. 'But perhaps Veronica has a say in who she is and isn't friends with?'

'Not in this house she doesn't,' Jared fired back.

I was instantly furious. I was on my own practically twenty-four-seven, while my sister lived her life away from me and they had the audacity to chase away the only friends I had.

'Jared, how dare you? I think it's you guys who should leave, right now!'

'Ronnie, this is your sister's house as much as it's yours and I won't have these thugs hanging around taking advantage of you. You have no idea what you're doing, you're just a child.'

'I'm just a child, but you're happy to leave me in the house my father died in, all alone until it suits the two of you? You know what? This house doesn't belong to either of us. Rachel...' I turned to her, 'Daddy spent all the money and didn't pay the mortgage. We have nothing.'

As the words left my mouth I wished I could suck then back in. Rachel's face twisted in disbelief, but it was Jared's reaction that shocked me the most.

'You lying little bitch!' he fumed, closing in on my face so fast I thought he might slap it. I was too shocked to respond, though I could see from the corner of my eye that Denver was moving towards us from the front gate so I knew I had to take a handle on things before they got out of control. I held a hand up in his direction to tell him I was okay, but that just enraged Jared all the more.

'Oh, so this your bodyguard now, is it? Don't think I'm scared of a teenager, Ronnie, because I'm not! You've always made your sister feel second best when it came to your father and now you're trying to take what is rightfully ours – hers,' he corrected. 'I won't have it. This house belongs to her and if I have to, I'll get my own lawyer to sort this out and you won't get anything because you're a minor.'

'Ha!' I retorted, hot tears stinging my eyes. 'Rachel wouldn't be in charge of her own head if it wasn't firmly attached to her neck!'

I heard myself yelling and both Rachel and Cloud crying, but not much was sinking in besides the notion that I'd always made my sister feel second best. It was a new low of sadness and I felt myself shrink back from the man yelling at me. I didn't care any more.

Jared's words were nothing more than a blur. '... So you can tell your boyfriend here to get stuffed, because I'm taking control of this situation from now on.'

'That's not her boyfriend,' came a voice from behind him. 'I am.'

Jared spun around. Startled by the new visitor standing inches from him, he tripped down the porch steps. Muttering a string of profanities, he steadied himself in front of Kal and pushed his chest out. 'So, which one are you?'

'I suggest you stop yelling at her,' Kalen's mouth pressed into a thin line, his fists clenched by his sides. In the time I'd known him, I'd never seen him overwhelmed with any type of emotion and though I was aware there was a lot I didn't know about him, his intense anger came as a shock to me.

Jared stared at Kalen. 'She's my sister-in-law. I'll talk to her how I like. Who the hell do you think you are to tell me any different?'

Kal took a step closer so they were toe to toe. 'It doesn't matter who I am. All you need to know is that I don't care who *you* are. I'm warning you, leave now.'

Scared Jared might throw a punch, I held my breath. Thankfully, Rachel stepped forward and placed a hand on his shoulder.

'Babe, don't yell at Ronnie, she's just a kid. She doesn't know what's what with the house. We'll look into it, okay?'

Jared's thin face darkened with rage as he looked wildly between me, Kal and Rachel. Finally, he grunted. 'Ronnie, I'm sorry I yelled,' he said flatly, clearly not sorry at all. 'But we're here to take care of you now. Rachel and I will deal with it.'

'Jared, Dad lost all the money. I wish he hadn't, but he did. If Rachel had bothered to turn up to the meeting with the solicitor she would know all of this. We have a bit in the bank, but after the funeral costs there's very little left. You can check it all you want,' I croaked, holding my chin up defensively, 'but I'm not wrong. I am sorry for the situation that Daddy got us into – but I'm not wrong.'

'We'll see. Rachel and I just want what's best for you and hanging out with these idiots is not a good start. We just worry about you, is all.'

'Thanks Jar, but I can take care of myself – just like I always have.'

Rachel clucked at that and stalked off towards their car with Cloud still whimpering unhappily in her arms. 'Leave her now, Jar,' she yelled over her shoulder. 'We come over to visit the little madam and this is the thanks we get.'

'Will I see you Christmas Day, Rach?' I called over, ignoring her insult.

'If your new friends aren't around, then of course I'll spend

Christmas here, like I do every year. It is my house too, Ronnie – don't forget that.'

Jared pushed past Kalen and darted down to the car with Rachel. As they pulled away Denver nodded a goodbye and left swiftly over a side fence, leaving me alone with Kal.

'It's not Rachel's fault,' I said, instinctively defending her. 'She's had a hard time and Jared is just looking out for her the best way he knows how, I guess.'

'So you keep saying, but it's not okay for anyone to yell at you like that,' he said, following me back inside and closing the door behind him.

I sighed. 'Still, you can't put me in that position, why did you all have to behave so violently?'

'I think a grown man yelling in the face of a teenage girl is quite violent, personally.'

'Look, I really appreciate you sticking up for me, but he's my sister's partner and for the sake of my tiny family, which is all I have, I have to try to keep the peace. It's what I've always done.'

His eyes softened. 'I'm not apologising for defending you, but I'll leave you alone if it'll make things easier for you with your family.'

'I don't want you to do that. I don't even know if we're friends or what? Where have you been?'

'I had to tend to some business out of town.'

'Business was it? What was her name?'

He frowned. 'That's a little juvenile. Not like you at all.'

'How would you know what I'm like?' I snapped.

'This is getting ridiculous. You said you just wanted to be friends. Are you jealous or do you want me to stay out of your life?'

'I want you to tell me who you are.'

He closed his eyes and let out a slow breath. 'I can't do

that.'

That was that then. If he couldn't be honest with me about who he was, how could I side with him over my own sister? My stomach knotted painfully.

'Then,' I struggled, 'it's best you leave me alone for a while. I need to take care of my family.'

He dragged one hand down his face and nodded. 'I won't go anywhere, Red. I'll be at the house if you need me.'

He left silently through the back door and I collapsed back on the settee.

Beirut, Lebanon — 25th December 2004

It was Christmas Day and colder than it had been all week. He'd checked in to a local motel with a single sponsor: the father, a humanitarian working for the Red Cross.

Every day for two weeks he'd sat on the same street, in the same cafés, playing football with the local boys, drinking tea and watching – waiting. Waiting for the call that was taking for ever to come. It had been seven months since his first job and there had been three others since – it all seemed second nature to him now. This was, however, his first war-zone assignment. It was also the first time things had gone wrong.

The call came at midday, the target someone he hadn't expected. He'd spoken with the man on more than one occasion; he was the owner of a market stall that sold small, and somewhat useless, handmade leather goods. The man had even stopped someone from stealing from K just a day before. K had seen the thief coming, but for a bit of sport he was going to let him take his wallet before breaking his arm. Yet the man had chased the pickpocket away. Shocked at receiving help from a stranger, K had accepted an invitation to join the man for coffee. He was learning English and K's cover was that he was a Swedish student. They conversed together, idle chitchat in broken sentences and misplaced words. The man often laughed at his attempts to explain the simplest of subjects.

Now, knowing he was supposed to kill him that very evening, K found he was quite perturbed. Having never pondered the reason for his job before, he couldn't help but consider it then. For the very first time, he was aware of what he was about to do and it bothered him.

The target was by his stall, just a hundred meters away when K received the call that sealed the man's fate. Tormented, he swallowed two espressos before leaving the bustling square to consider his plan of attack. The man was not even remotely covert, so he did not need to follow him. Down the back of his right trouser leg he placed a thin skewer, which he would later plunge into his target's heart before shoving him down a flight of stairs. It would be a long time – if ever – before anyone realised the cause of death wasn't an accidental fall resulting in a broken neck. By which time, both he and the sponsor would be safely back in the United States. The plan was made, it just needed to be executed. K picked up speed as he went over the arrangement in his mind.

His hair was shorter than usual and dyed a white blond; his skin tanned and dirty. He looked nothing like the boy from the room in France all those months ago. Today he was Karl, a schoolboy from Sweden.

He spent the day observing from a position where he could see the entire street without being noticed. He watched the man eat some food, watched him laugh at a joke as he drank from a pitcher of water after thanking the woman who handed it to him. All the while, as K studied the target, his stomach churned. He thought perhaps he was falling ill, yet somewhere inside he knew that was not the case.

Cursing, he turned from the street and entered a back alley, muttering to himself, desperate to pull himself together. Not completing the job would be a tremendous failure and he did not understand what it was to fail. It would be an entirely unacceptable outcome. Eventually, when his mind stopped racing he returned to his lookout. From what he knew of each local's routine, the target would be there for at least three more hours until the last of the tourists or potential shoppers had gone. He decided to return later, going back to his own room to read until the time came.

Following the target two and a half hours later was easy. He expected nothing and was completely unaware of any danger. It was the second time K wondered just who this man was and why he needed to be eliminated. Inside the target's apartment building, he waited as the old man scaled the first flight of stairs, before following silently after him. It was a long process, because his apartment was on the fifth floor and his right leg seemed to give him pain. Each step he took was agonisingly slow.

When finally he reached the top, K heard voices above him; the greeting of a wife and a young child. He hadn't been told there would be others. He had orders to kill the man and that meant whoever could witness it, but this was not what he had planned for. A quick decision to return later was just as swiftly quashed when, in turning to leave, he was stopped in his tracks by a voice calling down the stairwell to him in Arabic.

'What are you doing down there?'

The man was staring over the banister. That was it then, no going back. K looked up into the eyes of the man he was about to kill. He hoped the man would see it coming, would fight back and try to kill him, too. It would make everything so much easier.

But of course he didn't.

'Karl! It's you!' the man said happily in broken English. 'Come – I want you to meet my son, he is a little younger than you but he is smart! Learning English too – you come!'

With what felt like a lead weight inside him, K ascended the last flight of stairs to the man waiting with open arms. His tiny son's smile was more genuine than his own had ever been and the wife – a petite cherub-like woman, with rosy red cheeks – was beaming too. K swallowed, telling himself that he didn't care, that people were fickle, *life* was fickle, and if he didn't take the life of those he was supposed to, his own would be forfeit. Still, his weapon stayed hidden. His guard remained down.

'Come, Karl – come in,' repeated the man. Uncertainty clouded his features.

'I can't. I am very sorry,' K answered in fluent Arabic. The target's face dropped somewhat at the change. Confused that the boy from Sweden could suddenly converse so perfectly in his native tongue.

K leapt over the banister and dropped the four flights down. Landing in a crouch, he stood and fled the building. Outside in the bitterly cold winter air, he vomited onto the pavement. Wiping bile from his chin with the back of one dirty hand, K's first thought was that the man's reaction had not been one of any real suspicion. If anything, he had almost seemed impressed that K could speak Arabic. Surely, someone he was supposed to kill, a man who must know there were people who wanted him dead, would be more cautious of such a thing – even of a thirteen-year old boy?

K left Lebanon with the sponsor the next day. His mission failed.

13 — FAMILY

THE DAY WEIGHING ON MY MIND HAD FINALLY ARRIVED. I'd prepared most of what was going to be our traditional Christmas dinner and Rachel brought pudding and mince pies. She and I cried over brunch, which usually saw Dad leading us in Jingle Bells and other carols. Jared played with Cloud while my sister and I wept, tight in an embrace I wasn't used to. We spent the rest of the day making it as fun as possible for Cloud, which ended up making it really fun for us too.

I found myself smiling at my little family throughout the day and wishing Kalen could have shared it with us. He'd said he didn't have parents either and Christmas was not a time to be alone. I didn't ask Rachel of course, I was skating on thin ice as it was.

Shortly after dessert, Rachel announced they had to leave. It was seven o'clock.

'You're welcome to come with us. We're going to Jared's parents, though, so you might be bored,' said Rachel.

'I'll be fine here,' I lied. 'I'll watch some movies and get an early night.'

'Okay, call us if you change your mind.'

After a hug the click of the front door closing echoed inside me and I steeled myself to walk back into the empty front room. I hadn't even pulled myself away from the door, however, when I heard a quiet knock. I peered through the frosted glass. The crystalised outlines of several people formed in front of me and I pulled open the door to the faces of Kal, Ace, Laith, Denver and Nash, staring back at me from beneath dark hooded jumpers. I pressed my fingers to my mouth to suppress a laugh. As pleasant as it was, it looked a lot like I was about to be robbed by the Grim Reaper & Co.

'Hey, Ronnie,' Ace said, his grin bright in the darkness.

I opened the door wide and they walked in, each nodding hello. Kal stepped in last and stood in front of me, his face was dappled with water. I glanced outside to see tiny droplets of rain catching the wind beneath a street lamp. There was no car in sight.

'You saw them leave?' I asked.

He cocked his head to one side. 'We were... in the area.'

I nodded, fighting my smile. 'Thank you,' I whispered. I'd told him to leave me alone and yet, right when I needed him most, he was here. I couldn't ignore that.

'You shouldn't be alone tonight,' he said, lowering his eyes.

Not knowing how to respond, I led the way into the kitchen. The boys were already eating left over food, pulling apart the turkey, stuffing and cold potatoes.

'I can make something extra if you like?' I ventured from the doorway.

'Na, that's okay. Hope you don't mind us dropping by?' Denver replied with a mouthful of stuffing. 'Wow, Ronnie, this is awesome.'

'We brought you a gift,' said Ace, holding up a brown cardboard box with a large red bow tied crudely around it.

92

Stumped for words, I took the box and opened it while they stared at me with interest. Inside was a pile of wires and black plastic.

'Um–

'It's an alarm system for your house,' said Nash. 'I made it.'

I looked at Kalen, who was watching me intently. I could see they were serious about the gift.

'You made it?' I asked turning back to Nash. 'That is – quite amazing.' I wasn't lying. It was amazing. It was also the strangest gift I'd ever been given. 'Thank you all,' I added.

Ace looked pleased with himself and their attention went back to the table of food.

'Sorry about the present,' Kal whispered as we headed into the living room. 'I do understand it's not a standard Christmas gift.'

'No, it's – lovely,' I answered quickly. 'I guess I've never really felt unsafe here, but it's good to have. Nash is obviously very talented.'

'We just thought as you live alone now, it's something that might put your mind at ease – and mine. It doesn't call the police, of course.'

'Really?' I was confused. 'Who does it call then?'

'Me.'

'You don't have a phone,' I pointed out.

He smiled widely. 'Let's just say I have the alarm part and I can be here in an instant if you aren't safe.'

'Why wouldn't I be safe?'

'I'm sure you will, but for some reason I find I'm incapable of worrying about anything else.'

His eyes bore into mine and, as usual, my heart rate accelerated, catching me off guard. Suddenly, a house alarm was the best gift I'd ever received. If I could have hugged it in bed that night, I would have.

'Ace has never had Christmas, not a real one,' he changed the subject.

'Have you?' I countered.

Immediately, his eyes turned to stone and whatever moment we were having was over. I wanted to kick myself. I changed tact. 'Well, he's more than welcome. You're all welcome here. I thought I'd be alone all evening.'

A loud voice boomed from behind us. 'Hey you two, none of that!' Denver threw himself on the couch. The others followed into the room. I broke away from Kal and hurried to the kitchen to fetch some drinks. To my surprise each of them declined alcohol, so I made hot chocolate with marshmallows and whipped cream instead.

Denver was the most talkative. He made jokes for most of the evening and was very good at accents, so he would surprise us every so often doing "bits" from different television shows and while the others didn't laugh as much as I did, they seemed to appreciate his performance. I was quickly getting used to being around them – if it was possible, I almost felt like I was with family.

Nash installed the small box in record time and I noticed with relief that it was so discreet Rachel would never even notice. When he'd shown me how to activate it, the most silent of the group spent some time studying the carpentry throughout the house. All the units, shelves and tables had been handmade by Dad and I could see he was impressed. Even Laith – normally so stubbornly moody – appeared to be making an effort to be upbeat, though at one point he did say he hated Christmas. Ace rolled his eyes and called him Scrooge. It would have been funny, except that he looked confused and asked who Scrooge was. Not for the first time, I wondered about their past; they all seemed so lost.

Christmas Night turned into Boxing Day morning and I was falling asleep on Kalen's lap. Walking me to my room, he waited by the door until I was tucked under my duvet and then he left. I let sleep take me instantly, knowing it was only a few hours until morning. And as my eyelids cemented together in that incredible feeling of being so tired nothing can keep you awake, I knew I'd made it through Christmas okay.

14 — ENOUGH

I WOKE UP TO MY PHONE RINGING.

'Merry Christmas!' Mae sang.

'Merry Christmas,' I agreed. 'What time is it?'

'Did I wake you? It's like noon! What you doing today?'

'Nada.'

'Right, I'm coming to get you. Be ready in fifteen.'

I stumbled into the shower before pulling on jeans and the new grey mohair jumper my sister had given me. I was out of the house by five to twelve waiting down by the road. A silver Volkswagen Golf pulled up in front of me. I felt my jaw drop.

'Holy crap!'

'I know,' Mae beamed as I slipped inside. She wore a sequin beige jumper that made her skin appear iridescent and her long hair was tied back in a high ponytail. 'Mum and Dad bought it for me for Christmas. I haven't had much driving time since I passed my test, but this car practically drives itself so we should be sweet!'

'It's brand new!' I blurted, as I enviously slid my fingers along the leather interior.

'I can't believe it either, but Dad said as long as I'm going to be driving on my own now, he wants me to be safe. Means I can drive us everywhere from now on!'

'Yeah, that's great,' I nodded and we began the ten-minute journey to her house in Temberly.

'How was your day yesterday? What did you get?' said Mae, struggling with second gear.

'It was good, better than expected. I didn't get a car, that's for sure.'

The gearbox crunched and finally we rode smoothly along. Mae breathed a sigh of relief and her smile returned. 'Yeah, so what did you get? Why was it better than you hoped?'

'I got this,' I pointed to my jumper. 'You know, Rach always gets cool stuff from the magazine so I think it's a good designer. Though I wouldn't know either way.'

We both giggled while she pulled at the label to check.

'Hey watch the road! Anyway, Rachel and Jar left after dinner and I thought I'd be on my own, but then–'

'You could have stayed with us!'

'I know, I know, but it was okay. Kalen and his friends came over.' I cringed as I waited for her response. I didn't have to wait long, her tiny nose wrinkled and she eyed me seriously.

'Keep your eyes on the road,' I laughed for the second time.

'What am I going to do with you? Have you found out how he knew your dad yet?'

I was stuck at that. Being around people like Mae and my sister made me feel like an idiot for all the things I was ignoring about Kalen.

'No,' I admitted.

At that point, we pulled into the driveway of the Jensen's and Mae's mother came running out to greet me. Susan Jensen was from Hong Kong and had met Mae's father while studying in the States. Her American father Roy had got a job in London when Mae was four. They'd lived in Temberly ever since.

'Hi, Mrs. Jensen.'

'Veronica Rose! You naughty girl for staying away so long!'
The tiny woman pulled me in for a hug and ushered me inside.
I inhaled the familiar scent of jasmine blossom and vanilla as
I walked into their grand house. It took me back to my child-
hood, which at the moment felt like a million years ago.

After too much food and a round of Pictionary, Mae's father
caught me off guard by asking about the boys. 'Mae tells us
you're friendly with that group of young guys we hear so much
about.'

'Not really friendly,' I faltered, glaring at Mae over his
shoulder. 'Well, one of them – I see one of them – sometimes.'

He made a *hmmm* sound, before leaning onto his knees and
looking at me seriously. 'You should be careful Ronnie. We all
care about you and no one wants to see you get hurt. You're
vulnerable right now – some people will try to take advantage
of that.'

I couldn't believe it, she'd told on me! With a gulp, I returned my attention to him and nodded.

'I am careful Mr. Jensen. They're actually quite nice, from
what I can tell. But, you're right, and I promise I'm being careful.'

'Good!' he slapped his hands on his thighs, as if he were
pleased to have done what he could to save me.

'I've heard they're from The States, do you know where?'
he added as an afterthought.

'Um, I think New York, though not all of them are from
America, just a couple...' I was grappling for answers I didn't
have. Thankfully, Mae's mother called Roy into the kitchen
before I looked even more clueless.

I stared at Mae. 'I can't believe you did that.'

'I didn't do anything, I just mentioned it in passing the other
day and he jumped on it. Besides, if you aren't doing anything
wrong, then what's the big deal?'

'I'm not doing anything wrong.'

'But is he? You know,' she lowered her voice, 'I heard they're thieves. You have a lot of valuable stuff in your house, maybe that's why he's taken such an interest in you.'

'Mae that's ridiculous—'

'Is it? You know nothing about him, you said so yourself.'

'I know enough,' I stated angrily. She gave me her best 'whatever' look and sat back on the couch.

'I said I'd visit him tonight,' I croaked out the lie. Enough was enough. I was going to beg Kalen to tell me the truth if that's what it took. I needed to know I wasn't wrong about him.

'Now?'

I looked at my watch to pretend I had a time frame in mind. 'Yeah, I should leave now.'

After a long pause, she said, 'I'll drive you.'

The journey consisted of a thick silence, one that I knew she wanted to fill with advice for me. I didn't want to hear it, so I resisted the urge to make it easier for her. She'd chosen her side.

When we arrived the house looked dark. So dark that I started to worry how I would get home if they were out.

'I'll wait here,' said Mae, as if reading my mind. 'You have any luck just wave me off.'

'Why don't you come in?' I asked hopefully.

'Na, I don't think so. Mum would have a fit. Besides, I'm kind of seeing someone and I don't think he'd like it.' Even in the darkness I could see her blush.

'You didn't tell me. We've spent the whole day together.' I knew she had college and new friends now, but it was painful to think we were growing apart. There was a time when she would have told me everything.

'I know, but it's not been long. I don't want to jinx it.'

'Who is it?' I asked.

'It's Taz,' she said proudly, toying with her hair.

I gaped. 'Gym Taz? But he's in his thirties!'

'I know that,' she said indignantly. 'Thirty-two, actually. But I really like him. He's hot, right?'

Taz was my kickboxing instructor – it explained why Mae had been coy about going with me and why he'd made such a fuss of me. He was very good-looking, but oh boy did he know it. Everyone knew he was a womaniser and had been with most girls in town his age, my sister being one of them.

'He is hot,' I said reluctantly.

'Ronnie, you're a fine one to talk about men that are bad for us.'

'I know, I just, I didn't know you liked him, that's all.'

'Whatever,' she said. 'You want to go see your boyfriend and let me know how you get on?'

I muttered that he wasn't my boyfriend and got out of the car feeling dejected. I could hear the music before I reached the door. Classical. Up-tempo. I recognised the song, it was well known, but I couldn't place it. My knowledge of classical music was limited at best. I took a deep breath and stepped inside. Laith was the only one in the kitchen.

'Hey, Laith.'

'Veronica,' he nodded curtly.

'Is Kal here?' I asked, with my best attempt at light and breezy.

'Nope.'

'Do you know when he'll be back?'

'Not tonight.'

'Oh.' I wondered if any of the others were around, but I could see I was getting nowhere asking the most socially inept of the group. 'Okay. Well, when you see him please let him know I stopped by.' I turned to walk back out, but his dark laugh halted me in my tracks.

He took the remote control and turned the music down a

little. It was a polite gesture, but the look on his face told me he had meant it to be anything but.

'You like Nocturnes?'

'Um, yeah, I guess.'

'Of course you do. Guess, I mean.'

I had no idea what he meant. The song finished and was replaced with something else I didn't know.

'You two must have so much in common. You like, let me guess – Britney Spears? And K listens to Frederic Chopin. Did you know that?'

'Where is everyone?' I asked, ignoring his insult. I didn't particularly like Britney Spears. Maybe two years ago, but I wasn't going to tell him that.

'You know, Veronica, you are somewhat delusional. You think that because K seems to have some ridiculous infatuation with you, that you're special? Meeting him was every one of your worst nightmares combined. He's dragged us to this hellhole and since we've been here he's been on his best behaviour, but it's all lies. You have no idea who we are and just how much we shouldn't be here. We've stayed in this place too long and because of you we could all be in serious danger. And you'll find he won't care a damn about what happens to you if it means saving his own life.'

I tried to hold his gaze as he bore down on me, his dead blue eyes wide and rimmed red with rage. I wasn't sure if he meant to hurt me or not, but I prepared myself to scream just in case. If the other boys were in the house, I was sure they would help me. At least I hoped they would. I couldn't accept what he was saying, I couldn't have been so wrong about Kal.

'You're poison, Laith. Leave me alone or I'll tell Kal everything you've just said to me. How do you think he'd react to that?'

He smiled. 'Go ahead. Why don't you tell him now?'

I faltered. I didn't know Kal's whereabouts and Laith was

101

enjoying that.

'I can tell you where he is at this precise moment, if you like?' He sat back, casually placing his hands behind his head. 'You could learn something that might save your life. You want to know the truth don't you, Veronica? Don't take my word for it, go and witness with your own eyes just who we really are.'

Of course I accepted the challenge. I told myself it was so I could prove him wrong, but if I was honest, Laith was right: I needed to know the truth and so far Kal had told me absolutely nothing.

Mae dropped me home with a look that said I told you so, but when giving me a hug goodbye she told me the offer to stay with her family still stood. I thanked her and watched as she drove away in her new car.

It was seven in the evening, but it may as well have been the middle of the night it was so dark. I didn't care. As soon as I walked back into the safety of my warm house, I called a taxi and made my way to the nearest train station.

15 — ASSASSIN

I ARRIVED AT THE DOCKS WISHING I HADN'T. On my own in the darkness, all I knew for sure was that I was astonishingly cold and a long way from home. What was I expecting to see? From Laith's words I couldn't be sure what was going to happen, if anything.

It wasn't long, however, before I saw movement from inside one of the big white yachts, just as Laith had predicted. My stomach lurched as I thought about what I'd done. This was it – no turning back. If he told me something bad about my father, I'd have to say goodbye to him. With that thought, I had to force my feet not to run. Finding out the truth about the boy to whom my happiness was bound so tightly made me numb with fear.

Dressed entirely in black, he leapt silently from the boat and hotfooted it along the jetty in my direction. Up until that moment I'd been annoyed, but my anger quickly turned to fear when I saw his urgency. As he ran, his feet seemed to barely touch the floor beneath him; he looked lighter than air. I was reminding myself to be angry – not impressed – when two huge German Shepherds launched themselves from the boat and gave chase along the docks. Kalen reached me, his eyes widening. A flash of anger clouded his features.

'Dammit, Ronnie!' he said.

He grabbed my arm and forced me to run with him. I said nothing; there was no time. Being chased by two savage dogs gave me the adrenaline kick I needed and I ran faster than I ever thought I could. But I knew we couldn't outrun them. We reached a brick wall and I turned in horror, watching the two animals gaining on us, snarling and barking ferociously. I flinched against the wall, my heart pounding in my chest. Still holding me, Kalen glanced towards the black water then back to the dogs. Any second now they'd be mauling us... Then Kalen's arms were around me, lifting me off the ground, tossing me like a rugby ball into the air. I gasped. Flailed. Cold air rushed past me. I heard the yelp of a dog before I hit the freezing water. What felt like a thousand needles pierced my skin all at once, evaporating into hundreds of tiny bubbles. I gasped for air as I broke the surface.

Wiping my eyes, I looked around desperately. The sound of waves licking the concrete walls made for an eerie accompaniment to the dark water.

Though I couldn't see them, I could hear the dogs barking from somewhere above, the frustrated barking from animals denied their prey. If I hadn't been so cold, wet and miserable I might have sighed with relief.

Treading water, I searched for a way out, when Kalen's backpack slammed into the water a few feet from me. I looked up. Kal stood on the roof of a two-storey apartment block and threw himself into the air. His body rotated into a perfect dive and slipped into the river like an arrow from the night sky. The surface of the water remained as still as it had been before the impact, barely a ripple out of place.

Beside me, his head rose out of the water. 'Can you swim?' he asked harshly, his dark eyes glittering in the moonlight.

Bit late for that question, I thought. But I nodded mutely, through fear of crying if I spoke. I wasn't sure if the shock had truly hit me yet, but the tone of his voice had. I hated him being angry with me.

'Good. Swim next to me to that pier,' he pointed. 'The police are coming. Be quick.'

The pier didn't look too far. I took a deep breath, held back my rising panic and began to swim. Kalen was already up on the jetty and reaching an arm down to me as I neared it. With ease, he hoisted me up. His large hands ripped open the rucksack and from it he pulled a clear plastic bag containing a pair of khaki trousers and a jumper. He threw them to me.

'Get your clothes off. All of them, except your sneakers. Get these on.'

'What about you?' I asked through chattering teeth. The sound of police sirens began to wail in the distance.

'I'm fine, just hurry.' He turned his back to me and I did my best to tear off my jeans and jumper that were already stiff with ice. Trembling, I pulled on the dry clothes as quickly as I could. Just performing normal functions was a struggle. I was colder than seemed possible.

Kalen appeared behind me and threw my wet things into the river. I thought fleetingly about my sister's Christmas gift, but before I had time to dwell on it, he'd grabbed up the bag, my coat and my hand and started us running again.

The chill of the night air threatened to freeze my blood, but every time I wanted to give up I reminded myself he was still in his wet things and it forced me to press on. It wasn't long before we reached a grassy bank leading up to a back entrance to a train station, though I had no idea which one. He held back part of a broken fence. Without a word, I squeezed through the gap presented to me. Keeping my body so low to the ground that I could smell the wet grass under my nose, I made my way up towards the platform.

'Are we going to be okay?' I asked when we sat down. 'It's freezing and you're still soaking wet.' I choked out my words. My chattering teeth gave away just how cold I was. He looked at me, troubled, then at the electronic clock above us that indicated the next train was in twenty-three minutes.

After a brooding pause he spoke, as if to himself. 'No, this isn't okay.'

Taking my hand again, he led us both quickly out of the train station and into the car park. Fortunately being the day after Christmas, nobody was working at the station. It was empty, bar us.

'Wait here,' he instructed.

He shot off into the darkness. Seconds later I heard a car approaching and a navy blue Mercedes came to a stop in front of me.

The door swung open and I peered in. 'Did you steal this?'

'Get in, Red,' he answered darkly.

I didn't need much persuading. The air was so cold outside I wanted the warmth of the car more than I wanted to be law abiding. I jumped in. The tyres screeched away from the kerb as I was still closing the door. At the mouth to the main road Kalen swung the steering wheel so the car spun and faced the opposite direction and we were racing along the motorway as smoothly as if I were being rocked to sleep.

'The heater's on,' he said more kindly. 'You'll start to feel better soon, I promise.'

I nodded. The many questions cluttering my mind would have to wait until I wasn't so cold. Despite the heating inside the car, however, my body didn't seem to warm up. Thankfully, quicker than seemed possible, he cut the engine and I realised we'd reached my house. The lights were off so I knew Rachel had not returned, and for that I was grateful. I wasn't sure how I would explain my clothing or my late-night guest without a huge fight.

Inside I took him up to my room and hurriedly showed him to the shower room. Then I ran into my father's bedroom to find him some dry clothes before going to take a shower myself.

The water burned my skin at first, but I relished it after the cold. I dried, almost feeling back to normal and not being worried about dying of hypothermia meant I could consider exactly what we had just done. I'd been an accessory to car theft for one thing, but that was the least of my problems. Who the hell was Kalen Smith? We had broken the law, but how he'd done it made me think perhaps it was something he did on a regular basis. This could be a lot worse than I had imagined.

I pulled on sweat pants and a jumper and waited for him. I felt empty inside, but as soon as he emerged from my en-suite with a towel wrapped around his waist, his muscular body dappled with water, a pit of nerves filled my stomach. I grew hot, averting my eyes.

'I'll wait for you downstairs, I left some dry clothes for you there.'

I left the room, my heart threatening to burst out of my ribcage. I'd barely sat down in the living room when he walked in. Quietly thanking me for the clothes as he perched on the edge of a chair opposite me.

His eyes searched my face. 'Ronnie, why were you spying on me?'

'I need answers,' I said as boldly as I could manage.

'What answers?' he snapped. 'What do you want from me?'

'I want to know who you are.'

Pursing his lips tightly together, he stared at the carpet. 'Who told you I'd be there?'

Uh oh.

'Ronnie?' He lifted my chin so our eyes were forced to meet.

'I'll tell you when you tell me what I want to know,' I demanded.

His expression hardened, but suddenly, much to my own

surprise, he relented. 'Fine.'

He let out an exhausted sigh and my stomach responded with a lurch. I was about to learn information I'd wanted for weeks, but now I wasn't sure I was ready for it.

'What do you want to know first?' he asked solemnly.

After a brief hesitation, the words almost fell out of my mouth. 'How did you know my father?'

'He saved my life.'

My face must have been a picture, if it betrayed my shock. The answer was so blunt, yet of all the things I'd considered he might say, this had been furthest from all of them.

'About three years ago,' he continued, leaning his elbows on his knees and staring at the ground between his feet, 'I was in Portugal, running from people who were trying to kill me. I had been running for a long time. I was bleeding heavily and close to collapsing. Your father was driving and saw me on the side of the road. He stopped and picked me up, taking me back to the place you were staying at the time. You were on a family holiday. He fixed me up, gave me food and shelter for a full twenty-four hours, never once asking me who I was or what I was running from. All he said was: *'whatever you've done, it's not worth such a young boy's life.'* Your father was a good man. I haven't met many.'

I was dumbstruck. It was so far removed from the response I was expecting and I was filled with an overwhelming love for my father. I was hooked – I wanted to know everything.

'Portugal – Lisbon, I remember that holiday, did I meet you?'

'No, you were asleep when I arrived and by the time you woke up the next morning I was hiding in one of the unused guest rooms.'

I thought about that, him being so close to me without my knowledge. It was a peculiar feeling. 'Who were you running from? Why would anyone want to kill you?'

He sighed and pinched the bridge of his nose between his thumb and forefinger, his lovely face contorting into a frown of desolate sadness.

'I suppose I'd better start at the beginning. I need you to understand that what I'm going to share with you will put me in danger. But more importantly, it will put you in danger. I'm going to leave out information you don't need and you must never repeat any of this. Don't even discuss it with people you assume already know, such as my friends. The less you know the better, and the fewer people that know you know. Do you understand what I'm saying?'

I nodded mutely, every hair on my arms standing on end. Part of me didn't want to find out any more, but it was too late for that now.

'I'm an orphan, as I told you. We all are. When I was four, I was taken from an orphanage in Boston and given a home. I believed I was so lucky the day a loving couple came to collect me. I'd dreamed of a family and all of a sudden out of nowhere I was getting one.

'But, I never saw that perfect couple again. I was taken to a farm in the Midwest, operated by several men and women, none as caring as the actors they'd hired to collect me. I was the first, but soon after I arrived so did other boys around my age. We were home schooled to the highest standards in all subjects: economics, technology, sociology, languages. I speak four fluently and can get by in three others.'

He coughed into his hand and the way he spoke next made me reel. His accent suddenly reflected every American television show I'd grown up with. Absolutely flawless. This was so obviously his natural manner of speaking, yet his English pronunciation had appeared so normal I'd never suspected it.

'Accents were next,' he continued, 'acting or, I guess, lying. Though we didn't call it that, of course, nothing is called what you think it is where I grew up. For seven days a week, twenty-four hours a day I was conditioned on how to walk, talk and breathe so I could be nobody. Sounds ridiculous, right? But being invisible can be the difference between life and death for us. For that reason, I saw no other boys except those I lived with, unless absolutely necessary. I was treated like a man from a very young age, spoken to only when a situation required it. The point of such treatment was to strip us of normal human emotions.

'Soon after we'd become used to this routine, they slowly introduced the endurance and combat training. I was seven when I first abseiled off the side of a cliff and nine when I jumped out of a helicopter into the ocean.

'Fighting, climbing, running, driving... at first it was fun, but soon enough the real purpose of the strange farm became apparent. As we each turned thirteen, they told us what it was all for. That we were being trained to be the world's "best soldiers".' He laughed darkly. 'Soldiers – another word that has no meaning. Infiltration, insurgence, assassination; they told us we were saving the world. By then it was too late to have objections, it was all we knew and we were excited to move to the next level. We cared for nothing else.' He paused then and I could tell he was remembering times he would rather forget. I didn't know how to feel about what I'd heard. It was hard to believe, yet somehow, I knew he was telling the truth. Minutes passed in silence. I reached my hand across to his. It was fiery hot.

'Kal, you're burning up,' I whispered with concern. His eyes narrowed as he looked at me and he pulled his hand away sharply. I had no idea what he was thinking, or what I should do, so I clasped my own hands back on my lap in front of me.

'For three years, from the age of thirteen,' he continued gruffly, 'I worked for them. Spying on men three times my own age, gathering information and terminating anyone they ordered me to.' The same dark and painful laugh escaped his lips and intensified my goose bumps.

'As it turned out, such power isn't suitable for children.

Some of us couldn't be controlled, despite the punishments that were handed out when things went wrong, which of course they often did. Too many boys acted out and it was all too little, too late, when they realised none of us could ever be anything other than what they had made us: cold-blooded killers. We could never be integrated into society, go back to being normal kids. Or normal adults for that matter.'

I flinched at the word killers. I couldn't believe that of the boy I had such strong feelings for. Though my voice came out tiny and pathetically desperate, I forced myself to speak. 'I don't understand, what project? Who did that to you?'

'The government, Ronnie,' he said bleakly. 'The people you're supposed to trust the most.'

'Why would they make children do that?'

'Project Five Fifteen of the S.R.U. – Special Requirements Unit. *The Agency.* They thought child assassins would be the ultimate guise, a weapon no one would see coming. Most of us were recruited at the age of five – though I was younger – and used for their missions until we were fifteen. A lot of countries use children in war, so it's not that shocking. Not really.'

'But a child couldn't do those things, a child can't kill a grown man.'

Unhappily, he pursed his lips, staring at me with a mixture of sadness and regret, so I knew instantly how wrong I was. Images of Laith, Ace, Nash and Denver raced through my mind and so many things fell into place.

'So, they let you go?' I croaked, knowing the answer to my incredibly naïve question before he spoke.

'One man who worked for them – I'll call him Andrew for the sake of this conversation. Andrew looked after us more than anyone. He was what we call our handler. He found out that each of us were to be terminated before we turned sixteen and he took pity on me. He told me to get out. Long story short – I told others and we ran. We were lucky, I guess, or perhaps the

111

world was unlucky, who knows which.'

'Ace?' I uttered his name and a pain shot through me at the thought of him.

'Ace has never done anything wrong. He was only twelve when we ran so he'd never been sent on a job. Anyway, that was nearly four years ago. They were on my tail until your father saved my life. Since then, I haven't seen or heard from them. I sneaked onto a cargo ship over to the UK and haven't had much trouble keeping a low profile. I think we're safe – for now. We just want to survive. We have to steal sometimes, because there's no way any of us can get real jobs. We don't own anything, we don't keep anything; when we leave a place, all we take are the clothes on our backs. We know we can't expect much from our lives now, but we won't let them take us down. We won't let them win.

'They're out there, though. Any day they might turn up and we could all die. I expect many of the old team are dead already. There were nineteen of us in the beginning. After casualties and before the project ended, sixteen of us had survived.

'So that's my life, Ronnie Rose. Tell me, how do you feel about me now?'

Canter Creek training facility, Iowa – July 2003

'I can't do it,' A complained.

'That's your call, man.'

'Yeah, but I know what you're thinking!'

'Hey, I don't care what you do, but you know what it'll mean if you disobey an order.'

'I like this horse, K, it's a pet!'

'I think that's the point,' he answered without looking up from the firewood he was chopping outside the front of the big farmhouse they shared.

'But it's a horse! It's not a pig, or a cow – why the hell have

112

I got to kill it?'

'I know what a horse is!' K bellowed impatiently. The boy was young, but they had all been there, all done things they would rather not do. He didn't want to live someone else's pain; his own was quite enough.

'I just don't see the point,' the young boy finished quietly, his head dropping.

'You don't?' K threw his axe down and stepped forward, wiping sweat from his brow with the back of his hand. 'All this whining over an animal, how will you fare when it's a human being? You'll be sent out soon, what'll you do then? Huh? Now get lost, I'm busy, do what the hell you like.'

A swallowed the lump in his throat and stared at his teammate. Eventually K stopped chopping again and stared back. An unspoken understanding passed between them. K knew very well how it felt to kill an animal that trusted you, that you had treated as a friend. He knew the torture of it. What he didn't know was how to help his younger teammate when he couldn't even help himself.

Shortly after the exchange, the youngest of the group left the front yard dejected. An hour later, a shot rang out in the forest.

***

My mouth had completely dried up. I had to swallow several times before I could find enough voice to respond. 'I don't feel any different about you, Kal. I just feel so sorry–'

'Don't.' He almost growled the word.

I flinched, but it wasn't his tone that scared me. I couldn't believe something so horrific could be real – that he'd come through all that. I lowered my eyes.

'So,' I breathed, staring at my lap, 'You came to my father's funeral.'

113

'It's not difficult to keep tabs on someone who isn't hiding. His saving my life meant a lot to me. I was saddened when I learned he'd fallen ill so I came to Clanots to find out more. When he died I wanted to pay my respects. I saw you there and – I felt for you. You'd lost your father, a great man, and I wondered how you'd cope. I thought I owed it to him to ensure you did.'

'So you only visit me because you feel you owe it to my father?'

Some light returned to his eyes. 'You're worried about my motives for seeing you?'

'I guess I need some time to absorb it all.'

'Of course.'

He stood up and held out his hand to me. I looked at it. A large hand, slightly worn for someone so young – it was an instrument of death. I almost shuddered at the thought, but I took it quickly, hoping he hadn't noticed my hesitation.

'Oh, hang on. So tonight, who were you stealing from?'

'No, now it is your turn,' he said firmly.

'Oh, right.'

'Ronnie, I must know who told you where I'd be. I won't be angry with you.'

'You will be angry with him though.'

'That's not your concern. We had a deal.'

'Promise me you won't do anything *drastic*.'

He looked irritated, but I held on, anxious for Laith.

114

Though I had no reason to care about his welfare, I still felt responsible. 'Promise me!'

'Fine,' he relented with obvious impatience. Leading me to the front door, he said the words I needed to hear. 'I promise you, nothing drastic.'

The light of a full moon danced through the window on the door, casting spooky shapes across his face. He looked at me intently, awaiting my answer. I sighed. I could think of no reason to protect someone who'd been vile to me since the day we met.

'Laith,' I said.

'I see,' his brow furrowed.

'Kalen you promised, don't do anything you'll regret.'

'Ronnie, do you want to see me again?'

The question was unexpected, but I answered instantly, nodding yes. In my heart, there was no other answer.

'Good. Tomorrow then? We can talk some more then if you have any more questions for me. For now, you need to sleep. Before you do, make sure you drink a pint of water and maybe have a slice or two of toast. I don't want you to become ill after our little stint in the river.'

'What about that car?' I asked, as fear of repercussions flooded my mind. I'd never been involved in something illegal before. It was a terrifying prospect.

'You don't need to worry about that, Red. I'll return it, I promise. Don't worry about anything, okay? Just do as I've asked.'

I agreed, surprising myself at just how exhausted I was. I wanted to ask what was in the bag on his shoulder, and why Laith hated me so much, but I already had more information than I could cope with. Shimmering flakes of snow began to fall as he walked onto the porch and jogged through the front garden to the stolen car. I watched him leave. It was like seeing him though new eyes. Every movement, every step, was considered and perfect. I'd always been impressed by him. Now, with this new information, I was in awe. I probably should have been scared of who he was, of what we had just been through, but when my mind tried to think logically, my heart overruled it.

16 — WHO AM I?

AFTER A SURPRISINGLY DREAMLESS SLEEP, my body ached and my mind raced. I hadn't properly absorbed what Kalen had told me about his life but, strangely, I was more anxious about what I'd told him about Laith. Now I knew who they all were and what they were capable of, I was scared something horrible might have happened between them. Added to which, my job interview was in two hours.

Rolling out of bed, I glanced out the window and groaned. Everything was covered in a thin layer of sugar-white snow. I like snow. In all its white glory, it made familiar things look shiny and new, but the thought of getting to the Travel Shop when the roads were crusted with ice didn't fill me with joy.

After a shower, I began to feel more like myself again and tried to focus on the interview rather than my new secret. It was almost impossible. Mainly, I couldn't get my head round the fact that the five boys were deadly assassins. They were just kids – kids like me.

I dressed in my one-and-only suit, pulled my hair back into

a neat ponytail and hurried downstairs.

The ice in the air blasted me as soon as I opened the door, but a warm sensation quickly replaced it – Kal's Audi was waiting in the driveway.

The car door swung open, his tall frame following smoothly after. He walked towards me with his head down and his hands in his pockets.

'Thought you might need a ride to your interview,' he explained hesitantly, his eyes not quite meeting mine.

I tried to place my feelings. The truth was, seeing him standing there, his nose slightly pink from the chill of the weather, his American accent different yet mesmerising, I couldn't find one part of me that was unhappy to see him. I wasn't sure what that said about me.

He held out a hand to me, so putting any logic or reason to the back of my mind, I took it and we walked across the immaculate sheet of snow to the car. As my feet crunched on the gravel, I realised what a thin layer of snow it was and glanced upwards. The white sky was rimmed with a dark ominous grey. I wrinkled my nose.

'What's the matter?' he asked, when by some miracle we reached the passenger door without slipping.

'It's just that I know it's going to rain later, and wash away all the snow.'

'You like the snow?' His eyebrows arched.

'Well, it's not as good as sunshine, but it's better than the rain.'

'A happy medium, what more could one want? Here we go, Miss.' He held the door open for me and I slipped inside, contemplating the notion of *a happy medium*. Once, I would have been happy with medium anything. Average, normal, ordinary – that was me. But I didn't want the snow any more, I suddenly realised just how much I wanted the sun.

'Thanks for this,' I said, when he got in the driver's side.

'You really didn't have to.'

'The least I could do, seeing as you spent half of last night battling hypothermia because of me.' He shifted the car into gear and we pulled out of the driveway. I can't say he drove slowly in the snow, but the journey was calmer and more thoughtful than normal. Whether it was because of the weather or our conversation the night before, I wasn't sure.

'So,' I ventured, when I'd gone over it ten times in my head, 'did you talk with Laith?'

'I did.'

'Um,' I gulped, 'is he okay?'

A small smile formed on his lips. 'Laith's fine, you don't need to worry about him.'

'I was worried about you.'

'Well, you definitely don't need to do that.'

I sank into my seat. Not wanting to pry any further, I left the subject. Just glad to know no one had been hurt. It wasn't that I believed he'd harm Laith. Something about Kal told me he'd never hurt his friends, but my head was spinning. All I had wanted to know was how he knew my dad. I thought everything would become clear once I found out the truth, but if there was one thing I was learning it's that truth is complicated. I'd never been able to predict his reaction to things and now I knew who he was, I was even less sure. I thought about the way he'd dealt with Jared, when he'd clearly lost his temper but managed to control himself. I didn't think I had anything to worry about. Perhaps they were more disciplined than the rest of us. I wondered for the journey's entirety, not realising how silent and lost in my thoughts I'd become until the touch of his hand on my shoulder jolted me back to reality.

'Red, we're here,' he said gently.

I pressed the palms of my hands to my eyes. I needed to concentrate on the interview; this was what I needed to do to save my family home.

'You'll be fine,' his calm voiced soothed. I nodded, trying to drum up some confidence and opened the car door. Frozen air flooded the car.

'I'll wait for you. Afterwards you can come to ours if you want? Ace is keen to see you,' he added, as if I needed another reason to spend time with him. I walked up to the unlit store and tapped lightly on the door. The Greek owner, Chris Hanno, who I'd met a week before, opened it immediately. He smiled brightly.

'Veronica!' he beamed. 'Please come in, it's cold out! Here, this is my wife, Eleni.'

I shook the hand of the tiny woman who appeared behind him, her dyed blonde hair glowing almost luminous in the warm corridor light. Behind me, Kal drove away. Part of me was relieved. I didn't want them to see him and start asking questions, because they weren't the sort of questions I was prepared to answer.

I stepped inside the shop, my legs almost trembling beneath me, but I needn't have worried. My interview turned out to be an informal chat about when I could start and what the job would entail.

'So why do you want to work in the travel industry, Ronnie?' Eleni asked.

I opened my mouth, ready to give an answer I felt appropriate in a job interview, but the words that came out were not what I'd planned. 'My father died and now I have to take care of the house and my sister. I'm scared if I don't get a job like this, I'll never get out of Clanots Ocean.' Where had that come from?

My brain told me to say something better – to cover it up – when I saw Eleni nodding sympathetically. She smiled in a way that told me she'd heard about my father. Of course she had.

After a five-minute private chat with her husband, Eleni came back in and welcomed me to their travel firm with a hug.

'Thank you so much, Mrs. Hanno,' I said. 'I promise you won't regret it.'

She shooed me out after that, telling me to enjoy the rest of my Christmas. I thanked them again and stepped out onto the pavement in a trance. I'd done it. All I needed to do now was convince Rachel that the house was worth keeping and that if she and Jared could just re-mortgage, I would help pay the bills and we could keep our father's house. The Audi pulled up in front of me almost instantly, as the first drops of rain began to fall.

'You got it, then?' he asked with a knowing smile as I slid into the front seat.

'I got it,' I agreed, shocked to hear it from my own mouth.

Christmas lights still brightened the streets around us and the light flurry of snow that had fallen made everything sparkle. I felt like I was in a movie, or perhaps an extended version of one of my many daydreams.

I looked at the driver and smiled.

***

At the mansion I tried to behave like nothing had changed. But now that I knew what the boys were about, it was surreal being around them and I wasn't sure if I was pulling off acting natural. Nash sat with a laptop computer resting on his lap, wearing a frown as he stared at the screen. Denver and Laith threw a ball absently across the room to one another and Ace had his nose in a book. It was all so normal, yet it wasn't normal at all. I turned to Kalen and saw him watching me, watch his friends. I couldn't read what he was thinking, but as I looked in his eyes a chilling thought occurred to me: the similarities between them – the look of innocence they shared and smiles that belied any wrongdoing; I wondered if they had been handpicked as children for that exact reason, because when you looked at their faces you could be forgiven for believing they were angels. It

121

was only on closer inspection, looking into their eyes, that you could see the darkness that lurked inside – the torment and pain they carried with them. A look that can only be acquired from years of hardship and horror that any normal person would be unaccustomed to.

There was nothing angelic about that look.

17 — ONE GOOD DAY

'**S**O HOW COME YOU DON'T HAVE A PHONE?' I ASKED ON OUR WAY BACK TO MY HOUSE LATER THAT EVENING.

He rubbed one hand over his mouth. 'It's difficult,' he said eventually, 'but the boys and I agreed to it a long time ago. One less way for them to find us. If we separate, we have a few agreed meeting places and all the time in the world to find each other anyway.'

He glanced at me, one hand resting casually on the bottom of the steering wheel, the other on his leg. I wanted to reach out and hold it. I didn't.

Soon, we were pulling up outside my house. Rachel's BMW was in the driveway.

'Oh, great,' I mumbled. I wanted to stay and talk, but if I didn't go in soon she'd only come out and get me. It was more embarrassment than I could handle. I stepped out. 'Will I see you tomorrow?'

'If you want to,' he said softly.

'I want to.' I looked at him, so he knew I meant it.

His face remained impassive, but I thought I saw something in his eyes, as though he was half expecting me to tell him I wanted nothing more to do with him. I watched his car drive away, knowing in my heart I would never do that.

Rachel and Jared were sitting in the lounge. I checked my watch to make sure I hadn't imagined the time – it was past midnight.

'What's going on?'

'Cloud is in Dad's bed asleep. We thought we'd stay here tonight.' Rachel's tone was cutting, so I knew I was in for a lecture.

'Okay.' I tried to slip out and up to my room.

'You've changed, Ronnie.'

I slumped and fell back on the sofa.

'Your attitude, this attitude you have right now. Who are you these days?'

'Rachel, do you have a point?'

'Yes, I have a point! Mrs Carpenter told us that boy has been over here a lot. She called me. She's concerned you're being led astray.'

I slid even further into the depths of the settee, wishing it would suck me into the back of the cushions to a world where Mrs Nosey was mute.

'Ronnie, we care about you. Since you started hanging around with those boys your whole attitude has shifted. You don't care about anybody any more.'

'You mean I don't wait on you hand and foot any more.'

Jared flapped his arms. 'That's not fair!'

'I don't expect you to wait on me, Ronnie, I know you've always been the grown up in the family, but Dad isn't here any more and I know he wouldn't want you behaving this way. What about your old friends?' Rachel snapped.

'What old friends? If you opened you eyes for just a second you'd see that all I've ever done was take care of you and Dad – I have no other friends. This is the first time in my life I've had people to have fun with, what's so bad about that?'

124

'What about that My girl?'

'I still see Mae,' I stated pointedly.

'And what does she think of what you are doing?'

'Rach, Mae doesn't like Kalen either, but I do. I wish you'd just try to be happy for me, like I've been for you since–' I stopped myself from insulting Jared, much as I was tempted.

'Go on,' she insisted angrily, 'say something mean and prove everybody's point about what a nasty little cow you are these days.'

They both stared back at me like I was the worst person in the world. I got up; there was nothing left to say.

'I got a job today, Rach. I start work next week.' With that, I walked up to my room and closed the door.

***

The morning brought with it a feeling of guilt. I couldn't remember my dreams, but I was sure what Rachel had said had been on my mind all night. I headed for her room, tapping lightly on the door. There was no answer. Pushing gently, I peered in. The room was empty and the bed made. Letting out a sigh, I went back to my own room for my phone and called Mae, inviting her over to meet Kalen in an attempt to make peace. I needed at least one person on my side.

Reluctantly she agreed, but as soon as I hung up the phone rang again. My new boss, Chris Hanno, spoke with his heavy Greek accent, asking me to spend a few hours in the office training before I started in the New Year. Of course I said yes. I hurried to get ready and left the back door unlocked for Mae in case I didn't make it home on time.

A few hours turned into a whole day. I panicked as I pictured Mae arriving to meet Kal without me there. Chris was taking forever to type an email that he'd asked me to read. I offered to type it for him. His mouth turned down at the corners,

125

far enough to change the shape of his chin.

'Veronica, I can type an email. You see, watch me as I type! All I want is for you to tell me what you think of it once it is written. You don't mind, ah?'

'No, of course not.' Yes, actually, I really do!

Thirty minutes later, I was able to leave. I rushed home to find Mae walking out.

'Hey, sorry I'm late. Are you going already?' The disappointment in my voice was clear.

'Sorry, Ron, I have plans later.' She smiled in a sweet and reassuring way, like I imagine a mother might smile. 'I met Kalen and we had a nice chat. That's what you wanted, right?'

'Yeah, I guess.' I felt my shoulders slump. 'So what did you think?'

She sighed, 'He seems to care for you a lot. As long as you're happy and safe, that's what matters.'

Then she left, and I couldn't help but notice her parting words were louder than they needed to be.

'Is everything okay?' I asked a clearly brooding Kalen when I walked into the living room.

He looked up at me with a tight, forced smile. 'Of course.'

'Did you have a nice chat?'

'She's a great girl – you're lucky to have her as a friend.'

'Okaaay.'

'Are you okay?' Kalen tapped the seat beside him.

I threw myself down. 'I just wish I could have one day without the aggravation from my sister, or pointed looks from Mae – just a day when I don't miss Dad so much. I don't know what to do for the best any more. I seem to be hurting everyone at the moment.' I was surprised at the truth of my words. I hadn't meant to be so blunt.

He looked at me sympathetically, yet there seemed to be something more that he wanted to say. He remained quiet.

I gulped. 'Did Mae say something to upset you?'

'Let me take you out tomorrow,' he offered, without answering my question. 'I know we're just friends but, maybe for a day we could pretend nothing else matters. Let me try to give you that one good day.'

18 — SUBTERFUGE

I DIDN'T REMEMBER FALLING ASLEEP, but I was in bed when an alarm on my iPhone woke me. I reached for it, a reminder note had flashed up on the screen:

Be ready at 9. Warm casual clothes.

K

It was seven. I jumped up and into the shower. Hurriedly, I toweled my body dry, dressing in jeans and a navy hooded jumper and pulling my hair on top of my head. Outside, the sun was shining brightly, a sharp contrast to yesterday's rain.

He arrived punctually, wearing black cargo pants and a dark grey sweater pushed up to his elbows. His eyes were masked by a pair of Wayfarers.

'So, where are we going?' I asked, pulling the front door closed behind us.

'It's a surprise.'

I shielded my eyes from the brightness all around me, following him down off the porch.

'Have I mentioned I don't like surprises?'

'No, you haven't,' he said, with a smile.

I'd expected the Audi, or even the Ford, but to my surprise a shiny black motorcycle sat by the side of the road. The same one he'd sped away on the day we met. I glanced at him anxiously, but he wasn't looking at me. If it was possible, he was even quieter than usual.

Suddenly, my fear of riding on the back of a motorbike was the last thing on my mind. I wanted to ask if he was okay, but the words caught in my throat. He handed me a spare helmet.

'I've never been on a bike before,' I said instead.

'Are you afraid?' There wasn't a trace of humour in his voice, he wasn't joking or trying to scare me. His question demanded a legitimate answer. I should have been afraid, but somehow I knew this would be yet another thing he did with perfection.

'No.'

With a small nod, he swung one leg over the seat and straddled the bike.

'Can I ask a question?' I ventured.

'It seems so.'

'What?'

He smirked and I knew I'd missed some joke again. 'Where did you get this bike?'

'It belongs to Nash.'

'And the Audi?'

'That's mine.'

'How did you afford it?'

'They're not stolen if that's what you're asking.'

I wasn't blind to the fact that he hadn't answered my question, but I wasn't sure I really wanted to know. It was easier to accept if I didn't think about it.

'Hop on, Red.' Removing his sunglasses, he pulled on a black helmet, so I could see only his eyes. So often overshadowed by his distracting smile, alone they were more striking than I'd ever realised. The problem right now was that they looked sad. He was definitely hiding something. Before I could ask what, he flipped the visor down. I slid silently on behind him.

Once in my seat, which felt further from the ground than I'd anticipated, Kal reached back, taking both of my hands and wrapping them around him. My stomach flipped with the contact, but it was nothing compared to when the engine roared to life and we took off. I pressed myself tightly against him.

Eventually I dared to open my eyes. I doubted that any car in the world could go as fast as the bike and if it did, it wouldn't feel the same. There was no room in my head for negative thoughts – all I could focus on was the wind, the speed, and Kalen's firm body. At one point, I felt the front of the bike tip upwards, the engine roared even louder as we wheeled through a set of lights. I squealed, but it was all good. A jolt of pleasure pulsed through me.

When he pulled to a stop, I slipped off and rubbed my thighs. I'd been gripping so tightly it took a minute for the feeling to come back to them. As I glanced up, however, I became distracted by where we were.

'Oh, God,' I blurted, straightening and staring at the airfield in front of us.

'Don't panic, Red,' he smiled crookedly, 'you trust me, right?'

'Um... I think so.'

He laughed. 'Did you know when you're nervous, you tug at your hair?'

'No, I don't.' I let go of the strand I'd been holding.

'Yeah, you do. You twist and pull at it. It's cute. But hey, there's nothing to be scared of.'

He took my hand then, leading me across the field to a plane that looked small enough to be a toy.

'Hey, mate,' Kal greeted the pilot with a handshake and his fake British accent.

'Morning, Mr Smith. She's all ready for you both, pack is

over there on the ground, as you requested. I'll give you some time to get sorted. Just hop in when you're ready. Weather is great for it, which is surprising for this time of year.'

'Ah, Kevin, I told you not to worry. The weather's always on my side.'

The pilot hoisted himself into the plane after that, with a fleeting look in my direction. Kalen stepped over to a big piece of material on the floor. A parachute. It looked more like a shiny bed sheet.

'Don't we need two of these?' I asked nervously. Noticing I was twisting the end of my hair, I quickly shoved my hands in the pockets of my jeans.

'You want to jump on your own?' he looked up at me with a quizzical expression from his crouched position, where he was running his hands along the material and checking things I had no idea about.

'Of course not. I'm not even sure I want to jump.'

'That's okay,' he chuckled silently, 'I'll jump and you'll be attached to me so it's all good.'

'But what I mean is, don't we need to be strapped to people who do this all the time?'

'Yep, you're looking at him.'

I nodded to myself, another chill running through me. Kalen continued to check the chute without looking up at me again.

When we were in the plane the engine was so loud I couldn't muster the energy to yell above it and Kalen was without doubt the most excited I'd ever seen him. I pushed away the stirring in my stomach and repeated in my head that he knew what he was doing. Inside the plane was bitingly cold and as though feeling it too, Kalen wrapped his arms around me. The next thing I knew, the pilot was calling out something about twelve-thousand-feet. Kal stood us both up my heart went crashing into overdrive.

'Are you sure we're going to be okay, Kal?' I squeaked.

'Red, look down there.'

We shuffled together towards the edge, the icy air catching me off guard. I peered out and instantly felt sick. The feeling had no time to linger, however, because as I glanced over the edge, he used the motion to flip us both out the door. My stomach dropped and we were hurtling into the vast expanse of sky below.

I don't recall how many times we spun, or how long the fall took. The experience was just too overwhelming. I'd thought being on the motorcycle was freeing, but it had nothing on this. As we plummeted towards the earth, my life, my problems and even the cold all seemed like distant memories. It was the first time I had complete and utter peace. On top of that, it was the biggest kick! I screamed out, the wind caught in my mouth, ballooning it open. I laughed into it.

The sound of the parachute opening above us came before I felt it pull us upwards, and then it was as though everything stopped. From one intense rush to an entirely different one, we floated down towards Clanots Ocean, like a feather caught in the wind.

'Amazing, right?' Kalen's voice whispered in my ear, and in that moment I knew I didn't want to live without this. Whenever I was with him, I was happy and I didn't want it to end. Ever. I bobbed my head. Unable to form the words for how amazing it was.

As we neared the ground, which rushed up suddenly with a speed I hadn't expected, he told me to lift my legs and we landed smoothly after just a few steadying steps from Kal.

'Oh God,' I said for the second time, though my meaning had changed a lot.

When I was unhooked, my legs buckled like jelly. I let myself fall back onto the grass. Kalen laughed from above me.

'You okay?' he asked, the sunshine framing his face like a

halo. I squinted up at him, my smile practically splitting my face in half.

'I want to do it again!' I breathed eventually.

Grinning, he reached down, took me by the elbow and hoisted me to my feet. 'Wait here, I'll be two minutes.' He jogged off towards a small reception area.

While I waited, I tried to comprehend what had just happened: I, Ronnie Rose, had jumped out of a plane. And I'd loved it! Every fibre of my body was humming, I giggled to myself.

Hearing my name, I turned to where Kal stood waving me over. I skipped across to him, feeling lighter than air.

'I'm starving!' I announced.

'Yeah, it does that.'

'When was the last time you did this?'

'Too long ago and believe me, never in such pleasant circumstances. Come on, let's get you something to eat.'

'How much was that? What do I need to give you?' I asked, scuttling to catch up with him.

Kalen frowned, making a clucking sound of disapproval as we headed towards the bike.

I felt like a pro now. I let myself look around as we sped along the country lanes. I held on to him, but I didn't feel scared any more. I resisted the temptation to whoop with my hands in the air and settled on grinning into his back as I pressed my face against his jacket.

Underneath me, I felt the bike slow and the sound of the engine softened as we rounded a corner to the alleyway where he'd first dropped – as if out of the sky – in front of me. He pulled up to a stop. Kalen was his usual silent self as he broke the lock on the back door to the abandoned building and led us through to a staircase inside.

When we reached the top, the last door swung open easily and we were able to step out onto the roof. I stood in awed silence. High above Clanots Ocean, the liquid-gold sun had begun to set. It sparkled and shone, showing the town in a way I'd never seen it. Ahead, the ocean shimmered and behind us, building after building tapered off until there was nothing but rolling fields.

He smiled. 'You like it?'

'I didn't know it could look like this,' I said.

'Being up high, above the churn of every-day life, I can sometimes find solace,' he said, almost wistfully. 'Rooftops, the sky, they're my favourite places.'

'I saw you once, I think you were with Nash. You were both jumping from this building.'

He smiled. 'I remember.'

'Do you do that a lot?'

'I guess. It was something we were taught to help us evade people. You'd be surprised how little people ever really look up.'

'It was amazing. You ran along a wall!' When I thought about what I'd witnessed, now I knew what he was, I knew those things weren't flukes. I couldn't help but be impressed.

'Parkour.'

'Huh?'

'Free running. It's a sport – look it up on YouTube.'

'Can you show me some now?'

His expression grew cold and serious; there was a long silence before he spoke again. 'You're too forgiving of people, you know.'

I sighed and sat down on the blanket he had laid out in front of us. Where had that comment come from? 'How can someone be too forgiving?'

'Not many people are, but trust me, it's possible. You're a prime example.'

'Explain,' I pressed.

'Your sister, for one. When we first met, you told me she lived with you. You lied.'

'I didn't know you then, you might have wanted to rob me... or kill me. That's the only reason I lied. What does that have to do with me being a pushover?'

'I didn't say you were a pushover. How interesting that you would use that terminology.'

I groaned. 'You're confusing me now.'

The corners of his mouth twitched. I knew he enjoyed getting me tongue-tied. Huffing out a lungful of air, I peered over the edge of the roof, trying to clear my head.

'You've always taken care of your sister and now there's no one to take care of you. You don't see the bad in people. Your kindness is going to be your downfall.'

I felt him sit down next to me, but continued to stare down at the road as his words spun in my head. I didn't think I was too kind – how was that even possible? I shook my head adamantly. 'Rachel doesn't have bad in her, she's maybe a little selfish, but that's all.'

'What about her husband?'

'Jared? They're not married, though she always refers to him as my brother-in-law,' I said. 'He's not bad either.'

'What about me?'

'What about you?' I glanced over my shoulder at him. He didn't meet my eyes and I watched as the muscles in his jaw tensed.

'Am I a bad person?' he managed eventually, his voice tight. He threw a small stone. It bounced on the rooftop and over the edge.

'No,' I answered confidently.

From the set of his frown, I could tell he wasn't satisfied with my answer.

'You're too nice,' he concluded.

'Well, I must be balancing out the universe in compensation for you then!'

It was the first time he'd really laughed. He laughed so hard he threw his head back and clutched his stomach. It was a wonderful sound. My irritation vanished.

When he was quiet again, he glanced at me from the corner of his eye, hiding a mischievous grin.

'What?' I asked.

From where he sat, Kalen launched himself into a crouch and upwards into a flip, landing back down into the same sitting position he'd started, as though he'd never moved.

I stared, open-mouthed. We both burst out laughing again.

'Show off!'

'Hey, you asked!'

I replayed his stunt in my mind as we watched the last rays of sunlight melt like butterscotch behind the buildings ahead of us. Finally, the daylight disappeared completely.

Kalen took off his jumper, draping it over my shoulders, as I wrapped my arms around myself to ward off the chill that came with the absence of the sun. I sneaked a glance at his near-naked torso, my attention held once again by the scar that showed just above the collar of his undershirt, pale in contrast to his sun-kissed skin. I forced myself to look away, desperate to ask about it, yet too scared to know. Lying back, I stared at the sky and tried to stop my mind from racing.

'If you're cold–' I began.

'I've never felt so warm,' he interrupted simply, his body falling back next to mine. 'Tell me about your house. What's going to happen to it?'

'I really don't know. We owe a lot of money on it. I can't afford it, Rachel can't afford it.'

'How much is a lot?'

I faltered at that. The solicitor had told me but the number was so large that I had let my mind forget it almost as it had been spoken. What difference did it make how much, when the figure was too much?

'About one-hundred thousand, I think.'

'Do you want to live there?'

'Where else would I live?'

'I don't know, there's a big world out there, do you want to stay in Clanots Ocean all your life?'

He sounded impatient and I had no idea why, but I got lost in thought at that point anyway, mumbling something about it being all that was left of my dad and therefore I wanted to do what I could to keep it, but I was thinking about the world. I had always wanted to travel and assumed that one day I would. Now, if I took on the responsibility for keeping our family home, I'd never go anywhere.

The stars began to blink down at us and I felt his fingers intertwine with mine, the sensation breaking through my depressing thoughts and almost taking my breath away.

I woke up with my head resting on his chest and quickly sat up. 'I fell asleep?'

'It's not been long,' he said. 'An hour, maybe. I should get you home.'

I didn't want to leave, but it was getting colder by the minute and all he had on was a thin T-shirt. I stood up grudgingly, not letting go of his hand, which had remained in mine.

The ride back felt strange. I felt strange. Something about him was tense and I could feel it through the leather of his jacket. When we arrived in my driveway I slid off and removed my helmet, shaking out my hair.

'I don't want this day to end,' I told him.

'Everything has to end.'

My eyes flashed to his. I'd enjoyed what felt like one of the best days of my life, definitely the best day since Dad had died. I couldn't bear to think it was going to end badly. 'Are you okay?'

'I'm fine,' he said, as he took the black helmet from my hands. 'I – I had a good day,' he struggled.

I wanted to reach out and touch him, but I reminded myself we were just friends. I had made it that way.

'It's been so great, thank you, Kalen.'

'I hope it took your mind off everything?'

'It did, it was everything I needed. Do you want to come in and hang out?'

'I have some things I need to do tonight,' he said softly, his eyes lowering.

I was disappointed, but he pulled me towards him, his hand slipping behind my neck as he gently pressed his lips to my forehead.

The action was so sweet, so careful, that my breath caught. Something felt terribly wrong, but before I could get a grip on myself enough to speak, he was sliding his own helmet back on and the sound of the engine put an invisible wall between us.

Then he was gone.

PART II

19 — TIME AND PUNISHMENT

'I HEARD THEY LEFT TOWN,' SAID LARA, THE OF-FICE TEMP. I'd managed to avoid this topic of conversation for the two weeks I'd been working at the Travel Shop, but today they'd been talking about nothing else since work began an hour ago. Thankfully Lara wasn't speaking directly to me, so I was able to keep my head down. I mustn't have been doing a good job at hiding my feelings though, because I looked up to find my coworker, Alex, staring at me with interest.

The office was small, just Alex and I on phones, the office manager Damien and Ben, the luxury travel consultant, as well as a temp from time to time. Alex had been really helpful since I'd started, but our conversation had never veered beyond work, so while I didn't want to be rude, I didn't know how to respond to the way she was looking at me. I gave her a small smile.

'Did you know them?' she whispered.

I cleared my throat. 'What makes you say that?'

To my surprise, she suddenly looked sad for me, as though she was worried I might burst into tears. Did I look that bad?

'Kalen, was, a friend,' I mumbled.

'Oh my God!' she mouthed. "Kalen *Smith*?'

I sighed inwardly. My new job had gone a long way to helping keep my mind busy, but work and school only took up so much time.

My initial reaction when Kalen had left without even saying goodbye had been anger, but it was difficult to blame him for leaving – my colleague's elated reaction to his name spoke volumes. She was beaming at me, her large blue eyes wide with anticipation. Damien and Lara had fallen quiet and I could feel their glances in our direction.

Alex seemed to cotton on to them too, as her expression switched from excited to over-it in a millisecond. She stared at her computer screen, tapping the keyboard repeatedly, making out like she was busy. Lara lost interest and scuttled off to the kitchen.

I looked at Alex to find her smiling, like we were in on a secret together. I wanted to thank her for her tact. It wasn't something I was used to.

'Some girlfriends of mine think he's hot,' Alex added when no one was in earshot. 'I quite like the taller one myself.'

'Denver,' I nodded simply. Her choice was an obvious one. Denver was as beautiful as any actor or model. Though in my eyes, nobody compared to Kalen, not even remotely. My stomach tensed uncomfortably at the thought of him. 'I didn't realise people knew them,' I lied. They hadn't wanted people to know them, but they definitely did; the drawback of trying to be covert in a tiny village that had its own Neigbourhood Watch. He could never hope to be invisible when everyone in Clanots knew him by name.

'Er yeah! But, I didn't think they spoke to anyone – well, apart from the hot one, he's always out with like, a zillion girls around him – but that Kalen one, he's never even looked at me before. How did you meet?'

'He was a friend of my father's.'

Her enthusiasm was infectious. Even though I knew the

141

boys were gone for good, it was nice to have someone take notice of me. We continued to chat for most of the day, between
taking calls and hiding our conversation from people coming
and going.

At the end of my workday we swapped numbers and agreed
to meet up for a coffee. I didn't have the courage to tell her
what he'd really meant to me, or that he'd left without even a
word. I'd only come to terms with it myself, just days before.
It had taken ten days for me to finally believe it. New Year's
Eve had come and gone. At first I felt numb, wondering over
and over if I'd missed something, if I'd done something wrong,
something that would make him ignore me. I spent all my time
checking my bedroom window, listening for every sound until I
felt completely neurotic.

Then I became scared something might have happened to
him. The strange feelings I'd had when I was alone, the car
with the blacked out windows that I'd assumed was a debt
collector. Could that have been someone, not watching me, but
watching Kalen? Before I knew it, I was running through the
pouring rain like an escaped mental patient and banging desperately on his front door. It swung open to a cold dark shell,
no trace they ever existed.

Back at home I'd stumbled around in a trance. I lit the fire,
made a cup of tea and went through mundane motions to keep
my mind busy, like sweeping the floors and dusting the television cabinet. It wasn't until I sat down to drink the tea, which
had turned cold that I realised I'd done all of it without taking
off my jacket. Sitting in my soaking wet clothes, I didn't move
or attempt to take a shower. The cold and damp seeped right
through me. I let it.

I thought of our last day together and wondered how he
could have let me enjoy one of the greatest days of my life,
when he knew it would be followed by so many of the worst.
Was it a particularly cruel form of torture he'd learned as an
assassin, or was it designed especially for me?

I stared vacantly at the television, too afraid to think about what I'd lost.

Clanots Ocean – 30th December 2009

'You know, my friend is infatuated with you.'

Kalen looked at the tiny Chinese girl who was trying her best to appear threatening. He had to stifle a smile, because of all the threatening people in the world, she wasn't one of them.

'Don't be modest. You know she is, because you've constructed it to be just that way. You swoop in here, all dark and mysterious. You find her when she runs away from home, you stop her doing drugs in the bar, you save her from her inner demons, or whatever–'

'Mae, what are you getting at?' he asked, suddenly irritated. He wasn't used to people knowing anything about him, and a naïve little girl telling him how it was made him more than uncomfortable.

'What I'm getting at, is that you knew what you were doing – so now you have her right where you want her and I wanna know, what now?'

'Is that any of your business?'

'Frankly, yes. She's been my best friend for seven years and Ronnie doesn't make friends easily. She doesn't trust people, because even though she tries to pretend like her mother leaving never affected her – it did. She's actually very fragile. She's just lost her father and now you show up and I think you're going to hurt her, possibly in a way she might not recover from.'

'I'm not,' he managed through gritted teeth, unable to look her in the eye. What was wrong with him? Who was this girl to make him feel guilty for doing something he wanted to do?

'Really? So what – you're going to stay here, be her boyfriend, go for walks in the park, take her out for dinner, get married, live happily ever after?'

'What has she told you?'

'Nothing. Since you came along, she barely talks to me any more. But you think I can't see that you're bad news? What is it Kalen, drugs? I mean, come on – the whole town knows you're trouble, all we have to do is look at you and your friends to know something odd is going on.'

Kalen couldn't believe his ears. He was supposed to look sweet and innocent, like butter wouldn't melt – he wasn't supposed to radiate trouble. He was finding out a lot about himself lately.

A noise sounded at the back door. Ronnie was home. Kalen's palms began to sweat; it had been a very long time since that had happened.

'Look, I'm not saying you don't care about Ronnie,' Mae said quickly. 'All I am saying is that if you cared *enough*, you would leave her now before she's in too deep. She's a beautiful girl with her whole life ahead of her, Kalen. Do you really think you're good for her?'

'I hear you,' he growled, barely managing to control his rage.

Seeming to sense his inner turmoil and looking happy with her achievement, Mae delicately picked up her cardigan and left the house, just as Ronnie came in from the garden.

'Sorry I am late – are you leaving?'

'Sorry Ron, I have to, I have plans later. I stayed as long as I could.'

Pause.

'Ron, I met Kalen, we had a nice chat. That's what you wanted, right?'

'Yeah, I guess.'

'He seems to care for you a lot. As long as you're happy and safe, that's what matters.'

'Okay.'

Kal sat on the living-room sofa and fumed silently. He hated this girl who professed to know him. *She knew nothing,* he thought miserably. Yet somewhere deep inside, he was tormented. His feelings for Veronica overruled all sense and reason. He'd put his friends in danger – he'd put her in danger, all so he could keep enjoying the moments of serenity he found when he was close to her. He hated to think of another man having his hands on her slim body, in her long silky hair, but maybe that is what was best for her. After all, he really didn't deserve happiness... but she did.

'Is everything okay?' Ronnie asked, shocking him out of his reverie.

'Of course.'

'Did you and Mae have a good chat?' Her tone was light, but her eyes were questioning. There wasn't much that could get past her, he thought, with mixed feelings of pride and regret.

'Yeah, she's a great girl – you're lucky to have her as a friend.'

'I guess so,' Ronnie trailed off. He could see she had questions, but he also knew she wouldn't push it any further. Instead she curled up next to him on the sofa. He felt his pulse quicken.

'You sure you're okay?' she asked him sweetly. He loved the sound of her voice. No matter what was happening around her, there was optimism in her tone, a blindingly absurd belief in the people around her. Despite how ugly a person was inside, she still had faith in them - she had faith in him. His gut wrenched at the thought of her and of him without her. Her sunny face brightened his world, an otherwise desolate place. Being with her was the only time he felt any peace.

'Are *you* okay?' he asked, coughing to clear the tightness in his throat.

'Yeah. I guess I'd just like one day without the aggravation from my sister, or the concerned looks from Mae – just a day when I don't miss Dad so much. I don't know what to do for the best any more. I seem to be hurting everyone at the moment.'

'Let me take you out tomorrow,' he asked with more effort than he'd ever needed to exert to remain calm and unreadable, 'let me try to give you one good day.'

She looked elated at the possibility and he hated himself a little bit more.

20 — OLD FRIENDS

RACHEL HAD BEEN BUSY. Now the boys had left town, both she and Jared were less concerned with coming over to check up on me. My new class timetable meant I had Fridays off and I'd managed to fill the void with two and a half days a week at the Travel Shop. Still, I had a considerable amount of time to myself again.

I got in from work at four, rewired an old table lamp that hadn't worked in months and put the remaining boxed Christmas decorations back in the loft. Mae had called and agreed to come and hang out later in the evening. We had been back at school for nearly two weeks, but I'd barely seen her outside of classes. I was looking forward to a proper catch up.

I watched the clock on the kitchen wall while I waited for her and for what felt like the millionth time, I wondered what had become of me. My life had been dull before, but I hadn't been aware of it. I was happy in my ignorance. Now, knowing how it felt to have something I wanted, only to have it taken away, I had developed a newfound hatred for everything average. Even my old daydreams no longer helped. Once, I could have pictured my hero coming to my rescue and felt infinitely better. But now, when I tried to picture him, his face was nothing more than a blurry haze. The only thing that stood out was a pair of intensely dark-blue eyes, reminding me of everything

I wanted to forget.

I went to the computer and started it up. Google home page filled the screen. I typed in: *Project Five Fifteen*. A whole page of results popped up, but nothing remotely related to what I was looking for. Instead, a list of events occurring on or around the fifteenth of May. I started a new search, typing, *Special Requirements Unit*.

My finger hesitated over the button on the mouse. I'd watched enough movies to consider that looking for such things could get me in serious trouble with the wrong kind of people. And what did I expect? That his name and address would pop up? I shut down the computer and unplugged it from the wall, feeling ridiculous, desperate and scared all at once. The television it would have to be. I curled up on the sofa, glancing back at the computer. I felt like it was watching me.

When I heard the knock on the door, I felt the tightness in my chest ease. I hopped up from the sofa to let Mae in.

'Hey–' I did a double take. She had brought Cheryl along.

'How are you?' Mae asked, wrapping her arms around me.

'Okay,' I exaggerated. 'Hi Cheryl, how's it going?'

'Great, thanks,' she beamed, walking in and glancing around, examining the decor.

'Can I get you both a drink?'

In unison, Mae answered tea and Cheryl, coffee. I headed for the kitchen and filled the kettle.

'I hope you don't mind,' Mae asked from behind me. 'I couldn't really leave her, we've been shopping all day and I really wanted to come see you.'

'Of course not.' I hoped my lie wasn't as transparent as it felt.

Silence lingered while the water boiled. I filled the cups and stirred Mae's tea, suddenly infatuated with the whirlpool I'd created with my teaspoon.

'Ronnie, where is your bathroom?' Cheryl was looking at me as though I was crazy and I realised I'd zoned out again. I didn't know how many times she'd asked where my bathroom was, but Mae was casting me a look I can only describe as pity. I forced myself to perk up.

'Sorry, I was a million miles away,' I breezed, 'the bathroom's upstairs, first door on the left.'

With a pointed side-glance in Mae's direction, Cheryl swept out of the room.

'Ron,' Mae said as soon as Cheryl was out of earshot, 'you going to talk to me?'

'What do you mean?' I looked at my oldest friend. Her eyes were searching, trying to work me out. I missed her, but I could hardly tell her how I felt. She'd hated Kalen.

'I mean Kalen leaving town. I know it's hit you hard, but you won't talk about it. What good is it going to do to bottle it all up inside?'

'I'm not sure what there is to say.' Placing the drinks on the table, I sat down and wrapped my hands around the large mug of tea. The heat scolded my palms. I didn't let go.

'Did he say why he left?

I shook my head.

'Well, that's just plain rude, you see! He was never good enough for you. You must know that. No job, no prospects and obviously zero manners!'

'You're right,' I nodded, hoping that would be the end of it.

'But you seem so down. Have you been kickboxing recently?'

I eyed her curiously. 'Surely you know I haven't?'

'Taz doesn't really talk about work, but yeah he does ask after you. He's just worried about you. We all are.'

'Everyone's so worried about me, but–' I thought better of it. What was I going to gain by falling out with Mae? 'So, how's that all going with Taz?'

'Oh,' she brightened, 'he's so great. He buys me flowers all the time, takes me out for dinner. It's been nearly a month now!'

'That's nice.'

Her pretty face pulled into a grimace. 'Ron, that's nice? Is that all you can say?'

'Sorry, I just – I guess I'm just not myself lately. So, has he met your parents?'

'They don't know about him yet. Taz rents his own apartment in the town centre so I stay there most of the time. He's going to start giving personal training lessons soon and when he has enough money saved he's even mentioned us finding a place together – maybe in the next few months. To rent of course, I wouldn't buy this early on.'

I stared at my friend, forcing my gaping mouth to close. 'Mae, you just said it's only been a month!'

'I know that, but sometimes when it's right, you just know,' she beamed.

I considered the notion of knowing something was right. It seemed to me like you could know something in your heart and something else in your head, so what was so obvious about that?

'He has so many girls after him though. I have to be quick or he might get away.' She giggled as if she'd told a joke, but somehow I suspected there was a level of truth to her words.

'Have you decided on UEA or Kings yet?' I asked, desperate to talk about something else.

She shrugged. 'I'm not even sure about uni any more. I'll have to see what happens with Taz.'

I took a moment to absorb what she was telling me. 'Mae, don't you have to have a degree to be a doctor?' I asked before I could think better of it.

She lifted her shoulders a second time. 'Maybe I don't want to be a doctor any more. We don't all end up how we thought we would when we were kids, Ron. Dreams change as we get older.'

I opened my mouth to tell my friend how ridiculous she sounded, when Cheryl came back.

'You have a great house. I'm surprised,' she said, seemingly oblivious to her insult.

'I'm glad you approve,' I responded sharply.

'Someone's touchy.' Taking her coffee, Cheryl helped herself to more hot water from the kettle and, with what looked like a deliberate pose, she placed one hand on her hip and sighed.

'You know,' she began, 'I think you need to get out more. I mean, you had a great night out with us at White Lies before that stupid guy turned up and ruined all our fun.'

'Yeah, you're right, if only I'd been left to take drugs and wallow in self pity, it's just what I needed.'

Her eyes narrowed. 'You weren't wallowing, you were having fun, which is more than I can say for you now. I don't know you very well, but I'm just trying to give you some friendly advice. Mae really worries about you, which isn't fair on her if you ask me. You should come out with us more – put a smile on that face. If you put some make up on, you're actually not bad to look at.'

I was sure someone couldn't be so unaware of the insults they bandied about, but I refused to rise to her bitchy comments. For a while, ignoring her worked, but at every chance she got, Cheryl would turn the conversation back to Kalen and tell me how much of a loser he was. Even though he'd left town and broken my heart, I still couldn't listen to someone speaking badly of him. In the end, I yawned, pretending I was falling asleep. Eventually, they took the hint and left.

'Now, don't forget, okay, come out with us next weekend.

We're going to Tantra on Thursday. It's in London. Have you ever been to London, Ronnie? It really is so much cooler than Clanots. Though if that seems too much for you then maybe come out on Saturday instead, we'll just be going to White Lies like last time.'

'It really would be great if you hung out with us more, Ron,' Mae said softly as she hugged me goodbye.

I said I would call and closed the door behind them, taking myself straight up to bed. If nothing else, the conversation had exhausted me and so I thought maybe for once I might sleep well.

21 — NEW FRIENDS

IN THE OFFICE, Alex's short bobbed hair was even shorter than it had been the day before, her lips painted a bright vivacious red. She was so keen to talk about the boys that I almost wished I could continue to lie, but without even making a conscious decision, I took a chance and told her the truth: he'd left me.

She was so sympathetic it was actually a relief. Insisting that, from what I'd told her, he'd seemed far too keen to have left without a word. It felt good to have someone on my side, but with that thought I began to worry about him again. Maybe something terrible had happened, and I had no idea how or if I could do anything about it. Still, his parting words echoed in my mind: 'Everything has to end.' I shook the thought away. He'd left because he wanted to. I had to face it.

We both had a half-day and Alex suggested we spend the afternoon together to cheer me up.

'Starbucks?' I offered.

'No way,' she stated firmly. 'We're catching a train to Cowford. You don't need to be stuck here hoping to see him walk past. It won't help. Let's remove the possibility and we'll automatically have a better day.'

I was more than happy with her plan. Getting a train was

as exciting as my life had been lately. We paid our fare and sprinted along the platform to catch the Clanots to Cowford fast train, at the same time as a crack of lightening lit up the sky and the rain began to pour. We made it just before the doors closed, giggling as we tumbled into the carriage.

We found a seat and watched the sky glow and flicker as the storm picked up momentum. Heading out of Clanots was a relief. Cowford was only a thirty-minute train ride away, but it was at least three times the size of our little town and the anonymity was a welcome feeling. I was almost excited.

The rain had become lighter by the time we arrived. Still, we rushed through the cobbled streets to a small café that served homemade pies.

'I hate the rain. Any other weather I can handle, but the rain messes with my hair,' said Alex as she threw down the newspaper she'd been using as an umbrella.

'It looks good,' I said.

'It's short. No fuss, no muss. But I can't grow it anyway, it's too thin. You, on the other hand, have amazing thick hair. I'm totally jealous.'

Alexandra beckoned the waitress with a wave. 'Two of the beef and Stilton please. Babe, you're gonna love these pies, seriously,' she directed the last part at me and the waitress scuttled off.

I surprised myself at how hungry I was. It forced me to acknowledge I'd stopped cooking for myself again. Two weeks of eating cheese on toast for dinner.

Alexandra – as I found out she liked to be called – chatted about work and the men in the office. She had a crush on the office manager Damien and thought he liked her too. Everything she said was so genuine and friendly that I instantly felt at ease with her. We spent the afternoon moving between cafés and shops and, as the day wore on, I began to feel less like a shadow and more like Ronnie again.

'I guess we should get back,' I said regretfully when the shops started to close. I was reluctant to go home, scared my thoughts of Kalen, that had stayed at bay for the last few hours, would return.

'Storms suck. If you don't want to be alone tonight, stay with us. You have the morning shift right? We can go in together.'

I accepted hesitantly, not wanting to impose. Alexandra laughed musically, telling me to loosen up. 'You are one highly-strung chick, Ronnie. We need to sort you out, babe.'

That was how she spoke. Everyone was babe, chick or sweetie. She was dramatic and flamboyant, but the more time I spent with her, the more I liked her.

We swung by my house on the way home so I could pick up clothes for work. Rachel wasn't home and the house was silent and empty as usual, so running back out of the front door gave me great pleasure.

My new friend whistled appreciatively, 'Gorgeous house.'

'Yeah, it's great, but it's difficult to live here all alone.' I shrugged, not wanting to make a big deal. She was aware my dad had passed away and I knew it was difficult for people to broach the subject, but as she drove us to the apartment she shared with another girl her age, she looked thoughtful.

'I reckon you should sell it,' she said once we were inside. The flat was small but cosy, lit with fairy lights and a table lamp. 'Just leave your stuff in my room on the left, babe. Bathroom is opposite if you need it. We have a sofa bed in the living room so you can sleep there tonight. After a bottle or three of wine!'

I dropped my bag where I'd been told, pondering her offer of wine and how I hadn't had alcohol since Kalen had forced me to throw it up.

'I might have to sell it,' I admitted as I stepped back into the living area. 'It seems it isn't all paid for.'

'Good, that'll work out better for you.'

'It's our family house, I don't feel ready to let it go yet. I'm not sure Rachel will either.' It was impossible to be offended by Alexandra. Everything she said, though blunt, was filled with honest concern.

'But your sister's never there, right? It's not your responsibility to look after her. It's so terrible for you that your dad's passed away, but you have to start looking out for number one. It's the only way you're going to get through it.'

'Wow, Alexandra, the girl has just lost her dad. A little tact?'

I turned to see a striking girl with wild dark curls walk into the room. She was tall and slim with flawless skin the colour of coffee.

'Hi!' She held out a slender hand for me to shake. 'I'm Diana,' she beamed, 'I've heard a lot about you.'

I was as enchanted with her as I'd been with Alexandra. She radiated warmth and positivity.

'Diana Saunders, meet Ronnie Rose,' Alexandra announced.

'You'll have to excuse Alexandra's brash, no-nonsense approach to life. She means well, honestly, she's just a bit more pragmatic than the rest of us.'

'Oh please, chick! You're just as bad as me.'

Diana flopped down onto the sofa, her long dark limbs falling gracefully over the edges of the chair. She filled three glasses and we clinked them together.

'To new friends,' she toasted.

'Yes! To new friends,' Alexandra agreed happily, placing a bowl of pretzels on the table in front of us. 'Nothing like wine after a hard day at work.'

Diana threw a pretzel in the air and caught it effortlessly in her mouth. 'Hard shmard. You worked for three hours today!'

'Yeah, I know, I was just trying to make you feel better, it is Saturday after all. Diana's a hairdresser,' she directed at me.

'Saturdays are a rare commodity for her. As in, she doesn't get them.'

'It's true, but I hear Tuesday is the new Saturday anyway,' muttered Diana as we each took a sip of our drinks.

I savoured the tart taste of it on my tongue, I wasn't used to drinking wine, but I figured I could learn.

'Thanks, guys,' I said happily when we clinked our second glass. I knew I was getting lightheaded, but it wasn't the same as in the club. For a start, I didn't feel the need to dig my hand into my chest and rip out my aching heart. I just took part – or listened mostly – in conversations about men, work and life in Clanots Ocean with girls who seemed to manage just fine all alone. As it turned out, both Alexandra and Diana hated Clanots as much as I did and they were saving their money to move to London. They were both older than me and had fin- ished college, but it didn't seem to matter. Diana was fun and alternative, she read the zodiac and believed in soul mates, and it was to this notion that Alexandra rolled her eyes. The op- posite of Diana in every way, she didn't believe in anything except her motto of *make your own luck.*

We sat in animated conversation until late in the evening, and while in the back of my mind I couldn't erase thoughts of a certain teenage assassin, I found to my relief that I still had some optimism left in me. I believed things were going to get better. They had to.

22 — GOODBYE, RED

IF SOMEONE HAD ASKED ME A FEW WEEKS AGO IF I WOULD BE CELEBRATING MY EIGHTEEN BIRTHDAY, I would have given a resounding no way! Who would I celebrate with? I was expecting Mae to come over and we'd rent movies and eat popcorn. As it turned out, six days before my birthday, a knock on my door at seven in the evening changed everything. Diana and Alexandra stood on the doorstep, dressed to kill and holding up a bottle of champagne.

'What are you doing here, are you going out later?' They looked beautiful of course, Alexandra dressed in black figure-hugging trousers and a black top, her trademark red lipstick shining under the light in my hallway, and Diana, wearing a simple gold dress that clung snugly to her waif-like frame and showcased a pair of amazingly long legs.

'You both look amazing!'

'Thanks, doll. We'd better make sure you look just as good, because we're going out in Cowford tonight. All of us!' Diana chimed. 'Happy Birthday!'

Panic set in. I didn't want to go out and celebrate – my last club experience had not been a good one. I started stuttering clumsily, that I had nothing to wear, no money and I wasn't feeling like going out.

'Um, I'm not hearing you properly, babe. Did you say you were going to get dressed?' That was Alexandra, already rooting through my kitchen cabinets for glasses. I smiled and gave in.

'Come on,' she squealed, 'let's drink to the Birthday Girl and we'll help you get ready. The others should be here soon!'

'Others?' Instantly, I was nervous again.

'Yeah, your friend Mae and the other two girls you say you like, but we know you actually don't. Mae wouldn't come without them and we thought that with us here, maybe you'll feel better about it.'

Knowing Mae, Cheryl and Toni were coming out with us, I wasn't sure how to react. On the one hand it was great of my two newest friends to go to so much trouble, on the other, I wasn't sure how they would get along with Cheryl and Toni. As far as I was concerned it wasn't possible to combine sweet and genuine girls with spiteful superficial ones and get a pleasant cocktail. Mae, however, was a different story. I wanted her to meet the new friends I had in my life and I wanted us all to hang out. Before I had even decided, I was clinking glasses and saying thank you. Then the doorbell rang again.

The three girls that stood in front of me did not appear so enthusiastic. Mae smiled sheepishly, but the other two looked bored, as though they had come under duress.

'Hi, girls, thank you so much for coming.' I smiled warmly at Mae, realising how glad I was that she was there for my birthday surprise, but I barely acknowledged the others. I wasn't going to let them bring me down.

I introduced my new friends to my old ones and we all talked for a few minutes over our drinks. Alexandra and Diana made a constant fuss over me, which I could tell they were doing for the benefit of my more critical guests.

Getting dressed was less enjoyable. The five girls dressed me up like I was a doll, trying on different outfits with varying hair and make up combinations. I insisted not much could be done with my hair, but Diana managed to make it so that it was a huge mass of perfect shiny curls.

'See what a bit of effort does?' Mae noted. 'You're beautiful.'

'I didn't know my hair could look like this,' I said, pulling at one shiny ringlet and watching it bounce back into place. I swished my head from side to side.

'That's because your version of making an effort is washing it.'

I laughed. I couldn't be insulted by something that was true. I'd always just assumed my slightly wavy red hair was as good as it got, even having an older sister who was more obsessed with styling products than all my friends combined hadn't given me a clue.

When they were done primping, I looked in the mirror and almost didn't recognise the girl staring back at me. Despite Alexandra's protests, I'd insisted on jeans instead of the dress she wanted to lend me, but I'd paired them with unreasonably high heels and a silk black top that exposed most of my back. As I stared at the sparkling woman in the mirror I wished Kalen could see me. My heart ached at the thought of him, but I kept smiling. I promised myself my eighteenth birthday would be the day I grew up and lived in the real world. I wasn't the girlfriend of a secret agent who jumped out of planes on the weekends – I was just me: Ronnie Rose from Clanots Ocean. Sometimes I wondered if the whole thing hadn't been just another one of my fantasies.

We all tumbled into a cab and headed for the biggest nightclub in Cowford. On my second visit to the bar I ordered a bottle of champagne and six glasses. I was about to hand over the money, when a voice sounded from next to me.

'I've got that.'

I glanced up to my right, taking in the guy who'd spoken at

the same time as the barman took his card. He had a friendly face, with messy golden hair worthy of a gel commercial. His green eyes were staring at me playfully. 'I'm Adam.'

'Ro-Veronica,' I answered.

'So, d'you come here often, Veronica?' he asked while the bottle was being opened.

I felt myself relax and laughed. 'Really?'

'Sorry, that was lame. But I actually mean it, I've never seen you here before.'

'I take it that means *you* do come here often, then?'

He smiled in reply, just as an ice bucket filled with the champagne was handed to me.

'I'd better get back to my friends. Thanks for this.'

'Any time, gorgeous.'

Flicking my hair as I'd seen Rachel do hundreds of times, I headed back to the dance-floor. Alexandra cheered as I presented the bottle. All my friends seemed to be having a great time, even Mae, who'd been edgy around me recently, was her normal cheery self.

We danced until our feet hurt, spilling towards the exit with the crowd as the club started closing. A tap on my shoulder stopped me in my tracks. The girls carried on ahead of me.

'You're leaving?' Adam was staring down at me, wearing a look of exaggerated disappointment.

'Yeah sorry, it's past my bedtime.'

'But you forgot to give me your phone number.'

I played along, lifting my eyebrows. 'Did I say I would?'

'You definitely did, I remember it vividly.' His smile was infectious and I couldn't help but smile back, but as he handed me his Blackberry to tap my number in, I found myself thinking of someone I wished I didn't think of any more. It was hard not to: here was someone handing me a mobile phone and offering me direct contact whenever I wanted it – a stark difference from one who didn't own a phone and disappeared without word. I caught a look from Diana and her confused glare woke me from my trance. Quickly, I typed in my number, storing it under Veronica and left with a flirty wave in his direction. I didn't have any butterflies or nervous tingling sensations, but it felt nice. Nice was good.

Outside the club, we hailed a taxi, when loud yelling and cursing attracted all our attention. A man in a white tuxedo jacket and black shirt was kneeling on the pavement. He wailed and held his nose, the white of his blazer splashed with drops of blood. The bouncers appeared disinterested, so without thinking, I ran over and knelt next to him, asking if he was okay. I was instantly pulled upwards by a grip around my arm. Expecting to see one of my friends, I recoiled. Denver was staring down at me.

'Miss, don't get too close to him, he's – wow,' he stopped short, a wide grin spreading across his face. 'Ronnie?'

The ground seemed to tilt beneath me. I stumbled. But he steadied me. *Of course he did – just when I was getting myself together, here was one of the boys, back to haunt me!* What was more irritating was the sinking realisation that I was more excited than I'd been since they left. I scanned the crowd desperately hoping for a glimpse of Kal.

'It's Denver, right? Fancy seeing you here.' Mae's voice was defensive.

'Yeah, I was just out, having some fun.' His American accent was like music to my ears, I wanted so much to ask after Kalen, but somehow I resisted.

'Having some fun include beating people up?' She quipped, nodding towards the man on the floor.

He shrugged. 'He did that to himself.'

'I bet he did.' Mae gave me a loaded look and walked back towards our other friends.

Denver's eyes swept over me. 'Ron, you look great.'

'Hey Veronica, is this guy bothering you?'

I turned to see Adam behind me, staring at Denver.

'No, not at all, he's a... friend.' I smiled tightly, trying not to look at the girls, who I could sense were all enjoying the encounter way too much.

'Okay, good.' He let his gaze shift from Denver to me. 'I can make sure you get home safe if you want?'

'I think she can get a taxi with her girlfriends actually,' Denver interjected, taking a step towards him. Now inches apart with only my tiny self between them, I hastily told Adam I needed a minute. Reluctantly he stood a little farther back.

I glared at Denver. 'What are you doing?' I whispered furiously.

'K wouldn't like it if I let you go with him.'

My mouth fell open, but I quickly composed myself. 'I have no idea why Kalen would even care, but I know for sure it's none of his, or your business who I do, or don't go home with.' I wasn't ever planning on going home with Adam, but I wasn't about to tell Denver that.

'Ronnie, I'm sorry, but we don't keep secrets from each other. I'll have to tell him. That is just how it is with us.' His voice was tight, laced with a mixture of conviction and regret. 'So, you can be as angry with me as you want, but I can't let you get in a cab with that guy tonight.'

'You mean you won't,' I snapped.

He lifted his large shoulders. I was so angry I could barely speak. My fingers trembled at my side. Who the hell did he think he was, telling me what to do? It wasn't fair! If Kalen had never left, I'd be with him on my birthday. None of this was even my fault.

I held my chin up defiantly. 'Denver, nobody tells me what to do any more. Not you, or Kalen Smith. You can't stop me.' With that, I spun on my heel and began to walk away. Perhaps I would let Adam take me home after all, just to spite him. But before I could make it two steps Denver was in front of me again.

'You can't stop me,' I repeated, with slightly less confidence.

'Ronnie,' he began, his eyes deadpan, 'you know I can.'

I stared at him incredulously, but I knew all too well what he was capable of. My lame attempt at resistance was quashed and my chin slowly slipped back down. To make matters worse, Adam was next to me again, probably in some attempt at chivalry. I found myself babbling for him to call me to arrange our date just to get rid of him before Denver made good on his threat. I slid into a waiting taxi with the girls, each of them asking me to explain what had happened. I shook my head – I had absolutely no idea.

'That was the gorgeous one!' Alexandra giggled. 'You should have introduced me.'

'I wouldn't do that to you,' I muttered under my breath, glancing out of my window at Denver as we pulled away.

They were here. They were still in England, just a few miles away and Kalen hadn't come to see me. He wasn't in danger. He just didn't care any more.

My head was a mess, too many thoughts compounding one another and none of them making sense. Of one thing I was certain: none of those thoughts were of the pleasant guy I'd just met.

23 — CHANGE

'**C**ALL HIM BACK!' ALEXANDRA SAID FOR THE TENTH TIME. It was raining again and we'd fled into Starbucks on Clanots High Street after work, to wait it out.

'I'm not calling him.'

'Babe, he's called twice and left a message, if you don't call back he's gonna think you're not interested.'

'And I keep trying to tell you, I'm not.' Adam had seemed really nice. During all the fun on my birthday, giving him my number had felt like a good idea. Now it just seemed pointless. I couldn't even think of dating someone.

She chewed on her thumb and looked at me. 'It's been five days, babe. If Kalen was going to come back he would've by now,' she said quietly.

'This isn't about him.'

'Yeah right, like if Denver hadn't shown up out of the blue you wouldn't be down in the dumps again? You'd just started to pick yourself up. Just call Adam. Better still, text him! What harm can it do?'

I stared at my phone. Adam had left a voicemail. He wanted to take me out for dinner. It was so nice, *so normal*. But I didn't care, not like I should have cared anyhow.

'Here, let me.' Knocking the back of my hand so my phone flipped into the air, she caught it and flashed me a satisfied smile.

'Don't you dare,' I threatened, crossing my arms.

'You'll thank me later.'

I watched as she typed out a text. I could have easily snatched my phone back, but something was aching inside me to try it out. Curiosity. If Kalen was really never coming back, could I ever be happy again? The thought sent a chill through to the tips of my toes.

'Let me see what you've written then,' I sighed. Leaning forward to take a look, I instantly went to object, but she'd already hit send.

A reply came through almost straight away. I swiped my phone back. The text from Alex read: **Hey Adam, I'm free this weekend if u still wanna go out, let me know.**

His reply read: **Saturday night. Pick you up at 8. Text me your addy x**

I looked at Alexandra, who was sipping her drink, trying her best to look innocent.

'Dammit,' I mumbled. 'Now I'm gonna have to figure out what to wear.'

'Well now, babe, you know I can help with that.'

***

Alexandra and Diana were dragging me around the shops. I'd had a whole night to think about my impending date and considered canceling at least twenty times, but Alexandra had threatened me with blind dates if I did, so reluctantly I'd agreed to go to the mall with them. When I'd met Adam I was more glamorous than ever – a fact the girls kept reminding me of.

They started with underwear. I wanted M&S, they wanted Ann Summers – we settled on La Senza.

166

'Why does it matter what underwear I have on?'

'You have to feel good from the inside out,' Alexandra lectured.

'By good, do you mean like a porn star?' I grimaced as she held up a shear black bra, studded with Diamanté.

'She's right, babe, that's streetwalker material right there,' said Diana.

'I have this.' Alexandra looked mortified as she stared at us. Diana and I burst into fits of laughter.

It only got worse from there. Dresses, heels, handbags – I was exhausted by the time they dropped me off at my house. On the porch, I waved the girls off and was about to head in, but hesitated. A strange feeling crept over me. The same one I'd had in the supermarket before Christmas – like someone was watching me. Back then, I'd put it down to the fact the boys had been waiting outside, but right now I was all alone. I stared across the front garden at the trees that surrounded most of the house. Nothing stirred.

The feeling didn't go away, but I shoved it aside and headed indoors.

As the evening wore on, I started to plot ways I could get out of the date without telling Alex. I came up blank. Seven-thirty arrived and my phone rang.

'What you wearing?'

'Nothing yet.'

Alexandra giggled. 'I like your style. Naked – it's a statement.'

I felt myself flush. 'I'm going to wear dark-blue skinny-jeans and the black bandeau top you forced me to buy.'

'No dress?'

'Not tonight.'

'Heels?'

'Yes – *maybe.*'

167

'Heels!' she said more forcefully.

I said goodbye and threw my phone on my bed, reaching into my wardrobe rebelliously for my ballet flats.

In the mirror I fluffed my hair to give it some volume, the light in my room made it look redder than ever. Unfortunately, no matter what I did, I couldn't seem to forget the boy I wanted to forget. *Red.* His name for me would haunt me whenever I looked in the mirror. Frustrated with the never-ending thoughts of my past, I brushed some mascara onto my lashes and plumped my lips with too much gloss. Then I took myself downstairs to wait for Adam.

He arrived a little after eight. I opened the door to find he was better looking than I remembered. If anything his messy blond hair and bright green eyes reminded me of someone I used to dream about and I felt my cheeks grow hot at the comparison with my fantasy hero.

'Hi,' I said shyly.

He whistled. 'You look great.'

'Thanks, you too.' He was wearing dark jeans and a roll neck jumper and, from the looks of it, everything was some designer or another. *Rachel would be so proud,* I thought.

His car was parked close to the house – a brand new silver sports number.

'It's a company car,' he said, though I hadn't asked. 'One of the perks of working in the city.'

I slid inside. 'So, where we headed?'

'I thought we could see a movie.'

I let my head fall back against the seat. A movie was perfect – it meant minimal conversation. He drove us to the multiplex in Cowford and let me choose the film. I skipped everything remotely romantic and went for a thriller.

Inside the theatre, I glanced around at the other couples lit by the flashing screen, holding hands and cuddled close. I wondered to myself: maybe this is how it's supposed to be?

He took my hand in his and I resisted my instinct to pull away.

When the film ended, Adam dropped me home and we lingered in his car.

'So, Veronica, I don't think I've asked you how old you are.'

'I'm eighteen. Tomorrow actually, what about you?'

'Twenty-one. Funny, you seem older that eighteen.'

I laughed. 'Is that good or bad?'

He leaned towards me, his voice husky and low. 'A compliment. You're not like most of the girls I meet, all obsessed with celebrities and hairstyles. You're different.' He brushed a strand of my hair back from my face. Sensing he wanted to kiss me, I leaned away.

'So, you work in the city?' I said lightly.

I liked him, but I wasn't sure it was enough. I wasn't sure what it was.

'Yeah,' he said with a lazy grin, dropping his arm across the back of my seat. 'I'm a junior investment banker. It's long hours, but it's gonna make me rich and that's what it's all about, right?'

I smiled, not knowing how else to respond. He asked about my job at the Travel Shop and we made smalltalk about school and the differences between Clanots and Cowford. I was just starting to relax when he said, 'So, how come you don't have a boyfriend?'

And that was it. I needed to get out of the car. Suddenly, the space felt incredibly small, like it was going to fold in on me. I leaned forward and gave him a peck on the cheek, thanked him for a nice night and almost threw myself out of the Focus.

Once inside my front door I fell back against it and let out a long breath. I'd done it. It was over. As far as I was concerned, I could go back to being alone and no one could say I hadn't tried.

24 — NORMAL

THE MORNING WAS BRIGHT AND I DIDN'T HAVE TO WORK. I was trying to decide what to do, when the doorbell rang. I ran down the stairs and yanked the door open to find Rachel with Cloud in her arms.

'Where are your keys?'

'I forgot them, hey can you have Cloud this morning?'

'Sure,' I said, giving my niece a kiss and taking her from my sister.

'Happy Birthday. I'll take you shopping next weekend. There's some vouchers in the card.'

She handed me a sealed envelope as we walked through the house. I'd just ripped through the paper when the doorbell rang a second time.

'Expecting someone?' Rachel asked.

I put my niece down and headed back through the hallway. Adam greeted me at the door with a smile, wearing slim blue jeans and a button-up shirt and his blond hair perfectly styled so it hung over his face like a fringe. On his index finger he dangled my new grey cardigan. I'd obviously left it in his car.

'Hey Birthday Girl, thought you might miss this.'

Cursing internally, I tried to thank him and get him to leave without asking him in. But of course Rachel had other ideas.

She swung the door open wide. 'Who's this?' she asked with one of her best smiles.

'Rachel, this is Adam,' I wagged my finger between them. 'Adam this is my sister, Rachel.'

Ignoring my imploring glances, she invited him in and Adam sat in the kitchen with her while she grilled him about all sorts of personal things. *Where did you grow up? Where do you work? Do you have any tattoos?* My ears pricked up at that. He unbuttoned his shirt, showing us one on the top of his right arm: a dragon. I muffled a laugh and took Cloud into the garden, before he started explaining to Rachel what it meant.

Ten minutes later Adam poked his head out the back door and yelled goodbye. Knowing it was the polite thing to do, I followed inside.

'I'll see you on Friday then,' he said, as we reached the front of the house.

'Huh?' I almost choked.

'Your sister invited me over for the dinner you're cooking for her and your brother-in-law.'

It was my own fault – I should never have left them alone. Mentally I was killing Rachel, but I forced my face into a smile.

'Maybe it's a bit soon for a family get together.' I tried to make a joke out of what she'd done, but Rachel appeared behind me, swinging one arm around my shoulders and pinching my skin where Adam couldn't see.

'Don't be silly, Ron, it's only your big sis!'

I smiled and spoke through gritted teeth. 'See you Friday, then.'

He winked and headed back to his car.

I wanted to turn and slap my sister round the head, but I was too hung up on his gesture – the wink. A wink I wished was

171

someone else's. The thought caused a surge in my stomach and with it came a wave of determination. I would see him Friday for dinner and I would erase all memories of Kalen Smith, for ever.

***

Friday came and went. It was actually okay. Rachel and Jared both loved Adam and my seeing him appeared to have calmed whatever storm had been brewing in that part of my life. He was sweet and friendly, and more importantly he didn't make me feel like he wanted me one minute and couldn't wait to get away the next. Over the following few weeks, things changed. I changed. My clothes got more sophisticated, my heels got higher and on Adam's suggestion I'd dyed my hair a dark chocolate brown. It was only a semi permement colour and the box said it would be back to normal after twenty-eight washes, so I couldn't see the harm, but the more I thought about it the more I liked the idea anyway: new start, new me.

It was a Thursday night and Adam had brought over takea-way Chinese food and DVDs. It was the first time he'd been over when I had the house to myself. It got to that time, how-ever, where kissing leads to something more and I heard myself asking him to go.

'Okay,' he said, standing up grudgingly and running his hand through his tousled hair. 'See you tomorrow at The Half Moon?'

'Yeah, we're meeting the girls at eight.'

As we reached the front door, he leaned in, grazing his lips against mine. I wrapped my hand up around his neck and kissed him back. Kissing Adam wasn't the same as kissing Kal. It was softer, less intense and a little sloppier... but it wasn't altogether bad.

'See ya, babe,' he said, turning and heading down the front

porch to his car. His keys jingled as he walked, replaced by the sound of the engine as he drove away. Then there was quiet.

I was about to go indoors when a noise sounded from above me. I craned my neck to see up on the roof. There was nothing there – the sky was so black, I couldn't even see the moon. I stood for a moment, trying to work out what I'd heard, but the silence lingered. With a final glance around, I reached for the door handle.

Then another sound – thrrrump – as if something had fallen to the floor behind me. I froze. Fear knotted my insides, transforming me into a useless block of stone. The hairs on the back of my neck sprung to attention. I could sense that whoever (or whatever) was there, was incredibly close. I had nowhere to run.

My heart crashing in my chest, I turned around.

25 — OUT OF THE DARK

A LARGE SHADOW LOOMED IN FRONT OF ME. Instinctively I kicked out, making contact with his groin and sending him toppling backwards.

Turning to run, my foot caught. I fell. Through my panic I tried to think of some moves from the many self-defence classes I'd paid for over the years but, infuriatingly, when under immense pressure, I was completely unable to remember anything. I reached out for something I could use as a weapon instead. The branch of a tree, left on our porch for summer days when we would prop open the door, was the only thing within reach. I lunged for it, lifting it over my shoulder. With all my reserves of strength I stood up and swung.

Despite my erratic state, I managed to connect it with the dark figure now rushing towards me. The intruder caught the branch on impact and, too quickly for me to let go, pulled it towards him. I was dragged into his arms, which locked tightly around me so I was unable to move.

'Red. Calm down.'

All the air rushed out of me as though I'd been winded. Slowly, I turned my head and focused on the silhouetted face, now intimately close to mine. As my eyes adjusted to the dark, Kalen's eyes sparkled.

Torn between intense happiness and immeasurable fury, I couldn't control the sudden swell of emotion inside me – tears spilled down my cheeks.

Kalen scooped me up into his arms, kicking open the front door and walking inside. In my living room he gently placed me on the couch. After what felt like an eternity I managed to compose myself, wiping my wet face with the back of my hand.

He crouched by my side, his eyes showing such panic that it was almost funny. Almost. He must have seen the amusement in my expression, because his own features smoothed out and his face was, once again, unreadable.

'You frightened me,' he said with his usual level of indifference, before sitting back in the chair opposite mine.

'I frightened *you*?'

'Well, I thought I'd hurt you, which I tried very hard not to do. I'm not used to holding someone down without hurting them. It was new for me.' He smirked to himself, as if he were intrigued at having discovered something new about himself.

I didn't return the smile. 'If you don't want to hurt a person, maybe don't sneak up on them in the middle of the night.' I swung my legs from the sofa and stared at him. I was so happy to see him that inside me there wasn't one ounce of anger, but the pain I'd felt since he left still ached like an open wound.

He frowned. 'You look different, your hair's brown. Why?'

I didn't answer him, but I looked him over too. His hair had grown a little, it was less military than usual. His blue eyes were the same though: dark, brooding and annoyingly indecipherable. I gulped.

'You're back,' was all I could manage before my voice failed me and more tears trailed down my cheeks.

'Yes, I thought... I *hoped* you might be happy to see me, but you're still crying.'

'I'm not dignifying that with a response, Kal. Why did you

leave without even telling me?'

'I had to leave Clanots for a while.'

I met his eyes sharply. 'Is that all I get?'

'Red, please, let's not fight,' he said, standing up and walking to the window.

'I don't want to fight either, it's just, you left and I thought you were never coming back.'

'Would you rather I hadn't? I see you've moved on quite nicely.'

'Why would you say that? I didn't ask you to leave, Kal! I was so los…' I pursed my lips, determined not to pour my heart out.

'I thought our reunion would be nicer than this,' he said quietly, still gazing out into the night. 'I should have called.'

I laughed bitterly. He who didn't own a phone should have called – yes, that would have been a wonderful start! 'I thought we were friends,' I replied, instead of voicing my thoughts.

He made a *hmmm* sound without looking at me. 'Friends.'

'What did you mean anyway – I've moved on?'

'Your male visitor. I assume he's your boyfriend?'

'You don't *assume* anything, Kal, it is not in you to assume. How long have you been back?'

'Long enough.'

'And you're only just coming to see me now?' I got up and stood in front of him so he was forced to look me in the eyes. Any happiness at having him back was sullied by his nonchalance. He didn't owe me anything, but his talking to me like he couldn't have cared less was almost too much for me to take.

'What I told you about myself,' he said, 'it must have disgusted you. No matter what you said or how you pretended to be okay with what I am. I did you a favor leaving. You can't really want to be friends, or anything else, with me.'

'Don't tell me how I feel. If you're too far-gone to see when someone really cares about you, then you should go. You're right, Kalen, I am different and it's not just my hair! I am not the same weak, needy girl I was two months ago. Get out, do whatever it is you want to do with your life and do it without me.'

He stood perfectly still, his mouth set in a way that told me he was waiting for me take back what I'd said. When I didn't, he walked past me and out the front door. It fell shut and I closed my eyes. The sound of my heartbeat grew loud in my ears and the room wobbled around me. I fled up to my bedroom, turning off all the lights as I went, all the while trying desperately not to let him back inside my head. Had I really told him to leave? I almost retched involuntarily at the thought.

Finally, flicking off the main light in my room, I sat in the pale illumination the moon cast through my window. I'd got used to being alone, something I never thought I'd do. I no longer needed lights on in rooms I wasn't in. The feeling of comfort from having other people around was long gone for me. I no longer cared.

I turned back the bed covers in a trance and went to close my curtains.

Kalen was crouched on my windowsill.

I must have been becoming immune to shock because I didn't even flinch. Had I hoped he would come back – even known it?

'This must be the only window I didn't lock,' I said, walking back to my bed. It was true, but not because I'd forgotten it. I hadn't locked it since the day he left, hoping for this exact moment – his presence at my window. 'But I guess it wouldn't have made a difference. You could have got in anyway, right? What's a lock to you?'

'I'm sorry,' he said quietly.

Ignoring him, I found some lint that needed picking from the quilt cover.

'Red, look at me.'

'No.'

'Please.'

Reluctantly, I did as he asked, chewing on the inside of my cheek to prevent my hurt from showing in my face.

'I missed you. A lot. That's why I'm back. For no other reason would I be here. The boys – well, I'm not in their good books since I made us return, put it that way.'

I continued to stare, unblinking, trying to resist the urge to run to him.

'I wont leave again, if you tell me we can still be friends. I know you have a boyfriend and still, I want to be around you. Please forgive me. Ace wants to see you, too,' he added.

I smiled despite myself. 'Don't bring Ace into this, that was incredibly low, Kalen Smith.'

'Sorry.' A look of relief swept across his features and his dimples penetrated my heart. 'It was terribly low of me, but hey, you're smiling now.'

'You hurt me,' I croaked. 'I'd just lost my father and then I lost my – my friend. My only friend.'

'You have friends here now.'

'Yeah,' I admitted, 'I suppose I do.'

'I'm here now too.'

'Why did you leave?'

His jaw clenched, like he was searching for what to say. 'I thought it was better for you.'

It wasn't the entire truth, and I think he wanted me to know that. But at that moment it would do – I was too happy to pretend otherwise.

'Well, why are you back then?'

'Because it wasn't better for me,' he said with a rueful smile.

After a long silence, I closed the gap between us, unsure what to do once I reached him. He leaned in and took my hand.

'I'm glad you're back.' I admitted, my voice tiny.

'I never imagined I could be attached to another person. I didn't know I was capable of missing anything. I–' he faltered. 'You have no clue how much I've changed because of you.' His eyes were filled with such sincerity that I slipped my hand out of his, afraid I wouldn't have the strength to deny him anything he wanted.

I hadn't really given much thought to what Adam meant to me, but something stopped me from just pretending it didn't matter now because of how much I'd missed Kalen. Kalen had left me – he'd hurt me, but Adam had been nothing but great since the day we met. How could I ignore that? 'I'm seeing someone now,' I whispered.

'I know,' he said, lowering his eyes. 'I'm sorry I scared you earlier. I was just, over excited. You're tough for such a small person, you caught me off guard.'

'Ha! That's rich! God, you're a nightmare!'

His eyes glinted, 'Shame, I was hoping to make your dreams.'

'Get out now, please.' I said with mock authority, my heart feeling lighter than it had in weeks.

Just before he turned to leave the way he'd come in, he looked back. 'Ronnie, your hair – it was beautiful the way it was.'

'You know, you could leave through the front door.' I grinned.

'Where would be the fun in that? I wouldn't be able to show off then, would I – all those years of training gone to waste.'

He took my hand and kissed it, then sprang through the window and ran down the slanting roof. As he reached the edge he jumped, his arms latching onto the tree opposite. I giggled, watching him swing into a flip and land smoothly on the grass. He looked up and gave me a little bow, then sprinted off through the back garden, scaled the fence and disappeared.

New Orleans — October 2005

The city looked perfect from the rooftops – a far cry from the turmoil and strife of the fighting that had taken place below. He stopped to catch his breath, knowing it would be a short moment of respite. Soon enough they would be on his tail again and the helicopters would drive him from the rooftops. He needed to find cover – quickly.

Kalen looked around and listened for the tell-tale sound of the chopper. Nothing. Could he have finally outrun them? Unlikely. As his heart rate slowed he prepared for another burst of energy, knowing that to linger or rest would be fatal. He sprang into action once more and as he reached the edge of the building, threw himself from it. His legs flailed through the air. His heart missed a beat; miscalculation meant death. But he landed smoothly on the neighbouring roof and continued his sprint. The speed allowed him to move in a way many others couldn't, running up walls, flipping and somersaulting over stairwells or any obstacle blocked his path. Parkour had always been one of his favourite things to do – the closest a man could get to flying. That day, however, not long after he'd said goodbye to his only friends and the day he had truly begun to run for his life, it wasn't fun any more – it was terrifying. He continued to leap from building to building until finally a chasm below was far too vast to jump. Instead, he fled down the wall, using guttering to aid his descent, and found himself in a dumpster-lined alleyway.

Ahead of him, K could see the main road. He breathed out. He had made it to where he needed to be, just in time to hear the helicopter approaching in the distance.

Took them long enough, he thought, almost smiling. He pulled the hood of his black coat up, to conceal his face, and slipped casually from the side road onto the bustling street. The parade took place throughout the streets of New Orleans every year at the same time – it had been a lucky coincidence. Now, because he was amongst what was one of the largest crowds he could have hoped for, he regained his swagger and caught his breath, heading for the water's edge with confidence.

There he would begin his journey to the other side of the planet; as far away as he could get from the United States and the people who wanted him dead. K had no idea what he would do with himself once he arrived in Europe – if he wasn't an assassin, he didn't know what he was. He was sure of only one thing: he wanted to live. For now, that was enough.

26 — LIE TO ME

A T WORK I DECIDED TO TELL ALEXANDRA HE WAS BACK. I made tea for everyone in the office. As the new girl, it was an unwritten rule that tea making was part of my job when there was no temp around, until someone newer than me started at least. But I didn't mind doing it – time in the kitchen was time to dream. As I placed everyone's cups on their desks and approached Alexandra's, I couldn't hide my smile. I put her tea down last, next to mine. She stared at me intently.

'What's going on with you, chick?'

'What do you mean?' I asked innocently.

'I mean normally you seem to carry the weight of the world on your shoulders until I force you to snap out of it – yet today I can barely cope with your excitement. The sun is shining outside and we're working. What could possibly be worth smiling about?'

'Oh yeah, because there are so many other things to do in Clanots.'

'Hey, anything's better than being at work.'

'I'll pretend I didn't hear that, Fusco!' the voice of our manager boomed behind us. She beamed up at him and he walked away with a coy smile. Another affirmation that they were more than work associates. I raised my eyebrows when she looked at me again.

'Oh no you don't, you have to answer my question before I answer any of yours.'

'He came back,' I said before I took a sip of my scolding hot drink.

Her eyes grew large. 'No way!'

I grinned, quickly turning my attention back to my computer as Damien looked over in our direction again. An email popped up on my screen.

From: Alexandra Fusco

Subject: Tell me everything right now!

I typed back, stifling a laugh. *He turned up last night – at my house*

What did he say? Where's he been?

I don't know where he's been, as usual he doesn't tell me much… but he said he missed me. That's why he's back

OMG! What about Adam?

Well, I guess nothing changes… Kalen and I were never dating anyway, we still aren't.

Oh yeah you're just friends right? Pfffft!

What does pfffft mean?

It means you're full of sh!t, Rose... you love him!

No I don't!!!! Honestly you don't know what Kalen's about – he's not the sort of person a girl should love. Adam is good for me.

Yeah but babe – since when has anyone loved what's good for them?

My work phone rang at that point, bringing me back to reality. A woman wanted to take her husband and three children on holiday to Benidorm. I was pleased for the distraction because, honestly, I didn't know how to answer my friend.

***

I walked into the bar with Adam. Nestled below White Lies it was the only pub in town with a poolroom. Inside, the old red carpet and teak wooden bar made for the sort of pub you'd expect to find an older crowd of men playing darts, but because of the location it was the most popular place in town without even trying. I saw Mae immediately and waved over. She came running, leaving Cheryl and Toni at the bar. I noticed instantly the three of them were all wearing similar outfits. Strapless dresses, in varying bright colours. I'd kept on my black work trousers and changed my shirt for a bottle-blue spaghetti-strap top.

'Ommigod, Sally Cartwright has just thrown a drink in her boyfriend's face. You missed it.'

I smiled. I knew of Sally, but not well enough to care all that much. 'Taz is coming tonight, right?' I asked.

'I hope so,' Adam said looking around. 'I don't want to be the tag-along guy on a girls' night.'

'It's not a girls' night,' said Mae with a giggle. 'Taz should be here soon so you'll have someone to chat to.' She squeezed between us, linking her arms through ours to direct us to the bar.

'I take it you know they're back then?' she whispered to me while Adam got our drinks. My stomach tightened. Quickly I tried to decide whether or not to play dumb.

I chose not. 'How do you know?'

'Because he's here,' she said flatly.

I felt like I'd been hollowed out, my heart rate accelerated as I scanned the crowd.

'Where?'

She eyed me furiously. 'I knew you'd seen him!'

'He's a friend, Mae, I'm not gonna ignore him just because

all of you seem to hate him for no good reason.'

'Whatever,' she said with a flick of her long dark hair. 'Just remember he left you in pieces. I'm not gonna pick up the pieces a second time.'

'Where is he?' I asked, trying to keep my voice level so she wouldn't know how much her words hurt me.

'Here you go, ladies, one vodka cranberry and one Sauvignon Blanc for Veronica.' Adam handed us our drinks, cutting our conversation short.

'Ergh, can you believe those idiots are back in town?' Cheryl whined loudly as she joined us. She noticed Adam and stuck one hand out. 'Hi, I'm Cheryl.'

'We met, in Cowford,' he grinned.

'Oh, yeah, Ronnie's birthday, that's right!'

'What idiots?' he asked.

The girls all stared at me.

When I didn't answer, Cheryl stepped in. 'Oh, just some friends of Ronnie's. You should be careful Adam, this one likes to walk on the wild side.'

Rolling my eyes, I let the sounds of their chat fade and turned as casually as I could to scan the room. I saw him instantly, over by one of the pool tables. Dressed in black jeans and a grey fitted tee and leaning casually against the wall, pool cue in hand. He was speaking to someone... Denver! I recognised his height instantly. As if Kalen felt me looking at him, his dark eyes lifted and met mine. A small smile formed on his lips, but he didn't let it all the way out. A shiver ran through me. Denver glanced over, giving me a polite nod and leaning across the table. He sunk two balls with one shot.

Kalen dropped his gaze to take his turn. As he moved I noticed Laith standing close behind him, glaring at me venomously. I looked away.

'You gonna drink that?' Adam asked, turning to see where I was looking. I flipped my head back around to face my friends, ignoring the look I knew Mae was giving me. I wished Alexandra were here.

'I'm going to the bathroom,' I put my glass down and walked away from them. I needed air.

The toilet seat fell down with a thud. I sat and rested my head in my hands. My mind was reeling. He was here. He was here and I was with my boyfriend. Why did that feel so wrong? I sat for as long as I could without my presence being missed in the bar, then got to my feet, took a deep breath, left the bathroom.

A large hand wrapped around my arm, pulling me under the stairs. Kalen was looking down at me, a smile in his eyes. He smelled of fresh air, salt and wind – if wind had a smell.

'He seems, nice,' he said in a low voice that caused a twinge behind my navel.

'He is,' I hesitated. The proximity of his body meant I could almost feel his heartbeat. Or was that my own? Everything in my mind was a blur as I looked up at him.

'What are you doing here?'

He laughed.

'What?'

'You ask as though you think I'm following you.'

I lifted my chin. 'Are you?'

Lightly, he trailed one finger down the side of my face. 'Not this time,' he said, his voice barely more than a whisper. 'The boys wanted to play pool. This, is just a happy coincidence.' He stared at me for a long moment. 'I'll come say hi before you leave,' he said, and in a blink he was gone. The door to the main pub swung closed behind him.

I let out the breath I'd been holding, wanting to leave through the side door and escape into the night. Instead, I straightened and headed back into the main room. I stole a glance in the direction of the boys as I passed. A group of girls were talking to Denver. I watched as one of them broke away and stepped towards Kalen. His eyes flicked to mine and I quickly looked away. My insides twisted.

Back with my own group, Mae was whispering something to Cheryl. I ignored them and smiled at Adam. Staying on track with the conversation and ignoring my desire to look back in Kalen's direction proved difficult, but then the door to the pub flew open, shaking on its hinges as it rattled to a close. We all glanced around. Four men I didn't recognise had entered, their stance and expressions screaming trouble. The one who led them had coal-black hair and small shifty eyes, like pools of tar. He scanned the crowd and waded in our direction towards the bar. I could tell from people's reactions that the men had some sort of reputation. Everyone watched them without actually making eye contact. Subtle movements and small adjustments to people's stance and posture as the men walked past showed that no one wanted to get in their way.

As the group reached us, Shifty-eyes took a purposeful stride sideways, barging Adam from behind to get him to move. Adam lurched forward, his drink spilled from the glass, sloshing over Toni.

'Watch it, mate!' Adam exclaimed. They were all older than us, maybe in their early thirties, but something told me I couldn't count on them acting like adults. The guy smirked at Adam and then faced the bar, bumping him again in the process. The group found this hilarious. Adam turned back to us, slightly chagrined, but obviously having the sense to ignore them. Cheryl had other ideas. Irate that Toni had been doused in beer, and too drunk to think better of it, she tapped the guy on the shoulder and started yelling abuse at him.

'Hey, who the hell do you think you are? At least apologise to my mate, you got beer all over her, you idiot!'

The man sneered, looking over at Adam. 'Do me a favour, mate, get your bird out of my face.'

I glanced over in the direction of Kal. He was watching us intently. Laith whispered something in his ear.

'She's not my bird,' Adam said hesitantly, 'but there's no need to be rude.'

'Sorry, what was that?' Shifty was not much taller than Adam, but he was stockier, with a thick neck and muscles that almost popped through his shirt. He leaned in, cupping a hand over his ear, taunting Adam into saying it again.

'We're not looking for any trouble,' Adam said.

I stared between them, watching the looks on the faces of each of the men. We may not have been looking for trouble, but they definitely were.

'Now, now fellas,' said the barman, 'no fighting.'

'Get lost, Frank,' said Shifty. 'I think we have a big shot here.' He pushed Adam's chest with both hands so Adam stumbled backwards. I shot another glance at Kalen, he looked about to head over, but Laith grabbed his arm, holding him back.

Adam had his palms upwards, trying to diffuse the situation. Cheryl was still shouting in a shrill way that hurt my ears. Because of her, things were escalating out of control. Adam was going to get hit.

Unable to stand any more, I moved so I was in between them and looked up at Shifty. 'Please, can we just leave it? We haven't done anything to you guys,' I told him, with my best pleading voice. With one large hand he grabbed hold of my shoulder, about to shove me to one side. Another hand locked around his wrist before he had the chance.

'You heard the lady,' Kal's voice was deadly. In one hand he held Shifty's arm and in the other, a pool cue. Around us, people fell silent. For a second I thought Shifty might back down, but he didn't. He threw a punch with his free arm, putting all his weight behind it. Kal ducked. The swing went wide and in the second he lost his footing, Kal dropped the pool cue, grabbed Shifty's head in both hands and smashed it against the bar. Shifty collapsed to the floor, knocked out cold. His friends moved in. Bouncers were making their way across the floor too. The crowd backed away, so Kal was in the middle of a circle with me behind him. An arm hooked around me from behind, hoisting me away from the fight. I turned to see Denver, his eyes fixed on the situation unfolding in front of us.

'You can walk away from this,' Kal warned the three men.

They rushed him. Kalen knocked one of them on the floor with a move I didn't even see and in a split second had the second guy's arm bent behind his back. The third guy hesitated, as if contemplating what to do.

'You gonna help him?' I whispered at Denver.

With resignation he shook his head. 'He doesn't need my help.'

I heard the second guy's arm crack, followed by an ear-piercing scream, just as the third idiot lunged at Kal. Kal swiped the cue from the floor and used it to flip the last attacker off his feet.

On the dark-red carpet in front of us, four men lay, either knocked out cold or moaning in pain. The crowd stared in stunned silence. Kalen backed away and walked to me, taking both of my arms in his hands, just as security arrived.

'You – out!' The first one hollered at Kal.

'Mate, he helped us, it was these guys,' Adam said, coming forward and pointing to the men on the floor. While the bouncer's attention was distracted, Kalen ushered me outside. The others followed.

'You need to get home,' he said as we burst out into the fresh air. I spun to face him.

'Are you okay?'

'I'm fine.'

Laith stormed out and slammed the door closed after him. 'I can't believe you did that!' he yelled at Kal. Then he turned to me. 'You, this is all because of you!'

'L, back off.' Kalen stepped in front of me.

'A civilian brawl – you got involved in a civilian brawl, man! This is screwed. Hear that?' he asked, pointing in the air. We could all hear the sirens. 'That's coming for us. Are we done here?'

Kalen turned to me, his expression torn but, before he could speak, Adam was beside us. 'Thanks for that, mate, that was hardcore what you did back there.'

Kalen looked at him for the first time, his eyes narrowed. 'If you can't take care of her, don't take her to dives like this.'

'Kal–' I began, but he was still looking at Adam.

'Get her home safe,' he finished, with a less hostile tone, as though he could see he'd embarrassed Adam and felt bad about it. Then, without so much as another look at me, he turned away and the three boys walked swiftly towards the beach.

'Quick then, ladies – unless you want to spend all night explaining that to the police,' said Adam, clearing his throat. We didn't need to be told twice. We left the main street in a hurry. My heart was hammering, not because of what had happened, but through worry for Kal.

At the cab rank, Adam called one of his friends and filled him in on the events. From the sounds of it, he thought it made for the best night ever. I didn't share the feeling.

Cheryl and Toni stalked off, saying they were going to another bar, leaving Mae and I standing in silence, waiting for our taxis to arrive.

Mae shivered. 'Aren't you cold?' she asked.

I wasn't, I was numb. Kalen had got into a fight and nearly got arrested, because of me. The accusation in Laith's tone rang in my head.

'Well, no big shock our night got ruined,' she continued.

I looked at her sadly. 'Mae, what happened had nothing to do with Kalen.'

She made a dramatic choking sound as if I'd said something ludicrous. 'Funny, because to me it looked like he beat up four guys and practically turned The Half Moon upside down.'

'If he hadn't done that,' I pointed out, 'Adam would have got beaten up by those guys. They were looking for a fight. Kal was helping us.'

'I don't think we need that kind of help,' she spat. 'I'm calling Taz.'

'Where is he, by the way?' I asked airily.

She gave me a cold look and walked away with her phone pressed to her ear. A cab rolled up to the kerb at the same time. I decided to take it before she came back over. Adam came trotting up to me, slipping his phone in his back pocket.

'You okay, babe?' he asked with a smile.

'Just tired. I'm going home. Can you make sure Mae gets a cab okay?'

'Yeah sure. Hey – who was that guy earlier?'

I sighed, half in and out of the ride that would take me home to bed. 'He was a friend of my dad's.'

'Well, tell him I said thanks again, yeah? I'm gonna head out to Cowford and meet the lads. You okay to get home?'

'I'm fine.'

He kissed me then. It took me by surprise, and I found myself pulling away quickly. As I slid into the back seat I squeezed my eyes closed to press back my tears.

***

My dream was dark. Full of hazy forms and far-away voices. The bar was less crowded this time, just me, Kalen and the gang who'd attacked us. They sat on one side of the pub, while Kalen bought us drinks. I watched them watching us, I knew they wanted to start something, so we left the bar, finding our-

191

selves in a deserted car park. The men followed. I told Kalen to run. He laughed.

'I'll never let anyone hurt you, Red.'

Suddenly we were on the beach, in the pitch of night and the pouring rain. I was wearing my red raincoat. The men who'd followed us charged at Kal. I tried to wake up, but remained trapped inside, forced to watch as Kalen fought for our lives.

He took each of them down with ease, until one of them pulled out a knife.

I cried out.

Kalen swiped the weapon and threw it into the ocean and in one swift movement his arm wrapped around our attacker's neck. As the man's life began to drain away I screamed for Kalen to stop. He didn't hear me. Try as I might, I couldn't get my voice to rise above the sound of the sea crashing against the pier. My ears rang with noise, as if the beach was closing in on me. The wind, the ocean; a raven's call from somewhere above me. And then the man's lifeless body fell into the ocean with a splash that silenced everything else.

Kalen's dark eyes lifted to mine.

I sat bolt upright in bed, gasping for breath. 'Oh my God,' I said to the darkness around me. 'It was him.'

27 — KNIGHT IN NOT-SO-SHINING ARMOUR

ALL MY TIREDNESS EVAPOURATED. Images flashed through my mind like a shutter speed camera; the body falling into the ocean, my hero, my hope – who was ultimately not a hero at all, but as it turned out, a trained killer. Kal was the one who'd saved my life three years ago. It had been Kalen Smith who'd taken the life of my attacker that night.

I had to see him right away. It just couldn't wait for morning, or for the moment he decided to grace me with his presence. Everything I'd ever dreamed of hung in the balance. I needed him to admit it before I really believed it.

I looked at the clock next to my bed: three a.m. The night was pitch outside, but I didn't care. Determined, I dressed swiftly, grabbed my bag and shot out the front door. Outside, the air was stiller than usual, with a thickness that hung around me like an ominous warning that I should go back inside and wait until morning. Ignoring my instincts, I pulled my hooded jumper close to my body and hoisted myself into Dad's old Land Rover. It wasn't the most inconspicuous of cars and I only had my provisional licence, but I figured I could use the back roads and make it to the boys' mansion without anyone seeing me. I'd crossed over to a place of very little sanity, that was for sure. I said a quick thank you to the car when it roared to life and patted the steering wheel. Then I clicked the gear-stick into drive and slowly edged out onto the road. Dad had given me plenty of lessons on how to drive, so once I'd come to terms with what I was doing, instinct took over and my heart rate returned to normal. Twenty minutes later (ten minutes longer than it usually took Kal) I rolled into their driveway.

Once I'd turned off the engine I stared around into the darkness. The ride over had been anger and adrenaline fueled, but as the silence loomed around me I started to wish I'd listened to my gut and stayed at home.

Well, I've come this far, I thought. Forcing myself – nausea and all – to get out of the car and quietly close the door, I made my way up to the house. I needn't have bothered being discreet, the light was on in the one room they all used.

As I approached the kitchen door, the sound like a twig snapping came from behind me. I spun to face the sound. Laith stared back at me, with an amused smile that made me shudder.

'You should be careful, we don't expect visitors this late. I might have mistook you for someone else.'

I opened my mouth to respond, but another voice replaced my own.

'Laith.' Kal's tone was as dark as the night around us.

With a roll of his eyes, Laith turned and melted back into the shadows. I looked up at Kal, standing in the doorway.

'How did you get here?'

'I drove Dad's car.'

He peered around me. 'I didn't know you could drive?'

'Well, while we're talking of things we didn't know about each other,' I snapped.

He glanced over his shoulder and I noticed Nash and Denver sitting at the kitchen counter watching TV. They both nodded in my direction. I returned the gesture.

Kal stepped out onto the stoop and pulled the door closed

behind him.

'What's the matter?' he demanded crossly. His face seemed impassive enough in the darkness, but it was obvious he was cranky with me. Well, I was mad at him, too, so I ignored my compulsion to try to make him feel better.

'I need to talk to you.'

'Look, Veronica, I am not in the mood for this.'

'Oh, it's Veronica now is it? Do you think I'm in the mood to wake up at three in the morning, drive without a licence because there's no other way for me to contact you, and stand on your doorstep in the cold?'

He gave me a look of exasperation then took my hand and led me inside. Even in my flustered state, the touch of his hand on mine sent electricity bolting through me. We walked through the kitchen to chimes of hello, and I waved back at the boys, but Kal didn't allow me to stop. He took me upstairs to his bare room and stood in front of me, arms folded.

'Why are you being nasty?' I asked, caught off guard.

'I've had a bad night.'

I bit back the apology that nearly tumbled from my lips. 'You lied to me,' I breathed. 'I mean, you told me what I wanted to know, but you left information out. You didn't just turn up when you heard my father was ill, did you?'

Kal's eyes narrowed.

'Tell me if you saved me three years ago when I was attacked on the beach. Tell me the truth!'

He stared at me, his lips pressed together. 'What difference does it make?'

'It makes every difference!' I didn't need any further confirmation of course – his reply said it all. 'I know it was you. Kal, please!'

'Fine,' he almost shouted, raising his voice at me for the very first time. 'It was me. I did it for your father. Everything

I've done has been for your father. He saved me, I saved you. That's all.'

I flinched. Was he saying he didn't care about me? That everything he'd done had just been out of gratitude? My throat was suddenly so dry that even if I'd wanted to say something more I couldn't have. I turned and ran from the room.

28 — CONFESSIONS

I HAD TO FIGHT TO KEEP MY EYES OPEN AT MY DESK. I'd filled Alex in on what happened at The Half Moon – leaving out the part about my crazed three a.m. excursion, and she spent the morning cursing that she hadn't come out.

'Cheryl needs to get a clue. I hate girls that cause fights,' she said angrily.

'Yep, if only Mae saw it that way.'

Alexandra kept her thoughts about Mae to herself, but I could read them clear as day on her face. I shrugged to show I understood.

At five, just as the work day was ending, a knock on the window got my attention. Ace was waving through the glass, his white-toothed smile gleaming against his olive skin. It had only been three months, but it looked like he'd grown even in that time. In spite of him being younger than the others, I was sure he was as tall as Kal now. The anxious knot I had been carrying around all day disappeared.

Alexandra put a caller on hold and pulled her mouthpiece to one side. 'Which one's that?' she whispered.

After I'd told her, I took off my own headset and stepped outside.

'Hello, you,' I said.

Ace looked at me sheepishly. 'Hey, Ron.'

'You're a rubbish friend.'

'Oh, don't say that. I had to leave. If it helps any, I moaned about it the entire time.'

'I guess it helps a bit.'

He wrapped his arms around me, lifting me off the floor.

'Ace—' I choked.

'Oh, sorry!' He put me back on my feet.

'Good to see you too,' I smiled, straightening my blouse. 'I know you think you don't get a say when Kal tells you to do something, but you do. You should have at least said goodbye.'

'I really am sorry.'

'It's fine,' I said, realising just how pleased I was to see him again. 'Let me get my things.'

Back in the office, I happily ignored the questioning glances from my coworkers. I waved a big goodbye to everyone and winked in Alexandra's direction as I left. She was beaming. It felt good to have someone who understood how I felt and not judge me for it.

The first thing I noticed was that Ace had cut his hair since I saw him last. It made him look older, his boyish curtain style was now short and cropped close to his head, like most of the others.

'Did you hear about last night?' I asked, as we walked to the bus stop.

'Not from K, but Laith was pretty riled up when he came in.'

'He hates me.'

'Laith hates the whole world. Kal meeting you has thrown him a bit, because we never saw it coming. He can't understand because it wasn't part of the plan, you know? He'll get over it.'

I stared at his profile, contemplating all the things I knew about them. Mainly, how Ace had never killed a man and still, he was doomed to hide for the rest of his life.

A low whining made me look up, the bus had pulled up in front of us. I paid for us both and headed towards the back.

'So, how have you been?' I asked.

'Not bad, you know I turned sixteen while we were away.'

'I missed your birthday!'

'I know, I thought that day of all days I could have got another awesome home cooked meal, but–' he stopped himself as though he wished he hadn't brought up their departure.

'It's okay Ace, it wasn't your fault. I'll make you a birthday dinner tonight instead, how does that sound?'

He grinned in response, but then he seemed to think something over. His silence lingered until the bus stopped at the end of my road. We hopped off and

walked the gravel-lined track to my house, heading straight to the kitchen door round back. As we stepped up onto the verandah Ace's hand wrapped around my arm.

'Ron– I probably shouldn't say anything – it's none of my business, but I just wanted to tell you, I'm really glad K met you.'

I smiled, but the serious of Ace's expression made it clear he had more to say .

'I just mean, he didn't want to leave you – I think he believed he was doing the right thing, so, try not to be too mad at him.'

'Hey, leaving without saying goodbye to your friends is never the right thing!' I pointed out.

He grimaced. 'Yeah, sorry. I don't get a say in how things go. I'm the youngest. I fall in line.'

I frowned and sat on the chair that looked out across our back garden and the fields beyond.

'I don't mind,' he continued, leaning on the verandah and staring straight ahead. 'I'd rather that than be responsible for the lives of the team.'

I swallowed, my mind reeling as I tried to gauge how to respond. Kalen had told me not to mention anything to Ace about what I knew about them. But from what he was saying it was obvious he had somehow worked it out by himself.

I stayed silent. The air was damp and smelled of rain to come. I really liked spending time with Ace, when he was around I felt calm, like I'd known him all my life, but something wasn't quite right about him today.

'Ace, I'm so glad you're here, but I feel like there's something you want to tell me.'

He looked at me then, turning his head, but not his body. 'I'm just worried about you is all and I'm torn what to do about it. Kalen is like his old self since he met you. His *old*, old self - back when I first met him, and before he got sent out... well, you know. He smiles more. I'm really happy for him. But he left because he was worried about what our presence in your life might mean for you and though I was upset I didn't get to say goodbye, I understood. Now, we're back and I don't know if he'll ever be able to leave you again.'

We stared at each other. I was trying to digest the warning he was giving me. Because that's what it was - a warning. Right now, Kalen leaving was the last thing I wanted to think about.

'Hungry? I said eventually. He smiled and we both headed for the kitchen door. He made it first, reaching up and sliding the spare key from the top ledge.

'You really shouldn't keep this here.'

'Ace,' I said, taking a deep breath to prepare myself for what I was about to ask, 'should I be scared?'

His face fell. His eyes were serious, almost pained. 'I really don't know,' he said.

29 — DECISION

THE FOLLOWING MORNING, I was mulling over my conversation with Ace. It had taken a lot for him to be so honest with me, that I could tell, but what it meant to me was making my head hurt. I decided to inflict some pain of my own – Kickboxing would do nicely.

I opened the front door and slumped to find Rachel on the front porch with Cloud.

'Eight a.m.?' I said.

Rachel gave me a pursed-lipped smile. 'We thought we'd come to see you. I'm taking Cloud to ballet lessons in an hour.'

'Rach she's not even three.'

'They have to start that young if they're going to be any good. She's also started gymnastics, modeling and theatre school for toddlers.'

'Dear Lord,' I said under my breath as I stepped outside, then more loudly, 'Rach, I can't stay. I'm heading to the gym.'

She held her arm out in front of me so I couldn't walk past her. 'Just a coffee, Ron, I haven't seen you in over a week.'

'I am aware of that.'

'Well, I'm here now. Please stay.'

'Please stay with us, Aunty Wonnie.'

Relenting, I crouched down and gave Cloud a hug, taking her small hand and leading her back inside. 'You look bigger every time I see you, CJ.'

'We're off to Marbella on Sunday and it's her birthday not long after we get back, did you remember?'

'Of course.' I flicked the kettle on. I hadn't forgotten a family birthday yet. 'How long you away for?'

'Just a week. We're having a bouncy castle for her on the twentieth and we want you and Adam to be there.'

Adam... I hadn't considered him at all today. I'd have to see him later and the notion didn't fill me with the joy it should have. He was sweet, caring, happy and uncomplicated. He didn't walk around as though the world sat on his shoulders. More importantly, he wasn't a wanted criminal. My brain took no trouble at all in trying to rationalise the obvious, yet it still felt so wrong.

I sighed heavily. 'I'll be there.'

'What about Adam?'

'Yeah, maybe.'

My sister shook her head and placed her chin in her hands, her freshly rolled blonde curls bouncing with the movement. 'Ronnie, this is why I wanted to talk to you. I know that boy's back.'

'Which boy?'

'You know perfectly well which boy I mean. I saw his friend in town yesterday. You know, the tall good-looking one who thinks he's Mr Wonderful?'

I couldn't help but smile, even Rachel with all her prejudices wasn't immune to the charms of Denver. Wanting her to leave as soon as possible so I could get on with my day, I chose the smallest cup I could find to fill with coffee and placed it in front of her before I sat down.

'Okay, so what's your point?' I answered eventually.

'My point is, you're walking on thin ice. Ronnie. You're lucky to have a guy like Adam who wants to be with you. He's handsome and successful, he's someone Dad would be proud to see you with and quite frankly I don't know how you've managed it. Yet, you have that look in your eye.'

'Yeah, and what look is that?' The chances of my day being a good one were gradually lessening and I was seriously considering writing it off and going back to bed. Cloud was playing with a bucket of building bricks in the corner, taking no notice of us. I was thankful for her miraculous way of blocking out unpleasant experiences.

'The look that tells me you're about to do something rash.' Rachel leant forward then, so our faces were inches apart. 'Ronnie, you think I don't know my own sister? I know I can be into my own thing most of the time. You've always been the dependable one, the sensible one–'

'Rachel–'

'Wait, let me finish,' she insisted. 'What I mean is, you always seem like the dependable one, but I know how independent you actually are. All our lives, even though you were so much younger than me – you were always brave enough to try things first. You always did what you wanted to do, when you wanted to do it.'

'I think you're looking at the wrong sister, Rach.'

'Yeah, you didn't make a fuss when something didn't go your way like I did, but you had a way of doing exactly what you wanted without hurting anyone's feelings – so it went unnoticed. Dad may have seemed like he was always worrying about me, but really, you've always been the flight risk, because I needed him – I need you. You Ronnie, you don't need anyone.'

It wasn't true that I didn't need anyone. I'd been forced to cope on my own because when Mum left us, Dad felt compelled to try to keep Rachel from hurting. I'd always been on my own.

'Rachel, what are you trying to say?'

'I'm trying to say, I care about you and you look as though you're going to do something incredibly stupid for some whim of the heart. I know you're a dreamer, little sister, but this is real life, not a fairytale. Make the right choice.'

She left soon after. Dramatically sweeping out with Cloud in tow as if she had a million other places to be and had only dropped by to save my life. A hard-done-by air kiss later and she drove away. The clouds had turned a grotty looking grey during her visit and I could hear the distant rumbling of thunder. Perhaps I could go back to bed after all.

Back inside my warm house, I thought long and hard about what she'd said. Ironically, all Rachel had managed to do was compound my feelings. I knew I needed to end things with Adam, because regardless of whether Kalen was right for me, I couldn't live in the real world she wanted me to. As far as I was concerned, life was hard enough without taking away the few things that made a person happy. As long as Adam was in my life I'd be pushing away the one person I wanted. It didn't seem fair on anyone. I picked up the phone.

Adam came over after work and was sitting across from me in the same position I'd sat with Rachel. The storm had got into full swing and the wind was howling outside, rattling through the attic.

'I can't be with you any more,' I blurted, after a long silence. It wasn't quite how I'd planned it, but it wasn't like I'd done this kind of thing before and the words just fell out of my mouth. He dropped his head with a bitter laugh. I knew then, in spite of any pain he felt, I was actually doing him a huge favour. Maybe he knew it, too.

'This is because of that guy isn't it?' he asked without looking up at me.

'In some way, he's been the catalyst, but aside from him, I'm not in this one hundred percent and that's not fair on either of us.'

He nodded slowly and pulling back his tousled hair he let out an exaggerated breath. Finally he met my eyes and there was a fleeting moment where my stomach knotted and I experienced a dreadful sense of panic at what I'd done, but as his eyes left mine, the feeling faded. He got up to leave.

'You know, Veronica, I really cared about you and I know that guy is just going to cause you pain. I have no idea what it is with girls, they always want the bad boy.' He walked out the front door, letting it slam behind him.

I didn't move. Had I expected more of a scene? Maybe it was his use of the past tense when he'd said *he cared*. Surely you can't go from caring to cared, in just a few seconds. I laughed at myself; so it had been easier than expected. 'That's a good thing,' I said out loud. If he wasn't hurting then that was a very positive thing. It meant I'd made the right choice.

Kalen would have fought harder, I decided. Though really I wasn't sure. At the thought of his name, however, another idea occurred to me: perhaps it wasn't Adam's lack of grief for our break-up that bothered me, maybe it was his parting shot. Was I really one of those girls who wanted a bad-boy? No way. Though I couldn't help thinking about it for the rest of the evening, because, no matter which way I looked at it, Kalen wasn't just a bad boy – he was the *baddest*.

30 — THE CALM

THE NEXT DAY, SAID BAD BOY CALLED ME ON THE PHONE. To say I was shocked didn't cut it.

'Where are you calling me from?' I asked, incredulous.

'A pay phone. I wanted to see if you were busy today.'

'I have classes until four. Do you realise this is the first time you've called me on the phone?'

I imagined him smile at the other end of the line. 'Is that a good thing?'

'Yeah, it's great!'

'So, four o'clock, you want to have some dinner at my place?'

'What's this in aid of? Last time I saw you, you couldn't wait for me to leave.'

'I think we both know I tend to overreact at times. I guess – I'd like to make it up to you. You can bring your boyfriend if you like.' I heard him struggling to construct that sentence and I was touched. I told him I'd meet him and that he had some considerable making up to do.

'You seem bent on making me hate you and then you want to make up, what's that about?'

'Red, please–'

'Okay, okay, see you later.'

I laughed and hung up. By the time I got to school I was almost skipping. The storm had passed and the air was fresh and crisp. The realisation that it was Kalen who saved my life was a shock at first, but the more I considered it the more positive I became. I'd met him – the one I'd been waiting for longer than anything – and deep down I'd never really believed I would.

My final class of the day was History and it passed painfully slowly. I was obsessively clock watching, until four o'clock finally came and I glanced out towards the school gates to see the old sky-blue ford pull up outside.

'Is that his car?' Toni blurted, her nose screwing up in disgust. She and I had History together and recently she'd taken to sitting next to me. I stared out the window as the man I'd dreamed of for three years got out of his car and looked back at me. Even from the distance I could see the apologetic smile touching his lips.

'Yep, that's his car!' I beamed. 'See you guys later.' I swiped my bag from my desk and left my classmates staring after me.

'Red,' he nodded, as I stepped up to the gates.

'Hello, moody.'

'I'm sorry,' he said, and then with a glint of amusement in his eyes, added, 'everyone in your class is doing all they can not to press their faces up against the window. It seems we're creating quite a stir. You want to go?'

I held back a laugh. 'Don't let it go to your head, this always happens when I leave for the day.'

'I don't doubt it,' he grinned and slid back into the car. I followed suit, forcing myself not to look back at the faces I knew were all lined up watching us.

'So, where's your boyfriend? Didn't you want to bring him along?' he asked when we neared his house.

I stared out the window, wondering what game he was playing, 'That's very charitable of you Kal, how very unlike you.'

I was avoiding the whole boyfriend scenario. I wasn't sure if I could tell Kal yet, it meant telling my family to get stuffed and I didn't know if I could do that.

'He's your boyfriend and I respect that,' he explained awkwardly. The car came to a gentle stop and we both got out.

'You don't respect anyone,' I pointed out.

'That's not true,' he replied, coming around to me and taking my arms in his hands. 'I respect *you*.' His sudden seriousness left me lost for words.

'That's why I'm trying my very best to be nice. Of course I want you, Red, I only came back to this ridiculous town for you, but if you don't want me then I guess I'll have to accept that, and if I can't have you as my own then for the time being I would like at least to spend some time with you, as friends.'

'For the time being?'

'Until you change your mind, or... I leave through not being able to stand the thought of you with another man any longer.'

'You would leave here because of that?'

'What else is there? The boys hate every day we stay in the same place.'

'I thought maybe you wanted to stay in one place, live a normal life?'

'We can never have a normal life,' he replied coldly. I knew he was losing his cool because I wasn't giving him the response he wanted. That was the thing about Kal, he was constantly battling with himself over the line between right and wrong.

London – October 2006

'I hate this country, why are we here?' Denver said sullenly. It was unlike him to complain. It had been a trying time, almost three years had passed since their escape from the United States and they had nothing to show for it but memories of sleeping rough and stowing away on cargo ships.

'London is surely just as good as any other city in the world?' Kal questioned, not looking up from the game of chess he was engaged in with Nash.

'Yeah, but I'm over it now, It's been months and it's cold here. I'm bored. The girls are hard work, and to be honest, they're not that hot.'

Laith laughed from the tiny kitchen area of the apartment they'd rented in Islington. 'True,' he said.

'I think that's a rash generalisation. There are over seven million people in London, fifty percent of them female,' said Kal.

'Quality, not quantity, man,' Denver huffed, striding to the window. The problem was, he was too big – too big for the room, too big for London, even. He was six-foot-four and had the energy of ten boys his age. As he watched the rain pound against the grey streets he shivered; he felt like a caged animal.

Nash finally looked up from the game. He never said very much, but when he did, Kalen thought it was usually worth saying. His face screwed up momentarily as if something had just dawned on him. 'You know, I've never heard you complain like a little bitch before. You scared of a bit of rain now, D?'

Kalen smirked.

'Fine. I'm getting out of here, anyone wanna come for a run around London in the rain?' Denver boomed. The others waved him off without looking up from their own pursuits.

'See you guys later, then.' He jogged out of the front door and into the downpour.

'Why are we here anyway?' Laith asked.

Oh great, Kalen thought dismally, it was going to be one of *those* afternoons.

'Why not?'

'Well, I can think of plenty of reasons why not, but I'm

struggling to find a reason to stay.' Laith fell back on the sofa bed and began throwing a ball into the air, waiting until it almost hit him in the face before he caught it each time.

'I didn't ask you to come here with me. If I am not mistaken, you guys all tagged along.'

Laith's eyebrows shot upwards. 'That's a bit rich.'

'True though,' Kal looked grimly at Nash, who was shaking his head at the exchange. They were all on edge when Laith had a bee in his bonnet.

'I think you have a personal reason to be here.'

'I don't care what you think.'

'I'm right though, aren't I?'

'Man, shut up, will you? He's kicking my ass right now and you are not helping my concentration.' Nash stared at the board for a long time before making his move. Kalen moved to checkmate immediately.

'Damn, you're the only one who beats me at this.'

'Not often, this is a victory for me.'

'We should leave soon,' Laith continued. 'We've lingered here too long, become too complacent.'

'We are leaving soon,' Kal answered, resetting the board. Ace took up Nash's position opposite him. Winner stays on was a long game, but they were not short of time to kill.

'Good,' Laith sounded both jubilant and surprised. 'That's good! Where are we going?'

'*I* am going to a place further up the East coast. Clanots Ocean.'

'What? I meant that we have to get out of England. Let's go to Italy, Greece, Norway even. Why would we stay here?'

'Do what you like, I'm going to Clanots Ocean.'

Laith fumed silently in the corner, but Kalen knew he'd follow. None of them wanted to be alone, as much as it would probably be safer if they were.

***

'So what are we doing?' I asked as we walked in.

'Dinner to start with, I cooked spaghetti,' Kal pointed to the spread on the table. There was a huge bowl of pasta at each end, a dish of steaming red sauce in the middle and even a salad.

'I didn't realise you could cook.' I struggled to hide my surprise.

'Ah, you think I'm only good for one thing,' he said with resignation.

I started to fumble an apology, when the serious look fell away from his face and he burst out laughing.

I glared at him. His joking wasn't something I was used to.

'You're right,' he said when he'd stopped chuckling, 'I can't really cook. Ace helped – or I suppose I helped Ace. The boys are looking forward to seeing you. They'll be here soon.'

'Great,' I smiled hesitantly. I hadn't hung out with them all since they'd been back and knowing they weren't all as enthusiastic as Kal about their return made me nervous.

'Relax, Red,' Kalen eyed me kindly, reading my mind. 'Then tomorrow as you don't have to work until the afternoon, I thought maybe I could teach you how to drive.'

'I can already drive,' I pointed out.

'Well, clearly you can or you wouldn't have turned up at my house like a mad woman in the middle of the night. I would, however, like to ensure you can drive *well*. What d'you say?' His dark eyes were warmer than usual as he stared at me, waiting for my answer.

'I think I say, thank you.'

'Great. Let's eat.'

Laith didn't join us and though Denver made some excuse

for him, I could tell it was to try to keep me from feeling bad. Despite his absence the evening was upbeat and happy and they didn't seem to hold any resentment towards me. It was a huge relief.

'You know, Denver, you have an admirer,' I said after we'd eaten.

He looked skeptical. 'It's not you, is it? Because he may be smaller than me, but I know better than to get into it with K.'

I looked at Kalen, who was rolling his eyes, but all other eyes were focused on me now, so I continued. 'Um, no, it's not me. It's my friend Alexandra, from work.'

He paused for a moment's reflection, and then his face brightened. 'Oh, the blonde babe from the club, that night a couple of months ago? With the short hair?'

'Yeah, that's the one.'

'Smoking hot,' he smirked. 'Good to know, Ron, thanks.'

'I didn't say you could do anything, I just thought I'd let you know.'

'Ha!' Nash spoke directly to me for the first time all evening.

'You can't tell D a thing like that and not expect him to do something about it. That girl's in trouble now.'

I must have looked as worried as I felt because Kalen was stifling a laugh.

'Not that sort of trouble, Red. Just Denver-dating trouble – you may want to warn her to stay well clear.'

'Dude?' Denver interjected.

I smiled to show I understood, but I regretted saying anything. I didn't want Alexandra to be one of Denver's one-night stands. I'd have to warn her about him.

After Ace and I had washed the dishes, Kalen came into the kitchen and asked me if I wanted to go home. I didn't, but I figured it would be weird if I stayed the night so, reluctantly, I agreed.

'I can drive you, or we can walk into town if you like? It's a nice night. Then I can put you in a cab.'

I accepted the walk, wanting nothing more than a way to prolong my time with him.

We hadn't even got half way to the town centre when Kal put his arm around my waist. It should have felt good, but as he did it he leaned into my hair and told me to walk faster. My mouth dried up. His eyes were even more focused than usual, his gait determined. A flash of fear bolted through my body.

'What's wrong?'

Before he could answer me, I knew. Five men with baseball bats came out of the bushes and walked towards us.

31 — REVENGE

'**R**ED, LISTEN TO ME, THEY'RE BEHIND US TOO. I need you to run. We'll run together. Turn left when I squeeze your hand.'

His words were a blur. I had no time to digest what was happening, within a second my hand was being squeezed and I took a sharp left as I'd been instructed. We sprinted across the main road, my hand firmly in his. I didn't look back, but I was very aware of the sound of their feet pounding behind us. They were gaining on us and no matter how hard I tried, I couldn't get my legs to move as fast as Kal's. We would never outrun them. Sprinting around a corner, we found ourselves in a dark alleyway, blocked at the end by a high metal fence.

As we reached the wire mesh, he looked at me urgently. 'I'm going to lift you. I need you to grab the top of the fence and pull yourself up. You'll fall to the ground on the other side, so make sure you bend your knees on impact. Then run!'

I shook my head. 'No way, what about you?'

'I'll follow you, but you can't wait for me. Don't look back, don't stop running until you reach town. OK?'

I whimpered pathetically.

'Ronnie, you have to do as I say.'

I nodded and he interlocked his fingers in front of me so he could hoist me upwards.

'I'm sorry,' I whispered.

'*I'm* sorry, Red, this is all because of me.' His voice was grim. I wanted to tell him that none of it was his fault, but there was no time to try to make him feel better. I had to focus if we were going to get away.

Jeering sounded from the other end of the alley, as Kal elevated me upwards. I grabbed at the top of the fencing. My fingers found the metal I was after, wrapping desperately around it, but my hands were sweating. I slipped. Falling back heavily into his arms. Our eyes met, just as at least fifteen large shadows rounded the corner. There was no time to run and no way out. Standing me up straight, Kalen stepped in front of me.

'Red,' he whispered, 'when I start fighting, I want you to run past us. I won't let them touch you. Do not stop running.'

I felt myself slump miserably as he moved forward to protect me.

'Not so funny now, is it?' said of one of the masked men as he approached us. I couldn't recognise their voices, but obviously the same men Kal had fought in the bar were back for revenge. And they'd brought some serious back up.

'I don't remember laughing,' Kal replied aloud, using his false British accent. His amiable temperament told me he was trying to get out of the predicament without a fight. Somehow, that made me even more terrified.

'Oh, you were laughing, mate. You won't be soon,' said the smiling balaclava.

'Please just leave us alone,' I pleaded. Kal quieted me by touching my arm, moving me further behind him.

'Please leave us alone,' they mocked in unison.

'Are you really going to try to hurt a young girl here in the middle of town? Don't you think that'll attract far more attention than you'd like? That the police will let that go?' He asked calmly, never taking his eyes off of the one who appeared to be the leader.

'Not *try* mate.'

'He's right Joe,' one of them whispered.

'Shut up!' the leader hissed. 'Don't say my bloody name!'

'Why don't you let her leave and we can sort this out, you and me.'

The voice responded acidly, 'Not gonna happen. You've had this coming to you, boy. After what you did to our crew if you think you're walking away from this, you're sadly mistaken. We have a reputation, you know? Now you and your bitch girl-friend are gonna learn some manners.'

A guttural snarl came from within Kalen. 'If you hurt her, I promise it will be the last thing you ever do.'

'Let's see, shall we?'

Kalen grabbed my arm. 'Run,' he growled.

The pack descended and Kalen shoved me forcefully to one side. I flew some distance, crashing to the ground. Shifting so I could see what was going on, I got to my feet and pressed my back against the wall. The instant one of them reached him, Kal grabbed a metal dustbin lid and backhanded it into the at-tacker's face. He fell to the ground. Then Kal spun, kicking one of the others before breaking another's arm and using him as a battering ram into the next. The bin lid was used repeatedly, be-fore being thrown like a Frisbee. The metal disc hit one of our attackers in the neck, he fell to his knees clutching at his throat and struggling to breathe.

At the same time, one of the men turned in my direction and with a grin he launched himself at me. I braced myself. Kalen was behind him in an instant, throwing him backwards. Very soon, Kal had them all in one corner of the alley, either fighting him or cowering from him and he'd barely broken a sweat. I felt a surge of pleasure and admiration – the pathway was open for me to run as I'd been instructed.

But then a baseball bat connected with the back of Kal's

legs. No sound escaped his lips, but he collapsed forward. The hyenas leaped on him instantly, beating down with their weapons until I lost sight of him completely.

His words rang in my head: *'Don't stop running'*. Part of me wanted to oblige. I wanted to run and never look back, but I was rooted to the spot. I couldn't leave him there.

I was waiting – hoping – for him to get up and start fighting again. When he didn't, I scanned the ground frantically. What looked like the handle of a pickaxe was lying beside a large masked man Kal had managed to knock unconscious. With one more glance into the fray, I leaned over the body and picked up the heavy piece of wood. My hands trembled.

I don't remember much else, bar running into the din and launching the weapon down with all my strength. I had no idea if I was hurting them, or just succeeding in making them angrier. Somehow though, a path suddenly cleared and Kalen pushed through. He was battered and torn, with blood covering his once beautiful face, but he was alive! Relief washed over me, but it was gone just as quickly when I noticed the anger and distress that swept across his features as our eyes met.

Then something cracked against the back of my skull and my world turned black.

32 — GONE

I WAS UNNATURALLY COLD AND IT WAS AS THOUGH SOMEONE WAS SPEAKING MY NAME FROM THE END OF A LONG TUNNEL. My eyelids felt cemented together and my head throbbed with sickening pain. As my eyelashes parted, the unwelcome white light made me wonder if I was dead, but the smell of salt and seaweed was deeply familiar to me and I quickly understood I wasn't staring at the doorway to heaven, just a cold morning sky in Clanots Ocean.

Finally, my vision began to clear and a shape formed above me: the village butcher, Mr Reynolds, his silvery hair blending into the sky above him. He spoke my name again. His dog licked my face.

I tried to speak, but all that escaped was a groan.

'Veronica? Oh thank goodness. I've called an ambulance. Stay still, dear.'

'Kal?' I managed. Even the sound of my own voice was torture on my head.

'Shhh, dear don't speak. You've been badly hurt.'

My eyes fell shut and several curses ran through my head for the poor old man who was just trying to help me. Why couldn't he just tell me where Kalen was? I couldn't remember what had happened, but I knew something was wrong. I kept my eyes closed. Soon enough, sirens sounded around me, joining in with the crashing in my brain. More people stood around me now. I could hear them all talking. I called out for Kal, wanting them all to shut up so I could hear him. I just wanted to hear Kalen's voice.

When the throbbing began to subside, I let my eyes blink open. The white room suggested I was in hospital, the drip attached to my hand confirmed it. I lifted my hand to my head and felt it was wrapped in a bandage.

'Ronnie?'

I was so pleased to hear Rachel's voice.

'Ronnie, I'm here, darling, can you hear me?'

I managed to nod and she squealed with delight, 'Don't speak, love, the doc said you have to take it really easy, but the police will be here later on, they want to question you about what happened.'

My vision was still slightly blurred, but I could see she'd been crying.

'Rachel, where's Kal?' I struggled.

'Who?'

'Kalen.'

'Oh him. Is that who did this to you?' she demanded, standing up as if to make a declaration of war. I tried to grab her, but collapsed back onto the bed. The pain in my head made it almost impossible to move.

'He was with me,' I winced. I had to stop her from running straight out and telling the world Kalen had attacked me. I forced some volume into my voice. 'Some guys with baseball bats jumped us and–'

She was by my side again, hushing me and stroking my hair, all the while cursing Kalen and his friends. So, it wasn't good timing when a knock at the door revealed Denver and Ace holding a bunch of flowers.

Rachel was her usual dramatic and deafening self, immediately getting up from the visitor's chair to yell at them. In the world according to Rachel, they had brought this on us and until they'd come to town nothing bad had ever happened to her sister. Mercifully for my head, a nurse came running in and told them all to get out. Before they did, though, Ace managed to get across the room to me. He kissed my forehead and whispered he'd come back later.

'Ace, where is he?' I pleaded, grabbing his arm before security led him out. Ace shook his head sadly and mouthed that he didn't know.

I was alone in my room then, muted sounds of my sister's abuse carried from outside the closed door. Everything had got completely out of control and now Kalen was missing.

***

It was all surface stuff: a few scratches, bruises and a slight concussion. But there were no broken bones or internal bleeding, so I was allowed to leave two days later. My arm was in a sling, but it was only a sprain. I'd lied to the police. I told them I had no clue who'd attacked us, because I knew that's what the boys would have told me to do. It's what Kal would have wanted me to do. Still, I wasn't the best liar and I didn't feel good about it.

Rachel was too busy to pick me up. After she realised I was going to be okay, her concern had lessened somewhat. I told her I'd get Mae to give me a lift home, instead, getting myself on a bus and heading straight over to the mansion for some news on Kalen. I couldn't understand why I was okay and he was gone. It didn't make sense.

When I arrived, Laith was the only one home.

'I was wondering when you'd show up.'

I tried to ignore the cold reception. 'Is he okay?'

He shrugged from the barstool where he sat with a can of cola clasped in both hands. He stared at the blank wall in front of him. I shivered. The house was silent, even the television in the kitchen was off. It became obvious I was alone with him.

'Where are the others?'

'Searching for him.' He looked at me intensely. 'You know, if K hasn't turned up by now, it's likely he's dead.'

I sucked in a breath and he smiled widely. If he had it in him to laugh, I'm sure he would have. He wanted to scare me, that was for sure.

'Why would you say that?'

'You know about us,' he stated as though it were a question.

'I don't know anything.'

Laith leant forward, his eyes glistening. 'You can't lie to me, Ver-on-i-ca.'

I flinched. He sat back, his grin growing wider until he looked almost deranged. 'You think you can lie to one of us? You can't. I'm particularly good at that side of things. K is more about the action, he lacks a bit in the smarts department. Well, he must do, because here we all are,' he waved his hands dramatically towards the room, 'stuck in this poor excuse for a town, waiting to be found. I'm just surprised it was civilians that finally managed to take out the all-powerful Kalen. Ironic really, don't you think?'

'Enough,' a deep voice sounded from the back doorway. I looked over with relief to see Nash glaring at Laith.

'Hi, Nash,' my voice trembled annoyingly. I tried to be polite, more grateful for the interruption than he would know, but I was still alone in the house with the two boys I felt least comfortable with. The two assassins, I corrected myself.

'Hey, Ronnie, I'm glad you're okay. Perhaps you'd like to come with me? We have a lead.'

'Really?' I perked up immediately, 'I really want to help, what can I do?'

'Come. Laith, stay. And – try to think happy thoughts.'

'Bite me, N,' he muttered, turning away from us.

I hurried across the room towards Nash and followed him outside without looking back. The Audi sat with the engine running.

'We have to take the car, D has the bike, but then, I don't think K would want you on the bike with me,' he half smiled to himself.

'So you think he's okay?'

'Ignore Laith, he's just a cranky shit.'

I nodded, though I was conscious he hadn't really answered my question. *How well they all seemed to do that.* I slid into the passenger seat of the car. Nash was taking a while so I looked in the rear-view mirror. I saw him slip a gun into the back of his jeans before he ran round and jumped into the driver seat. I gulped, my hands were clammy.

'Where are we going?'

'To meet Ace and Denver, they have a lead.' He reached out and lifted my chin. 'Chin-up Ron, we'll find him. Oh, by the way, I drive pretty fast. Brace yourself.'

'Kal drives fast, I guess you all do,' I babbled nervously.

'No one drives like me,' he winked and then the engine roared to life and I gripped the seat beneath me as he sped onto the main street.

'So what's happened?' I managed to squeeze out the words through gritted teeth as I flinched around each curve in the road.

'Denver did some digging and found out the guys who jumped you both a week ago were boasting about locking him up somewhere. Some storage garage. I checked the listings of lockups and found one listed to a Michael Corleone. Not too creative but I'm fairly sure we're not dealing with a group of Einsteins.'

I stared at him blankly.

'It's a film reference, Ron,' he said, looking between me and the road, as if waiting for some penny to drop. 'Um, not a movie fan, huh?'

We swerved around a corner. I closed my eyes. The thought of Kalen locked in a garage was better than some of the scenarios I'd considered, but it still caused bile to rise in my throat. Nash chatted as he raced along the motorway, ignoring the loud honking from irked drivers as he wove in and out of lanes.

'Why did you come back for me?'

'I didn't, I was coming for Laith, I thought we might need him. Numbers and all that – Laith does have some uses. But when I overheard what he was saying to you, I changed my mind.'

'So why bring me? Don't you think you'll need him now?'

'It was a spur of the moment thing, Ronnie. I'm sure K will be pleased to see you.'

'I dunno about that,' I mumbled.

'Yeah, maybe you're right.' His mouth pulled to one side, as he undercut a lorry that was doing sixty miles an hour in the fast lane. 'He might be annoyed at me, come to think of it, especially if it all kicks off and you get hurt, or if he's in a bad way, a way he won't want you to see him in. Wow I really didn't think that one through! Ha!'

'Nash.' I pleaded, desperate for him to stop thinking the worst.

'Sorry, Ronnie, let's just get there, see how it all pans out. We may have the wrong place anyway.'

As it turned out, I was certain they didn't have the wrong place. I'm not sure if was better or worse that way, because as Ace busted the lock that secured the garage, the smell hit us before we saw what was inside.

I had a hamster once – Cotton. Tame as a kitten. He used to scurry around my bedroom, tire himself out then return to his cage to sleep. Till one day Rachel left my bedroom door open and he didn't come back. We only found him in the end by following the smell, which finally led us to a radiator he'd managed to get stuck behind.

The moment Ace lifted the garage door the stench reminded me of finding Cotton's body, but the odour was so bad I knew nothing so small as a hamster would have caused it. The boys looked at one another with expressions that made my skin crawl.

33 — BROKEN

ACE FOUND A LIGHT SWITCH AND THE DARK ROOM GLOWED YELLOW. All that sat in the huge container was a chair, some rope and some dark stains on the floor. Kalen wasn't there.

Denver crouched down and touched one of the marks, rubbing the residue between his fingers. 'Blood,' he said flatly, 'some new, some old. They must use this place a lot.'

'Gang central,' Nash muttered, kicking away a pile of boxes.

'Where is he?' I asked, my voice breaking.

'You shouldn't have brought her,' Denver said to Nash without looking up.

'I see that now. Laith was being – never mind. Yes, I realise she shouldn't be here. Ronnie, let me take you home.'

I backed away from them. 'No! I want to know what's happened. Are we going to keep looking?'

Denver unfurled so he was standing. 'From the looks of things, they bring people here to torture them. Typical gang mentality – keeps people scared of them. The guy Kal had a tussle with in the bar has gone into hiding, as have his cronies. They probably know we're looking for them.'

'Well, have you asked around? Maybe I can–'

'I've done more than ask around Ronnie, but short of torturing random civilians until I find someone who knows something, there are limits to what I can do.'

I felt dizzy. Ace was next to me in an instant.

'Deep breaths, Ron, this doesn't mean anything.'

'He's right. It would be worse if there was a body,' said Nash matter-of-factly.

I flinched and caught Ace shooting Nash a dark look.

'We'll keep looking. Go home. We'll contact you if there's any news,' said Denver.

I didn't move.

'I'll take her,' said Ace gently, taking my hand and leading me outside to the car.

On the journey my chest ached like I needed to sob, but my eyes remained dry. My heart wouldn't accept what was happening. I point blank refused to believe I wouldn't see him again.

***

Ace dropped me home and said they'd get in touch. They didn't. Nearly a week passed and there was still no sign of Kalen. I couldn't face classes so I avoided school altogether. Study and exams were the last thing on my mind, but news I'd been attacked spread fast and once again the teachers took pity on me, only this time I took advantage of their sympathy.

Every day went by in much the same way. I'd wake up, scour the high street, pubs and beach in the hope of seeing one of the men who'd jumped us. On the third day I forced Alexandra to go with me to Cowford and we spent twelve hours moving from lunchtime pubs to evening bars and clubs. She was the only person who was sympathetic, yet it took its toll, even on her. Rachel, of course, was adamant that he'd just left again of his own accord and I hadn't seen Mae since I got out of hospital. I knew she was still dating Taz and I was angry and hurt that she hadn't been more understanding, but I kept promising myself I would visit her once I knew Kalen was safe. I would try to sort things out with my best friend – even if she no longer cared about our friendship, I did.

On day six I went to the mansion to find out if there was any news. The response I got left me desolate. *'No news, Ronnie. And we're going to leave soon if he doesn't show up.'* That was Denver, and while he came across less upbeat than usual, there wasn't the slightest hesitation in his tone – they were leaving and that was that. I looked at Ace, who glanced back at me contritely. My legs wobbled. If they couldn't find him, what hope did I have?

Ace insisted on dropping me home, but even the youngest and most sympathetic had no words of comfort for me during the ride.

I'd not long been in when I heard a light tap on the door. It was Alexandra and Diana. I couldn't remember the last time I'd looked in a mirror, but Alexandra's mouth dropped as she took me in. She shoved me inside, wrapping her thumb and index finger around the top of my arm and grunting in disgust. 'We're here to cook for you.'

'We'll hand-feed you if we have to, you look like shit,' Diana added. She could always be counted on to tell it how it was, but I didn't care how I looked, or if I ate anything.

'I'm not hungry,' I told them, ignoring the looks of concern they exchanged.

'I'll force it down your throat, Ronnie, don't think I won't,' said Diana.

Then Alexandra added, 'Also, we're taking you out this weekend, babe, this moping has to stop.'

I shook my head adamantly. 'No way.'

'To London. I have theatre tickets to see a show and you're coming with. Have you ever been to London?'

'Of course,' I mumbled throwing myself on the sofa.

The girls stayed as long as they could. They cooked, watched me eat and cleaned up afterwards, but I didn't make the process easy or enjoyable and soon enough they left me alone. I couldn't blame them – I was surprised they'd lasted so long.

I went to the same window I'd sat by each night and stared out into the darkness, imagining him rounding the corner and walking up my gravel driveway. I'd questioned getting the police involved, a resounding No coming from the other as-sassins. Now I couldn't help but wonder if I'd done that first, maybe they would have found him. Of course it could have led to their covers being blown, and Kal wouldn't have wanted that. It was the only thing stopping me.

I stared at the full moon, wracking my brains for places Kalen might be if he were hiding or hurt. Out of nowhere an idea occurred to me. It was a long shot, but I hopped up, pushed my arms through the sleeves of my duffle coat and yanked on my Wellington boots before I could talk myself out of it. I only had on my pajama shorts, but the cold was the last thing on my mind.

I sprinted through my back garden, leaning into the chilly night air that was biting my nose and ears. The grass was wet, even though it hadn't been raining; damp with a layer of even-ing dew that flicked up against my bare legs as I ran.

Stepping into the woods was the only thing that slowed me down. I couldn't run through the thicket even if I'd wanted to. I pushed my way through, twigs cracking under my feet as I fumbled towards the clearing. I considered how afraid I used to be of the forest. I wasn't any more. Different things frightened me now.

Finally, after pushing aside the low hanging branches block-ing my way, I saw the dark silhouette of the hut rise out of the darkness.

Hesitantly, I shoved on the door and stepped inside. A

hunched figure crouched in the corner of the room, hidden amongst shadows. I gasped.

'Kal?' I whispered.

A slight movement and the shadow spoke. 'Don't be scared, Red. It's me.'

I stifled a cry and ran forward. 'How long have you been here?' My voice escaped in a tight rasp. I knelt by his side, trying to steady my shaking hands. He smelled like sweat and blood and when my eyes had adjusted to the blackness I could make out his face was swollen and bruised.

I reached out and touched his cheek, unable to stop the tears from tumbling down my own. I traced my finger lightly down the scar I knew so well. He closed his eyes, sighing gratefully at the contact.

'Oh my God, Kal, I'm so sorry. I'm so, so sorry. Forgive me, please.'

'Red, this isn't your fault.'

'Of course it is,' my voice broke. 'Why didn't you go back to the mansion? I started to think you were de–'

'It'll take more than some drunk, overweight civilians to take me down, Red. You know me.'

From the struggled grate of his breath and the tiny decibel of his voice, I knew there was no time for my questions about why or how. I needed to get him into the house, I had to make him well again.

'Is anything broken, can you walk?' I asked, pulling myself together and wiping the tears from my face.

'I will, but not yet. Sit here with me, I just want to be close to you.'

'Kalen, come on, you made it here and I won't let you give up now. Your friends have been worried sick, they've been searching nonstop for you.'

'You're a horrible liar, Miss Rose,' he managed with a half

smile.

I swallowed a lump in my throat. 'They did, Kal – they did at first.'

'It's okay, Red, I know how it goes – we're all the same, after all. It's not their fault.'

'I didn't stop,' I told him, wishing his life could be different. 'Kalen, do as I say, please, no games. We have to get you inside and get you washed up, you look terrible, but nothing a bath and some food won't fix.' I hoped.

Eventually, he nodded. I eased his arm round my shoulder, focusing all my strength into lifting him. Slowly, I inched us forward as he forced his legs to move. He didn't make a sound, though I could tell he was in pain. There were about two acres of garden between us and the house, but I didn't dwell on the distance. We made our way slowly across the grass until we reached the back porch.

Once inside, things became more difficult. He wavered and I wasn't even sure he was fully conscious, because he turned into a dead weight against me. I steadied myself on the kitchen table, took a lungful of air and shuffled us both to the living room. Knowing I'd never make it up the stairs without help, I let him fall gently on the sofa and collapsed next to him.

I only allowed myself a moment's rest. I ran to the bedroom, grabbing pillows and a blanket. Back beside him, I straightened him out on the couch and tucked the blanket around him. I stared, wondering what to do for the best. In the lamp-lit living room I could see the purple discoloration on his face, the dark circles under his eyes and the cuts that covered most of his skin.

'Kal,' my voice quavered, 'I don't know what to do. I want to call a doctor.'

Though he didn't reply, I saw his frown pull together at the mere mention of the word. I gulped. Internally, I cursed the boys for not owning phones. It was ludicrous – if they had at least one between them, I'd be able to call and ask their advice. But they didn't, so I needed to pull myself together. I fled for the kitchen, filled a jug with water and scurried back in to him. Rousing him wasn't easy, but I was able to drip some water into his mouth. I hurried to the bathroom, digging through the cabinet until I found the first aid kit.

Looking after Dad when he was ill had given me a good idea on how to make someone comfortable, but it wasn't translating to Kal's injuries. Mostly, he was covered in bruises, but some of his skin was cut and the wounds seemed fairly deep. I wiped them clean as best I could, biting back my hysteria as I washed him down. Around the lacerations, his skin was either red raw, or filled with a sticky yellow liquid. I had no clue how to get rid of the infection.

I looked at his face – still unconscious – and fell back so I was sitting on the floor, praying I wasn't going to burst into tears. I felt so helpless.

With that thought, a surge of anger got me to my feet.

'Kal,' I said, though I was fairly certain he couldn't hear me. 'I'm an idiot and I don't know what I'm doing, so I'm going to get the boys. They'll know how to help you. I'm sorry.' Grabbing up the keys to the Land Rover, I placed a careful kiss on his forehead and shot out the front door.

I drove as quickly as I dared along the back roads, promising myself it would be the last time I did anything so illegal. Somehow, though, I wasn't convinced it was a promise I would get to keep.

All the lights were off inside as I pulled up the gravel driveway, but knowing none of them slept particularly well, I wasn't worried about disturbing them. I dashed up the steps, my hand poised to knock when the door swung open. Nash stood in front of me.

'Hello, Ronnie,' he nodded carefully, having reverted to the deadpan state I was used to before Kal had gone missing.

'Hey,' I said bluntly. I was getting really sick of treading on eggshells around them all. 'I have some news: Kal's alive, he's at my house now.'

His aloofness disappeared and for the first time I thought he showed signs of joy. His smile combined with a relaxation of his stance told me he'd been more upset than he was letting on, so I continued more politely.

'I need your help. He's in a bad way,' I choked on the last word and looked away.

Nash had more tact than to try to comfort me. He told me to get back in the car; he'd drive. He disappeared into the house and a moment later he and Denver came jogging out. Denver greeted me with a high five and a short time later – much faster than my journey over had been – we arrived back at my farmhouse. The boys carried a sleeping Kalen to my father's bedroom opposite mine as I watched nervously. Nash seemed to take the reins after that, he stitched a cut on Kalen's chest and bandaged some of the others.

'You did well Ronnie. By the looks of things he's not eaten in a while, and I doubt he's had much water so that's probably the worst of his injuries. I think you found him just in time,' he said.

I nodded and followed them downstairs.

'It's okay, Ron,' Denver whispered before they left, 'he's lived through a lot worse.'

I wasn't comforted by that notion, but it was the only thought on my mind when I went to bed that night. I slept fitfully, afraid he would wake in need of my help.

Canter Creek, Iowa – January 2005

'What happened?'

'I don't know, Sir. I couldn't kill him. He – he had a family.'

The man stared at the boy in front of him, his expression

unreadable. K, however, was aware of what he was thinking. He lowered his gaze.

'He had a family,' the bearded man repeated. 'Mm-hmm. Well, K, this is a problem, because you're here on God's green earth, to do nothing else but what I order you to do. If you can't do that, you are no good for anything.'

'With all due respect, Sir, you know I'm good at my job–'

'Don't interrupt me,' the man shot back, his first break in an otherwise affable manner.

'Yes, Sir.'

'You're right,' the man continued more calmly. 'I may have expected this from some of the others, but not you. You, who we've spared no expense on training. Who we held in such high regard as the success story of this project. I'd like an explanation.'

'Sir, I've no excuse except that I failed.'

The man got out of his black leather chair and walked across the wood-panelled office. He turned his back to K, looking out the window. K wondered where the other boys were. They couldn't all be out on missions, yet he hadn't seen any of them since he'd arrived back from Lebanon two days before.

The huge man sighed loudly, bringing K back to the current situation.

'I don't know what to do for the best. You're fortunate that your record so far this year has been impeccable. You haven't once aroused anyone's suspicions – you play the sweet innocent teenager with exceptional accuracy. You have, however, failed your first test and if you think we'll go easy on you because you're a child–' he took a deep breath, filling his lungs and pushing his chest out, 'then, you would be wrong. You are anything but a child, because we made you anything but. Childhood is a state of mind, lad, and your mind is more adult than most of the men I've worked with. Now, I know you might hate me right now, I know you would like to hurt me, but

233

you will bear it. You will take it on the chin like the soldier you are, because what you need to realise is that emotion is no good to you, and it's definitely no good to me. I won't tolerate it.

'What if I told you, the man you failed to terminate later detonated a suicide bomb, killing not only his own family, but four others and six US soldiers?'

K didn't flinch and he didn't reply, he knew the question was rhetorical and, if he was honest, he didn't have any feeling about it either way. He guessed that was what they wanted, for him to have no views or emotions about death and murder and to some extent he didn't. Until that Christmas evening, he'd thought he was a breed above every other person, able to remove himself completely from what he liked to refer to as the "human condition". His reaction to the target and the mission had surprised him as much as it had surprised his superiors and he'd accept whatever punishment came his way.

'I'd be lying anyway. It was a test, K – a test you failed. The man was an innocent. However, we chose him to see if you would follow orders so perfectly if your situation were more *complicated*. You didn't. For this, I'm afraid, you must be trained.'

As the words were spoken, the door to the office opened and three men in suits entered. K stood immediately and faced them, preparing himself for a fight. It didn't last long – he managed to land a good punch on the jaw of one of the agents before a bag was thrown over his head and he was beaten until he lost consciousness.

When he awoke, he could barely move and his hands were cuffed behind his back. K opened his eyes and waited for them to adjust to the darkness around him, but they never did. The dark was too black, there wasn't even a patch of light to infiltrate it. He forced his body to move when he realised nothing was broken. K knew they wouldn't break any of his bones, to ensure he wasn't beyond repair when they were done with him. After all, that would be a waste of everyone's time and money.

The point was to train him, not kill him. Otherwise, he'd be dead already. The notion didn't comfort him. They had many other ways of inflicting pain if it helped break any element of his humanity that remained intact.

Self-preservation forced him to his feet and he shuffled around the room, inching backwards and feeling his way along the walls. It was solid stone; a closed box, and from the smell and the thickness of the air, he was sure it was underground.

There was no way out.

K blinked. If he knew what it was to cry, he might have cried then. He'd been a prisoner of sorts for many years, but this was the first time he felt trapped and the first time he had ever been scared. Then the steel door in front of him opened and an artificial white light poured into the room. The bag was thrown back over his head, and the next beating ensued.

And so the days went on.

34 — RECOVERY

I WAS AWAKE AT SIX. I wanted to see him, but I knew he needed to sleep. After almost an hour, which felt more like a hundred, I allowed myself to creep to my father's old room and peek in. To my surprise, Kal was sitting on the edge of the bed, staring at the window.

I pushed the door open. 'Hey, how are you feeling?'

He glanced up, studying my face as if he didn't recognise me. A horrible suffocating sensation filled my chest. Could he have amnesia? Panic. If he no longer knew me, my life wouldn't be the same.

'You've been taking care of me,' he croaked, as though he hated to have been a burden.

My relief was so intense I almost laughed. I bit my lip. I wanted to tell him the joy I felt at seeing him recovering. Instead, I asked if I could get him anything.

He shook his head mutely.

'Well – please don't go. I think you need to rest some more, just get back into bed. It's okay, no one knows you're here. I mean, your friends do, but no one else and Rachel's on holiday.'

He stared fixedly at the floor for a long while, before finally lifting his legs back onto the bed and closing his eyes. I lingered for a moment and wondered how I would have fared if things had been different – if he'd died. Realising my hands were shaking, I left the room and busied myself with other things.

He slept for the rest of the day, waking only to eat. I sat by his bedside most of the time, reading through course notes my tutors had emailed to me. I washed the last of the brown dye out of my hair, ditching the dresses and wearing my jeans again. It felt like I was finally throwing away a mask I'd been wearing for everyone around me.

The following morning he was wide-awake, but I had to work. It was the last thing I wanted to do. I called in sick and made him breakfast instead. He was sitting on the sofa in front of the open fire when I came downstairs from my shower.

'It's spring out there, you know. You wanna sit in the garden?'

'I like the fire,' he said absently. Then he turned his head in my direction. 'Come and sit with me.'

I perched on the arm of a chair by his, pulling my feet up underneath me. The burning heat from the fire was almost too much, but I didn't move. Silently, we stared at the flames dancing in the grate.

'I need to ask you something,' he said. 'You do understand what the word run means, right?' His sarcasm was only slight, he was actually annoyed with me.

'Yes, but was I supposed to just leave you there without even trying to help?'

'That's exactly what you were supposed to do!' He looked at me seriously, his expression evaluating. Then he let out a thoughtful sigh. 'Not many people would do what you did, Red. Thank you.'

It's my fault you got hurt. Don't thank me for that. 'What I don't understand, is why I was left there, but you were taken.

Are you going to tell me what happened, should we call the police?'

He lowered his eyes. 'No and no.'

I swallowed. 'We went to the garage. There was so much blood–'

His head snapped up. 'The boys took you *there*?'

I didn't answer, the conversation was going nowhere good.

'That wasn't all my blood,' he said eventually. 'They moved me from there, worried the boys would find me. Honestly Red, all of this,' he looked down at himself, 'is mostly because I was locked up for so long with no food or water. They began to panic, and none of them having what it took to actually kill me, they left me there, hoping I would die. It took me too long to escape and when I got to the woods at the back of your house, I passed out. How long was I gone?'

I twisted the sleeves of my jumper, my eyes burning with the threat of tears. 'Nearly a week.'

'Red, please don't be upset.'

'I'm so sorry.' It seemed completely inadequate, but I could see my moping was only making him more uncomfortable. I tried to think of a way to change the subject. I said the first thing that came to me, 'So, is Kalen your real name?'

He grinned. 'That depends.'

'On?'

'On what you class as a real name.'

I reached over and playfully prodded his arm. 'What name were you born with?'

'I have no idea. I was so young when they took me from the orphanage, I don't remember.'

'Oh.' That was possibly the saddest thing he'd ever said. I pulled my knees up to my chest, but he shrugged it off as though he'd come to terms with it long ago.

'The Agency gave me K, and Kalen was the first name I was

assigned on my very first job. It can be oddly comforting to see your picture next to a name when you've never had one. Anyway that's what the few people who know me refer to me as, so in that respect I suppose it's my real name.'

'And Smith?'

'The same,' he shrugged.

'And how do you all survive, I know you were stealing from someone that night in London.'

His head dropped. 'Sometimes D and I get door work in the bigger cities we visit. Nash does some encryption work. He's real good with computers. But really, jobs aren't an option for us. It's not like we steal from little old ladies,' he added as an afterthought. 'We don't take much. Just what we need, when we need it, which believe me, is not a lot. The house we have right now, for example, Nash and I scoped Clanots for a while before we came here, we knew this house was vacant, and we monitor the owner's movements. He doesn't know we're here... so while we don't pay rent, we don't rob anyone either.'

'He doesn't know you're living in his house?'

'No, and if he ever planned to pay his holiday house in Clanots Ocean a visit we would know about it.'

I thought about that and decided they were making the best of a bad situation. What did I want from him? That he would go and get a job filing in an office? It was foolish of me to hope for something normal to come out of something so abnormal, but inside me my emotions were tearing at each other. Would he ever be able to live like a regular person, if not, what did that mean for us? Though there was no "us" as such, I didn't think I could stand not having him in my life. Even just as we were right now.

'So, you can never have a normal life?'

Something glimmered in his eyes then. Hope. It wasn't an expression I was used to seeing on him.

'When my handler told me what was happening, I agreed

to disappear; to leave and let the other boys die. He gave me money – a lot of money – to help me get gone. I have it hidden away. One day I hope to get my freedom and that money will be waiting for me. Maybe I can have some semblance of a life. Probably not, but everyone needs a dream, right?'

A dream. I knew the feeling. 'You changed your mind about leaving the boys, then?'

'I was never going to leave them, but I was angry and wanted his money. I'd earned it. So I told him what he wanted to hear and then I screwed him over the way he screwed us.'

I tried to imagine what he must have gone through, I came up blank – it was too hard to fathom. 'You're very brave,' I said lamely.

'Not brave,' he said. 'It's fear that drives us all in the end, Ronnie. We might be scared of something, but there'll always be something else that frightens us more. We're scared of taking a human life, but more scared of failure. Scared to get found in a group, but more scared of living our pointless lives alone... scared of loving someone, yet terrified not to.' He lifted his eyes to mine. All the air had left my lungs. I felt like I was in a vacuum.

'I didn't want to die when they terminated the project, but I couldn't live with myself if, after everything I'd done, I let those who trusted me most die in my place. I was more scared of who that would make me than I was of any form of death they could deliver.'

'That's a sad way of looking at things.' I cleared my throat, finding my breath once more. 'You're saying every good thing people do has a selfish motive behind it. That would mean no hero is ever really heroic.'

'I wouldn't disagree with that.'

'No,' I responded adamantly. 'You sell yourself short, and other people. You should have a little faith in the human race.'

'Ah, the human race,' he sighed.

'Let's not think about that anyway,' I ventured, wanting to lighten the intense mood I had inadvertently created. 'Let's think about what we can do with that all that money one day!'

It worked; his eyes softened. 'Where's your boyfriend? Does he know I'm here?'

When I didn't answer, he stretched his arms up behind his head. I watched him, in awe of his strength. He seemed fighting fit after such a short time. Though I hoped there would be no more fighting – ever.

'He's out of town,' I said eventually. I wanted to tell him I'd broken up with Adam, but I was scared of what saying it meant. It wasn't the danger Ace had warned me about that was frightening me, it was the notion that no matter what Kal and I did, or how much we cared for each other, I wasn't going to get to keep him.

35 — STAY WITH ME

IN THE DAYS THAT FOLLOWED, I BARELY LEFT THE
HOUSE, finding things that needed fixing or cleaning to
keep me occupied, all while Kalen sat close by my side
helping me study and talking about the different countries he'd
seen. He never delved too deeply into the subject of himself
and I didn't ask about the jobs he'd been sent on, but his de-
scriptions of strange and far away places were enough to keep
me hanging on every word.

On the verandah we sat looking out at the afternoon sun,
rocking lazily back and forth on the porch swing. The cold
edge to the weather had softened. Spring was all around us; the
scents throughout the garden sweet like freshly cut grass and
dandelions.

'I want to travel one day,' I said wistfully, when he'd finished describing Nepal.

'You do?'

'I've always wanted to, but, I don't know if I'll get the
chance now.'

'I'll show you the world, Red. Just say when.'

I laughed. The feeling warmed me from the inside. 'Where
would we go?'

'Anywhere you want.'

'Egypt?'

'Of course.'

'Fiji?'

A wicked smile pressed at his dimples. 'Pack your things.'

I thought about that, letting my imagination wander to far away places. I'd only ever been to Portugal. Our one and only trip abroad as a family and it had resulted in Dad saving Kalen's life. And that had resulted in him finding me when I was about to be killed. I toyed with a word in my head, one that until very recently I had never been a fan of. Fate.

A knock on the front door jolted me upright.

'I'll be back in a sec,' I said, hopping up and running through the house.

Alexandra stood on the front step, disappointment shining in her large eyes.

'Oh, Al, I'm so sorry!'

She frowned. 'You don't return my calls, you skip work, I've been worried sick about you, babe. What's going on?'

'I'm so sorry, really, but when you come in you'll understand everything.'

She looked at me skeptically. I moved aside and eventually she sighed and stepped into the house. I led her through the hallway and when she reached the garden a slow smile formed on her lips.

'Alexandra Fusco, this is Kalen Smith.'

Kalen stood, moving towards Alexandra with a polite but reserved smile, and extended his hand to her.

Alexandra shook it, her expression full of interest. 'Good to finally meet you, Kalen, I've heard so much about you. I have to say I'm happy you're safe and sound.'

Kalen's eyes flicked in my direction and I knew he was wondering what I'd told her. His face remained unreadable, of course, and suddenly he grinned widely, catching her off guard just as he'd done with me. 'Well,' he said with a smooth and intoxicating voice, 'thanks to Ronnie I'm fit as a fiddle again.'

With a look towards me that said she agreed with his description, Alexandra sat down on one of the wooden deck chairs.

'Ron,' she said. 'Seeing as you've had me worried sick for nearly a week, I guess you can start making it up to me with a cup of tea.'

I laughed. 'Kal, would you like a drink?'

'Water,' he said, taking a seat back on the swing, 'thank you.'

I stepped inside a little hesitantly; the last time I'd put Kal with one of my friends he left town the next day. I'd never blamed Mae for what happened, but the coincidence wasn't lost on me. I hovered by the door for a moment longer than I should have, catching the beginning of their conversation.

'So, Mr Smith, where have you been this last week and a half?'

'Actually, I've been back a few days so I was only–'

'Oh, that explains why I haven't heard from Madam then.'

'Sorry about that, I didn't realise she was skipping work.' I heard the smile in his voice and I knew Alexandra wasn't giving him a hard time. I headed across the kitchen and filled the kettle with water.

When I returned with their drinks they were both laughing. It wasn't often I saw Kalen laugh with anyone and I experienced a mix of feelings, the first being jealousy. The pangs I felt were too strong to pretend I didn't, but as he raised his eyes to meet mine, the feeling instantly melted away.

'What are you two laughing at?'

Alexandra looked up at me, pursing a smile. 'Kalen was just telling me how you carried him from the forest to the house. I didn't believe you could do it, but he insists you're stronger than you look.'

With relief, I sat down and joined in the conversation. Alexandra knew some guys had jumped us and soon I cottoned on that Kal hadn't told her anything too revealing. Just that he'd hit his head so hard that he'd been concussed for a couple of days.

Alexandra appeared comfortable around him and began talking of other things: her relationship with our boss at work, Damien, which she now spoke openly about, then finally something she said she'd wanted to tell me for a while.

'Diana and I finally have the money to move to London, Ron. We have a few months' rent saved up so we can start looking for jobs there.'

'You're leaving Clanots?' I couldn't hide the distress in my voice. Kalen shifted in his seat next to me.

'Not just yet, but if I find something good then – probably.'

I took a deep breath. I was happy for my friend, but it also meant I'd be alone again. Work wouldn't be the same.

'I'm pleased for you, but, I'm going to miss you, that's all.'

'Kalen, will you please explain to Miss Clanots Ocean here that London is only an hour away on a train.'

'She's right, Red,' Kal nodded, smiling sympathetically. 'It's about forty minutes if I drive,' he added with a wink.

'See!' Alexandra declared. 'You and I will probably spend more quality time together because you can come to London and stay with us on weekends.'

I tried to smile. I knew I had to grow up and accept that not everyone was going to stay forever in Clanots. *Except maybe me,* I thought grimly.

Alexandra stayed for over three hours. I was walking her to the door when she turned and stared at me seriously.

'You look happy, babe,' she said, throwing her arms around me. 'Next time, make sure that Denver guy is here.'

'Hmmm, maybe London is the best place for you,' I

laughed.

'Oh, that bad, huh?'

'Let's just say he takes advantage of those good looks.'

'I may take advantage of them myself one day. Not every-one is looking for Mr Right, Ron.'

'Well, don't say I didn't warn you.'

'Cross my heart,' she giggled and skipped down towards her Jeep. I turned and headed back through the house.

'I really appreciate the effort you made with Alex,' I said to Kalen when I was back on the porch.

'I think you mean Alexandra,' he pointed out with a grin. 'It was no effort really.'

'Are you tired?' I asked. The night had fallen while we'd all been talking, I could see the weariness in his eyes.

'A little, but I've slept enough.'

'You should rest. Dad used to say rest is everything.'

'I guess I could lie down. Will you come and talk with me?'

I nodded and we walked inside. He pressed numbers on the alarm as we passed it. A strange bleep told me it was set. I cringed.

'I haven't told Rachel the code, I'd better not set it till I have.'

He clicked some more numbers on the grey box with a brief look of disapproval in my direction, before leading the way up-stairs. 'All that time I was away, you didn't use it,' he muttered.

'I guess I forgot.'

'Please don't forget.'

I smiled to myself as I followed him up the stairs. In my father's old room he perched on the bed. I pulled a chair next to it for myself and turned on the television to provide some distraction.

'I have to tell you something,' he said, looking at me in

a way that made me fear something was wrong. 'To explain some things I've kept from you, which you once asked me to be honest about.

'When I first arrived in Clanots Ocean I'm not sure what I was expecting. I'd seen you before, asleep in Portugal and you'd stuck in my head, but when I came to England I told myself I was just visiting William – I mean, your dad – just checking on him to make sure the man who saved my life was doing okay. Yet–' he chewed his bottom lip, 'I'd travelled from Portugal, hidden in the storage hold of a cargo ship for days and in my heart, though I couldn't explain why, I knew I was doing it to see *you* again.

'Let me be clear, there has been nothing in my life that's driven me to do anything impulsive – ever. I plan everything, maybe not on paper, but in my head. Every little detail of every move I make is laid out exactly how it should be, with plan b and c ready to be executed should the need arise. It's all I've ever known. So on the cold October morning that I arrived in England and made my way across the country on three trains and a bus to your tiny town, with no plan of action whatsoever... I felt to some extent free. It was exhilarating.

'I hadn't expected to come across you before I even found your father's house. You were walking along the beachfront in pouring rain and pitch darkness, your face covered by the red hood of your raincoat. I knew immediately it was you. You reminded me of a book I owned as a child – the only thing I ever owned as a child, actually – do you know the one I mean?'

'Little Red Riding Hood?' I ventured, realising I'd been holding my breath. I remembered the night well, though it had never been recited back to me from another perspective.

'Yes, that's the one. That's why I call you Red, though you thought it was because of your hair. You were embarrassed about it,' he remembered. A smile touched his lips. 'I watched you through the rain, from the edge of the pier. You came closer, and I was actually nervous, for the first time in my life.

247

'But that's when I saw the guy. He walked past you at first. You didn't see him because you were shielding your face, walking blindly on your route home. Something in the way he hesitated as he passed you made me stand up. When he stopped and doubled back, I started down the pier towards you, but I couldn't run along the beach in the shortest direction without losing sight of you, so I was forced to go along the pier and down onto the footpath.

'As I ran, I couldn't understand why you weren't screaming. From what I could see, he was on top of you, holding you down.'

He paused then, visibly quivering with anger. He'd closed his eyes, in what seemed to be an effort to find calm.

'So I increased my speed,' he continued with his eyes closed. 'Cursing the distance between us as I watched you both tumble over the seawall and onto the sand. I knew if I didn't get to you quickly, I'd be too late. I was so angry. I was flat out sprinting when I reached you and tackled him. I hadn't killed a man in over a year and until that night I'd never killed anyone in anger.'

He looked at me sadly. 'After that, I left the country. I'd tried to be a better person once we escaped the project, and failed the moment I lost my temper. I was no good to anyone, let alone an innocent young girl. I was, and still am, the epitome of evil.'

'You're not evil,' I whipered. Despite what he had done in his past I couldn't let him condemn himself for having saved my life. 'You're not evil, Kal. I've seen your goodness, all the times you've helped me, saved me! All the times you–' I faltered.

'Exactly,' he let out a short unamused laugh. 'I haven't done a decent thing for anyone apart from you and that's only because I wanted you to be mine. I don't have any decency in me because they drove it out. I care about no one and nothing except you, and only because it would hurt me if something happened to you.'

'That's not true. Why did you stop me taking drugs that night? Why did you stop yourself sleeping with me when I practically handed myself to you on a plate? Why didn't you kill any of those men when they attacked us? You are a good person, Kalen. The people who brought you up have convinced you otherwise, but you can't let a bunch of old men, too frightened to do their own dirty work, decide who you are. They don't know a thing about you. That night you saved me, if it hadn't been for you I'd be dead now. Do you get that? That man had raped and murdered–' I took a breath to steady my voice. 'Why do you want to live your life in the darkness, hating yourself for everything you've done, rather than trying to move forward and make amends?'

He stared at me for a long time. 'Will you lie with me?' he asked eventually. 'I won't do anything, I just don't want you to leave my side. Stay with me tonight, Ronnie?' His voice was so soft, so small and almost desperate that I didn't know how to respond. Without speaking, I lay down beside him, tucking my body into the curve of his.

36 — GAME OVER

I OPENED MY EYES TO DARKNESS. It was late and the bed empty beside me. I blinked, scanning the room. Kal sat on a chair in the corner.

'How long have you been up?' I asked, my voice still full of sleep.

'A while,' he returned flatly.

I pushed myself onto my elbows, my jeans uncomfortable and rigid against my skin where I'd slept in them.

'What's wrong?'

'Would your boyfriend be happy to know you slept with me?' His tone was cold. It was quite obvious he was mad at me.

'We didn't sleep together,' I pointed out.

'What would you call it?'

'Why are you being like this?'

He stared at me without feeling. 'I just wondered what you're doing here with me - does any of this mean anything to you?'

I sighed and fell back onto the pillow, all remnants of my blissful sleep gone. I had come to know Kalen well enough to understand he was angry because he'd opened up to me, and now he felt exposed and vulnerable. I wanted to tell him the truth, but inside me a flame of anger suddenly ignited.

'What's your problem?' I snapped, hoisting myself out of bed. 'I've been worried sick about you for days. I looked for you every day, I cried for you every night! I hold on to every nice thing you say to me – you know why?' Growing louder by the second, my voice no longer sounded like my own. 'Because nice words from you are so few and far between, most of the time I spend heartbroken!' I stormed out of the room to regain some control and in my own en-suite I yanked a brush through my tangled hair and splashed my face with water, before running down the stairs and throwing open the back door in desperate need of air.

Seconds later his footsteps approached from behind me.

'Ever since you found out it was me who saved your life you've been trying to make me into some sort of hero. I'm truly sorry, Ronnie, that I'm such a disappointment to you.'

'I never said you were a disappointment, that's not fair.'

'No, it's not fair.' He walked past me and out into the garden, heading for my fence where I knew he would duck out and not come back again until he decided it was time.

Calm left me. 'Don't you walk out of here, Kalen Smith! I'm so sick of you leaving on a one-liner and thinking that's an acceptable end to an argument – it isn't! You can't walk out on me all the time. This relationship is never going to work if you keep leaving whenever we talk about something that makes you uncomfortable!' My breathing was shallow and escalating out of control. To my surprise, however, his confrontational stance had vanished and the corners of his mouth were pulling upwards. He placed a hand casually in front of his mouth in an attempt to hide his smile, but it was obvious something amused him.

I frowned, my heart rate regaining some rhythm as he walked towards me. Now only inches apart, he looked down into my eyes, raising one eyebrow.

'Relationship?'

Ah. Had I said relationship? Yes, yes I definitely had. I panicked. Instead of removing bricks carefully from the wall between us, they were falling down around me. Yet a warm sensation ran through me all the same. I couldn't hold back my smile.

'I didn't say that.'

'Yes,' he whispered into my mouth, 'you did.' His warm breath swept down my neck and his lips followed. I didn't object. I inhaled his familiar scent of wind and rain and everything outdoors. I tilted my head, willing him to touch my skin. It had been months of fantasising – years even, considering he had literally turned out to be the man of my dreams.

'Are you mine, Veronica?' his smooth voice asked into the nape of my neck, still without touching me. I didn't respond at first, desperate to hold on to some restraint as my emotions spun my whole world out of focus. But when he asked again, his mouth burning against my shoulder, I heard myself saying yes.

In a split second his kiss was on me, his grip tightened fiercely around my back and I finally let myself go. Kalen's large hands lifted me so my legs wrapped around his waist. Still kissing me, he carried me inside the house and upstairs. His eyes were ravenous, and though my body yearned for him in return, my nerves were beginning to kick in. We reached my bedroom door and I wrapped my fingers around the frame to stop us going in. I knew I wanted him – I was more certain of it than I'd ever been of anything – but I hadn't a clue what to do. I suddenly felt incredibly shy.

His eyes were questioning, searching mine and I cringed at what I was about to say. I opened my mouth, but no words came. Cursing internally, I bit my lip. In the same moment, Kal seemed to read my thoughts, his expression softened and while I could see in his eyes that the knowledge he'd be my first definitely excited him, he gently set me down on the ground and tipped my head up so I was forced to meet his gaze.

'We don't have to do this,' he said softly.

'I want to,' I blurted.

His mouth stretched into a slow grin. He took a step towards me, pulling me against him. 'Just relax Red. I'll take care of you.'

I nodded and his lips found mine. This time I didn't hesitate. I melted into submission as he scooped me up and carried me to the bed.

I've always scoffed when people told me they were in love, or that they *fell* in love. Maybe because Mum walked out on us, or because Rachel and Jared do nothing but argue. Whatever it was, I'd been totally naïve. Kissing Kalen now, his tongue searching mine, his hands gripping my body, I felt as though a light had been turned on inside me and I finally realised who I was.

Nothing good could possibly come from falling in love with an assassin on the run from the government, a criminal who could kill with his bare hands. But the fact was – I loved him. Game Over.

Lisbon, Portugal — September 2006

K had to go back to the apartment because he'd made a crucial mistake. He'd left behind his book. It wasn't the object so much as it was what the object signified. It was the only thing he owned – that he had ever owned. Even his clothes were stolen from clotheslines and dumped on a regular basis. His copy of *Little Red Riding Hood* was the only thing he had from the orphanage. It had been a gift on the only birthday he'd ever celebrated and he had an urgent need to keep it. So, against all his training, he made his way back to the Lisbon town centre to retrieve it. He wasn't armed. He'd chosen this consciously since they'd found refuge in Portugal. Carrying a weapon meant looking for trouble. It was the opposite of what he wanted, though now he was regretting the decision.

He scoped the building from a distance. Whatever car Ace had seen was no longer around. It could be Ace had the whole thing wrong, though Kalen doubted it. He had a lot of faith in Ace's abilities, had he trained for longer he'd probably have been the best of them all. So despite the quiet surroundings, the lack of any ominous vehicle, Kal sat for over three hours watching the apartment block. Finally, he moved in. Ducking and hiding where possible – never running – he kept his gait and demeanor that of the sixteen-year-old he was supposed to be and not the trained assassin he was. He managed to get all the way to the side of the apartment block without being seen. Then:

'Vasco!' A voice cried from the apartment next door. Kalen cursed under his breath. The old man had invited Kalen and Denver over for dinner one evening after they'd helped him fix a broken window. His wife had cooked them the best meal they'd eaten all year.

Kalen nodded hello and hoped the man would go away, but he came rushing down the fire stairs from his balcony, holding a hot loaf of bread and waving it in Kalen's direction.

'My wife has baked this for you,' he yelled in Portuguese. Kalen stopped because there was no other option, and let the man greet him with a hug. He wasn't used to affectionate contact but managed to hide his unease and pat the man on the back.

'Thank you, sir,' Kalen replied in the same tongue, trying to make excuses as to why he couldn't stay and chat. The man wouldn't listen, he spoke of strange men he'd seen going into the building where the boys lived. Kalen's interest picked up at that, but he knew he was blown. He told the man to get inside and stay there, but his warning was too late. The old man went down like a lead weight, a look of surprise on his pudgy face.

The bullet was meant for Kalen so he knew he had no time

to help the man, but he managed to drag him to the side of the road.

'I'm sorry, old friend,' he said in Portuguese. Looking quickly at the wound, he smiled. 'But you'll be okay.'

Then he ran.

A line of bullets followed him, blowing out dust and pieces of concrete from the ground as they barely missed. He threw himself into the side streets using every building he could to shield himself, leaping over anything that crossed his path; taking short cuts he had memorised. He headed for somewhere safe to hide. What he hadn't anticipated was how many of them there were. They had positioned themselves all across town. No matter how he outran one, there was always another waiting. He was shot at four more times, surprised they managed to miss, but not dwelling on the reason for his good fortune.

Kalen paused to catch his breath when he burst through the bushes and shrubbery to find he was standing at the edge of a freeway. Footsteps were approaching behind him at a run. The one who finally caught up with him was a man armed with a Glock. Kalen hid in the low hanging branches of a tree. He waited. As the assassin approached, he launched down feet first, knocking the weapon from the killer's grip. It fell into the undergrowth, but the assassin quickly drew out a knife. Kalen unfurled into a standing position, they began to circle one another.

Despite his own reflexes and speed, his opponent managed to get a shot in at Kalen's face, slicing his cheek open beneath the eye. Kalen had to think fast; blood was pouring out of the wound, blurring his vision. All he had on him was the key to his front door but it was small, which meant he'd have to be incredibly close for it to be of any use. He took it from his pocket anyway. Strength wouldn't be on his side, so he had to try to use his youth and speed to his advantage. If the assassin caught him again, Kalen knew it would be the end.

The assassin's eyes glittered as he slashed out at Kalen.

Kalen batted the arm away and got in a punch of his own. A side kick came at him next, almost clipping his shoulder, but Kalen grabbed hold of the leg and flipped his attacker to the ground. Like a spring, the man whipped back up. Kalen took his moment and got in close, slamming the key into his opponent's eye.

It didn't kill him, but the moment was all Kalen needed. The assassin screamed and fell backwards, the key hanging out of his mangled eye socket. Kalen began running once more.

He could hear the sound of others flooding the canopy of trees and knew his chances of escape were slim. Still, he refused to give up and shot out onto the main road in what would possibly be the final run of his life. Had he been out in the open for more than five minutes he'd have been shot or captured for certain, but something happened that Kalen never expected. A car pulled over.

Kalen held the knife he'd taken from the assassin and waited for the final fight of his life, but the man who got out of the car wasn't one of them, he was a civilian. In the dim lights of the street lamps Kalen could see the man was tall and red haired, with a mustache. He was squinting into the night, shading his eyes. He asked if Kalen was okay. Kalen slipped the blade under the cover of his shirt and breathed a sigh of relief.

Once close, the old man took one look at Kalen's bleeding face and gasped. 'Dear Lord what's happened to you? Son, do you speak English?' The man was British and well spoken.

'Yes, sir, I do,' Kalen spoke with his own American accent, not thinking straight enough to fake it.

'Here, let's get you in the car.'

Inside the car the man offered to take him to a hospital. Kalen refused. The Good Samaritan thought this over, the edges of his mouth turned down as if he knew he was doing something very wrong. Eventually he nodded in agreement.

'Whatever you've done, lad, it's not worth such a young

boy's life. What can I do for you?'

'Sir, I just need somewhere to stay the night, if that's okay?'

He thought it over. 'I can manage that. Though, I'd prefer it if my girls didn't know you were at the house.'

'Sure. How old are they?'

'Twenty-two and thirteen.'

'What are they like?'

'Here, hold this towel against your face to stop the bleeding, we'll be back at our holiday house soon, are you sure you don't want a doctor?'

K didn't answer, but he took the towel and pressed it against his slashed cheek, trying to push the protruding flap of skin back where it belonged. The man saw him flinch and sped up. Kalen couldn't help wondering at the man saving his life, with no explanation and apparently no fear. Few people ever impressed Kalen, yet here he was feeling a wave of admiration for a man he'd only just met.

'My eldest daughter you won't have to worry about,' the man said eventually. 'She's always at the beach or by the pool. She wouldn't notice a stranger in our house if you danced around her with a cat on your head.'

Kalen felt the corner of his mouth twitch upwards at the thought. It was a bizarre thing for the man to say.

'Ronnie, however – that's my littlest – she's another story. Very inquisitive and smart, if she hears a noise, she'll investigate.'

'I'll be quiet as a mouse, sir.'

'Okay, now here we are. It's on a complex, but as it's so late it's unlikely we'll see anyone.'

Kalen stared at row upon row of white houses separated by iron gates and swimming pools. It was even more impressive that a person who had so much could be so gracious. He hadn't experienced this before.

'Can I ask your name?' asked K.

'Can I ask yours?'

'You can. I may not tell you the truth.'

'Okay, I appreciate your candor. What can I call you then?'

There was a long pause. 'Kal. You can call me Kal.'

'Okay, Kal. Thank you. I'm William – William Rose.'

'Mr Rose, thank you for what you've done tonight, I'm fortunate you were out so late.'

The man coughed awkwardly. 'I, yes, I just like to get out of the house every now and then, I'm never gone long.'

The garage opened by remote mechanism and the jeep drove smoothly inside. Kal peered over his shoulder as the door automatically closing after them, but already knew they hadn't been followed.

Kalen walked into the warm family home, holding the towel tightly to his face so blood didn't drip on the marble floor. He found the bathroom and headed inside. A moment later there was a light knock on the door. Kalen pulled it open.

'Here,' William handed him a first-aid kit, a pile of cotton wool and a bottle of Jack Daniels.

'I can help, if you like?'

'No, I can manage. Thank you.'

The door closed and Kalen lifted the towel away and looked at his reflection. The wound was deep, but it would heal, though his stomach was churning and his vision beginning to blur.

'Screw it,' he whispered to his reflection as he removed the lid on the bottle of Jack Daniels. He swallowed two mouthfuls and then, after a few deep breaths, began to stitch his own face.

When he was finished he cleaned the bathroom scrupulously and slipped out towards the room where he was to spend the night. He had to creep past the youngest daughter, asleep on the couch. He stopped as he saw her, unable to keep walking. She was sleeping soundly, a mass of long red hair fanned out across the pillow and a small smile touching her pink lips. He stood transfixed, in awe of the angelic beauty in front of him. He wondered what she was dreaming about.

He was about to reach out, compelled to touch her face, when a large hand locked around his arm. William stared back at him.

'I'll be sleeping with one eye open, boy. I'm giving you the benefit of the doubt tonight, but if you hurt a hair on the heads of either of my girls, you won't live to tell the tale.'

'You can trust me, sir. All I want is to get some rest. I'll be out of your hair at first light.'

'Fine. Now let's get you in that room before she wakes up and we're both blown.'

With one glance back at the sleeping beauty Kalen went to the room he had been assigned and caught up on some much needed – albeit, broken – sleep.

37 — ASTOUNDING THE SPY

KALEN WAS STARING DOWN AT ME WHEN I WOKE UP.

'Morning.' His dimples jumped out happily with his smile.

'Morning,' I agreed.

'So, do you have to work today?'

'I do,' I groaned at the thought.

'Can I help you wake up?'

His grin was dangerous. I was more nervous than last night. In the daylight I was starkly aware of my naked body, my bed hair and a need to brush my teeth. He took my silence as a yes, however, and I was grateful because he pulled me under the sheets before my embarrassment could do any damage. His lips pressed against my neck and shoulders, tenderly at first and then more urgently. His large hands gripped me as though he was afraid I'd vanish if he let go. Within minutes I was completely at ease again and entirely overwhelmed.

'I've never been this happy,' he whispered in my ear. I felt my face break into the biggest smile, until I saw the clock hanging on my wall. If I was late for work after taking so much time off, I was sure to lose my job. I sat up, hesitating before I threw back the covers.

'Can you close your eyes?'

'You're kidding?' he scoffed.

'No! Please, Kal, just do it.'

'Okay, okay,' he held up his hands in defeat and pulled a pillow over his face. I wrapped my fluffy robe around me, making a mental note to buy a sexier one on the weekend, and rushed to the bathroom.

In the shower I couldn't stop grinning. I smiled into the water as it rushed over my face and closed my eyes to scenes replaying in my mind. I had expected my first time to be awkward and painful, but it had been neither. Well, maybe a little painful, but Kalen had been so careful with me, it had felt completely natural. I would have laughed out loud had he not been in the next room. I showered quickly, conscious of the time. Thankfully, when I emerged he was already in his jeans. Just his torso was naked. I swallowed.

'I'll drop you there,' he said as he stared at me. 'Do you have any idea how beautiful you are? Your hair, that mouth–'

'Are you sure you're well enough to be out and about?' I interrupted, feeling my cheeks flush.

'I've been well enough for days. I'm just dragging out our time together.'

'Oh. So, you're going back to the mansion?'

'I guess I should go see the boys, but I'll come back tonight if that's okay?' Then he said, 'Although, maybe you need some time?'

'Time for what?' I hadn't washed my hair, so I was pulling it up into a knot on top of my head and grabbing my blazer while he spoke.

'Time to tell Adam – that you're no longer seeing him,' he faltered, but he kept his eyes on me and I knew he was trying to work out what I was thinking. Truth was, I wanted to laugh – I had completely forgotten the reason behind the argument that had finally brought us together.

'Oh, right. Yeah, I don't really need any time.' I pretended to fluff my hair in the mirror and applied lip-gloss to drag out the moment. From the corner of my eye I could see his expression harden, as I expected, and he looked deadly serious as he held his chin up proudly.

'Are you going to end it with him?'

Unable to hold it in any longer, I began to laugh. I knew I was being mean.

'Sorry,' I said quickly, when his eyes grew dark. 'I don't need time, Kalen,' I walked up to him and slid my arms around his waist, suddenly feeling more confident in my own skin than ever before, 'because I broke it off with him nearly two weeks ago.'

It's not often you get to astound a spy, so I was mighty pleased with myself when his face betrayed the shock he felt.

'You didn't tell me.' His expression melted into the smile of the sweet boy I was in love with.

'No, I didn't. Now, do you want to get me in trouble at work, or can you drop me off now? I have ten minutes to get there.'

'I only need five,' he grinned, and with that he took my hand tightly in his and we left the house.

I arrived at work with six minutes to spare. Turned out, he only needed four.

***

I took all my calls in a trance, replaying the last twenty-four hours of my life over in my mind. I heard nothing Alexandra said to me and eventually she slapped my hand with her ruler and told me to snap out of it. Staring at my computer screen, I began flagging emails that needed my attention. Then I created a to-do-list with Post-its, sticking them across my monitor and desk. It was futile. I could think of nothing else but Kalen; his strong arms, the small of his back. Each perfectly defined muscle and the feel of his body close to mine. My cheeks began to burn with the thought and I glanced around to see if anyone had noticed.

The third time I scanned the room I caught Alexandra's glum expression. I'd been too wrapped up in my own thoughts to see she was quiet and unlike her usual self.

'Hey, lovely, what's up with you today?'

She looked at me, her eyes glassy, then her attention flicked towards another part of the room. I followed her gaze and saw Damien speaking with the new administration temp. She was blonde and pretty enough, though she had nothing on Alexandra. But from the way Damien was leaning in, hanging on her every word, it didn't take me long to figure out what was going on.

I looked back at my friend. *'Loser,'* I mouthed.

She nodded and continued typing. I'd never seen her so subdued. I stared back angrily at the flirtatious couple. If nothing else, Damien was a manger and should have known better. I wished I could think of some awesome quip to call out to him, but I came up blank. Instead I whispered to Alexandra, 'Want to go out later?'

She gave me a small smile, but shook her head. 'It's okay. I just want to chill out and eat ice cream.'

I sat back on my chair and tried to think. I wanted more than anything to rush straight home after work in the hope Kalen would be there, but my newest friend had quickly become my closest. I didn't know what I would have done without her when Kal left. I wanted to be there for her.

'We're going out,' I insisted. 'You can drive us to mine after work so I can grab some things and then we'll go and change at yours.'

With a glance back in Damien's direction, Alexandra finally tipped her head. 'Thanks, babe.'

'No problem.'

My only slight problem was that I couldn't contact Kalen to tell him I was going out, but I couldn't do anything about that.

'So what's going on?' I asked as we drove to her apartment.

'He's a prat!' she said flippantly, suddenly back to the fiery girl I was used to. 'He told me last night we couldn't see each other any more. Tells me it's because people at work are beginning to notice and all that crap. Pretends he's really upset, blah, blah, blah. Then today he starts flirting outrageously with that Tanya chick. The guy's a prat.'

'You're right. He is. I'm so sorry, Al.'

She clicked her tongue and pouted her red lips in the rearview mirror as if checking her lipstick was still in place. 'Don't be. He's just a guy. I didn't even care that much, but I guess I just think – ergh! It's so annoying. He isn't even that good looking and he chased me and chased me. It's always the same. This stupid small-town mentality. He was the best of a bad bunch and so I let my guard down and now he's screwed me over. Prat.'

After her rant, and an extended silence, we both got the giggles.

'So, is Diana going to come out with us?' I said when we finally stopped laughing.

'Babe, I really don't want to go out tonight. I'm not wallowing, I promise. I just know what I'm like. I'll rebound on the first guy I see, and that's not what I need right now.'

'Okay,' I said, seeing her point. 'You wanna just hang out at yours then? Drink some wine?'

'I'd love that. I'll stop and get some Ben & Jerry's too. Chunky Monkey?'

'Phish Food.'

'Both.'

We laughed again.

Two tubs of ice cream later and Alexandra fell asleep on the sofa. I said goodbye to Diana and caught a taxi home. I was completely exhausted and wishing Kalen had a phone so I could call him. As I walked into my bedroom and kicked off my shoes, however, he was already lying back on my bed, one foot folded over the other, a book in his hands. My bed had never looked so inviting. I resisted the urge to run to him. I held up my index finger to let him know I needed a minute, then went to my bathroom to brush my teeth and change into my pyjamas.

He welcomed me into my bed silently and I slipped into the nook between his arm and chest. It was my very own slice of heaven.

'You're late tonight,' he whispered into my hair.

'You should have a phone,' I pointed out. When he didn't respond I said, 'I had a lousy day.'

'Wanna tell me about it?'

'The guy Alexandra was seeing at work broke it off with her. He's flirting with another girl in the office. It was harsh. I felt really sorry for her.'

He didn't reply, but he wrapped his arms tighter around me and kissed the back of my neck. Very swiftly, my day drifted away from me.

It felt as though we'd been sleeping for hours when he woke up suddenly, sitting bolt upright and holding his chest as though someone had driven a sword through it.

'Kal?' I whispered. 'Are you okay?'

He nodded.

'Bad dreams?'

'Hideous nightmares,' he muttered.

The look of sadness on his face caught me off guard, so that I almost couldn't breathe.

'Here,' I said, fluffing the pillows behind me so I could sit up and make room for him in my arms for once. Hesitantly, he laid his head on me.

Determined to keep his nightmares at bay, I stayed awake for the rest of the night while he slept. Finally, when the sound of birds singing alerted me to the proximity of daylight, I let my eyes close.

Clanots Ocean – March 2010

'Stop!'

They were re-grouping. Men who he'd taken down were slowly getting to their feet. The leader – whom he'd heard called Joe – held his gaze, standing behind Ronnie's unconscious body.

'You don't get to call timeout, boy.'

'I'll stop fighting,' Kalen responded blackly.

The man pulled his black balaclava from his head. Kalen recognised him instantly – he'd broken his nose in the pub. Black and purple bruises still hung under his eyes.

'I'll let you take me now. Just call an ambulance so they can help her.'

They all started laughing. Joe turned back to smile at his comrades. 'Is this guy for real?' he asked them, before looking at Kalen once more. 'That's not how this works–'

'She'll be missed,' Kalen interrupted. 'She's well liked in this town and you know the police won't let it drop. Nobody will miss me and I'm the one you want anyway. Let her go and I'll let you tie me up and take me where you want.'

The men laughed again, a spiteful sound that Kalen wanted to make them choke on, but the leader wasn't laughing and Kalen knew he had his full attention. His dark brown eyes narrowed as he considered Kalen's offer.

'Take her down to the beach, boys, leave her where she'll be found,' Joe said, without taking his eyes from Kalen. 'And get the van for this one.'

'That's not the deal. She needs medical help,' said Kalen.

'It's the only deal you're gonna get. Take it or leave it.'

Gritting his teeth, Kalen nodded, watching the men pick up Ronnie's tiny body and carry her across the road to a grassy bank beside the beach.

'I'm gonna enjoy this,' said Joe, rubbing his jaw between his thumb and forefinger.

Without comment, Kalen stepped forward and held out his hands.

38 — LAITH

KALEN HAD FORCED ME TO GO BACK TO SCHOOL, which I didn't find fair, seeing as he didn't have to go, but he'd told me rather cockily that he already knew everything. Somehow, I found it impossible to argue. In return, he agreed to let me watch him and the boys train later in the evening. It was the only thing getting me through the day. Mae had barely acknowledged me in registration and even though we sat together in French she found a way to ignore me. Exams were in three weeks and we were going over old ground – purely revision. I knew Mae would ace the tests; she and I had got straight As all year. Still, she kept her head down, scribbling furiously as though she was too busy to even look in my direction.

'Mae,' the word caught in my throat. Painful tears burned behind my eyes. I wasn't sure what to say. I'd been about to apologise, but what was I sorry for? That she didn't like my boyfriend? As far as I knew, she no longer wanted our friendship and I wasn't sure what I could have done that was bad enough to deserve how she had cut me off. The bell rang before I could think of something to say. She scooted out of her seat.

'Ron, sorry, I've got to go meet the girls. Let's catch up this weekend, yeah? If you're not too busy with your new boyfriend of course.'

With that, she hurried from the room. I sat where I was until the last student had left. Mae had visited me while I was in hospital, but I knew it was everything she could do to keep from telling me *'I told you so.'* Now, if it were possible, we were drifting further apart than ever.

Slowly, I packed up my things and headed out to where I knew Kal would be waiting. He was leaning on the bonnet of his car, his eyes hidden by sunglasses. From the smile he was trying to suppress, I sensed he was more than comfortable in his new civilian skin, especially as he seemed to command an audience. I ignored the stares of students milling around, but it didn't mean I wasn't aware of them. I walked up to him and tiptoed into a kiss. He responded by pulling me closer, lacing his fingers through my hair.

'Hello to you too,' he said when we parted, stepping to my side of the car and opening the door.

Leaving my problems at the gate, I slipped inside. It was a relief to drive out of the school grounds. Kalen let go of my hand to change into fifth gear then slid his fingers back through mine. The familiar fields that surrounded Clanots Ocean flew past as we drove to the mansion. I wound down the window. Though it was only April, we were experiencing a fluke summer's day, the perfect blue sky broken only by a few scattered cotton-ball clouds. It was twenty-two degrees and I had on my favourite frayed denim shorts and a white lace smock. Kalen was wearing his jeans and a short-sleeved fitted tee and, for once, a bright unaffected smile.

'What's it going to be like?' I asked, focusing on what I was about to witness.

Kalen laughed and gunned the accelerator. I didn't have a problem with how fast he drove anymore, if anything I kind of liked it.

'Like I mentioned this morning,' he said, 'we all get a bit antsy sometimes. Stuck indoors, no weapons, no missions. Though I'm glad to be free of the latter, I still crave the training.'

'So you guys set up your own courses now, your own training?'

'Well, it's not really training any more. It's like – exercise.'

I was about to watch them doing some of what they did best. Kal said it was the first time any of them would have trained in front of a civilian. By all accounts the boys were quite revved up.

'Before we go in,' he said as we headed up the winding driveway, 'I have two things to give you. Well, one's for me actually. Please don't make a fuss, they're both very small.'

'What? Like *presents*?'

'Yes – well, one part's a gift, but it's no big deal.'

'Why have you got me a present?'

'Ronnie, you're making this very difficult,' he frowned. 'Do you have to ask so many questions?'

'Sorry.' I gestured with my hand as if I were locking my mouth and throwing away the key.

He held out a clenched fist in front of my face and as he opened his hand a silver heart dropped down from a delicate chain.

'Happy belated Birthday.'

I gasped, but quickly held back any inclination to gush – as instructed.

'Open it,' he said. It glittered in front of me.

I took it in my palm and popped the tiny clasp. It sprung open to reveal a picture of Dad and me when I was five. The photo had been one of many in our living room; he must have taken it and had it re-sized. It was the most thoughtful present I had ever been given. It was lucky he didn't want me to make a fuss, because I was lost for words. Taking it from me, he swiped my hair up and gently fastened the chain around my neck.

'You still have one left and this you're going to like,' he quickly drew my attention away from the necklace, when from his inside pocket he withdrew a small mobile phone. My jaw dropped.

'Only you will have the number and it's for text messages only.' He tossed it to me and got out of the car before I could speak. Through the window he beckoned me with his index finger and a crooked smile.

I scuttled out and stood beside him.

'Thank you so much,' I said seriously.

'The second half of the gift was long overdue. I apologise for that. You should be able to contact me whenever you need to.'

He slid one arm around my waist, leading us through the back garden. The boys were already waiting. A pile of rope, tires and some equipment I didn't have the first idea about, sat in the middle of the lawn.

Very quickly, they began and I watched in awe as they interacted with each other. More than friends, more than brothers even; like one person split into five parts. Watching them play fighting was like watching a pack of lions: fast, beautiful... lethal. One wrong move and any of them could have been killed.

Through it all they laughed. Insults were thrown around for bad form or less-than-amazing performance and somehow I was the judge. Even Laith seemed to get a kick out of having someone impartial watch them. I lapped it up, crowning Laith the champion of climbing. He'd scaled the side of the mansion faster than any of the others; although I thought there was nothing to grip on to, they all scurried up like spider monkeys. He was more than happy until Kal received the same title for knife throwing. Laith actually threw his last knife in Kal's direction with such force that I screamed, but Kal caught it with ease and, with a genuine laugh, branded his friend a bad loser. Laith stalked off to his room.

'Shall we have some lunch?' I asked quickly. Everyone agreed, wanting – as I did – the awkward moment to pass.

Inside, Laith joined us again, his eyes fixed on the mobile phone I'd left lying on the counter. I cringed. Kal hadn't asked me to keep it a secret, but while I'd had enough sense not to mention it, I didn't have enough sense to hide it.

'Whose is this?' Laith asked, holding it up.

'Mine,' I lied.

He lifted one white-blond eyebrow with a look that cut through my façade and made my cheeks burn. I couldn't lie to any of them even if I wanted to.

Kalen interjected immediately. 'It's mine,' he said, looking directly at his teammate.

Laith instantly looked appalled. 'Why do you have a phone?'

The boys glanced between one another.

'I have one so Ronnie can contact me, Laith. You have a problem with that?' The question was directed at everyone in the room. He'd obviously broken their pact, but I knew he wouldn't apologise, so it was a standoff. Eventually, Laith shook his head and stalked out.

'It's just for Ronnie,' Kal explained to the others.

'Leave him,' said Nash. 'We'll go sit outside. He'll come to us when he's bored.'

We made a batch of ham and cheese sandwiches and headed back out. Eventually, as Nash predicted, Laith joined us – at a distance. He began throwing knives at a nearby tree, just as they'd been doing earlier.

Nash was retelling a story of when he first visited Thailand. He didn't mention anything about the job he had been sent on, but he did recall it was his favourite country.

'You can just be yourself, you know? Hell, you can be anyone you like in Thailand and nobody cares. Awesome place, seriously.'

The sound was like the humming of a bee or a tiny mosquito too close to my ear, follwed by a thump. Had it not been for the look on the faces of Kal and Denver, I might not have reacted to it. Their expressions caused me to turn to my right. Directly in front of my eyes, an inch or so from my nose was a long shiny throwing knife embedded into the tree I was leaning against. I jumped away in fright. A delayed reaction, but the only one appropriate when finding someone has thrown a knife at your head. I looked over at Laith who was staring back, his face void of any emotion.

'Laith!' roared Kal, jumping up from the rock he'd been perched on and stepping in front of me. 'What the hell are you doing?'

'Chill out, mate, I was just playing,' Laith had continued to use a British accent despite the fact that I knew about them. It was unsettling.

'It's not funny, you could have killed her.'

'Only if I'd wanted to,' he responded, his eyes narrowing.

'K, leave it,' Denver warned from where he sat. Though clearly as shocked as the rest of us, I could tell he was trying to prevent a blowout. 'It's not worth it.'

'What if he'd missed, D, huh? What then?'

'He wouldn't have missed man, you know that.'

Kal opened him mouth to yell something towards Laith, but seemed to think better of it. Instead he walked to me, taking my face in his hands.

'Are you okay?'

I nodded.

'I'm taking you home,' he said, looking back over his shoulder towards Laith. But Laith had already turned away. I watched as Kal fought with himself, pulled between his relationship with his friend and me.

I waved goodbye to Ace, Nash and Denver, who all wore matching expressions of guilt for Laith's behaviour. Ace more than any of them looked desperate to say something to make it better. I smiled at him and then Kalen took my hand and led me down towards the driveway.

Before we got in the car, I glanced over in Laith's direction. He was throwing knives at the tree again and though he had his back to me, I felt he knew I was watching. He threw each knife with perfect precision, lined up at exactly the same height only a centimeter apart. But before I looked away one of the knives slipped, its handle hit the bark and it fell clumsily to the ground.

I gulped and slid into my seat. I didn't look back again; I wouldn't give Laith the satisfaction.

Gaza Strip — June 2005

'Mineral.'

'Is it man-made?'

'Yup.'

'Does it have a purpose?'

'Yes.'

'Is it bigger than a tank?'

'No.'

'Is it smaller than a tank?'

'No.'

'Is it a tank?'

'Yeah.' Laith stared out in front of them at the dusty street. His muscles aching from the fever he'd only just recovered from.

'You know, you could try to make this more interesting.'

'Why?'

'I dunno, man – why not?' K couldn't be bothered to play

274

either, but it seemed better than sitting and waiting in silence, and a lot less conspicuous. 'You pick the first thing you see, you make the game more boring than necessary.'

'I'm sick, I can't deal with this shit.'

'I thought you didn't get sick?'

'Well, obviously this hideous country has worn me down. How long have we been here now?'

'Five weeks, four days and,' Kalen glanced at his watch, 'fourteen hours.'

Laith made a hmmm sound and toyed with the brim of his cap, pulling it down over his eyes to prevent glare from the sun that seemed to come from every direction, even bouncing up off of the sidewalk. 'I'm so sick of this heat,' he muttered.

'Please stop complaining, we don't have much longer.'

'What if we die out here? Our bodies will rot in this godless country for ever.'

'It's not godless, dude.'

'I'm telling you, man, this country is devoid of God. Look around us – killing is all they know. '

'Yeah, and what more do we know?'

'Hey,' Laith said with a serious tone 'we fight evil! We're like, superheroes or something, we only kill the bad guys.'

K gave a short, mirthless laugh. 'Whatever helps you sleep at night, L.'

'Hello you two, where is your father today?' the voice of the café owner sounded from behind them in broken English. The boys both turned in their seats to look at him.

'He's teaching at the university,' K replied amiably.

'Ah, you tell him next time, I have some fresh pastries for him. Okay?'

'Thank you, Isaac.'

The man walked back to his kitchen and they were by themselves again.

275

K took a sip of the tea that had gone cold in front of him. 'You know, it doesn't matter where we die; here, back home, what difference will it make? The things we've done, we'll all end up in the same damned place anyhow.'

Laith didn't reply and they both stared out at the sand-swept sidewalks, waiting for the call that would send them on their way to kill.

39 — TOO COMFORTABLE

THE RAIN WOKE ME WITH A START. It pounded my window and the deck outside. Usually I liked the sound; being inside my warm house while the weather went crazy around it. But right now I had a strange feeling – something in the house didn't feel right. I thought about calling Kalen, just to hear his voice, but stopped myself. After Laith's outburst he'd dropped me home and I could tell he was furious. I figured they probably needed some time alone without me bothering them. I looked at the clock – seven a.m.

I got out of bed and walked down the hall to Rachel's old room to check if she'd stayed the night. It was empty and the bed was made. No big surprise there. My stomach was growling so I pulled on my dressing gown and made my way down to the kitchen, peering into each room I passed. I'd never felt unsafe in my house, it was big and kind of in the middle of nowhere, but I'd always felt secure. Right now, however, even though every room was empty, my uneasy feeling refused to go.

I glanced around my kitchen: everything was as it should be. Nothing out of place and no sound apart from the rain. Pulling at the fridge door, I took out a carton of milk. Drinking straight from it, I pictured Dad telling me to use a glass, like he always did. The memory was cut short by cool steel pressed against my temple, followed by a noise I'd heard in a thousand movies: a gun being cocked.

It was like all the air got sucked from the room. My body turned to sponge, threatening to collapse in on me. The carton dropped from my grasp. Milk leaked between my toes, across the floor.

'Don't scream,' said the owner of the gun, his voice eerily calm. 'Do you understand?'

I nodded carefully, momentarily remembering the alarm I'd been given – the alarm I'd chosen not to use, even though Kalen had asked me to.

'I'm not going to hurt you and I'm going to lower my weapon. Don't run and don't scream if you value your life. Nod if you comply.'

I tipped my head again, conscious of the gun and not wanting to give it a reason to go off. Slowly, the intruder stepped away from me. I blinked. My body was rigid with fear so I could barely move, but I steadied myself on the kitchen counter and forced myself to face him.

The man wasn't what I expected. He was older for a start, old enough to be my father and smartly dressed: he wore jeans and a suit jacket – and leather gloves. I wasn't happy about the gloves, that part was more disconcerting than anything, perhaps even more than the gun. I met his blue eyes and tried to think of what Kalen would tell me to do.

'Who are you and what do you want?' I asked, trying unsuccessfully to hold my voice steady.

'You can call me Andrews.' He slid the gun inside his jacket and I found myself eyeing the block of knives on the counter.

'Please don't even think about it, Veronica. Just listen and I'll be out of your life very quickly.'

'What do you want?'

'Kalen,' he said simply.

I regarded him contemptuously. 'Is that a name? It's stupid,'

I answered.

'Don't play games with me, child, there isn't time. Just hear me out. I know K, tell him Andrews was here and he won't be angry with you for talking to me. I'm fond of him. More than you can imagine. It was because of me that he escaped, but he should not have taken the others, it's caused untold problems. If K hands over those he's still in contact with, his life will be spared.'

I pictured Ace being led by the person he loved most, into the hands of people who wanted him dead. It made me want to gag. I had a strong desire to hit the man giving me such an option, but I wasn't that foolish. I waited, hoping he had nothing else to say. I had never really hated anyone before, until today.

'I don't know who or what you're talking about, you sound crazy to me.'

'Ms Rose, while I understand your loyalty, I don't care for it. Just know this. I've been here long enough to know that K is here because of you. I believe in his own warped way, he thinks he loves you and now you have the chance to save his life. Don't you want that?'

I swallowed as something very sinister came into my mind. I had been so blind not to see it before. 'You!' I blurted. 'You've been following me. I've seen your car – you've been watching me for months!'

He stared back at my blackly. 'I needed to know what you meant to him. Kalen won't talk to me, he won't entertain anything I have to say. If he gets even the slightest inkling I'm here, he'll flee. I had no idea this opportunity would present itself with you, but it has. Convince him to turn himself in, Veronica, because I believe there's no one else who can. He must do this to save his life, and the lives of the others must be the forfeit. Don't delude yourself – these boys do not have any bond save that of habit. They have not been brought up to care about one another, only the mission. His loyalty to them will only be his own pride; he hates to fail. You must convince him otherwise.'

I swallowed. I had to be careful not to say too much. 'You don't think he cares for his friends?' I asked.

'They are not friends, they don't know the meaning of the word. They're a unit.'

'So, you don't think he cares about his unit?'

The man sighed impatiently. 'He doesn't care about anything. He can't.'

'But, you just said you thought he loved me. Bit of a contradiction, don't you think?'

Andrews scowled, inhaling a deep breath through his nose. It was a good ten seconds before he spoke again and tiny beads of sweat were beginning to form all over my body.

'I can't comment on his feelings for you, or the selfishness of his infatuation. It's not my concern. But I will tell you one thing before I leave: those boys are not soldiers – they're killers. They're dangerous, Veronica, and you are putting yourself and everyone you love in grave danger, not to mention breaking the law, by harbouring them. If you don't care about that, then consider this: out in the world on their own, they have no means by which to fight the US government. They will all die. It is up to you to decide if we can at least save one of them – the one we both care for the most. Think it over.'

He turned away from me and walked towards my front door, dropping a card on the counter as he passed. It was blank apart from a hand written telephone number. I stared after him.

'Five are already terminated,' he called over his shoulder, 'there are only eleven left. You have the chance to save one of them.'

Then he was gone. The door slammed behind him, echoing his departing words.

40 — CONFRONTATION

I RAN UPSTAIRS FOR MY PHONE. My heart was thundering, my hands shaking, but I hesitated. Andrews had said if I told Kalen he was here, he would run again, but I didn't think that was the case. Not now. Now, he would probably try to stay with me and because of that, he could end up dying. I didn't know what to do for the best. I had to tell him something, I had to get him away from here and as far away from Andrews and The Agency as possible. I typed out a text.

Need to talk. Pick me up from school at 4?

I needed to get my head straight. It seemed Andrews didn't want to hurt Kal. He had given me time to speak with him so at the very least I had a few hours to figure out what to do.

At school, I played out scenarios in my head. If I told Kal about Andrews, I knew he wouldn't turn his friends in, but it might make him leave. But more likely, it might not, and once again he'd be endangering his own life and the lives of the boys just to be with me.

I thought about calling Alexandra, but telling her would put her in danger and that was the last thing I wanted. My mind formed two conclusions: I could tell him the truth and let him decide what to do, or I tell him nothing except that I want him to leave town. The second option broke my heart, but would mean Kalen would be safe. Away from Andrews and whoever was hunting him. The more I thought about it, the more I could see no other way. If I loved him enough, I wouldn't want him to risk getting caught so we could be together. It was everything I could do not to throw up at the thought.

'Veronica?'

Ms Jones –or Ruby, as I was now permitted to call her – was staring at me. I glanced around and saw the rest of the class was, too.

I gulped. 'Can you repeat the question?'

As if to save me, the bell rang. Everyone rose from their seats and headed to the door. I took my chance and pushed my way through the crowd. Ruby called after me, but I ignored her.

Kal was waiting in the Audi as I jogged through the front gates, but his face wasn't light as it had been yesterday. His expression was serious – urgent. I slid into the front seat and we pulled away quickly. I tried my best to appear nonchalant, but he could tell something was up. I felt his concerned expression flicking between the road and me, but he didn't ask what was wrong and I had a full ten minutes to continuously change my mind as to my course of action.

As we arrived at my house, I groaned. We were faced with a new problem. The dark blue Mazda in front of the house told me Jared had come to visit.

Silently we walked indoors. Jared greeted me with a hug.

'I just called round to talk to you about this house nonsense.' He looked at Kal. 'Do you mind giving us some space?'

Kalen looked at me and I nodded.

'I'll be in the kitchen.' He walked from the room, with Jared's eyes following him. Then Jared turned to me.

'I know you've spoken to Rachel about keeping the house, but I think that's a bad idea. You and her are too close to this, you need me to take the reins.'

'Can we talk about this another time, Jar?'

His eyes narrowed. 'This is exactly my point. You have your priorities all wrong. We'll talk about it now.'

I sighed, sitting down on the sofa. 'Fine. Well, I'm not ready to give up so easily. I think it's a great chance for all of us to have something that will be worth a lot one day. If we sell it now, in this tough market, we won't make anything and everything Dad worked for will have gone to waste. Please, let's just try it for a year or so. I can pay for more than half of the mortgage repayments using my wages, I just can't borrow the money is all. I just need your help.'

Jared remained standing, so he was looking down at me. 'Ronnie, you're talking like a child! I know you love this house, but you need to think realistically.'

'I am thinking realistically, where will I live? You're telling me to sell my home!'

'You know you can live with us. You can look after Cloud while we're at work, which would pay for your rent.'

Was I hearing correctly? He wanted me to sell my father's house and move into their tiny flat so I could be their nanny?

'I'm not asking you for anything. With Rachel's job she can borrow the money by herself. This is her decision too,' I pointed out proudly, in an attempt to disguise my hurt feelings. 'You can't force us to sell it.'

'Actually, I've spoken to Rachel and she wants what I want. The sooner we can put all this business behind us the better. Without her, you don't have a choice Ronnie, so I suggest you stop fighting this. I'll have some paperwork for you to sign in the next couple of days.'

What felt like a fever swelled through my body, hot tears sprang to my eyes. 'No please! I might be able to raise the money, perhaps Mae's parents will help me get a loan.'

Jared shook his head and turned to leave. I pushed myself up and ran in front of him.

'Rachel loves this house! I know this isn't really her decision. You can't do this! Daddy worked hard–'

Jared's eyes blazed. 'Oh, for crying out loud! I'm sorry to be the one to point this out Ronnie, but your father is the reason you're both in this mess!'

Whether it was Jared's voice raising or the mention of my father, Kalen stepped into the hallway from the kitchen and leaned against the doorframe. He stared at Jared.

'Jar,' I said calmly, hoping my serenity would carry itself to Kalen, 'Please, let's talk about this with Rachel here too.'

'Rachel has enough to deal with. I'm taking charge. We're selling the house and you and Rachel will each get half of whatever profit is made.'

I opened my mouth to tell him there wouldn't be any profit, but it was too late. Kal was in front of me and my heart sank even further.

'This is none of your business, boy,' Jared spat.

'Kal, I'm fine,' I said quickly.

'No, Ronnie, you're not.' Kal's voice, thick and deep, burned with anger. 'Jared, if I may make a suggestion. How about, you back off and stop trying to intimidate my girlfriend, and I won't throw you through the window.'

I watched Jared's eyes widen in disgust. He would never have been spoken to in such a way before, especially not by someone he considered a child. I could feel the atmosphere closing in around me.

'It's Kalen, right?'

Kal's lip curled in response.

'Well, *Kalen*, don't you dare threaten me! I'm not scared of you.'

'Perhaps,' Kalen said, stepping forward so they were toe to toe, 'you should rethink your stance there.'

'Please don't!' I wailed, suddenly terrified. I knew nothing would happen to Kal, but I didn't want him to hurt Jared. Through all his faults, I had no doubt he was just trying to look out for my sister and I couldn't hate him for that. They ignored me, continuing to stare each other down.

Eventually, Jared stepped back, glaring at us both before turning and heading for the door. Tears stung my eyes. I didn't want any of this. It was too hard to think of my family hating me. I just wanted to make it better and I opened my mouth to tell him so, but Kalen cut me off.

'Jared.'

Holding the front door open, Jared looked back.

'Ronnie loves her sister and for some reason she loves you. I understand that she has a small family and she cares deeply about that, but I want you to know the only reason you are still able to walk, is because she wishes it so.'

Jared stood frozen, a look of pure shock written across his long face. With a final grimace in my direction, he walked out.

As the door closed behind him, I broke down.

'That was so stupid! How are you and I ever going to work if you talk to my family like that?' I yelled, storming into the living room.

He followed me. 'You can't be serious? We won't work if I can't get on with *him*?'

'Kalen, it's my family and I'll handle it my way!' I actually had no idea what I meant. All I knew was that I once held my family together and now it felt as if I were driving it apart.

'Family,' he muttered.

Kalen had no family, how could I ever expect him to understand? 'How would you feel if I didn't get on with any of your friends?' I said.

'Nothing and no one could ever change the way I feel about you.'

I swallowed back a moan. 'You left once.'

'I left because–' he stopped himself, his eyes narrowing. 'It's different now. I can't – I won't let anyone talk to you that way. You deserve so much better. I'm trying to take care of you.'

'I've managed to take care of my family and myself for the last six years without your help. In fact, I attracted a lot less trouble before you came along!' Instantly I regretted my words, but it was too late, they were out there.

'You're right,' he said, turning to stone in a millisecond. 'I apologise.'

'Kalen, that's not what I meant, please–'

'You'll always put your family before me. I suppose that's to be expected, though I won't pretend to understand it. All I want is you and I'd take down the whole world if it meant we could be together.'

'But we can't go around treating people badly just to get what we want, Kal. It's not right.'

He nodded and looked around, shoving his hands deep in his pockets. I knew he wanted to walk out, but I had called him out on doing that, so instead he was trying to decide what to do next. I had no idea either. Silence lingered.

'Kal, I need to tell you something–' I began, but that's when I heard it. It had taken Rachel less than ten minutes to arrive. The sound of her car pulling up, the door slamming and her key being erratically forced into the lock were as familiar to me as my own name.

Kalen glanced at the door. 'Shall I leave you to it?' he asked quietly.

I nodded, cringing as I waited for the front door to slam and the living room door to fly open. Both things seemed to happen simultaneously. Kalen had slipped through the back just in time.

'Where is he?' she wailed.

'Not here.'

'I heard he threatened Jared! This has gone on long enough, Ronnie. You're allowing him to split this family apart!'

'Rachel. Please don't do this. I'm not splitting anything apart, he's done nothing wrong, I know he yelled at Jar but Jar was yelling at me! Kal was just defending me.'

'Against Jared? Think about it, since when have you needed protecting from us, Ron?'

'Rachel, he's not a bad person, he's my boyfriend and I want us all to get along.' I pressed my fingers to my temples, to ease the pounding.

'I can't believe Daddy did this to us,' her voice softened and she perched on the edge of the sofa. Looking at her nails, her gaze never met mine. Rachel wasn't good at saying sorry. I pulled her so she slipped into the leather cushions beside me and wrapped my arms around her.

'It's going to be okay, Rach. I have my job, you have yours. We can keep our house, we just need to sort out some finances. We'll be okay.'

I watched as a tear ran down her cheek. It had been a long time since I'd seen her so upset.

'I promise you, it's going to be okay,' I repeated, tucking a strand of her silk blonde hair behind one ear.

'It's just so hard to believe he left us with nothing. I never knew. All that time and I never knew he had a gambling problem.'

'I didn't know either. He kept it from both of us.' I squeezed her tightly. 'We just have to stick together now. You and me.'

She whipped her head away from me and sat back with her arms folded across her chest.

I flinched. 'What's wrong now?'

'Sticking together doesn't seem to be an option for us any more, Ronnie. Not while you're seeing that hooligan boyfriend of yours. You have to choose.'

'Oh, come on, Rachel, don't be ridiculous!'

'Ridiculous? So you don't believe me or you just like murderers?' She was screaming now, suddenly hysterical again.

'Murderer? You're being melodramatic.' I began to panic. What did she know? Had Andrews been to visit her?

'You should have made the right choice on your own, Veronica. I didn't want to have to tell you this, but your thug boyfriend has killed four people!'

I sucked in a breath.

'Enough,' I said without looking at her. 'I can't listen to you any more. Sometimes I think I'm the adult and you're the child.'

Pushing her hair back from her face, she grabbed at the remote control, flicked on the television and found BBC News.

I forced myself to watch. A wave of nausea ripped through me. Rachel was muttering that she was sorry she had to be the one to tell me and I tried to block her out, reading the words running along the bottom of the screen.

FOUR MEN KILLED IN KITCHEN BLAZE

"A HOUSE FIRE, HAS TODAY CLAIMED THE LIVES OF FOUR MEN IN THEIR THIRTIES. THE VICTIMS WERE SAID TO BE PART OF AN INFAMOUS COWFORD GANG AND WERE WANTED FOR QUESTIONING IN A NUMBER OF GANG-RELATED INCIDENTS. NO FOUL PLAY IS SUSPECTED."

Photos of the victims filled the screen, like a silent alarm shattering my world.

'That's them, right? You told me who they were, the ones who jumped you and your boyfriend. They used to come to The Chasers Arms when I was younger. I remember them.'

'They were, killed – in a kitchen fire.' My eyes refused to look away. Pictures of the building in flames flashed up on the screen, burning into my soul.

'Oh, please, Veronica, open your eyes! The police may be foolish enough to believe that, but I don't believe in coincidences and from the look on your face neither do you.'

'Get out,' I managed, my voice a hoarse whisper.

'Ronnie, I'm sorry I had to be the one to–'

'GET OUT!' I heard myself scream, but I couldn't believe the sound came from inside me. I looked at my sister before she left. Despite her apology there was no sympathy in her eyes. I suppose I didn't deserve any, but I couldn't understand her smugness. Did my own sister really hate me that much?

41 — CONSEQUENCES

SLEEP REFUSED TO COME. I willed it at first, desperate for a few hours' peace, but after tossing and turning for what felt like an eternity I wrapped myself in an old sleeping bag and sat on a bench in the back garden. Even at night I could see the tall trees of the forest, adjacent to the rolling fields that seemed to go on for ever, only instead of being the usual shades of green, yellow and gold, they were covered in night's purple, blue and silver.

Kalen was ignoring my text messages, but I didn't know what to say to him even if he replied. What was I supposed to do now? The question weighted me down. I knew what Kalen was; it wasn't right, of that I was certain. He had killed people before – probably more than I was willing to believe – but did that mean he was guilty of what Rachel accused him? And if he were, if he really had gone back and murdered his captors in cold blood, could I still love him? I considered his past, telling myself that the people he had killed were bad people, dangerous people. His actions were just like those of anyone who joins the army, anyone who has to fight in a war. But I knew nothing of war. I'd never had to experience anything to make me question my morals or my soul. Until now.

I sighed as I wondered if Kalen had taken four lives in the

short time we had been apart. It was possible, and after what they did to him it should have been probable. Still, something didn't feel right. Kalen was better than that. I was sure of it.

I awoke to a squirrel foraging on the bench next to me. The sun had already risen. As I moved, the tiny animal scurried away. I'd fallen asleep. Cursing, I rushed to get ready and headed for the mansion. I owed Kalen a chance to explain and I still hadn't told him about Andrews.

But he wasn't there. None of them were. Ignoring my rising panic, I wandered back through town. *It didn't mean anything*, I told myself. They could all be out running. It didn't mean they'd left.

Eventually noticing my surroundings, I realised I'd gravitated to the alleyway where Kal had first dropped into my life. The same one where he'd shown me Clanots Ocean from the sky. In that moment a swell of emotion balled like a fist in my chest. A feeling I knew to be complete unconditional love for him.

Closing my eyes, I tried to tell myself that I wasn't a bad person, that *he* wasn't a bad person. Yet, at the back of my mind, my sister's voice grew louder. She'd warned me, more than once, and it was as if the truth of her words had been lost on me because of how I felt about him. But in the harsh light of day – in a blinding light I couldn't hide from, away from the dreaming and fantasy – I was dating a killer who had potentially killed as recently as yesterday in a fit of rage.

I sank to the ground and sat among the rubbish. I felt as though I belonged there.

***

'Where have you been?' Kal asked when I arrived home some three hours later to find he was already there. 'I got a phone so we could keep in contact and you don't even take yours out with you?'

I discarded my bag on the kitchen counter. 'I thought you were mad at me?' I pointed out. 'You didn't answer my texts.'

He softened. 'I could never stay mad at you, Red. You're the only thing that makes me happy.'

I gazed at his kind sweet smile and my fears began to melt, but as I reached his eyes, I saw the one part of him that told me what I feared could be true. I looked away.

'How did you get in?' I asked, without caring about the answer.

'I broke in. Don't worry, everything's as it should be, no damage. Hey I have a gift for you.' He looked pleased with himself, his voice brimming with excitement, but his smile quickly faltered. 'Red, what's wrong?'

I searched his eyes for the truth, better yet, a magic spell that would take away any responsibility I felt for the deaths hanging over my head.

'Tell me what's happened,' he repeated with more authority.

'I found something out last night.'

'You're going somewhere with this?' His dark eyes penetrated mine. I wanted to ignore my feelings, to pretend everything was okay because of those eyes, yet it was exactly those eyes that told me I was far from okay.

'Kal, have you seen the news?'

'I have,' he stated blackly. 'I had nothing to do with that.'

'I want to believe you, but they hurt you so badly, I almost couldn't blame you for wanting revenge. Someone like you, so strong and capable, it would be naive of me to think you wouldn't want retribution. But in ignoring it, I'm responsible too.'

His shoulders slumped. He stood by the window and stared out. When he finally spoke, his voice was low and tight. He barely sounded like himself.

'It was difficult. You know me well, Ronnie, but you don't

know everything. I think you underestimate me, or the effect you've had on me. I didn't take any revenge, because of *you*. It's really that simple. They mean nothing in the scheme of my life now. What happened with them is nothing in comparison to the things I've seen and been through – things I've already done.

'Leaving the project was my freedom. I never wanted to take a life and I don't intend to again. I could have killed every one of them while they were torturing me if I'd wanted. Do you know that? You really think some thugs would be all it took for me to ruin what I have with you? If anything, it's because of that incident that we're together. I'd thank them if I could. It hurts to believe you think that of me. You of all people.'

'I'm just scared,' I whispered, what felt like a rock was lodged in my throat.

'Of?'

'Of being a bad person, of turning a blind eye because of the way I feel about you. I'm scared my father would be disappointed in me.'

He was by my side in a second, crouched down and looking up at my face. 'You could never be a bad person. Your goodness is why I am so in lo– please, Red, please don't do this. If you don't believe in me, I have nothing.'

I tried to contemplate how I was going to make things good again. Good for Rachel, good for Kalen and somewhere in the scheme of things, good for me. As long as there were people I loved who hated Kal, I'd always be hurting someone.

'Kal, I have to tell you something,' I began, my gut wrenching with each word. 'I had a visit yesterday–'

A loud banging sounded from the front door. I got up and looked out the bay window, with Kal close behind me. I mouth dropped open at the scene in front of me. At least twenty people were gathered in my front garden – and they didn't look happy.

42 — THE MOB

KALEN MUTTERED SOMETHING IN A LANGUAGE I DIDN'T RECOGNISE. Definitely a curse. 'Do you know what they're doing here?' I asked.

'I'm assuming they're here to see me off.'

'They're morons! Please, let's just ignore them.'

Lifting his shoulders he said, 'Morons or not, this means my time's run out, I have to leave. So I guess you can sleep easy.'

'I'll handle this,' I almost begged. I cursed Rachel and her stupid misplaced loyalty, trying now to be my parent after so many years. Storming out of the living room and towards the front door, I yanked it open, coming face to face with Jared, a group of his friends gathered close behind him, looking ready to carry Kalen out if they had to. *I'd like to see them try,* I thought darkly.

'Jared,' I fumed, 'why are you doing this?'

'Ronnie, you've been given every opportunity to get rid of these hooligans. I won't be threatened by a teenager. We're going to do something about it if you're not.'

I looked behind him at the sea of faces. I recognised them all. I could see from their expressions that some were there to back up Jared, but some were just interested to see what was going to happen.

'Jar, you and Rachel can't tell me what to do any more. I'm eighteen.'

His face contorted into a sneer and in that instant I knew he hated me. He'd instigated it all – I should have known Rachel wasn't remotely vicious enough to come up with such a plan.

'You're living in this big house all by yourself Ronnie, you're just a child and you're putting everyone here in danger.'

'Oh really, how's that? Seeing as you guys are the ones at my door, not the other way around.'

'He killed those men.'

'Oh the men who put me in hospital, you mean? You have no proof that their deaths were anything but an accident.'

'We don't need proof!' The yell came from one of his friends, but I didn't even glance up to see which one. They all began to chime in then anyway, their voices causing me to flinch backwards.

Jared turned and held up one hand to quieten them and then faced me again with what I can only describe as a smirk. 'There's nine of us here Ronnie. I'm not sure he'll be so confident against those odds.'

I almost laughed. Jared really had no clue at all, but I felt as though someone had thrown a bucket of ice water all over me. I was frozen to my core. 'Jared, why are you doing this?'

'I'm taking charge. Something I should have done ages ago.'

'That's funny,' Kalen's voice sounded from behind me. He put his hand on my shoulder and moved me so my body was behind his. 'I can't imagine you taking charge of a school fete, Jared. Why don't you show me what you mean and leave Ronnie alone – I'm quite sure I've warned you twice now.'

The crowd behind Jared became deathly silent, bar a few animated whispers. They were witnesses to what was about to take place and while I knew they didn't have a hope in hell of removing Kalen from my house, the result would be Kalen's undoing. Maybe that was Jared's plan after all.

295

'You really think you're something special, don't you, boy?' Jared spat.

Kalen stepped forward. I couldn't watch him go down because of my sister's boyfriend. Panic twisted my stomach.

'I think he's pretty special,' came a voice behind us. 'What do you think, boys?' A large hand on Kal's shoulder stopped him in his tracks and in that second, everything changed. Denver, Ace and Nash had appeared behind us. I glanced over my shoulder towards the back door to see where they had come from. Their presence appeared to temper the group and I watched with pleasure as some of them inched backwards.

I had to think quickly, before the boys did something they would definitely get arrested for. There was only one thing left. Kal would never understand, but it was my chance to do the right thing and I reminded myself what was at stake. I was trying to save his life.

'Stop it!' I yelled, finally squeezing through the barricade and standing between Jared and my friends. 'Jar. You win, okay? The boys will leave town. You'll never see them again.'

I could feel Kal's eyes on me, but I avoided his gaze and stood firm. 'Now, all of you leave and let me say goodbye.'

Jared stared at me for a long moment, his eyes scrutinising me, but Kal pulled me further behind him. Jared dropped his gaze almost immediately, turning to his friends and nodding. They began to disperse.

'I hope you're not lying to me, Ronnie. We won't let this drop,' he said with a look back, before stepping down off my front porch.

'Oh, I know you won't, Jared,' I called after him. 'By the way, where's Rachel? Does she know you're doing this?'

He ignored me and I watched as the group left down my long front drive, laughing about a job well done. I pushed the boys inside and closed the door.

'I always thought British people were more polite,' said

Denver.

'I guess that means we have to go now, right K?' Ace asked sadly.

Kal sent them into another room with a tip of his chin. The three of them went into my kitchen while Kal and I remained in the hallway.

'You believe them,' he said, his jaw clenched.

I wanted to tell him I knew he was good, that he was everything to me and I'd never take anyone else's side over his. But if I did, he wouldn't leave and even if The Agency didn't find him, the police in Clanots Ocean would. One way or another, staying with me would destroy him and this was the only way to guarantee he would run again. I swallowed, preparing for my heart to break. I'd feared for so long that I would lose him, but I never imagined I'd be the one telling him to go.

'I don't know,' I answered, hoping to lie with some conviction. 'I don't know what to believe any more.'

'Don't do this, Ronnie. Please don't do this to me – not you.'

'Kal, I just–' I struggled. I couldn't believe what I was saying. 'I just–'

'Forget it,' he said desolately and in that second I saw exactly how much I had hurt him.

'Boys, we're gone.'

In desperation, I tried to grab his arm before he walked out the front door, but trying to grab the arm of an assassin is like trying to catch hold of the tail of a lizard, the door had closed behind him before I even realised I was empty handed.

43 — COUNTDOWN

LATER THAT EVENING, Rachel and Jared came back to the house and I closed myself in my bedroom. There was no way I was talking to them. I paced back and forth, trying to get a handle on my thoughts.

I picked up my phone and dialed Kalen's new number. I knew it was for text messages only, but I was desperate. I needed to hear his voice.

It rang out.

I tried again, becoming more frantic with each failed attempt. Of one thing I was sure: I had made a horrible decision. I wasn't strong enough to do it this way. When he wouldn't answer, I called the only person I could think of who would help me.

'Alexandra.' My voice wavered instantly.

'Babe, what's the matter?'

'Al, I wouldn't ask you if it wasn't important, but I need to get to Kalen's quickly. I can't take the car, because my sister's here and I need to get out without her knowing.'

'Ronnie, what the–'

'I'll explain when you get here, can you pick me up?'

'Of course.'

'Thanks, I'll meet you on the back lane. Do you know Turner Drive?'

'Yeah, I know it. Babe, I'm worried.'

'Don't be. I'm fine, but I'm going to lose him, Al. I need to get to the house now.'

'See you in fifteen.'

We hung up and I set to work. I locked my bedroom door and turned the television up loud, hoping if Rachel decided to try and talk to me she'd think I was sulking and leave me alone. Throwing open my window, I swung my legs out onto the roof. The ground looked impossibly far away, but I told myself Kalen did it almost every day.

Slowly shimmying down the slate, I reached the edge and began to lower myself using the guttering as leverage. It crossed my mind that in all my life I'd never been compelled to sneak out. How ironic that now, at eighteen and my father not even here, I needed to do it.

I dangled, my legs flailing, before dropping the rest of the way and rolling onto the grass. A spiny hedge scraped at my arms. I bit back a curse and, after ducking into the shadows to make sure no one came out to investigate the noise, I sprinted off through my back garden.

Alexandra was waiting in her truck as I burst through the trees onto Turner Drive.

'Thanks so much,' I breathed as I opened the passenger door and leapt inside.

'So the old Taylor mansion, right?' she asked, sensing my urgency.

I nodded and we sped away.

'Are you gonna tell me what's going on?'

'I'm surprised you haven't heard,' I said darkly.

'Ron, stop with all the riddles.'

'Have you seen the news about that Cowford gang who died

in a fire?'

'Yeah, what about it?'

'Take the back road past the seafront, I don't want anyone to see us.' I pointed and she took a sharp left. 'The guys who died were some of the men who jumped Kalen and me.'

'Oh, right. Oh!' Her expression fell.

'He didn't do it,' I cut into her thoughts. 'But Jared has taken great pleasure in winding up all his friends and probably half the town to think he did. Him and his mates were outside my house earlier today – and then some. They told the boys to leave.'

'What the hell? Who do they think they are, frickin vigilantes?'

'Tell me about it. I could kill Jared.'

'Why does he care about those guys anyway after what they did to you?'

'Good question,' I seethed. 'But to be honest it's not even about that. Jared hates Kal and he wants him gone. This has given him the perfect excuse.'

Alexandra chewed her lip. 'Ron, I'll only ask you this once, I hate small towns with their small mindedness, and this one is about as bad as they get, but are you sure Kalen didn't have anything to do with the fire?'

I looked at my friend. I wasn't angry, just frustrated. No one knew him as I did. 'I'm positive, Alexandra. I'm more sure than I've been of anything in my life.'

'Okay,' she nodded with a warm smile, 'so who cares what judge and jury of Clanots Ocean says. They've got no proof, right? So Kalen doesn't have to leave.'

'It's more complicated than that.' I grimaced and willed her to drive faster. He was angry and hurt with me, I had a small window of opportunity to tell him how I really felt before he left my life for ever. 'I told him to leave, too.'

Her jaw dropped. 'But... you love him!'

'Yeah, I do.' With my words, came a sharp pain in the pit of my stomach. I gripped the door handle.

'So why side with them? If you're right and he hasn't done anything wrong then they can go to hell!'

'Alexandra, do you trust me?'

'Course I do, babe. What are you thinking? You're scaring me.'

'If you trust me, try to understand – I want to tell you so much, but it's better for you if I don't.'

'Right.' She frowned, her eyes told me she was unconvinced.

'Al, I guess – he's a good person, he really is, but he's done some bad things. That's the best way I can explain it right now.'

We were nearing the house and she hadn't answered me. 'Do you think I should let him go?' I asked.

She took her time over her answer as we pulled up on the street where the house loomed ahead, perched on the cliff-edge away from the rest of the town.

'Ronnie, you haven't told me anything so it's hard to know, but my instinct is to tell you to follow your heart. I would.'

My heartbeat raced. I wasn't sure why I needed to hear it from someone else, maybe just so I knew I hadn't gone completely insane. 'Thanks, Al. Listen, you better go.'

'Please call me tomorrow, okay?'

'Thanks.' I leaned over and threw my arms around her neck before hopping out of the car.

'Be careful, Ron,' she called after me. 'I'm sure Kalen would never intentionally hurt you, but this all sounds terribly wrong somehow. I don't want anything bad to happen to you.'

I nodded and ran towards the house. Her truck pulled away behind me. As I reached the gates I could see the boys were still there, but something wasn't right. Denver, Nash and Ace were outside, crouched down below the kitchen window frame. I jogged towards them. Ace's eyes widened when he saw me, he held up his index finger to his mouth – an order to be quiet. I ducked down next to him, instantly hearing the voices carrying from inside the house.

'...Doing here?' Kalen's ice-cold tone was a dead giveaway.

'She didn't tell you?'

'She, who?'

'K, let's not play games.' The voice was impatient. I recognised it as Andrews immediately. Nausea swept over me, I had got everything so wrong.

'What do you want?'

'I want to help you. Veronica is only–'

'DO NOT, say her name,' Kalen growled.

'K, I'm not here to hurt her. If I'd thought it would help I would have disposed of her on my last visit.'

'I highly recommend you don't say anything like that to me again.'

There was a long pause before Andrews continued. I was only able to catch parts of the conversation. *'... can she have any sort of a life with you in it? You're always on the run, K. Do you think that will ever change, that they'll ever leave you alone? You're not a man, you are a weapon – a deadly weapon.'*

At the mention of weapons, Denver produced a knife from inside his jacket. By his side, it glinted and winked, catching the light of the moon. I held back a whimper.

He pressed his body close to the wall and edged forward.

'...I want to help you. You're better than this.'

'I don't need your help.'

'Five have already been terminated. Including J, F and B,' said Andrews.

A bleak silence followed. I wondered what was going

302

through Kalen's mind. Next to me, Ace closed his eyes, silently mouthing words I couldn't make out.

'Jesse wouldn't even have been sixteen,' Kalen's voice was raspy and full of pain.

'I'm aware of his age. I did not sanction what's happening K, you of all people know that.'

'But you haven't tried to stop it either, have you?'

The man laughed darkly. *'... You have me do? If I take this any higher all it'll serve to do is get me killed.'*

'God forbid.'

'You don't mean that. I've done all I can for you now. I've tried beyond what is safe and reasonable for myself to help you. Now you're on your own. I will say this, however...'

I strained to hear.

'...Never be allowed to live a normal life, K. If you come with me now we can find something for you. Your talent is too good to waste.'

'Get out.'

'Put the knife down, I'm leaving. But think about what I'm about to say to you. I found you. How long do you think it will be before they do? Barker won't let this go. He's taken your escape very personally. He won't stop until you're all dead.'

We listened to him walk out and I sat frozen to my place on the back porch, thankful the man had chosen to leave through the front. Once I was sure the unwanted guest had gone, I ran forward so I could see through the gap in the door. Kal was trying to steady his breathing, clenching and unclenching the fist not holding a kitchen knife. The boys stepped inside. I followed them in.

'Kal?' I said.

He cast the knife of the countertop, where it clattered and fell in the sink. 'You heard everything,' he said.

I moved closer to him, reaching out my hand, but Nash

stepped between us before we could touch.

'K, we have to split. Andrews was right, if he found us the others won't be far behind. The civilians want us out – they think you killed those men and it's only a matter of time before the police come around asking questions. It's attention we don't need!'

I'd never heard Nash rattled before. It made me very aware of the danger they were all in.

'Yeah, I know, N. We'll leave at first light.'

'Are you sure it's a good idea to leave it so late?' he pressed. 'K, I have a very bad feeling about this. I think we should go now.' He looked at me fleetingly and I knew it was me he had a bad feeling about.

Kalen sighed, pinching the bridge of his nose. 'Fine, you're right. Let me talk with Ronnie. Find Laith, let's empty the place out. We need to get rid of the cars too. Ace, you know what to do with the Ford. D, get rid of the bike. We leave in an hour in the Audi.'

Without further word, the boys left the room.

'Please, don't go,' I begged.

'I thought you wanted me to?' His arms remained heavy by his sides.

'You know I didn't mean that.'

'Really? And what did you mean? I'm nothing more than a killer, right?'

'Kal, please–'

Laith walked in at that moment, dusting sand off of his solid torso and drying his white blond hair with a towel. 'What's going on?' he asked as he looked at us both. 'You guys still together then?' he added with a sneer.

'We're leaving,' Kalen announced.

Laith's eyebrows jumped into perfect half moons. 'We who?'

'We, the unit.'

'Really?' His eyes sparkled and I knew it was the best news he'd received in some time.

'We had a visit. Andrews. Jesse's dead. So are B, Fix and apparently two others.'

Laith nodded solemnly and mouthed the same thing Ace had. It looked like, God Have Mercy. I'd never considered if they were religious, it seemed impossible because of some of the things they'd done, but I reminded myself that they hadn't chosen their lives, it had been forced upon them. Perhaps they needed God more than anyone.

'We'll head for Sweden as planned and then I might leave you all for a while.' Kal's eyes flashed in my direction and a darkness swept across Laith's features, as visible as if he were a cartoon. His brow knitted together and his blue eyes turned to stone.

'Why?'

'Because it's not safe for us to be in a group any more.'

'A lot of things aren't safe, K, yet you've had us doing them for months now.'

'I know. I'm sorry – that's why I'm putting a stop to it.'

'So you can come back for her?' he almost yelled.

'I don't know yet, but it's my decision.'

'You're putting her in front of your team again. This is ridiculous! I've tried everything, but nothing makes you see sense!'

'What do you mean by that, L?' Kal asked, suspicion lacing his tone as he stepped towards his friend.

'Nothing,' Laith muttered, his teeth clenched.

'Don't lie to me. It was you wasn't it – you killed those men?'

Laith's breathing had become tight and shallow, his shoulders lifting with each frustrated breath. 'I was just doing what you should have! Being with this girl has made you weak! How could you have let them do what they did to you?'

Kalen laughed, but it was anything but a happy sound. 'L, let's not pretend you were avenging me. We both know you did it to try and split Ronnie and I apart, to ruin what I have here. I'm so sick of your games. If you can't fall in line, you can go it alone. We're not supposed to be killing, we agreed–'

'We agreed to a lot of things!' Laith snapped, looking more frantic and enraged than I'd ever seen him. 'I can't let you do this to us. I can't let you change everything because of a chick. I won't!' he seethed. Then, without waiting for a response he fled back out the way he'd come.

Canter Creek, Iowa – October 2005

'So, what you're telling me, is that we were never going to live past fifteen?'

'I didn't know that was the plan, I wasn't read-in to that level until recently.'

'But why are we of no use after fifteen? We're good. R is one of the best snipers–'

'Once you're no longer children, you're not fit for the project.'

'What about other jobs? Other units? Surely they aren't really going to terminate us all? N turns sixteen next week.'

Tom Andrews stared back at Kalen, his expression resigned. 'You can't be reassigned. Taking you on so young, it's made you all unstable, unpredictable. You don't fit the profile for any agency.'

So in other words: they couldn't be *controlled*. The government's mistake meant destroying the lives of nineteen boys who'd had no choice in their destiny.

'Why are you telling me this?' Kalen whispered at length.

'I'm telling you because I care about you, K, I care what

happens to you.'

'But you don't care what happens to any of the others, right? Jesse? Ace? Your loyal unit?' Kalen knew his sarcasm was pointless, but the news was hard to digest, and while he wasn't afraid of dying, he felt sick to his stomach that it would be at the hands of those who'd made him into what he was. They'd been told Vass and X had both died on missions, but as Kalen thought about it now, it became clear. They were the eldest, they had both recently turned sixteen.

'I can't save everybody, you have no idea what I'm risking just by telling you, but I've known you the longest, I hand picked you myself – I feel I owe you something.'

'You owe me a lot more than this.'

'I am truly sorry for what's happened, for this whole projec–'

'Don't,' Kal interjected. 'Don't give me your lame apologies. I know no different, so who cares, right?'

Tom Andrew's bowed his head. It might almost have been in shame but Kalen knew men like his handler knew no shame.

'It can only be you,' he said quietly. 'Do you understand? If you tell any of the others, I can't help you, and I'll have to cut you off completely. If you leave now – just you, I'll tell them I sent you on one last mission, I will fake your death, give you money. You can get a place to live, spend your life on a beach somewhere.'

'Oh, wonderful,' Kal snarled, his patience running thin. Finally after a prolonged silence, Kal stood up to dismiss the meeting. 'What do you want me to say?'

'Say you'll do as I ask, I need to save you, K.'

'Why?'

'Because–'

'Is it to save your soul?'

For a brief moment, the man actually looked scared and

Kalen knew he'd touched a sore nerve.

'Kalen? That's what you call yourself, isn't it? Funny, how you act so stoic, yet you wanted to be named. To have something to define you. Well, *Kalen*, I'm offering you a chance at life – at freedom. Do you want it or not?'

'You know what I think's funny?' Kalen mused. 'I think it's funny how you pretend to be offended, when I question the notion of your soul. You've killed so many, but you're afraid to die.'

'Yes or no?' the man growled. 'Last chance, kid. Last chance to save your life. What's your decision?'

44 — BETRAYAL

'**W**E'VE COVERED OUR TRACKS HERE.** Just the
vehicles left. When can we discuss the plan?'
Nash asked as we walked into the dusty living
room where they all sat cross-legged on packing crates.

'We can discuss it now,' Kalen replied.

Each boy in turn looked up at Kalen and then at me. In
response he merely stared back at them. I glanced sheepishly at
my feet.

'Is there a problem?' asked Kalen.

At first I didn't think they would answer, but Nash looked
at Kal and, with an apologetic tone, said, 'It's just that, maybe
Laith doesn't go about it in the right way, but he does have a
point. We're endangering Ronnie by involving her.'

'Ronnie has a right to know the precarious situation I've
put her in. We can trust her. Do any of you have an issue with
that?'

After a moment's pause, each of them shook their heads.

'So here's the deal,' Kal continued, 'as we always agreed,
we know which country's next.'

'What then?' asked Nash.

'I don't know yet. I may come back here for a while, when

things calm down. Alone.'

'We're splitting up?' asked Denver.

'Let's just get there, okay? Then we'll decide what's best, for all of us.'

I gulped, watching all their expressions, knowing they regarded me as the reason Kal wanted to go it alone. One by one they all agreed and Kalen and I joined them on the crates. They started to discuss the plan in more detail.

'A, let's sort the car and the bike,' said Denver. At that moment, however, Laith came into the room.

I cringed inwardly, expecting another argument. But something was different: he didn't look as smug or arrogant as usual, if anything he was sheepish. I wasn't the only one who sensed it, because in just a few seconds the boys fell silent and stared at him with concern. I looked between each of them, suddenly apprehensive.

'Laith?' Kal asked, slowly standing up. 'What have you done?'

'I'm sorry–' he muttered, shaking his head, 'I just didn't know what else to do – I'm – I'm sorry.'

Kalen's head dropped, as did the heads of the others around me.

'How long do we have?'

There was no response.

'HOW LONG?' Kalen's voice boomed.

Laith stood up straight, as if to attention. Remorse flickered briefly in his eyes before he responded. 'Maybe thirty minutes, depending on how far away the closest asset is.'

'Do they know about her?'

'I – I don't –'

'Dammit, Laith! Just tell me the truth, do they know about Ronnie?'

'No.'

'Okay.' Kalen breathed out. Then, like a different person –
fully composed and deadly – he turned to face the rest of us.
'Ace, get her out of here. Run with her, get her to a motel until
you think it's safe to go back to her house, then you can leave
yourself.'

'No, K, I want to help you,' Ace pleaded.

'Ace, don't question me! N, D, get out of here now. Laith–'

'He's gone,' said Nash.

A thick silence fell over us and they all looked incredibly
solemn. For a brief moment, their eyes met and I watched as
they said goodbye to each other with those looks. Before I
could process another thought Kal was walking me by the arm
into an empty room.

My heart was thundering, everything was happening too
quickly. 'What are we going to do? Are you still going to come
back?'

'Red, we don't have much time, listen to me.' He brushed
my hair out of my face and looked into my eyes. 'I love you.
I've loved you since the moment I saw you sleeping in that
apartment in Lisbon four years ago. You've been the only thing
in this world that has made me happy and I'm sorry, for all of
this.'

I grabbed his shirt, burying my face into his chest. 'Please
don't leave, this isn't enough time! I don't want to say good-
bye⌐–'

The lights in the house went out, plunging us into darkness
and killing the rest of my sentence on my lips. Kal pulled me
close to him. Before I knew what was happening, I was hurtling through the air encased in his arms. A noise like firecrack-
ers filled the room around us as we hit the floor and he rolled
us into the next room. Kal stood fluidly, dragging me up behind
him. I pressed myself hard against the wall. Though I'd never
heard a gun being shot in real life, it didn't take long for my
mind to catch up. We were under attack. Our time had run out.

The spate of gunshots grew silent. Everything was so still, I could feel my heart pounding in my chest. Had Ace and the other boys got out in time? Slowly, without looking away from the doorway, Kal's hand reached down to a leather pouch fastened around his thigh, emerging upwards holding a knife around six inches long, with a black handle and curved blade.

A creaking sound from above us caused Kal to freeze. In one movement he spun us both so that I was behind him and he was facing the noise. Though the moon cast a light into the room, my eyes hadn't fully adjusted. I didn't see where the assassin came from, but I screamed as a foot knocked Kalen's knife out of his hand. He was flung backwards. A man dressed entirely in black swung from a rafter in the ceiling and stood over him. In the second it took Kal to flip upwards, I saw the cold, determined eyes of our attacker. Another gunshot went off. I screamed. Then I heard it clatter to the floor. Somehow Kalen had disarmed him and then they began fighting.

'Run and hide!' Kal yelled at me, startling me into action.

Though I felt rooted to the spot, I recalled the last time he'd ordered me to run. Ignoring him then had almost got him killed and as much as I didn't want to leave him, I knew this time I had to do as I was told.

I fled through the house, trying to block out the sound of their combat. The hallway was so dark I couldn't see my hand in front of my face, but fighting back the hysteria bubbling inside me, I felt along the wall for where I thought I'd once seen the door to a basement. My limbs trembled uncontrollably. Clenching my fists, I bit my lip and took a deep breath though my nose; I needed to get a grip! Panicking now was not going to help Kalen and it definitely wasn't going to save my life. A few assertive breaths and I managed to stop shaking, continuing to feel along the wall and almost crying out in relief when my fingers gripped the handle I was after. Carefully – quietly – I pried it open and peered down into the musty stairwell. I didn't want to go down there – I'd be trapped. But before

I could think it over, a window shattered somewhere in the house. My feet found some bravery and propelled me forward.

With each step into the basement the air became thicker. The damp smell of mould stung the inside of my nose. Finding the ground, I tiptoed gently towards the back of the room, trying to avoid the boxes and furniture while searching for something I could crawl into and hide. I found what felt like a shelving unit up against a back wall and slid my hands over it. My fingers picked up dust as I worked out its shape and size. It appeared big enough for me to get inside.

I was half bent over when a tremendous rolling thunder sounded from the floors above me. The house vibrated and shook. I fought back a cry. I didn't have to be an assassin to know a helicopter when I heard one. One, two, even three assassins and I thought Kal might triumph – but a helicopter meant a team. A team of killers had come for us.

I dived into the bottom shelf of the unit and pulled my knees up to my chest. Seconds later, the cellar door practically flew off its hinges.

'Down here!' said a loud British voice I didn't recognise. I strained to listen, but I wasn't surprised I heard nothing else. If assassins couldn't move quietly I suppose they'd be in the wrong job. As my eyes adjusted to the darkness I could faintly make out at least four silhouettes making their way around the room. My whole body trembled, I pushed myself further back against the back of the cabinet, clutching to the hope that I was as well hidden from them as they were from me.

'This looks promising,' said the same voice I'd heard before, extinguishing any hope I'd had. A torch shone down onto my face. The bright light stopped me from seeing much, but I felt a large hand wrap around my arm. I was dragged upwards.

'A girl,' the voice of the man holding me sounded confused and satisfied at the same time.

The others joined him in staring at me. The light shone into my eyes again.

313

'Please stop doing that,' I spat.

'Trust me, love, this is the least of your worries.'

Pain shot through my arm as he hauled me forward and threw me to one of the others. I glanced around, frustrated and disorientated by the darkness.

'Call in. We need to know what to do with her.'

One of them spoke quickly and quietly, as if to someone on a phone, or some sort of communication device. I couldn't hear what was said, but then to the other men in the room he announced, 'She may draw out the targets. Bring her in.'

'Bring me in? Bring me in where? You can't take me anywhere, it's kidnapping! I won't go anywhere with you people! Who the hell are you?' Anger was the only thing stopping me from bursting into tears and I refused to give them that. As I was being towed towards the stairs all I could think was that I'd let Kalen down. I couldn't even hide well.

'Gag her.' The one holding me dismissed my outburst and one who felt smaller in build responded to the order by pushing me up against the wall.

'Do as they say,' he whispered in my ear. 'I won't let them hurt you, but you need to stop fighting us.'

I held my breath. Had I heard correctly? Was he really trying to help?

He used one hand to pin mine behind my back and tried to fix tape over my mouth. From the top of the stairs, the one in charge threw open the door and called down. 'I suggest you come quietly, little lady. The more you fight us the more painful it's gonna be, all right?'

I knew I couldn't trust any of them. I whipped my head from side to side and just before my mouth was covered, I took my chance and screamed out, 'Kal will kill you if you don't let me go!'

He shone his torch down at me. 'Well, you see, I don't know who Kal is, love. What I do know is all them boys we came for have done a runner. They ran off and left you here to die. So, as for killing me, that might be difficult while he's doing all that running. What d'you reckon?' His words trailed into a vile laugh and my will to fight dissolved. I stopped struggling. The tape was finally pressed into place.

But his laughter stopped abruptly. There was a second of complete silence before his large body tumbled down the stairs and landed in a heap in front of us.

'You can't say she didn't warn him,' said a perfect voice from the top of the stairs.

The man holding me let go and raised his weapon in Kalen's direction.

'Red, down!'

I dropped to the floor as the sound of gunshots filled the room. I covered my ears. Above me, the soldiers were firing up at the open door, I forced my eyes open and glanced around, looking for some way out, thankfully his torch had stayed intact when it hit the floor – it was providing some light. The first thing I noticed is that we weren't alone: two shadows formed in the darkness behind the men shooting at Kalen. I was astounded. I squinted to make sure I wasn't imagining it, but I knew the faces well. Though I had no idea how they got into the room without any of us knowing, relief washed over me.

And just as quickly as it began, the noise ebbed. Without fight or struggle each of the men in the room with me dropped to the ground like lead weights. The room was suddenly flooded with light and Kalen descended the stairs in a single leap, pulling me up and into his embrace. His lip bleeding and one arm hanging limply at his side, he tried to carefully peal the gag from my mouth with his good hand.

I ripped it off myself and smiled, despite the sting the tape left behind. I'd never been so happy to see anyone in my entire life. 'I knew you'd come for me,' I breathed.

'Guys, I'm not sure we have time for this,' said Denver with a grin.

'Where's Ace?' I panicked.

'Here.' Ace slid down the banister to join us. 'Just sorting out the lights.'

I almost laughed. We were all alive! With that thought, I glanced at the bodies on the floor.

'They're just knocked out,' said Denver as though reading my mind. 'Tranquiliser.'

'Right, guys, great as this reunion is, we need to get out of here. I'd say this is well and truly game over,' Nash stated grimly.

'N, sort this out, will you?' Kalen pointed to his limp arm. Taking his bicep and his shoulder in his grip, Nash gave it an almighty shove. Kalen's shoulder clicked into the space it had been meant for. He grunted through gritted teeth.

'What now?' asked Denver.

His breathing ragged through the pain, Kalen looked at Ace. 'The pilot?'

'Sorted.'

'Okay,' he blinked slowly, collecting his thoughts. 'Boys, burn this place down. I suggest we make it look as though we died in here too. Fire exit, level one.'

'What about these guys?' said Denver. 'British SAS, I think.'

Kal looked at me apologetically. 'Ronnie, they saw you. They may be able to find out who you are.' He was asking my permission to kill them.

'No!' I exclaimed. 'Kal, they barely got a look at me!'

'You don't know what these men are capable of, Red. Do you think they'd show you the same mercy? They'll do whatever is asked of them and they probably know who you are now.'

'No, they won't. Please! They're just soldiers, Kal, like you guys.' I looked desperately at his friends but they refused to meet my gaze. I didn't care. It was one thing to kill someone in self-defense, but another to do it in cold-blood, *just in case*.

'Kal, this one was decent. He tried to help me.' I pointed at the man who'd whispered to me. For the first time I could see his face; he didn't look much older than us.

Kal stared at me, debating with himself before turning to the others. 'Put them outside, well away from the house, but hidden. Ace, fix the chopper.'

Nash lifted one of the unconscious bodies and marched up the stairs. Denver did the same.

'Others won't be far behind,' said Kal as we headed out of the basement. 'We need to get out of here. N, you're with Ace.'

'We can take them, K, especially if they underestimate us like these guys did,' Denver's voice came from ahead of us. 'I've got to admit, this has been kind of fun. It's been a long time!'

'No,' Kalen said, impatiently, 'not with Ronnie here. I need you all to do as I said: fire exit and get yourselves out.'

I stood by the front door helplessly while they dragged the unconscious men out of sight and Ace rummaged around inside the huge helicopter. I prayed he wasn't trying to fly it. Kalen and the other boys ran from room to room with their rucksacks. I guessed, to start the fire, covering their tracks. *Fire exit one.*

Finally, they all gathered beside me. I felt a clamp around my heart as Nash caught my eye. With his cap turned backwards, his long hair and boyish looks, he looked like an angel incapable of hurting a fly, but spoke with an assertiveness of a man three times his age. I wondered if he had any idea how impressive he was.

'Ronnie, I've enjoyed knowing you and despite what you think, none of this has been your fault. Take care of yourself.'

I wanted to say something, but he'd already moved to give Ace room. I gulped as he stepped forward, his eyes trained on his feet.

'Ron, I really wish things had been different.'

'Ace–' I choked.

He silenced me with a shake of his head. In contrast to his friend, Ace had never looked as old as he did right now. 'Miss you,' he said, finally looking me in the eyes.

My voice failed me completely. I reached out and squeezed his hand.

As his eyes glassed, he looked away from me and with a clear of his throat he said to Nash, 'Land or sea?'

Nash looked at him sympathetically. 'I'm thinking sea this time, buddy.'

The youngest nodded and without hesitation the two of them took off running to the cliff's edge, launching into the air in perfect unison and disappearing from sight, headed to what I knew was the ocean below. I wondered how far they could swim. I wondered where they would swim to; I wondered a lot of things as my time with Kalen began to run out and I was forced to prepare myself to lose the only thing I wanted in the whole world.

Police sirens sounded in the distance. 'I'll take the bike and lead the cops away from here,' said Denver to Kalen before he looked at me. 'Bye, Ron. What N said, yeah?' Without waiting for my response, he fled the house.

'How will he get away?' I asked Kalen robotically.

'He'll be fine. The police are the least of our worries.'

I managed to nod.

'We need to get out of here, Red. That helicopter is going to explode in about three and a half minutes. Then this place.' He closed his eyes, and when he looked at me again his face crumpled. 'I don't know how to say goodbye to you.'

In that second I would have happily remained in the house with him while it went up in flames. The tears I had been holding back flooded down my cheeks.

'Take my hand,' he said quietly, 'We need to run.'

I did as I was asked and we left the house, the cold air giving us the jolt we needed to pick up our pace. All of my thoughts were of him leaving. I hadn't even considered we might die before that happened. We reached the car and Kal opened the driver's side door, I was about to jump in and crawl across to my side, when something ahead of us caught my eye. A man in a dark grey suit walked out causally from behind the bushes and stood in front of us. The moon was bright, lighting his face. I could see he was older, perhaps in his late forties, with dark hair combed into a side parting. His mouth pulled into a smirk as he eyed us both. I didn't see a gun, but in the shadows I couldn't be sure. The way Kalen stopped in his tracks told me – gun or not – this was bad, bad news.

'Dave Steinberg.'

'Agent K,' the man nodded.

Keeping the door open, Kalen took a step forward so he was between me and the new threat.

'You boys have been a thorn in my side now for some time. Barker has been beside himself.'

'I'm real sorry about that,' Kalen said humourlessly.

The man's pleasant demeanor faltered. 'They want you alive, K. Come quietly and tell us where we can find the others and I'll let the girl go.'

'What others?'

'Let's not play games.'

I was very aware that our three-minute count down was running out fast. Shortly, we would all be dead.

'Did they only send you?' asked Kalen. 'You guys don't think much of us, do you?'

The man's scowl intensified. 'No, as a mater of fact I don't. I never understood why they'd send children to do a man's job and I can't fathom why they don't just let me kill you now.'

'Maybe I'm better than you think?'

'I doubt that,' he sneered. 'And to answer your question, no, I didn't come alone. You're surrounded. There's no way out. You either take the deal, or a body-bag for you and your girl-friend. This is a man's game, K. You lose.'

Kalen glanced swiftly in the direction of the roof before ushering me inside. I scrambled over to the passenger seat, confused as to what was happening and sure we were about to be blown to pieces. Before Kalen got in, he leaned casually on the open door frame and stared at the one he'd called Steinberg.

'Were you there when they killed Jesse? Did that make you feel like a man?'

'J died crying like a little girl.'

'Come on now, Dave, you know I don't believe that. Jesse was way tougher than you and he was just a kid.'

'Last chance, K.'

'Na... it's yours.' Kalen said and slipped in front of the wheel, starting the car before he had even fully got in his seat. We sped forward, leaving a trail of dust surrounding Steinberg as he stepped easily out of our path wearing a satisfied smile. I couldn't understand why he was letting us go - or why he ap-peared so smug about it. Then it became clear.

'Head down!' Kalen growled.

I watched in horror as at least ten men holding guns stepped out of the trees, blocking our exit. We had no way out. I screamed and ducked. Bullets rained down on the car. Kalen slammed his foot on the brake and shifted the car into reverse, flooring the accelerator once more. We rocketed in the direction of the cliff's edge.

'Red, sit up and put your seatbelt on.'

In the midst of so much carnage my adrenalin kicked in. I no longer wanted to cry or scream. I lifted my head and clicked my belt into place. Ahead, the line of agents stood firing at us.

Behind us, the cliff edge was approaching at high speed.

'Kal?'

Kalen looked at me, his eyes holding my focus.

'Do you trust me?' he asked.

I nodded. I could no longer hear the screaming engine or the torrent of bullets. Every sound fell away until there was only us.

'It's going to be okay, Red. I promise.'

And then the mansion exploded into a ball of flames and we drove off the edge of the cliff.

45 — CHOICE

I WOKE UP IN MY BED AND BLINKED AWAY THE SLEEP. The ceiling was moving above me in uncontrolled waves and my gut wrenched in a way that told me something was very wrong. In a split second, the haze cleared and the previous night's events rushed back into my mind.
I sprang upright.

Patting myself down, I scanned my room, everything was just as I'd left it and my clothes – how come I was in my pyjamas? I remembered us crashing into the ocean! How was I not dead?

My phone lay beside me, the screen black and waterlogged. It was the only proof I hadn't dreamed the entire thing. I pressed one hand to my forehead, trying desperately to recall what had happened. Images and sounds flashed through my mind. Kalen's soothing voice: *'Stay calm Red. Water's going to rush into the car now...'* and then he'd kissed me. The icy water flooded in quickly. I was crying. *'When the pressure is the same inside...'* and *'take a deep breath now, okay? Look at me, Red...'* Then the water had taken me under.

I could remember nothing else, but I was here – I was alive. That meant Kalen was, too. With that thought, an envelope at the end of my bed caught my eye. I threw back my covers and lunged for it, my fingers trembling as I tore open the paper.

Red,

As I sit here and watch you sleep, I find I'm almost incapable of doing the right thing, but I told you once that it is fear which drives us all in the end. Well, the only thing that scares me more than not being with you, is you dying because of me. I can't let that happen. I hope one day you'll forgive me.

In the top draw of your dresser is the gift I wanted to give you yesterday. I hope it makes you happy. If it gives you a tenth of the happiness you have given me then, for once in my life, I will have done something right.

Know that I love you. I love you like I've never loved anything in this world and I'll love you with my last breath.

K

I doubled over, a pain like nothing I'd ever experienced twisting my gut. Stumbling to my dresser, I struggled to breathe as I yanked open the top drawer. A thin black velvet box sat inside. I pried it open with trembling fingers, a stack of papers burst out. I scanned them, confused, it looked like the deeds to my house, bought and paid for in the names of Rachel and Veronica Rose.

Kalen had bought me my house.

It was everything I'd thought I wanted – my father's legacy, my home. I fell back on the bed as numbness crept through me, afraid my legs wouldn't hold me up much longer. The sound of the front door closing downstairs interrupted my thoughts. I recognised my sister's footsteps running up the stairs.

'Hey,' Rachel said, stepping into my room with an uncertain smile.

I wiped my cheeks to catch the stray tears.

'I heard what happened with Jar. I didn't get to talk to you last night, but I'm sorry it came to that.'

I managed to shrug as I took her in. She was going to be twenty-seven this year. She had a boyfriend, a daughter, a great job and now a house. *She'd be fine,* I told myself.

'What you got there?' she ventured.

'Nothing.' I folded the papers and stuffed them back in the box.

Rachel shifted awkwardly, toying with her hair the way Kalen once told me I did. 'Did you see the news? There was an explosion at the old Taylor mansion. A gas leak apparently. The whole thing burned down.'

'I haven't watched the news.'

'Isn't that where those boys were staying?'

'Not any more.'

'Ronnie, I'm trying to be nice here. Throw me a bone?'

'What do you want me to say?'

'Well, have you made a decision?'

'They've gone, if that's what you mean. For good.'

'Oh, thank God,' she sighed. 'You know, you've made the right choice, Ronnie. It's very grown up of you. This is the right thing – for all of us. Now we can get back to normal.'

I gave her a small smile. It was all I had.

'Are you going to be okay?' she asked.

I swallowed, trying not to cry. 'I am.'

'Okay, well, I have to go. I'm meeting some friends from work. Maybe we can have dinner tomorrow? Cook something lovely and I'll bring Jar and Cloud.' She rushed to me, kissing my cheek before turning to leave.

'Rachel,' I called, as she reached the door.

'Yeah?'

'I love you.'

'Me too, sweetie. Everything will be great now, you'll see. He really was no good for you. We'll find you someone better, okay?'

The door fell shut behind her. Her words resonating inside me as I stared at the void she'd left behind.

I fell back so I was staring at the ceiling and tried to collect my thoughts. It was six p.m.; I'd slept most of the day. But I still had time. I didn't believe Kalen would have left yet. He'd be watching me to make sure I was safe first, I was sure of it. With that thought, I knew what I had to do.

I got myself up, dressed swiftly and filled a small rucksack with my passport, a toothbrush and a change of clothes, leaving the velvet box in the middle of my bed where Rachel would find it. Then, rummaging through a trunk of my childhood things, I found my copy of *Little Red Riding Hood* and placed it in my bag with the rest of my stuff, lingering for a moment over the image of the wolf standing in front of the girl in her famous red cloak. To me, the wolf didn't seem so bad... perhaps just misunderstood.

Finally, clasping the silver locket that hung around my neck, I took a deep breath, and walked out the door.

EPILOGUE

THE DOCKS WERE QUIET, but there were more people around than there had been on my first visit. I was nervous. Not because of what I had decided, or that a killer could jump out at me at any moment, but because I might have been wrong. All my hopes were pinned on him watching me from the shadows and me being able to draw him out by doing something reckless. If I was wrong and he'd already left, I wasn't sure my heart could take it.

As I wandered between the huge boats, images of him flashed in my mind: his eyes, his smile, his laugh. I couldn't bear the thought of living the rest of my life with only my memories of him. The prospect felt as though I were being cut, from the inside out. My watch showed eight-thirty and with every step I took, my panic increased until I thought it might consume me.

And then he was there.

As if out of thin air, Kalen appeared in front of me, his arms folded across his chest, his eyes betraying conflicting emotions of joy and sorrow.

'Going somewhere?'

The pain inside me dissolved. It was everything I could do not to throw myself at him. But I held back – he was not getting off that lightly. 'Yes, actually, I'm looking for my pigheaded boyfriend, who seems to think he knows what's best for me.'

He lifted one eyebrow. 'Pigheaded? Maybe he was trying to do the right thing?'

'Maybe I couldn't care less about the right thing. Kal, I'm coming with you.'

'Ronnie.' He said my name like it was painful to him, but hearing it from his lips made my choice even clearer.

'I'm leaving England tonight, Kalen Smith. With or without you. What's it gonna be?'

For a while he just stared, his jaw set as a silent battle took place behind his eyes.

'You said you'd show me the world,' I added hesitantly. 'Remember?'

Finally, a whisper of a smile tugged at one corner of his mouth. He laughed darkly, linking his fingers behind his neck and glancing at the sky before back at me. 'Do you know what you're saying, Red? I mean, are you really sure about this?'

'I'm sure that I love you. It's the only thing I've been sure of in my entire life and I can't lose you again.' And as I spoke the words, I knew I meant them. I knew I'd now be a wanted fugitive too, and that while we may have triumphed for the moment, an inevitable confrontation with the people who wanted him dead probably awaited us somewhere in our future, but I didn't care about any of that now. Right now, I was exactly where I wanted to be and nothing else mattered.

Stepping towards me, he brushed a strand of hair from my face, studying my eyes like he couldn't believe I was real.

'Well?' I said. 'You gonna kiss me, or what?'

He smiled. 'Yes, ma'am.'

ACKNOWLEDGEMENTS

A BIG THANK YOU... first and foremost to my mum, Helen, for your unwavering encouragement and always telling me to follow my dreams no matter what. To Phil, for listening to me talk about my fictional world for the last three years and still smiling about it - I really couldn't have done this without you. To Kay at klediting.co.uk, I can't tell you how grateful I am for your patience and guidance in helping me turn First Light into something I'm proud of. You're the best! Danielle - the sister I never had - thanks for being you, for loving Kalen and Ronnie along with me and always telling me how great I am... even if you are biased! Janusz for everything www - you're my favourite nerd ;) and to Jaime for "Five Fifteen".

To my family, for all your support. I love you all to pieces. Particular thanks to Errol, my oracle! Your love and guidance really means everything to me. Paula, I don't know what I'd do - or what I would have ever done - without you. Catherine and Lizanne, for being there for me no matter what and telling me what I need to hear, even when sometimes I don't want to hear it! And Tiki, for my childhood... things could have sucked, but you were there, making sure they didn't.

Last but not least, a special thank you to someone who can't be named. Interviewing you was a surreal, eye opening experience and your input not only helped bring the world of Project Five Fifteen to life, but also made me realise that kick-ass heroes really do exist. You know who you are.

Thank you all so much, from the bottom of my heart x

BOOK 2

Project Five Fifteen

as you were

Coming soon.

For more information visit:

www.projectfivefifteen.com